MW00861997

Atomic Love

A Heavy Metal Memoir

Jessie Rose

Black Summer Press

Atomic Love: A Heavy Metal Memoir (Fiction) Copyright © 2019 by Jessie Rose. All Rights Reserved.

No part of this book may be reproduced in any form or by any electronic or mechanical means including information storage and retrieval systems, without permission in writing from the author. The only exception is by a reviewer, who may quote short excerpts in a review.

Cover designed by J. Rose using Canva Pro.

This book is a work of fiction. Names, characters, places, and incidents either are products of the author's imagination or are used fictitiously. Any resemblance to actual persons, living or dead, events, or locales is entirely coincidental.

Jessie Rose

Visit my website at www.jessieroseauthor.com

Printed in the United States of America

First Printing: Dec. 2019

ISBN- 978-0-578-56416-6

Black Summer Press

Content Note

Due to the sensitive subject matter in *Atomic Love*, I have decided to include a list of warnings below for readers who may need them. If you don't, skip to the next page.

Novel contains: Discussion of mental health, dissociation, anxiety, PTSD, and trauma. Instances of violence, sexual assault, miscarriage, suicide ideation and the death of a child.

For my son, Riley, whose father gave him music and rage and whose mother gave him art and fear. May you learn the difference between the two. Maybe someday you'll understand.

P.S. Don't let monsters in your bed.

- Love you forever,
Jennifer

PROLOGUE

I came to, naked in a hotel shower. Water, full blast, turned from hot to glacial. Saliva, thick with blood, dripped from my swollen lips and swirled down the drain. Electric static, frequency unknown. Maybe it was that damn radio. Or the valley my fingers traced along my skull. My bet was on the dent in my head, but the radio wasn't helping.

I pressed my palm against the tile to brace myself. A sharp edge of bone cut into my skin. Water from the showerhead washed across my hand, flushing blood from the wound.

A tooth. My tooth. Buried in my palm.

How long have I been here?

Guttural groans escaped my cracked lips. Forehead pressed to tile. Ice water struck my raw flesh like shards of glass. Tooth gripped in fist. Body recoiling in pain. This was not supposed to happen. Not to me. Not to anyone.

I was an artist once. My paintings were alive, robust, and colorful.

Until I became fractured into nothing—which, by the way, only comes in blues and blacks. Dull plum and drab olive if you are lucky enough to heal.

Broken. Undone. Cracked.

Somewhere in London? Los Angeles? Dallas? Somewhere on the road. Not like Kerouac, but somewhere far, far away from my mother.

A collision of two paths, where on the road became on the run. This is not a story about Dallas. Or my mother. Actually, it's not a story at all. It's a manual. A guidebook. What not to do.

Buy a good pair of running shoes. Don't believe anything you hear on the radio. Hide his matches. Hold on to your teeth.

Call your mother... maybe do that first.

Red is the color that streams from pokes and punctures. Pull hard enough and I'll fall to pieces.

A towel was placed on my burnt skin.

"You can't stay here." Suit Man screamed into my left ear. "Can you fucking hear me?"

My brain hemispheres were not communicating. This was some Jeffrey Dahmer shit. Five to one, baby.

Would I have stepped foot on that bus to Los Angeles if I had known what the universe had in store for me? Number 322, the overnight Greyhound from Phoenix; one-way express to hell. All aboard! Next stop: blood loss and broken teeth.

I wish something had stopped me—a flat tire, an earthquake, the apocalypse. There would have been another night, another bus. Years later, I still wish for a bus to a different city.

If God were real, she would have sent me a different man.

Chapter One

Summer, 1986

"You're coming with us," the goth girl with purple dreads said. A ripped Bauhaus "Bela Lugosi's Dead" tank slid off her shoulder. Shit-kicking combat boots, a sleeve of tattoos and vinyl hot pants completed her look. "I'm Kaley, this is Kevin."

A lanky, bookish guy in a long, white button up, and black-rimmed glasses gave me a part shy, part apologetic half wave.

Kaley grabbed my hand, pulling me out of a university art fair and my life as a studious painter at the Institute of Art, dragging me straight into the L.A. underworld.

Doubling up on classes, I had made no time for friends or a social life. Los Angeles' grit and grime was not for me. I wanted to get home to Arizona, visit my hippie parents, take a break to backpack across Europe, then move to the East Coast after graduation. I was fearless, adventurous, but my sweet parents had made me an overachiever and avid rule follower.

As an only child, I had to compete with the entire neighborhood. I'd never fit in with other girls. They wanted to talk about high school boys. I wanted to talk about Bowie, Warhol and Pop. I loved dirt bikes and nail polish. A mixture of mud and glitter were the precursor to expensive oil paints—now running off the edge of the neglected table in booth eighteen of the art fair while a total stranger pulled me around the building, down a wooded path.

Kissing ass had never been my strong point. If another Beverly Hills housewife dripping in diamonds asked me to take half off a painting I'd spent six months perfecting, I would scream.

Of course, I went with the purple-haired goth girl.

It was more than that. My world was vanilla. My classes were vanilla, my boyfriends had been vanilla. Not French vanilla, but cheap soft serve, without toppings. Kaley was the sprinkles to my vanilla-strawberry twist. She was the Pop Rocks and Red Hots, too. A performance artist, she lit her painted canvases on fire, then jumped through them. Spray-painted herself blue when bored. Kevin was her film student boyfriend with hair band credentials. He learned a few songs on his keyboard to say he was a musician, so he could make connections in the '80s glam scene.

Kaley's energy was intoxicating. Her perfect skin and green eyes gave her an ethereal glow, her black clothes a shield. A contrast to my dull, blonde, whiteness. I hid behind my colorful palette. Pretty, not plain, but a barrier, nonetheless. Bravery ending at surfboards and dirt bikes. Oil paints keeping others at a distance.

Endless, hyper chatter poured from Kaley's black-lined lips—filling a void. Spilling her life story like glitter in the wind, hoping it would stick.

I listened attentively, not wanting to miss a beat before this flittering black bird of a girl landed on her next captive audience. Her father, Freddie Dean, was a jazz musician from New Orleans. Quite famous at one point in his career, Freddie played with greats like Nina Simone and Fats Domino. The drifting bass player shacked up with Kaley's mother—a London-based fashion designer named Bridgette. Bridgette's goals included moving to California and obtaining a green card. Things had not worked out between the two. At ten, Kaley was left stateside to raise herself with her alcoholic father. This betrayal gave her grit and determination. (Along with a slight British accent, which erupted into a spew of Creole dialect when she phoned her father). Freddie never forgave Kaley for petitioning to have his guardianship revoked. Her case was denied. She ran away, living in the home goods section of a J. C. Penney, at a mall in Ventura County for a week (making her an "expert in uptight consumerism"—her words, not mine). Her father moved away from California, leaving Kaley behind. She sought temporary refuge with a cult leader named David who was twice her age. "Shit got a little too Charlie in the valley, so I bailed," Kaley said.

The night we met, I made my first major sale. In hindsight, I'm pretty sure that's why Kaley grabbed my hand. She'd been fidgeting through the sale, picking up items, flipping them over to look at the price. She cornered me outside the restroom, using the universal conversation starter, "Hey girl—love your hair."

"Thanks—um, yours too."

"Yeah, so, our car is out front. We're out of gas. Can you spare five bucks? I'm good for it."

Eager to please and naïve to the city, I pulled the money from my pocket.

She scanned it and smiled. "You passed the test. But never pull out cash in L.A. You'll get stabbed in the eye. This art fair thing looks boring as shit. Me and the beau are gonna go smoke some weed, wanna come?"

It was 1986. I was nineteen. Only one thing mattered: *Be cool.* "Sure." I shrugged.

Kaley grabbed my hand, told me her name then snatched a cone of pink cotton candy from the snack stand. Off we went, down a dirt path, into the trees.

"Sit here." Kaley plopped onto a large rock. A lucky rabbit's foot dangled from a chain on her purse. Hers was the real hoodoo charm, dyed lilac, faded. She carried her bag open (the better for slipping things inside). Unzipping a travel pouch, she smiled. "Pick your poison, girly." A massive joint, a rainbow assortment of pills and a strip of blotter tabs covered in cherries and bombs filled her mini-drug buffet.

D.A.R.E., "Just Say No," and President Reagan's War on Drugs conditioning ran through my head. My hippie parents smoked pot, they didn't care if I did. Anything more was a solid no. But... dare...

"Too late." Kaley popped her drug of choice on her tongue before sticking a matching acid tab on mine. She lit a joint, passed it to Kevin and leaned back on the rock.

I lay beside this strange, energetic creature, listening to her ramble for an hour about crumpets and gumbo sandwiches (a million dollar idea), President Reagan's Strategic Defense Initiative (Cult leader David was not a fan—he said it was the people's duty to bring on the apocalypse through mind control, not weapons). Whether or not David Bowie's appearance in the upcoming *Labyrinth* film was an indication that he was, "assuming his rightful place as God of the Goths" (not yet). And on the topic of Davids: "Is David Lee Roth hot—or not?" (Undecided).

I liked this girl already. She was so far beyond the norm I'd grown accustomed to.

My body tingled. The acid hit as the sky darkened. Shadow trees crept around us

Kaley waved to the left. "Look." Her hand scattered the full moon into a cascade of stars as her fingers floated across the sky, breaking my paranoia. The Hollywood sign burst forth like sunlight, shooting its rays across the universe. Yellow, orange, red—an entire spectrum of color entering my artistic brain. Paranoid to peace. Why had I not done this drug before? Our veins pulsed together in a secret code of some shared past. Kaley moved her hand—sparkling stars fell across our bodies. Hollywood in all her prismatic glory. Universal fragments connected, it all made sense.

That's the moment I fell in love with L.A.

We weren't exactly in the woods, just a small patch of trees between Griffith Park Observatory and a parking lot. If I'd looked in that direction earlier, between two particular trees, I would've seen the Hollywood sign. I'd seen it from transit buses, but never under the stars with the moon pulsing and reflecting a kaleidoscope of colors. An expert trip-sitter, Kevin sat behind us, wiping his black-rimmed glasses. Unobtrusive, never interrupting a Kaley moment.

"We're meant to be here, you know?" Kaley squeezed my hand. "Right here, right now. The universe brought us together for a reason."

I'd never been superstitious or spiritual, so maybe it was the acid. But I believed her. I looked at our arms and saw the veins rising in the air, twisting and entwining with each other. Alien molecules communicating on a different plane. I stored her words deep into my D.N.A.

Or something.

Kaley sang Foreigner's "Jukebox Hero" but couldn't remember where the stars went.

"Stars in his chin!" I laughed. "No, no, it was somewhere else."

"What's your favorite band in the entire world Jelly-Jell-O-June Bug? What is your name?" Kaley asked.

"Jennifer. And The Sound, I guess."

"Of silence?" Kaley said.

"No, just The Sound."

"Oh." Her pupils widened.

"How did the Jukebox guy get stars on his chin?" I asked.

"Bowie." She giggled.

Kaley and Kevin offered me a ride as we made our way up the hill and helped me pack my paintings into Kevin's tangerine Ford Pinto. Its bumper stickers read "Feed Artists" and "Nerds Need Love Too." Kevin carefully rearranged his film equipment in the trunk. Kaley pushed my long canvas roll through the back window, sliding her tiny body in with it. Laughing as her ass hit the seat, her boot-clad feet dangling out the window.

A voice followed us. "Miss Stone, you forgot your check." The art fair clerk took a moment to catch his breath.

"I didn't realize I'd sold anything else."

He smiled. "Girl, please. There was a bidding war after you disappeared."

Kaley piped over my shoulder, eyes wide. "$1,500? Holy fucking shit. You can buy a fucking car."

"This is a mistake." My heart pounded and my still-high brain wavered between disbelief and excitement.

Kaley hit the seat. "See what I told you? This is all meant to be. Fancy Pants, you're buying dinner. Curry in Thai Town, drinks to celebrate!"

Confirmed by the universe and Kaley Dean, I fell asleep on their sofa with acid emblazoned words on the back of my eyelids—*You're an artist now. It's always who you were meant to be, and these were always the people you were meant to be with.*

We were inseparable from that night on. Kaley connected me with an art dealer and eagerly stretched my canvases. The paintings sold fast. With my money, her tips and what Kevin managed to squeeze out of his student loans, we rented an apartment on Sunset.

College had served its purpose. A little goth angel was in my ear, telling me to dump the bourgeois and join the revolution. Convinced I had learned all the theory and technique I needed, I feared sacrificing my artistic style and vision. I'd pick the rest up off the streets.

Sunset Boulevard was an acid trip gone wrong and right at the same time. The colors—brilliant and grotesque; from the hobo's urine stain to Kaley's ever-changing hair color. It was a constant Warholian party. I painted, Kaley set things on fire, and Kevin put it all on video.

Racing on white crosses—the gas station pills we called "trucker speed,"—I completed a series of paintings titled *Looking Glass*. Abstract images mirroring each other, line-to-line, opposing forces—angel and demon. With any abstract, the object is what the viewer sees. A client purchased the entire series. I took home $2,000 after the dealer's cut. It was unheard of for a fresh out of the dorm artist. Honing my craft and studying Picasso, Pollack, Warhol, and Mapplethorpe had paid off.

Art in L.A. featured me in their "Young Artists" series. Kaley demanded I have a signature look for the photo shoot. We cut my sun-kissed hair into a short, choppy bob and bleached it white. Kaley tossed me a pair of her torn fishnets to slide on under a t-shirt and handed me a tube of Mac's Russian Red lipstick. I made a kissy face at her, sealing a pact with her demons. I'd never considered my art deep or dark, but it had hit a nerve.

I pouted my lips for the camera, pretending to smoke a Marlboro Red, curling my lip into a snarl. Taking Kaley's advice, "Don't smile. Look at that photographer like you could eat him for dinner."

I sent my parents a check, a copy of the magazine article and a well-thought-out letter on why I left school. Kissing the envelope with my new lipstick, I gave it to Kaley to mail before I changed my mind.

The partying resumed.

Ours wasn't the typical L.A. scene—no spandex, no hairspray. We added three more roommates, John, Livia and Fish, and rented a house outside of L.A. We needed the extra space to focus on our work. When we lived on The Strip, we took yellow jackets and white crosses to work faster. I wasn't brave enough to try anything dangerous. Sure, those pills might make your heart explode, but we didn't know that. When you're with the cool kids, you take what the cool kids take.

As nouveau-hippie valley dwellers, we minimized partying and increased productivity. We shared food, bathrooms and boyfriends. Except Kevin who was always off and on with Kaley. Abuzz with creativity, the house was much calmer than L.A. Life was perfect. Art, laughter, friendship—what more could I want?

The pace was too slow for Kaley. Whispering behind closed doors, she and Kevin were more off than on. He announced they were moving to a new apartment on Sunset, his eyes dry and red. *How many more late nights will he chase her around Hollywood?*

Kevin never mentioned her pawning his film equipment. He covered for her when she stole his checks and followed a trail of drugs to keep her safe.

Calm settled over the valley house. My roommates and I spent our days philosophizing, reading books and napping. (You don't get a lot of sleep when you have a 95lb, goth belly dancer, high on cocaine, teaching herself to breathe fire off the front porch).

It didn't take long for Kaley and Kevin to pull us back to Sunset. Kevin scored a gig shooting a video for a band called Neon God at the Rainbow Bar & Grille and needed help designing a set. The guys and I scouted the venue. Kevin had a measly $500 budget for supplies, lighting and labor, which meant working for free beer.

Kaley begged me to go to the band's private party with her. On edge, she fluctuated between Kevin and her ex; a drug dealer and biker named Michael who kept her strung out on heroin. She'd lost weight since I had last seen her—she looked sick. You don't tell a girl with body issues that. You tell her she's beautiful.

"Is everything alright, K?" I asked from the Rainbow bathroom stall, hoping she wouldn't shut me out. An extra coat of Cover Girl, three shades too pale, hid sores and marks where she'd picked at her once smooth skin.

"Pneumonia in the middle of summer—in Cali. Can you imagine?" Her fingers brushed against her trusty rabbit's foot. Conversation over. She touched up her mascara and walked out the door.

The Rainbow was packed. The band, their entourage—roadies, groupies, musicians from other bands, supermodels, and professional basketball players—crammed into the tight space. Kaley nudged me every time some Vince Neil wannabe walked by.

Despite her ghostly, waifish figure, Kaley looked cute. She'd lined the white shadow over her green eyes with black and purple eyeliner. Her matching dreads were pulled back, exposing harsh punk blush contour lines on her pale skin. A black vinyl mini dress and purple combat boots completed her look.

Sporting my surfer girl tan, I wore a belly-baring black halter. Skin-tight Levi's hugged my hips. My red lipstick had disappeared in the floorboard of Kevin's Pinto during the move. I hadn't been able to pull off my punk makeover for long. It seemed like a look you had to earn. I preferred to keep it simple. I wasn't bad looking. I had done art modeling. But I was nothing compared to the supermodels in the room. Kaley and I joked that they could see their reflections in their collagen and plastic—hot on paper, but it's not real life. Even so, they were supermodels; we weren't.

We were surprised when a security person came over and told us the singer had invited us to sit with him. I loved looking at the hairband boys in their colorful makeup and wild hair. But they weren't my type.

This band was different—black denim, black leather. The blond singer at the head of the table wore a Motörhead shirt and Jim Morrison aviator-style sunglasses. His bandmates looked like they'd rolled out of coffins full of pythons and porn stars. I imagined they smelled like old Harley grease mingled with whatever the latest fragrance Victoria's Secret models were wearing. Ripped jeans, leather, and torn lace. Not my scene either.

A hundred people crowded tight around the table, waiting for a handshake or a nod from someone in the band. And the band were staring at us. I had no interest in appearing like the groupies in the bar. Clad in cropped leather bustiers, shredded jean shorts with barely an inseam left to cover their asses. Their bleach blonde hair teased into the rafters.

I pretended to nurse an empty drink so Kaley wouldn't buy me another. She tugged my elbow and insisted we go over. "Don't you know who that is, Jenny? It's Evan Reed." Rarely star struck, Kaley's eyes dazzled when she said his name.

"Who?" I asked. These musicians belonged in a motorcycle gang instead of a rock band. Well on their way to prison and bad endings, these weren't Sunset Strip glam boys.

"First of all," Kaley slurred, fishing for a cherry with her pinky finger, sloshing her drink in my direction. "He's the singer in the band we're doing the video for. Second, he's like the most famous guy in music right now. Third, he's the hottest guy in the room and he's looking at you."

I'm not sure how she ascertained that through his sunglasses. But I felt watched. I gave in and followed Kaley into the VIP room, but the crowd changed my mind. This band had a flashing red danger sign above their heads.

Kaley, who loved to dip her toes in danger before diving in headfirst, said she wanted to wait for Michael. That was reason enough to leave.

Kaley never showed up to the video set the next morning. I assumed she was still with Michael, and Kevin didn't ask. Honestly, we were relieved—no hard drugs, no drama meant we could work. I hated myself for thinking that, but it was true.

Painting props, I wore faded overalls and a paint-covered black t-shirt. One overall strap dangled as I brushed up a tall set piece with a cobalt blue. It wasn't doing the trick. Apparently, I squint and wiggle my nose when I get into hardcore *Jenny the painter* mode. No one else noticed the paint shade was off. I needed a D43 Cinnabar Green to correct it, but I wasn't about to spend my money.

Exposure, ha! Even rich artists devalue the work of the strugglers. We were lucky to get free beer.

Our roommate, Fish, walked by in a huff, scratching his scruffy, dyed red goatee against his dark skin. "Can you believe this prick wants us to work a grand piano into the video? We have to change everything."

"Did anyone tell you about the piano?" Kevin panted moments later, the corner of his mouth and left eye twitched in unison.

"The big white thing that has nothing to do with this set? Yeah, I heard." My concentration broke, too frustrated to calm him. A truckload of green paint would not fix this.

Fish came back. "How'd they even fucking get it in here? They can't serve food, it's blocking the kitchen. They had to take booths out because he wanted it at 'his table.' Who does that?"

"There's something we can do, right?" Kevin sweated. "The bartender said they want it in the party room."

"Hell-fucking-no," Fish said. "I'm not moving that shit upstairs. They're fucking with you, Kev. Don't let 'em fuck with you."

I took the set sketches from Kevin's hands. "Ignore the bartender. I'll figure it out."

Relief spread across Kevin's face. "You're a lifesaver. Did you talk to him last night?"

"Who?"

"The singer."

"Nope."

"Go say hi. He's been asking about you," Kevin said.

"Why?"

"He digs your work—he asked for you to be on this project."

"Explain?" I crossed my arms against my breasts, wishing both overall straps were tightly secured.

"He watched the submission you and Kaley helped me with and asked for you, specifically. See if you can figure out what he wants us to do with this ridiculous piano. Heads up, I think he's your buyer."

"From the gallery?"

"I might have heard that somewhere." Kevin smiled. "Please go talk to him. I need this to go well. You're an artist with buyers. I'm a film student, with film and no one buying it. I need this to look good so someone will buy my film and give me food and weed money."

Rolling my eyes, I walked towards the stupid piano.

I may as well have walked off a cliff.

Chapter Two

E van Reed held a glass of blood-red wine in his right hand. His left hand ran across the white piano keys, looking for the perfect note. Black-mirrored sunglasses. Dimly lit bar. Shoulder length, dark blonde hair pulled in a loose ponytail. A bleached white strand curved down his defined cheekbone, resting against his tanned skin. A small silver cross dangled from his right ear. Jeans, black tank top and his hands adorned with silver rings and bracelets. Fingers trailing the piano keys, he looked at me over his sunglasses. A fierce dark explosion of blue emanated from his pupils.

I had walked over to that piano angry, but his eyes caught me off guard, making me uneasy. I would spend years trying to capture that particular blue in my paintings. Those eyes, shifting from sweet, calm waves of love to dark seas of anger and rage, would be the undoing of me. Artists sometimes see people as objects, things to paint, draw, adore, idolize. From the moment I saw Evan Reed's blue eyes, his pink lips, the loose hair brushing against his chin stubble, I was painting him in my mind.

An abrupt last note startled me. I rubbed my hands on my overalls. "Hi, I'm Jennifer... Jennifer Stone. We need to talk about your piano."

My offer of a handshake went unanswered, his eyes cold. How dare I interrupt the prince in his element? I got it. Interrupting any artist mid-thought is not permissible.

Stammering, I gathered my nerve.

"Your piano doesn't fit the set. Frankly, it doesn't work with the song either." I couldn't help running my finger across the piano edge as I spoke. I'd never seen something so expensively white.

"I know who you are," the rock star said. "And I'm changing the song."

"What?" *Keep it together for Kevin, Jenny. Come on...Nope.* "Are you fucking serious, dude? We've listened to your song for three days trying to get ideas."

"Serious." His *why are you invading my space?* look hadn't left his face.

I countered with a solid, *test me again motherfucker* glare. "Sweetheart" was on the tip of his tongue.

He wasn't sizing me up the way most guys did, he was staring through me. He tapped his fingers against his knee and twisted his massive skull rings. Cracking, flexing his knuckles instead of deep breathing. No doubt pulling himself from the creative cloud to deal with me, a mere mortal. He shook the stiffened fingers on his left hand. A handicap he didn't mean for me to see. "Look, this is a quick little promo for a Japanese gig. That's why we didn't hound the label for the big shot MTV guys. Can't be that hard—it's a piano—in a music video. Our editor will slap Kanji text on it, and we're done. Kid's play."

The hair on my skin stood. "The piano doesn't fit. The song is punk rock disguised as heavy metal, not 'Bennie & The Jets.' It's all wrong." I didn't like being a hired hand to some spoiled rock star, no matter how striking his bright blue eyes were. He was toying with me. I took the bait, which made me angrier.

"Your friend—nervous kid, rocking on his feet by the bar, jonesing for a drink he doesn't have the nerve to order on the clock—said he'd handle it. If you can't do it, I'll hire someone else."

Tempted as I was to flip him off and walk out the door, I reminded myself, *Kevin needs this.* I sighed. "If you keep the song, I'll throw a paint cloth on top of it so it's not visible. I don't see another solution."

"Well, you could set it on fire, but I'm kind of attached to it." He laughed. "Honey, I'm kidding with you. I had the piano brought over to test a few songs before the bar opens. I hoped we could throw a few black and white shots into the video, but if you can't make that work..."

My work revolved around color. If he'd seen my paintings, he knew that. "I'll figure it out."

"We can get out of here if you want to talk about it."

"Nope. Not into the rock star groupie thing, Mr. Reed."

"Just Reed. My middle name. I'm twenty-five, not your old-ass uncle. I was gonna suggest getting a hamburger before my manager brings out the Cristal and heroin on a silver platter. But if you're going to be a dick about it..."

"You done? I'm here to work," I said.

"Well, I kinda hoped we'd get off on better footing. Yet, here you are, stepping on my boots."

"You and I are already off the wrong side of your precious steel-toed boots."

"Damn, girl, come on, you blew me off at my party. Now you're giving me attitude. How many paintings does a guy have to buy to meet you? I guess I'm a glutton for punishment if I'm willing to pay you to insult me, too."

"You've really been buying my paintings?"

"Fan of your work. Not into the whole artist groupie thing." He cupped his hand, lighting a cigarette. "Occasionally, I indulge myself with a meal between backstage orgies."

Great, Jenny, insult the boss. That's what Kevin needs.

Reed pulled his sunglasses off. He grinned, playfully. Johnny Depp cool with curb-stomping motorcycle boots and a platinum record smile. A living, breathing contradiction.

"Could you quit playing hard to get?" He smiled.

My cheeks went red. I hated him, but my heart fluttered like the teenage girls plastering his posters across their bedroom walls. *Men can be dicks and still be hot, Jenny.* David Lee Roth and the guys from Mötley Crüe trolling around Sunset made that more than clear.

Reed raised an eyebrow. "Is that a yes? Or go screw yourself, Reed, you're not as good looking as all those magazines said?"

My stomach rumbled. The house grocery fund was low. Fish had been eyeing the band's buffet spread for an hour. "The guys are coming with us."

"Of course." Reed waved his hand. "All the people need to eat."

I gathered the troops and attempted to wash paint off my hands, drying them on the knees of my overalls.

"Can I get a vodka?" I asked the bartender. "And one for him." I pointed at Kevin.

Reed smiled. "Put that on my tab, Charlie."

Fish, Kevin and I piled into Reed's black Jeep Cherokee, speeding across town, wind whipping my hair. The rest of the crew followed us in a van.

Reed navigated with his knee while lighting a cigarette and sliding a tape of demos into the tape deck. He softened his demeanor towards me, cranking the radio and turning on the charm—only bristling up towards the guys. *It's a game.* It was strange watching a rock star do normal things—I mean, you're a god, and you drive?

He pulled into the lot at Pann's Diner on LaTijera Boulevard. A 1950s relic known for architects Eldon Davis and Helen Liu Fong's Googie space age design, '50s décor, and iconic neon sign. Its appropriate motto: "Just food, service and rock & roll."

Reed ran his hand through his dark blond hair and held the diner door. A sweet gesture, but every eye focused on him. The rock star king had entered the building. His *I will fuck you or fuck you up* stride was hard to miss. So damn smooth, cooler than Brando in his prime—sliding off his leather biker jacket.

I wasn't immune to him. If Jim Morrison walked in the room, wouldn't you want to lick the heroin-drenched sweat off his body?

Still, I'd seen Evan Reed at the Rainbow—the king and his court of celebrities and models fawning at his feet. Arrogant was the word that came to mind. *Maybe he was bored?* How many times can you hear strangers, who never listened to your music in the first place, tell you how amazing you are?

He leaned his arm behind me on the vinyl booth. A simple touch brought the heavy pressure of envy as fans stopped by the table to take a Polaroid.

It had to be the tequila-spiked drinks, but an electricity ran through us when my finger touched his. I was glad the fans interrupted.

"Get me and the crew," Reed said after signing their napkins. They obliged, sneaking a photo after he'd said something so funny that even Kevin laughed, his face red as soda dripped from his nose.

That was the first photo taken of Reed and me, sitting in a booth at Pann's Diner—unknowing, youthful smiles. My face and hair covered in a confetti of paint. His arm resting behind me. When people post collages of how our love "really was"—this is the photo they use. That beautiful, perfect moment in time that ultimately sealed my fate. That was when I became a girl rock stars write songs about. They weren't always nice songs—but that's for later. And that photo he slid in his pocket; a breadcrumb for lost souls who would never find their way home.

Reed stole my fries and informed the waitress we were sharing our drink with two straws. He sipped from mine. He joked with the guys but kept his eyes on me, blatantly flirting. Flasks and bottles of wine that weren't on the menu appeared from under the table throughout the night.

Despite the wide grin on my face, instinct told me to leave. My roommates, my protectors, slipped away from me, lost in booze and celebrity.

"What's your mama's name?" Reed asked, nuzzling his mouth against my ear, his breath tickling the spot on my neck that makes a girl shiver.

"You're drunk." I laughed, pulling away.

"I'm not drunk. I want to know everything about you."

I wasn't falling for it.

Reed was an open book. One that required a compass, a decoder, a glossary, index, and companion guide to decipher and read between the lines. He had a way of telling you everything, revealing nothing. Born Evan Reed Williams, he grew up in a small Kentucky town in Barren County he swore wasn't worth visiting. Dry like its name, "There's shit to do. Nothing to drink. Nowhere to go. And the Kentucky Chicken Fucking Sucks." He loved practical jokes and could make you feel like you were the only person in a room of thousands. When he took off his sunglasses in stadiums, every girl in the crowd swore he was singing to her. That night he projected that witchery on me.

He was pretty fucking cute, but I was not stupid.

"Need a ride?" Reed asked as we left the diner. Before I answered, he pulled me close and kissed me, his lips hot and sweet like whiskey and Cherry Cola.

I pointed at the bus sign. "My stop. Thanks for dinner."

Before he could charm me into staying, I jumped aboard and dropped coins in the designated slot.

I put the night out of my mind. I didn't have time to think about kissing Evan Reed. It was Hollywood in the mid-80s; if you were a girl (or guy) you'd kissed someone famous at some point or the other. For every famous guy you kissed, that guy kissed a thousand other girls. I didn't have time to dwell on it.

It was only a kiss.

Hungover, Fish ranted on the morning bus. "Dumb rock stars demanding a grand piano in the middle of a gritty nightclub scene. He totally put the moves on you."

"He was alright," I said.

"You need to burn that fucker down. I'm serious."

"Fish, you genius!" Remembering Reed's comment about setting the piano on fire, I snatched Fish's notebook, and sketched a new set design. At the Rainbow, I told the boys to tear down the set and pull the white piano to the middle of the floor. I called Danny, a pyro guy, and told him to bring lighter fluid. By noon, we finished our final run through with the video crew.

The band rolled in two hours behind schedule. Matty, the blond, frizzy-haired bass player tried to chat me up. His words slurred so badly, I couldn't understand him.

"Bathroom is behind the bar," I said.

Dene, the band's lead guitarist had a side-cut and massive mane of jet-black hair. "I'm digging this setup," he said. His hipbones jutted from his slick leather pants. It was impossible not to catch a glimpse of his hot ass.

Watch the paint, girl! These were not the kind of guys anyone should take home to their mother. They dripped with whiskey and intoxicating sexuality—and sweat, lots of sweat. Darrian Starr was the band's drummer—"not the original"—something constantly pointed out in a way that didn't reflect his playing, or when he joined the band, but to say, "We wouldn't normally hire a black dude." It signaled a bigger problem in the white, male-dominated metal scene.

Understandably, Fish didn't trust them.

Levon Steele was the rhythm guitarist shooting up heroin in the bathroom. Evan Reed, the habitually late singer, was nowhere to be found.

The director filmed test shots of the band while they became increasingly inebriated waiting for Reed. Fish and I sat out back laughing and getting high on weed & paint fumes. Kevin was furious.

"Guys, please?" He pulled at his messy blond hair. "You destroyed the set. Did you not consider calling the guy responsible for filming this video—you know, the guy who got you the job?"

Fish always had the best weed. We kept laughing.

"Screw you guys," Kevin spat. "Come inside. Pretend to be sober, if you can."

Giggling like school kids, we found refuge behind the bar. "Whiskey, yes?" Fish swiped a bottle. We took turns swigging long drinks when Kevin wasn't looking. Fish rolled his eyes. "Dude's wearing a tie. Can't believe he's falling for this shit."

"I know." I smiled in Kevin's direction, proud.

Fish grumbled, downing a shot. "These assholes don't care about any of this."

Evan Reed finally graced the bar with his presence, a stripper on each arm—never acknowledging my existence. *It was one kiss. Not a big deal.* He did have those blue eyes and dreamy lips, but what rock star doesn't? I was satisfied. I had orchestrated these ladies to dance in fire on top of a flaming grand piano. It was like a silly high school prank, only you're legal age and you're about to get busted.

"Reed, here is where you come in. We need a couple of close shots of you playing the piano before they set it on fire," the director said. Fish and I ducked behind the bar to avoid Kevin's gaze as that piano went up in flames.

The rest, as they say, is music video history. Look me up online. I won an award for art direction. If I had gone to the ceremony, I would have seen the band perform the song, flaming piano and all. But I wasn't a rock star. I had shit to deal with. Real life was about to come down hard, psycho killer hatchet style—destroying everyone I loved.

Chapter Three

A cryptic message waited for me on the answering machine a month after the video shoot. My name was listed as the next of kin on a hospital intake form for Kaley Dean.

"I'm not supposed to give details," a nurse said. "It's imperative she comes back for treatment. It's a public safety issue. I'm sorry."

Kaley had AIDS. Full-blown AIDS. She didn't know until her ex-boyfriend, Michael the junkie, got sick. While I'd been filming music videos and living the hippie commune life at the house in the woods, she'd been in the hospital for a drug overdose. No one had seen her since the band's pre-video party.

A hedonistic little creature, turning up when she wanted to—we hadn't missed her. Kevin always worried but he'd been focused on editing that damn video. By the time word got back, no one could tell us where she was.

You don't catch AIDS like a cold, but a plague had hit—first New York City, then San Francisco, then the world. Eight people had been in and out of our place, and there was that *sharing boyfriends* thing. Fish and I were okay. Kevin assumed the worst but refused to take the test. He wanted to find Kaley before it was too late.

We tracked Michael to a Sunset club. Once a terrifying presence, he was bone thin, covered in sores. So drunk he could barely stand.

"Where is Kaley?" I demanded.

Staring at me with hollow, dying eyes, he hissed. "Bitch got what she deserved. You will too."

My skin pricked as every tiny hair stood on edge. I paid Michael's tab and collected his ID from the bartender. Kevin and I slipped out of the building.

The address on the license was twenty minutes away from the club. Barred and boarded businesses lined an eerily quiet neighborhood. Graffiti announced: "Welcome to Hell."

The small white house, toxic lead paint peeling away from the siding, was half surrounded by a rusted, damaged chain-link fence. A sign read: "Beware of Dog." Crushed beer cans and broken glass littered the front yard. Second and third eviction notices taped to the front door blew in the wind. We banged on the door and after getting no response, looked through the windows.

Kaley's purple leather handbag, a gift Kevin had given her for her last birthday, lay spilled across the kitchen floor.

Kevin grabbed a rock and busted the window. He used the elbow of his jeans jacket to clear the glass shards and pulled me in behind him.

"Kaley?" I called out, checking each room. Kevin and I watched for junkies in the shadows.

The bathroom door was closed. Kevin pushed it open and stumbled back.

The bathtub was full of bloody water that had spilled over onto the floor.

Adrenaline pumped through my veins. My heart was beating so hard I was certain it would explode. Whatever had been in the bathtub had been dragged through the opposite door into a locked bedroom. We used our shoulders as battering rams until the lock broke.

Blood-saturated carpet greeted us. We followed dried rusty streaks through the bedroom to a utility closet.

Get out of this place now! My brain screamed.

I called out, hoping for a whisper, a whimper, a gasp of air. "Kaley? Kaley, baby, are you there?" I hated the way my voice sounded like a desperate Jamie Lee Curtis in the first *Halloween* movie, a girl desperate to find her best friend. I flicked on the lamp by the door, illuminating a white freezer covered in bloody handprints. *Stop. Go home, Jenny.* I slid my long shirtsleeves down, covering my palms and pushed the freezer lid open.

I choked.

"Kevin! Don't! Get away!" I shouted. But he'd already seen her. A ghastly sight. One we'd never forget. And, god, the smell.

AIDS did not kill Kaley. Kaley killed Kaley. She filled the bath with warm water and penned a short note to her dad. Then put a needle in the vein on her neck and slit her wrists with a pink disposable razor. The cheap, useless kind made for women.

She woke up and tried to get out of the tub, slipped, and hit her head on the porcelain sink.

Michael had found her bloody on the bathroom floor. He thought he'd killed her. Can you imagine not knowing if you've murdered someone?

I promise, it's not something you forget.

Michael had dragged Kaley down the hall, stuffing her limp, 90-pound body into the freezer—a bad attempt at covering tracks he wasn't sure he left in the first place. At least that's the drunken story he told in the end. It's not the one I believe, nor is it the one that haunts me. Unaware of Kaley's death, police across town had dismissed his rambling confession as words of a paranoid junkie.

He overdosed on heroin before he was picked up again.

When the coroner showed up to collect Kaley's body, I heard her say on her radio, "Don't rush, it's just another junkie suicide." And that's all it was. No one went to jail, nobody cared.

Cops were so unconcerned with Kaley's death that Kevin managed to slip out of Michael's house with her purple purse and a small, black Armani bag full of needles. "That's not her kit," Kevin said, tossing it on his dashboard. He reached for the purse zipper; the lucky rabbit's foot was missing. We were thinking the same thing—Kaley died because we weren't paying attention.

Kaley's ashes were stuffed in a USPS box with a bright orange "cremated remains" sticker and mailed to her dad and stepmom in Iowa. I will never forget the image of her in that freezer. Her body contorted into an unnatural geometric shape. Skin blue, her mouth frozen shut, eyebrows covered in frost. I'm certain I saw the scratches of a bloody handprint on the inside of the freezer. Cracked nails of a broken girl who tried to claw her way out. The blood covering her flesh—a black sticky mess

If you know my work, you've seen the painting.

I was not aware of, nor did I care about any award for art direction in a music video. Everyone went their separate ways. I canceled the lease over the phone and mailed a check for the damages.

I moved home with my parents. Seeking refuge in my teenage bedroom, beneath the scrap blanket my great-grandmother hand-stitched. Grateful for every guilt-filled cup of warm tea my mother sat on the nightstand, I wondered how one bright little soul felt so lost, so unloved that she managed to turn her own suicide into a murder. I remembered Kaley saying, "Pneumonia in Cali," like it was a thing. She was stabbing poisoned needles in her veins, while Fish and I laughed, hiding behind the Rainbow Bar as everything around us went up in flames.

My brain couldn't accept Kaley had frozen. Trapped. Alone. An instant replay haunted me—her begging me to stay at the band's party. Michael's chilling words. That damn white house with peeling paint, the blood—her tiny body contorted and alone.

I cried myself to sleep. There was nothing else I could do.

Chapter Four

When I returned to California, the summer after Kaley's death, I was different. After months of moping in my old room, and barely holding a job at the local coffee shop, I resolved to get my shit together. I washed my greasy hair and pulled up my metaphorical bootstraps. *Breathe deep.* My mom registered me for my last classes at The Institute of Art. I pretended the life before didn't happen. I had to prove that this horrific death had not consumed me. *If I lose myself, the drugs win. Michael wins. Death wins.*

Using the last of my savings to buy a used car, I made the drive, taking a detour along the coast by myself. Tanned surfers braved the breaking waves. Blonde girls with perfect smiles and glistening skin basked in the heat. I stayed in Mar Vista, taking a part-time gallery job.

My new dream was to own a studio. I could get what I wanted if I worked hard enough. Life owed me a reset.

I wanted to distance myself from the free love hippie lifestyle I'd fallen into before. Convincing myself I had integrity—the gallery owner was great, the art was local. I desperately tried to create this persona—someone who might have been Jennifer Stone if I'd never followed that girl in the Bauhaus shirt and purple dreads down her psychedelic path. I enjoyed the company of other people, but I kept them at a distance. You never know when someone you love is going to turn up in a deep freezer, right?

It was a good plan until management changed.

You can do this, Jenny. Get the fuck out of bed. My thin wrists gave me away—shaking after my third refill of lukewarm coffee in a Styrofoam cup. If Kaley had taught me anything, it was that a good coat of foundation, lashes to die for, and a smile with a fresh swipe of red lipstick can hide anything.

A corporate owner took over the gallery. Instead of giving me, the chick who'd been to art school a promotion, they hired the Suit; a sleazy car salesman to boss me around.

Out went the cool works from local artists.

In came socially irrelevant mass printings.

I hit a roadblock at university. It turns out that when you ditch your scholarship mid-semester, you have to pay the money back. My dad was having terrible coughing spells, unable to catch his breath. Mom was worried. I didn't want my debt to fall on my parents. Leaving school was my mistake, not theirs. I had to grow up and figure shit out fast.

Pressured by the gray cloud hovering over my parent's barely existent income, I forged my way into corporate, plastic America. The only way to disrupt the establishment is to jump into the pit of it, right? I scraped up change for rent and one class. At that rate, it would take at least two years to finish my degree.

Then what? I hadn't painted since I'd returned to California. No inspiration, no money for paint. I put on my pretend face in the mornings, with my air-attendant attire and fake smile, to get away from the girl in torn jeans and tank tops who'd stopped leaving her apartment.

I watched the clock and the exit for my chance to escape, aching for my old life. Not because I was happy and carefree or any of that bullshit—but because it was real.

Evan Reed made his grand re-entrance into my life that September. The gallery hosted a corporate event for a local law firm. Hair pinned up, my lips ruby red, I wore a black pencil skirt, white top and respectable heels. Determined to get a bonus and a transfer away from Suit. I'd be able to pay my bills for the month and send my mom money to fix her station wagon.

Suit towered above me in his office before the event. His triple XL suit stretched to accommodate his girth. His face drew into a plump, red-cheeked snout. He squinted, explaining things as if I was a child, grunting as he spoke. The squinting had given him a child-like quality at first. I'd hoped to find his pig-like presence endearing. The snorting cut that short. The long labored breaths he made the time he'd had the nerve to grab my ass, made me want to vomit.

Wheezing, Suit settled behind his desk. His knees splayed out, taking up the room while he leaned back, stretching his arms and locking his fingers behind his balding head. His cheeks flapped like they were full of lumpy chicken paste. His voice came in a sing-song whistle, blowing his ignorant man-thoughts out an empty tooth hole. "It wouldn't hurt you to smile,

Jennifer. People don't like girls who don't smile. It's off putting." When he inhaled, it felt like he might swallow up the entire room. *Wisp-swoosh.*

When he called corporate, he talked up my sales figures as though they were his own.

I wanted to stab him in the eye with my pointy red nails. I kept them filed sharp in case the opportunity arose.

"This is a very important night. Don't pull any of that quirky, artsy nonsense, Jennifer. These clients give zero shits about pigmentation or brush strokes. They don't know the difference between a Rimbaud or a Rembrandt."

I rolled my eyes. "Rimbaud was a poet."

"Exactly, child. Men don't want to be corrected by women. They want something original to hang above their desks. You and I both know the only people that will get a long look at these paintings are the secretaries they pound into after work. Maybe you'll get lucky and score a date. Gotta use those ass...ets, you know what I'm saying?" He chuckled.

I pinched the spot between my thumb and forefinger and gritted my teeth. *Paycheck, Jenny. Clock in. Clock out.* Suit was wrong. I didn't care how irrelevant the paint by numbers art was. And I did not need a man.

But, Jennifer, the confident, sexy, side piece greeted the clients. "Let me take your coat. Wine is to your left. Let me know if you have any questions." I was determined to stay focused to meet the night's goal.

First step: go for the clients who can't stay late—they can't afford anything in the gallery. The trick was the payment plan—a fast, easy sale, and a brochure to get them on their way. Then we could focus on the high rollers.

One young Reaganite grabbed my arm when I stepped out of the back supply room to replenish the cheese tray. He wasn't a repeat customer, but an entitled stalker. He stared at a painting of a bald eagle and American Flag. "I'm still interested in this one. Have you thought about my offer?" He nodded towards his crotch.

The pungent Gruyere and Limburger burned my nose.

He gripped my arm tighter. "You don't want me to tell your boss you're not being helpful, do you?"

Suit looked over with his *keep the transaction going* nod.

Not happening. I tried to move.

Yuppie scum blocked me.

I glanced at the red fire extinguisher on the wall, wondering how fast I could bash it into his head. Instead, I pushed the cheese tray into his hands. "Take your tiny dick out the door before I make a scene your co-workers will never forget."

The old me, the one who spent nights in overalls covered in paint, would have dick-punched him and taken his wallet. Here I was—being as polite as one can be, while being sexually harassed. This wasn't new—it was normal. Men were always doing this sort of thing. And not just to me. Every woman I know had stories like this.

Expensive cheese slid from the tray as he let it clatter to the floor.

I bit my lip. *Do not let him get to you, Jenny.* He didn't care about getting a blow job. These men got off on making women uncomfortable. To succeed in their world, I had to smile and pretend a grown man hadn't just told me to suck his dick in the middle of an art gallery.

Chaos erupted in the front lobby. A group of long-haired hellions walked into the pristine gallery. Thundering boots on tile. Leather, chains and furs—a far cry from the polyester suits in the room. A roaming Jack Daniels distillery mixed with motor oil, Calvin Klein Obsession, and the bottom of an ashtray.

Well, that's a hot damn mess waiting to happen! I would take any opportunity to get away from this jerk. I pushed past him.

Across the room, leather and fur coats were removed. A cigarette lit. Long hair—now darker, grown past his shoulders. Same blue eyes. A familiar face.

Evan Reed looked in my direction.

Creep boy tried to grab my arm again. "Are you seriously walking away from me? Do you have any idea who my father is?"

I snapped. "Your daddy can shove his money up his ass."

In hindsight, perhaps I should've been a "good girl," taken the yuppie scum upstairs, and given him an easy ride. Was that my fork in the road? Surely that can't be where I lost my way. Was that my warning from the universe? Give rich scum bags free blow jobs, but don't get too close to some rock star's blue eyes or you might drown!

Suit rushed the rowdy crew of rockers off the sales floor. "Gentlemen, let me show you our special selection in the back." He saw the chance to sell the nude knock offs he couldn't display out front.

I stepped between them. "Mr. Reed, thank you for coming. Unfortunately, there's not one piece of trash in this building worth wasting your time on."

"Jennifer!" Suit hissed.

Reed smiled. "It's okay—whatever you said your name is. I'm acquainted with Ms. Stone. We've done business before."

"I apologize for her behavior. What can I help you with?" Suit put his hand up, reminding me to stay in my place. I was merely a prop. A tits and ass mannequin, articulated in the jaw and wrist for the sole purpose of pleasing men—a cunt who ought to know her place was in the kitchen. Not a living, breathing human being.

"I wouldn't mess with Miss Stone if I were you. She's quite the little arsonist," Reed said.

"Jennifer, go help your clients," Suit said.

Evan Reed raised an eyebrow—challenging me to be the tough girl he'd met at the Rainbow, inspiring a sense of courage I'd misplaced. Reed's gaze made me want to be the woman grown men write kick-ass songs about. *Done.*

"Boys—wine." I pointed Reed's entourage towards the free wine and hors d'oeuvres. I grabbed my bag. I didn't want to be this corporate robot, selling generic paintings of mallards to dentists and lawyers who couldn't find their way through a Dick Blick art store without a map.

"Walk out that door, honey, and you're fired," Suit growled, reaching for my shoulder.

I dropped my bag and punched Suit in the dick.

Eyes bulging, mouth puckered, his face puffed bright red like a blowfish.

Reed laughed. "I think she quit, dude." He slipped his hand around mine. "Come on, killer, I'll walk you to your bus stop."

At Pann's Diner, the same blonde waitress led us to our booth. "You happy selling out with that dude?" Reed asked.

"It used to be an okay gig."

"Honey, that ain't a gig. It's a one-way ticket to obscurity. Why are you working for him? He should be working for you."

I sipped my drink. "My art doesn't appeal to the current clientele."

"Is that so? Well, it sucks you got fired." Reed thumped the saltshaker.

"It's a good thing."

"No, it sucks 'cause you can't pay me back."

"For what?"

"We have a little legal issue between us." He laughed.

"Are you kidding?" I stiffened up.

"You set a stripper's hair extensions on fire. They melted off in clumps. Man, she was pissed! It was funny as shit."

"Wow." I laughed. "That's a tragedy. Was she okay?"

"Yeah, she's fine. The smell of that woman though—I'm not talking bleach and smoke."

"Yikes."

"I had to fork over five thousand for that. Oh wait... there was that $60,000 piano." He laughed to the waitress. "Can you believe this girl owes me $60,000? And I'm buying her dessert?"

Her thin Hollywood lip liner turned into a genuine smile. "She must be a special lady."

"She's something alright."

"What brought you to the gallery tonight?" I asked, laying a napkin across my lap.

"Pure piano rage. Saw your name on the program, something had to be done."

"Wait, do you still have the piano?"

"Fire damage and all. Took her on tour and pyro-ed the shit out of her. I'm never gonna tell you who she belonged to before you set her on fire."

"It wasn't a well thought-out plan."

"You didn't bother to show up for your award."

"Things... happened."

Evan Reed twirled a strand of my hair between his fingers. "Yeah, I know."

I didn't know if he knew about Kaley—something told me he understood.

"Thanks for dinner. I'd buy, but you know, unemployed and all. Speaking of, I've got to get up early and find a job."

"Ah, you commoners always remind me what life is like in the real world." He dropped a hundred-dollar bill on the table.

Quiet streets were lit by the moon and flickering streetlights. A cool breeze blew through my hair. Reed pulled me close, into a hug.

"Is this the part where I kiss you and you run away on your bus again?" He brushed his hand against my cheek, our lips met—it wasn't just one kiss now.

Deja vu. I smiled. "This is the part where you buy us a bottle of wine in a paper bag and we take the bus to my place."

"Public transportation... It's been a while." He laughed.

"It's always an adventure."

"I'm up for adventure." Reed smiled.

"Alright." I pulled off my heels, grabbed his hand. We ran down the sidewalk to the liquor store. He bought two bottles of L.A.s finest—Absolut Vodka.

"Sir, I like your taste."

We chased my bus, jumping on before it rounded the corner. Downing vodka in the back, we made out shamelessly. We barely made it across the patch of grass to my apartment with our clothes on. I dropped my heels at some point, too drunk to unlock the door. He took my keys, picked me up, and managed to get inside.

Overeager hands and lips. Missed buttons and misplaced kisses. My head hit the wall; the ripped fabric of my skirt slid up my hips. Reed wasted no time sealing the deal. Warm flesh inside warm flesh, I gasped. *Damn, I guess Suit was right—I needed this.* I remembered the girls at the Rainbow, lining up after shows for guys like Reed. *Fuck that.* I bit into his lip hard and shoved him away with my knee, my palm hit his chest.

Backing away, he rubbed blood from his lip with his thumb. He grinned, waiting for my next move.

This was not his territory. I'd be damned if he came first. I conjured the girl I'd been at the Art in L.A. photo shoot, Russian red lips, fishnets. Power. Kaley's welcome voice in my ear—*make him think you'll eat him alive.* Reed didn't resist when his back hit the kitchen table, my knees tight against his ribs, twisting his long hair into my fist—I wanted to light a fire in him. Moonlight from the kitchen window cascaded down my bare chest. I showed no mercy, it would be me first if I had to break him.

On the edge, Reed gripped my chin. "You don't come without me. Not tonight. Not ever." My palm hit the table; books, drawing pads and art pencils knocked aside. He didn't make me wait, but his eyes never left mine. He gripped my wrists against his chest. Trapped in *la petit mort*—the little death—shuddering thighs, my knees gone weak. Cataclysm or ecstasy, it was too early to tell.

Nothing is more intense than two damaged people coming together for the first time.

Maybe he was the guy in the magazines, the videos—a line of groupies queued against his hotel door ready to blow him—but tonight, he was mine.

We moved from the kitchen to the shower. His kisses on my neck, chest, and stomach as gentle as the water droplets hitting our flesh. Each moment vivid. His fingertips smooth against my skin, my nails digging into his back. Nothing else in the world existed. No art, no music, just two beautiful, naked bodies with broken souls pressed tight against each other. That brief dizzy moment of insanity, believing you've found the missing piece and can't imagine you existed without them. Being with your soulmate the first time is like fucking in the stars. The skies open. It changes your soul.

Or maybe it was the vodka?

It was definitely the vodka.

I fell asleep in a mass of pillows and blankets on my bedroom floor, sleeping soundly for the first time in months.

My new favorite rock star made eggs and toast for breakfast. I put on his white tank top, a pair of black shorts and draped the long strands of wooden rosary beads he'd worn the night before around my neck. We ate our eggs at the kitchen table and read the newspaper. He doused his toast with hot sauce, eating it with a fork and butter knife like someone who'd had far too many Waffle House meals on the run, savoring each bite.

"Hey, I've got this band thing. You, okay? About last night. You had fun?"

I smiled. "Yes."

"Good."

We spent ten minutes searching for his snakeskin boots and wallet. The old ladies across the street watched the bare-chested, long-haired, tan guy search for his clothes outside my apartment. A dog had eaten my thong. My shoes were gone.

"Here, take your shirt," I said.

He kissed me. "Keep it."

I found an old Aerosmith "Back in The Saddle" tour shirt in my closet for him and watched it glide down his chest. He slid his wallet in his pocket. "How do I get in touch with you? What's your number?"

"No phone. No job." The vodka and pheromones had worn off, sanity had set in. "Really, you don't have to. I know how dessert and sex with a hot random rock star works. You're free to go, Evan Reed."

"It's Reed. And you know I'm not random." He pulled on his boots. "I've got somewhere I need to be, but I'm not going anywhere." He kissed me. "How do I get in touch with you, no phone?"

I pushed him out the door. "You know my bus stop." I didn't lie to myself that I would see him again. It was a fun night, but I knew a player when I met one.

Chapter Five

I scanned the classifieds, circling potential jobs and studio apartments. Sipping a warm cup of tea, Reed's used cup next to mine on the counter. My fingers absentmindedly traced his beaded rosary.

Bummed about my unemployment, I visited my friend Sasha who owned a beauty salon in L.A. A tiny place that smelled a bit like cats––but mostly chamomile, hair dye, the faint ghost of tamales—she'd inherited it from her Hispanic grandmother and lived in the apartment upstairs.

"You had sex," Sasha said when I plopped into her dryer chair. Her dark hair fell into gorgeous chestnut waves.

I laughed. "God, what?"

"You're glowing."

"I didn't have sex, I had coffee." I wanted to tell her about work, and yes, getting laid. Her client—a purple-haired seventy-year-old in curlers was holding a copy of *Rolling Stone*. Evan Reed was on the cover. *Wow, he's that famous now?* "Heavy Metal's Bad Boy Makes Good" was the story lead. My stomach turned. Skipping the sex, I went straight to my job woes.

"Good for you. Your boss is such a creep." Sasha foiled her second client, brushing bright red color against golden wheat hair. Her specialty was stripping layers of Sunset Strip Aqua Net, turning other people's bleached nightmares into something shiny and new. "If you need extra cash, you can do a couple of washouts for me." She knew I needed more than cash. I needed to watch fresh dye run across latex gloves and swirl down the drain. She had begged me, "Go to color school. All my clients love you."

Bright red hair twisted and twirled beneath her hair dryer. It was enticing—but beautician school would require more student loans to go along with the one I was already missing payments on. I grabbed a copy of the weekly job circular.

The next day, a dozen red roses waited at my apartment with a note signed: *For a special lady.* Evan Reed was suddenly everywhere. His latest ballad played in the dairy section of the grocery store; his face was on a magazine at the register. When I took my portfolio to an ad agency, the muzak version of his song played in the elevator.

A dozen pink roses sat on my doorstep.

Two days later, white roses.

Where is he? My kitchen was full by the end of the week. Monday brought another delivery, pink daisies, purple lilacs—the scent reminded me of my mother's kitchen, the calming safety of my childhood.

The note read: *Get a phone—it's the 20th Century! ~ Reed*

The only way to keep guys like Reed interested is to let them suffer. A part of me wanted him to suffer—and beg. I smiled. Kaley would love this!

A pain hit the pit of my stomach, reminding me she wasn't there.

Tuesday, I dressed for a job interview.

My doorbell rang. Reed leaned in the doorway, wearing his rock star sunglasses, holding a single red rose against his lips.

"Hi." I smiled.

He glimpsed my flower-filled kitchen. "Maybe I went a little overboard?"

"A little."

"The only way I could reach you, no phone..."

"There's a payphone across the street. Mrs. Ellie next door takes my messages. I can't afford a phone. No job, remember? I'm heading to an interview. Rain check?"

"I'm not gonna come inside unless you invite me in. So, invite me in."

"What are you, a vampire? I can't invite you in. I'm leaving."

"Not a vampire. A gentleman."

I laughed. "Is that what you tell your mother?"

"My mom's dead," he said.

"Oh shit, I'm sorry."

He rolled his eyes. "She's not dead, just a terrible person—a dude can be hopeful, right? I bet your mom's nice though. Invite me inside and tell me about her."

"You still want to know about my mom?"

"And your daddy and your dog from when you were five."

I laughed. "Didn't have a dog."

"Your five-headed lizard and the witchcraft book you kept in your nightstand? Secret pack of Marlboro Reds you hid under your mattress? Am I close?"

"Not even."

"I'm coming inside."

"Again?" I laughed.

"Damn, I like you." Reed eased inside my door and put his arms around my waist. "Little black business skirt, bright red lips, high heels. All my favorite things in one package. You sure you can't stay?"

"You're tempting, but no."

"After I took the bus and everything?"

"I'm flattered." I gently bit his bottom lip. "Any other time and I'd be down for this, but I need this job."

"Pretty please?"

Why does he have to smell so damn good?

He pulled my hair back, kissing my neck. "I don't want you to go." He pushed his hands up my skirt, pulled down my black lace panties, lifted me onto the kitchen counter and did things with his tongue that would put Mick Jagger to shame. Gripping his hair, my toes dug into his hips, riding the waves when he made me come so hard, I almost punched him.

Clock hands pulled me into reality.

Nudging him away, I adjusted my clothes.

"You want to leave after that?" He smiled, wiping his wet lips.

"Wait here if you want."

Reed kissed my neck. "Waiting is not my thing, honey." He ran his hand down the front of my skirt and pulled it up, pushing me forward onto the table. Slow at first. Then fast, hard. Almost too hard, but good. If there's one thing I've learned about musicians, they have impeccable rhythm. *Okay, maybe I can stay home... a few more... minutes...* My cold morning coffee spilled across the table, staining my blouse. *Fuck.*

We ordered Chinese for lunch using the last of my crumpled cash, while he rambled on about a million-dollar music video.

"There's an abandoned military hangar in Death Valley I wanted to use." He moved his chopsticks through his lo-mein. "Permits are a nightmare, no easy access for helicopters to refuel. It's 115 degrees during summer, too risky for film equipment. The record company rented Giants Stadium instead. My manager said I can use the new contract as leverage to get what I want next time."

Giants Fucking Stadium. I glanced over his shoulder at the clock, thinking maybe I could make it to a phone and call the hiring manager. *Sorry, this jerk rock star showed up on my doorstep.*

"Hey, you there?" Reed raised an eyebrow. "It was a good concept, right?"

"Yeah, sounds great."

He sat down his food carton. "Look, I'm sorry, this was a mistake."

"Huh?" I asked, pulled out of my *I'll be broke and desolate forever* daze.

"I never should've let you out of your bed." He jumped from the floor, pulled me over his shoulder and carried me up the loft steps. I laughed when I hit the sheets. Forgetting my problems, slipping into bliss.

At five, when there wasn't a chance of reaching the HR manager, Reed said he had to leave for a meeting. "Will you be home this week? I'll stop by since you won't get a phone." He kissed me at the door. "Listen, Jenny—can I call you Jenny? You were gorgeous this morning all dressed up. But you look better in your overalls, covered in paint."

I blushed.

He kissed my fingers. "You're beautiful. But don't take your talent for granted to score some shit job. I've got friends, y'know? I can connect you with some people. Hell, you could always work for me. My favorite painter bailed, she's not putting any new work out. I've checked all over town."

"I haven't really painted since Kaley -"

"I know about your friend."

"How?"

"That skinny kid from the video shoot. I can't imagine what that was like."

"I haven't painted since that night."

"Maybe I can inspire you a little?"

"And how exactly do you plan to do that?"

"I have my ways. Right now, I've gotta jet. I'll be back soon. I promise. You'll have to guess when since I can't call you. Don't wait up tonight."

"Oh, I won't."

"That terrifies me. But I like it." He glanced at the clock. "I'm late."

"Go, do whatever rock stars do."

He pulled me close. "That's not what this is. None of that exists when we're together. I'd blow it off, but it's kind of a big deal."

"It's fine, blow in with the wind."

"Honey, I'm a fucking hurricane."

Maybe he was a Scorpions' song, but to me he always felt a little more Blue Oyster Cult "Burnin' For You." He randomly turned up on my doorstep at all hours. After a while, he stayed over more nights than not. My rock star boyfriend was the same as your boyfriend—we ordered pizza, watched *E.T.* on a laser disc player, played Trivial Pursuit and Twister. He left his keys on my dresser, stole my toothbrush, and left the toilet seat up. His latest vinyl acquisitions mixed with mine. He said, "Jenny, let me play this album for you," a thousand times—Iron Maiden, Motörhead, N.W.A., Prince, Dinosaur Jr. and Peter Gabriel—everything except U2's *Joshua Tree* which he refused to listen to.

I had no clue he was blowing off rehearsals and wasting precious studio time.

We were normal together. It was easy to forget he was *that guy*. Things were different for Reed. Fans and paparazzi mobbed him in Hollywood. He couldn't take the bus to my apartment without being hassled. His driver dropped him off at a convenience store near my place. He went inside the store, bought a pack of cigarettes, went out the back and walked three blocks to my apartment.

He rarely mentioned his music other than complaining that his bandmates were always wasted.

In his mind, it was always them.

I found work at a small gallery and taught an art class at a youth center twice a week. Reed insisted on loaning me the money to register for my last two courses to finish my degree. I didn't tell him about my massive debt or my parent's money problems. My dad's health was failing; all their funds going to medical bills.

After Kaley, I wasn't ready to deal with someone else's illness. I was terrified to lose my dad, but I couldn't tell Reed.

He took my spare key. I would come home for lunch to find him asleep on my sofa or playing my old Atari. He never asked if he could do these things; he was used to getting what he wanted when he wanted it. Those things seem harmless when they involve sofas and video games.

The first nasty thing his fans wrote about me was in some fanzine. Megan Wocnyzik announced to the world that I was after Reed's money. Megan, if you're out there—know this—your favorite musician crashed at my place. He used my electricity, ate the last of my Cornflakes, and put the empty box back in the cabinet. He drank straight from the milk carton and always left his boots on the floor at the foot of my bed (no matter how many times I cursed while tripping over them). He never washed his own laundry. He did hang out with me at the laundromat, scribbling away in his lyric book. I used my own quarters. I knew nothing about his money or his six million dollar house in the hills—he didn't talk about it. I didn't ask. If money and fame were so great, why was he knocking on my door at 2 a.m.?

Lions don't like cages, no matter how big they are. Reed was trapped in that mansion. He could have and do whatever he wanted but at what cost? Fans and stalkers (like you Megan!) lined outside his gate. Paparazzi were arrested for trespassing on his property. He was safe with me in our little world.

The first six months we dated, I never saw his band play. It was a job. And some days he hated his job. He wasn't a sixteen-year-old, writing songs and drinking beer in his grandmother's basement anymore. Or the guy who slept on the floor of a studio apartment with four musicians, trying not to roll over onto broken glass or used needles. I didn't comprehend the magnitude of his fame. Fearing it would scare me away, he went to great lengths to make sure it didn't touch us.

When I saw Reed in a magazine, I turned the page. It felt wrong and invasive to read those things. That was his job, and he was a human being.

A former friend of mine was a tabloid "journalist." Inventing a cause célèbre, she wrote an exploitative gore piece that managed to tie Kaley's death to her estranged father's music career. I knew firsthand the lies printed in those rags, I didn't want to contribute to that culture.

We weren't like those people on television and newsstands. We were normal. We took road trips and went camping and canoeing. We surfed along the coastal highway. With his hair pulled back and piercings out, my casual friends from our camping group didn't recognize him. Reed loved the lack of pressure. Of just being—*Jenny from the gallery's boyfriend.*

He was creating a persona to get away from something—like I had after Kaley's death. When our camping friends asked what he did, he told them he worked at a recording studio.

"Really, dude? Meet anyone cool?" A friend asked.

"Nah, I sweep the floors, man." Reed winked at me and used a stick to roast a marshmallow in the campfire.

Later, lying in our tent, we heard a loud crash from the trash cans. He poked his head out.

"Shit, coyotes. They're gone now. I should have brought my gun."

I adjusted in the sleeping bag. "You have a gun?"

He stared at me like I was an alien from another planet. His forehead crinkled. "Yeah, I have a few. Why? Does that bother you?"

"I mean... I didn't know. My parents were super hippies. I've never seen a gun up close. It's strange, that's all."

He shrugged. "I'm from Kentucky. It's the law of the land out there. You alright? You seem a little freaked out."

"No, it's your money. You're a grown man."

"I can take you shooting sometime if you want."

"No."

Guns bothered me. I couldn't show weakness around him, and I wasn't sure why.

Sex with Reed was something else. He was up for it anytime, anywhere—but cuddling was like his jam. Maybe he didn't get enough love as a child. He constantly wanted to be held and doted over.

"You wear me out," I said. I loved being with him—his taste, his scent, his touch—but his constant neediness was draining. Three a.m. was the witching hour. That's when things got kinky. Three would become four, then five... I loved his spontaneity, and he made it clear he was up for anything. Leather, fire play, handcuffs. He was my Pandora's box. If we stayed up too late, I might unlock something I could not close.

A co-worker who knew Fish insisted on going to party on Sunset Boulevard for Halloween. I was super stoked to see my old friend.

"Do we have to go?" Reed grumbled.

I tugged him out of my bed. "I'm in fishnets, dressed like a Playboy Bunny. It's the least feminist thing I've done in my life. Of course, we're going."

"Or you could not wear that, and we could stay here," he groaned.

"Or you could get dressed now, so we won't be late to meet my friends. Come on, lazy bones."

He grabbed my shopping bag from the floor. "You want me to dress as a cop?"

"A hot, sexy cop. Hurry."

He pulled on the blue uniform. "Seriously?" He held out a plastic badge and rolled his eyes. "The badge of hotness?"

"Um, yeah because you're totally hot. Don't close those cuffs, there's no key."

Reed hooked them on his belt loop. He pulled his hair back and slid on the peaked police cap and his mirrored sunglasses.

He eyed my skimpy costume. "You'll get cold in that—put on a jacket."

I rolled my eyes. "Yes, master." I grabbed his leather jacket. "Better?"

"No. I can still see your ass."

"Well, don't look."

"I'm not worried about me."

"You're not going to be in a bad mood all night, are you?"

"I'm fine."

Fish mouthed a sarcastic, "Wow," when he saw me with Reed. Party drugs were passed around our costumed crowd before boarding the bus to the Strip. I was worried Reed would be a drag the entire night, but after a couple of pills, his charm and wit kicked in.

Halloween on Sunset was a Mardi Gras parade of Aqua-net, neon, fishnets and cheetah print. Only the coolest of the cool managed to make it into Whisky a Go Go and the Troubadour that night. Pop metal poured from the club doors. Reed was nervous about someone recognizing him—dressed up, having a good time. Our group ran through the crowd laughing, bumping into rave kids and drag queens I hadn't seen in ages.

"We rented rooms at a hotel near the Cathouse Club," Fish said, handing us a key. "Hourly rate!" He laughed.

We piled into a taxi and headed to the In & Out Burger. Reed paid the tab on each stop. Party goers packed the streets in every direction.

Fish managed to get me alone while Reed ordered a round of drinks at the next bar. "What are you doing with that guy, Jenny?"

"What do you mean?"

"Nothing. Forget it." His eyes were distant. There was something he wasn't saying. "You need to call Kevin."

I had Kevin's number, but I'd avoided dialing it since I'd come back to L.A. I missed him but I just couldn't think about that night. About Kaley.

I smiled when Reed came back over with my drink.

"Cathouse?" Fish said.

Fish's friends grabbed me. "Come on Jenny, we can go flirt and get past the line." They didn't recognize Reed in costume. He could have walked to the front of any line in Hollywood and never pay a single cover charge. The girls pulled me away from him, into the crowd, laughing.

I felt a click on my wrist. I jolted to a stop and turned around. "No—you did not just do that! There's no key!" I shouted at Reed.

He smiled, lifting his cuffed hand. "You're under arrest, hotness. No Cathouse for you."

Disappointed, I waved my friends off.

"Come on, I know somewhere we can go." Reed hailed a cab back to Sunset. Across the street from The Roxy, we entered a clothing store with a "rooms to let" sign. A group of girls ran towards us screaming.

"Oh my god! It's him!"

One girl kissed Reed on the cheek while another pushed me out of the way to get her arms around him.

"We loved your last movie, Johnny!"

"Who?" Reed said.

"They think you're Johnny Depp."

"Shit, okay." He signed Depp's name on several pieces of paper. He grabbed my hand, and we ran into the clothing store and up a set of stairs. He located a spare key and unlocked the door.

"Please tell me this is not your place." I followed him into a hoarder's bedroom, full of flowing fabric, candles, patchouli, incense and Indian rugs.

"Nah, a place I used to get high in. The owner is cool. Front of the building was a hotel in the '50s. Whorehouse in the late '70s. She rents the back rooms." He kissed me and leaned against the dresser.

"You were miserable tonight. You hate this whole scene, don't you?" I asked.

"It's alright."

I opened my bag and pulled out my eye makeup.

"What's that for?"

"You need eyeliner." I smiled.

He laughed but didn't resist. I braced my knees on top of his lap to get a good angle. I loved putting him in a position of vulnerability.

"All done!" I smiled.

"You like this? Cop uniform and eyeliner?"

"You're hot as hell right now." I laughed. "All rock starred up."

"Day job, honey."

"You always look like you walked out of some 1960's Hells Angels movie. I mean, you're the pretty one—but you're dirty and mean."

"I'm not mean." He smiled. "I don't like all this Sunset shit. There are photos floating around with my hair teased higher than Poison and Mötley Crüe. But I've done that scene. The Roxy, The Whisky, Troubadour. I paid my dues. I don't particularly want to relive that time in my life."

"You're forgetting we met at the Rainbow."

He touched my hair. "Yeah, filming an homage to all those things and places I left behind. Yet here we are in Miss Kitty's Bordello."

"If it bothers you, take the eyeliner off."

"Oh, no, I'm gonna fuck you wearing this because I can tell it's driving you crazy. Then, can we ditch this place?"

"Yes!" I grabbed his shoulders, and he kissed me.

"Hang on, I gotta smoke a cigarette real quick." He opened the window that looked over the crowded Strip. It was Halloween in Hollywood and the vodka was warming my entire body. I thought I would die before he dropped his cigarette out the window. He pulled me close, kissed me and grabbed my hips with his free hand. Trying not to twist our cuffed wrists, he held my palm against the edge of the window trim.

"Did I tell you about the Sunset Screamer?" Reed laughed.

"What's that?"

"It's when you fuck a girl so hard at one end of the strip you can hear her screaming all the way down to Sierra Drive."

"You sound like an expert." I laughed.

"First time, I swear." He smiled.

After echoing off the Sunset Boulevard billboards, we left for home, his leather jacket draped across our cuffed wrists in the cab. His hair messy, his eyes smudged with black liner. My body was warm, satisfied, I could taste his skin—but there was something else.

I'm falling for him. Shit. This was meant to be fun, an escape. I was too smart, too cool to accidentally fall in love. Yet, here I was, handcuffed to the baddest guy in rock n' roll, my heart aflutter.

Reed could have any girl in Hollywood, and he was content playing house with me. Something had to give.

At my apartment, he tried his best to shimmy out of the police uniform with his hand cuffed to mine.

"In a hurry to get into your biker clothes? You hate that whole hair band vibe, don't you?"

"I told you, been there. Done that. I want a career in ten years."

"You think dressing like Vance in *The Loveless* will accomplish that? I always expect you to pull up on a Harley."

"You mean the '55 Panhead Hydra Glide I bought from that film?"

"Tough guy. No, you didn't."

"I did."

"Then why don't you drive it here?"

"Because you live in a terrible neighborhood and it's an expensive bike. I don't want some gangbanger stealing it. Or those old ladies across the street. I hear they're pretty wild."

"Then take me to your place?" I'd been trying to find a way to approach it for weeks.

"You don't want to go to my house."

"You have a secret girlfriend or something?"

"No. I have a dog," he said.

"I want to meet your dog."

"Not this dog. She's mean."

I grimaced. "Sometimes, I feel like don't know you."

"You know me. You don't know him—the rock star fuck up. You don't want to. Besides, I like coming here. You're fun."

Crossing one arm defensively in a huff, the other wrist still attached to his. "Okay, tell me why you like it here."

Reed sighed. "Jenny, we need to address the elephant in the room. I think there's something we've both felt for a while and neither of us has had the nerve to say it."

A million thoughts ran through my head about what he might say. Was I ready to hear it? Was it too soon? Should I say it back? *Wait, is he breaking up with me?*

"Say it."

"Jenny—I, uhm. Look, honey. I gotta piss like a racehorse. We either find hedge trimmers or you're gonna have to hold my dick while I pee. You're into some freaky shit but I don't think that's it."

I sighed. "Out back." I took him to Mrs. Ellie's shed behind the condos. He found hedge trimmers and carried them to my place so we could use the table as a prop.

I held my arm out, waiting for him to step inside. Impulsively, I closed the door shut against the long chain between our hands.

"Jenny, Seriously? I can't do this with one hand."

We'd been cuffed together all night. I needed a few inches of distance. Him on one side of the door with his dick and hedge trimmers, and me on the other side trying to figure out what the hell was going on between us. I heard him pissing—the longest, loudest piss ever taken on this planet. He'd been holding a lot in.

"Hi, Miss Ellie," Reed said from the other side of the door.

My 83-year-old widowed neighbor used hedge trimmers to cut handcuffs off a rock star and his slutty girlfriend, while he stood in his own piss, trying to zip his dick back into his pants.

Miss Ellie became heavy metal legend with one swift clip.

After the pissing-handcuff incident, I tried my best to avoid thinking about our relationship. At times, we were too perfect. The fabric would tear. Little lies and arguments slipped through. He always apologized in the end, saying it was stress.

There were three words he would not say. I refused to say them until he did. I felt stupid for thinking I was falling in love. What did I know about him?

He had demanded downtime after his last tour. The free time he had with me was temporary. He warned me about his seasonal depression.

"It's not you, I need to be alone to write." He was pushing me away.

I know better than to get attached to him. I kept my tears to myself. Taking a deep breath, my hands pressed against my 1950s yellow bathroom sink. *Don't let him see you cry.*

Winter turned to spring; Reed came around less and less. Writing and planning a promo tour consumed his time. Occasionally he worked out a few notes and lyrics on an acoustic guitar he kept in my apartment. But he was a perfectionist, sleeping on the floor of the studio until the record was finished.

This was the *Dream Lie?* album. Record execs pressured the producer to cut songs and forced the band to alter the lyrics. Big chains refused to carry the album due to the cover art and explicit content. Dene, the guitarist, walked out mid-day from yet another stint in rehab.

Reed lived two lives.

The first time we slept together, he was late to a meeting where he signed a $30 million record deal. His real life was full of sex, drugs, fame and excess. Writing and recording had pulled him back into that world.

A world where I did not exist.

"I need to know where we stand?" I asked, after the third missed date in two weeks.

"It's complicated."

"Is there someone else?" The question had lingered in my mind for weeks.

He rolled his eyes. "Why would you ask me that?"

"You're different—everything is different."

"You knew who I was. Nothing has changed."

"Not for you," I mumbled, tugging at the thread of his faded flannel shirt on my arm.

Reed stepped off the condo porch and walked out to the street. He'd grown a beard, managed to slip out of the studio in a baseball cap to see me. You would've thought he was any other asshole standing at the end of my sidewalk ready to walk away; not some rock star. One question was all it took to widen the divide between us. *Where do we stand?*

I'd known the minute I let myself fall for this jerk, he'd turn out like all the other guys in Hollywood. The minute I needed something from him, he'd leave.

Reed turned around and walked back up the sidewalk towards me. He grabbed my hand.

"We need to talk," he said. I followed him inside, upstairs to my bedroom. I sat on the edge of the bed, he sat in front of me on the floor. "Jenny, I will never forgive you if you tell a living soul what I'm about to say."

I agreed. And I've never told anyone what he said. I never will.

We made love, but something was different. It felt final. We both stared at the ceiling, knowing what was coming and that neither of us had control over it.

"What are you thinking?" I asked, like some desperate teenager.

"You. Me. What I've been trying to protect you from."

"I'm not a child."

"We're from different worlds, Jenny. In your world people stay together. They go on vacations and send their kids off to college. That's foreign to me. I know trailers without electricity and back alley drug deals. Never knowing where you'll sleep at night or if you'll wake up. You're a decent human. You expect goodness in return. That's doesn't exist in my world."

"What do you mean?"

"You asked why I like coming here. It reminds me of when I was young—I'd hang out with whatever girl I was dating from the time she woke, 'til her dad kicked me out. It was safe, warm and there was always food on the table. I didn't have to deal with the shitty things in my life. Eventually they'd figure out what a piece of shit I was, or their daddy would kick my ass back to my side of town. When I met you, I needed a break from the chaos, the drugs, the music, the noise. Somewhere safe from Hollywood. I'm like a kid, wishing I could have things I don't get to have."

"Wow. So, I'm a thing you did until it was time to record your new album. Thanks," I said.

"You know that's not what I said at all." He lit a cigarette. "There are things you don't understand. Fame is a cannibal witch. She exists for little boys ditched in forests without a dime to call home. Fame waits below the Hollywood sign, mouth and cunt spread wide, tongue ready, salivating, luring you in with mescaline and amphetamines, her ovens hot and ready for the burn—spitting you out for sport—eating you raw."

"That's one way to describe it. If you were talking to *Rolling Stone*, but you're not. I don't know that part of your life because you haven't let me. If you're breaking up with me, tell me."

"I'm not breaking up with you. Contrary to what you may believe, my entire life doesn't revolve around you."

"I didn't say that."

"You don't understand what I deal with. No one does. How fucked is it, in my profession, my life expectancy ends at twenty-seven?" He held his fingers to his temple and mimicked pulling a trigger. "When I go in the studio tomorrow and sign off on the new album, that's it. We're lucky as hell the second album did as well as it did. It doesn't happen on album three. It doesn't matter if it outsells the Beatles, it's the beginning of the end of everything we struggled for. In this industry, you crash, burn—or get shot outside The Dakota."

"Reed, that's not true."

"Isn't it? There's no joy in putting this album out when I know I could walk into Void Records tomorrow, put a bullet in my head and outsell any of my peers. It was about the music with The Beatles. It's never been about the music in this band—and we're a really good band." He took a drag from the cigarette and smashed it into the ashtray. "*Rolling Stone* don't write about my lyrics or that insane guitar riff from "Hell's Break." They want to know if Dene's in rehab or if I'll lose it at some heckler at The Forum."

"You're right, I don't get it. But I care."

He stared off into space. "I wish that was enough, honey. I do. The only way to fuck fame is to beat her at her own game—become infamous, right?"

"Reed, are you okay?"

He rubbed his tired eyes. "No, I'm not. The band has no idea where my head is. I can't get these assholes to show up sober enough to play. I wrote half of Dene's guitar parts on this album. I don't have the heart to fire him or take his name off the credits. He's like a brother to me. But this band is a bullet train heading for a dead end, and they don't know I've got off yet. I'm the engineer." He half-laughed. "And the brakeman, and the conductor."

"Talk to them."

Reed laughed. "Yeah sure. Can you get them in the same room, sober? No one understands the pressure of being a leader of a band like this. If I can get them propped up on stage, they'll play a damn good show—but that's selfish, right? They can't keep up. It's pissing the fans off. I'm watching my best friends die in front of me. Do I kill them so I can play my songs? I wanted to make music. I never imagined I'd have their lives in my hands."

"Babe, I'm sorry."

He lit another cigarette. "They were too stoned to read the contract. I don't need a vote to fire them anymore. It's the only thing I can do to save their lives. Otherwise, I'm feeding their addictions. At least everyone is onboard about Matty. He's done. Dude doesn't write. He misses every bass note on tour. How's that my fault?" Reed stretched his tight fingers. "I'm the face of this band. I have to think about how people perceive us. I'm not a saint. I did all the coke on the first big tour—like, all of it—every suitcase stashed with a kilo. Ozzy Osbourne had nothing on us that year. These Hollywood bands dress up like the New York Dolls and write pretty party songs about their coke dealers and Sid Vicious—it's all glam and excess. Our albums tell the other side—the beat downs in the alley behind The Roxy, the drug dealer I watched put a gun in Matty's mouth on tour. I had to get an advance check cut to his dealer so he wouldn't kill him. I've saved his life more times than I can count. I'm protecting what the rest of us worked for. I'm sick of the world seeing us as the junkie band that can't stay straight for a five-minute interview."

I put my arm around him. "Why don't you talk to me, babe?"

"I just told you a $30 million dollar secret. Every time I open my mouth with you, I'm afraid I'll say something I shouldn't. I can't trust anyone in California. Anywhere. You shouldn't either."

"I know you don't want to disappoint the fans—"

"My fans don't give a shit about me. I'm playing a part. Being this character on stage, that's who people think I am, and I'm not. If I succeed, I've failed in their eyes because I haven't given them the show—the big payoff. The crash and burn. I'm twenty-six. I shouldn't be contemplating whether or not I'll be irrelevant or dead in a year." He pursed his lips.

"You're my escape from this insanity. And what we have doesn't belong in that world. These last six months with you are the only normal thing I've ever done."

"What are you going to do about it then?" I said.

He touched my hair. "That's what I love about you. You don't coddle me. I even like it when you treat me like shit. I'd rather have you kicking my ass to fix your toilet or Miss Ellie's sink, than spend a week getting my dick sucked on some prick's yacht. That says more about me than you, but it's true. Sometimes I tell myself I should give back the money and fame and get us out of here while we still can. I have a cool Mustang. We could drive away from here tonight. Never come back."

To this day, I wish we had done just that.

Reed confirmed my fears and broke my heart without taking a pause. *What we have does not belong in his world.*

Well, the man tried to warn me, didn't he?

Chapter Six

A few weeks later, Reed was gone. He traveled to Dallas, Chicago, and Boston for interviews. Two weeks in Toronto to master the album, band rehearsals, and a full week scheduled in New York. He installed a phone in my apartment before he left. He called every night until the album's final mixing in Toronto.

No conversation about whether or not we would try to make this work. Truthfully, I needed a break from him. I enjoyed him but his presence consumed everything in my life. His normal was not normal. I refused to wait around for his calls—which he noticed.

"I miss you," he mumbled into the receiver. "Did you get the package I sent?"

"Yes. You sound tired. Have you slept?"

"Last week," he groaned. "Dene swears he doesn't remember the conversation about firing Matty. Every damn time we see each other he goes off. I'm this close to leaving, babe. I can't keep doing this. How can they expect Matty to go on this tour when he didn't play a note on the album? Darrian and Levon swore they'd have my back on this if Dene flaked but I'm getting shit from them. I'm trying to save this band. If one more fucker mouths off to me tonight, I'm done. I swear to god, I'll put a bullet in my head. Better me than them, huh?"

"Don't say things like that."

"I'm sorry. You're right, I need rest." He groaned. "Flight to New York is in three hours." He fell asleep on the phone.

Shit, I can't have anyone check in on him because I don't know anyone.

He left a message before his flight apologizing. "Everything is okay. I'll call you from New York."

Neon God were scheduled to perform on a late night television show Wednesday. Thursday morning, they were playing a short acoustic set in Central Park. Saturday they were set to open the MTV VMAs. None of that would happen.

Reed's manager scheduled him for a radio show Wednesday morning. The DJ insulted Reed on air. Asking off limit questions about his past and personal life, belittling Reed.

"Change the subject, dude," Reed said. The guy pushed until he got a reaction. Reed called him a "Redneck little cocksucker." (On air)

"Watch yourself."

"I'm shaking in my boots, big rock star's gonna get me, call my lawyer." The DJ laughed, from behind his booth. "Word is your little band is falling apart at the seams. You heard it here first, Neon God is dead."

Reed threw a metal chair into the DJ booth shattering the glass, then charged for the exit. He wandered through Manhattan, back to the hotel where he ran into Dene. They tore into each other in the lobby like rabid dogs. The band's repulsive manager, Phil Watson, was searching the city to find Reed and put out fires as he went. The DJ filed an assault report.

Phil convinced the police to make the arrest after the Central Park show or there would be riots. NYPD agreed to a catch and release.

Phil caught up to Reed in the hotel. "Stop acting like a spoiled rock star."

Reed slammed the hotel room door in Phil's face, trashed the room and threw a TV out the window—a block from Times Square.

"There's your rock star, you prick!" Reed supposedly shouted. According to legend, Reed threw a lit match into the room. Who knows when it came to Evan Reed and Phil Watson?

Clueless, I sat in California, studying for my Art History final and playing Nintendo games. I hoped Reed's late night calls were a sign he was willing to work on things between us. I had no idea about the chaos erupting across New York City.

The rock star who stormed across Manhattan was not the man I loved. Life wasn't the internet free-for-all you see these days. By the time the tales trickled home, these men had time to cover their asses.

Usually.

Not this time. Not when the entire world was watching, anticipating this album. The one that would become their biggest selling to date.

One of the few times we'd gone at each other those first months we were together—Reed was drunk, pissed that I'd asked him where he'd disappeared to in the middle of the night. He told me it was none of my business and punched a hole in the wall, leaving me stunned and afraid. I left him passed out in the bed and slept on the couch near the door. The next morning, he apologized. Then I caught him going through my unopened mail. Collection bills and my dad's hospital bills I'd had forwarded to my place so my mom wouldn't have to deal with them.

"Why didn't you tell me about this?" Reed insisted on writing a check to cover the payments, a gesture that made me forgive and forget the fight the night before.

In his world, it was a different story.

Reed left the hotel in Manhattan before police arrived. He went to the bank, withdrew $10,000 and stuffed the money in his jacket. He booked the first flight out of JFK to L.A.X. and was on a plane home without a word to anyone.

I'd promised I would watch him on TV that night. I'd bought him a little hemp bracelet at the beach. He said he would wear it.

The Late Night Show played a rerun but didn't explain why. I dozed off on the sofa.

At 3 a.m., Reed stood on my doorstep, pale-skinned, soaked, and shivering from the cold rain, wearing a leather jacket and tight black leather pants with a huge belt buckle. He'd shaved one side of his head for promo pics and re-pierced the left side of his lip. He had a leather hat and sunglasses on in the middle of the night, in the pouring rain.

It was very Elvis-esque.

"What are you doing here, babe? Come inside. You're freezing."

He kissed me and slid out of his leather jacket. I peeled his leather pants off his cold skin. He tossed me a cassette to put on. We had sex on the couch to the screeching vocals and wailing guitars of "Think About You" from *Appetite for Destruction*. I'd never been so thankful for Guns N' Fucking Roses.

"Please promise you won't leave me?" He buried his cold lips against my ear.

"I'm not going anywhere."

The roof leaked in my apartment during storms. While drying the floor, I discovered on the morning news that "international rock star Evan Reed" was missing. Ridiculous headlines bombarded the newscasts.

What the hell? This rock star was not missing. He was passed out on my bed. Leather-clad boyfriend charging across Manhattan like Godzilla was a bit concerning. I went to check on him.

"Reed, babe?"

Ice cold, he wouldn't budge. *Oh, shit. Oh no. Oh god. What...*

The thought that I should call his driver or manager before I dialed 911 was a wake-up call. *Fuck that.* I dialed 911, gave the responder my name and address.

That was the end of my anonymity.

Chapter Seven

EMTs pushed Reed's eyelids back, shining a flashlight in his pupils. I'd cowered in the corner while they shouted at me repeatedly, "What did he take?"

Cold, unmoving bodies weren't my thing after finding Kaley.

"Look, you're not in trouble. I need to know what he took," the EMT said.

"I...I...I don't know. I don't think he took anything."

They asked me to fill out his insurance paperwork in the emergency room. My hands shook trying to hold the clipboard. "I'm sorry," I told the clerk, "I don't know the answers."

I knew his real name. *Known allergies?* I don't think so. *Is the address listed on his driver's license current?* "I don't know." I handed the woman his insurance card—everything in his wallet was soaked from the rain.

"Will he be okay? Can someone please help him?" Recognizing Reed, the hospital staff moved him to a private room. Nurses came in fifteen-minute intervals. It would not surprise me if people died because the entire staff of Cedars Sinai was in and out of Evan Reed's room.

Bundles of hundred dollar bills fell out of his jacket when I laid it out in the room to dry. I jumped back. How do you explain ten thousand dollars in cash? I didn't know what to do or who to call. I put the money in my bag for safekeeping. I dozed off holding Reed's hand.

Fighting off images of blue lips and claw marks in deep freezers, I woke gasping for air. The TV was on. Everyone in the world knew Evan Reed was at Cedars Sinai with pneumonia. Except me. Because the nurses and doctors wouldn't tell me anything.

He'll be okay, Jenny. People get pneumonia. *Not healthy twenty-six-year-olds, mid-summer. You know that, you dumb bitch.* There wasn't a nurse or doctor who could convince me this wasn't somehow my fault.

Reed was awake the next time I opened my eyes. "Oh my god, baby, are you okay?" I asked.

He half-laughed. "I'm high as shit. Am I in the hospital?" He had a sore throat and a slight fever, a drastic improvement from the morning. He drank warm tea and soup. He was barely holding his head up and a nurse asked for his damn autograph! His voice was his only concern.

Major Dickhead Phil, Reed's tour manager, stormed in at dinnertime. Phil's potbelly drooped over his heavy metal belt buckle and too-tight jeans. Patches for Lynyrd Skynyrd and Steppenwolf covered his frayed denim vest. He was angry the media found Reed first.

I'd waited hours not hearing anything and the doctor was going over the entire chart with Phil.

"You can leave," Phil said. When Phil Watson walked into a room, you wanted to walk out.

I wasn't budging. "I don't think so, person."

He gave me a dirty look. "Sweetheart..."

"I'm not going anywhere."

Phil glared at Reed. "You have royally fucked up this time."

Reed shrugged.

Heat rose red from Phil's chest, the vein in his neck throbbed. "Two separate counts of assault, destruction of property and disturbing the peace. You'll be fined by the FCC for what you said on the radio. You missed a talk show, and the set in Central Park. Those kids went apeshit and two of them got beat down by the pigs." Phil's face went redder. "Now you've lost your damn voice. There goes another million dollars, you asshole."

"You need to go," I said.

"Who are you, anyway?" Phil shouted.

Reed's voice was hoarse and deep. "You heard the woman. Get out."

I pushed Phil out the door and told the nurse not to let anyone else inside.

Reed took my hand and whispered, "Thanks."

"It's okay, I'll make it all better." *Pneumonia. Reed takes Manhattan. $10,000 cash. Telling off a scary tour manager. Yeah, Jenny, you've got this. Yeah, right!*

Reed's voice cracked. "You make everything better. I'm sorry about all this."

He could be hot headed at times. For the most part, he'd been kind and gentle around me. The character he swore wasn't the real him didn't seem like the greatest catch.

Looking out the hospital window, I could see a crowd of people waiting outside to get a glimpse of him. If I needed to leave the room to go pee, I had to go through two massive bodyguards.

Reed wrote a list of things he needed and the number for his driver. His driver would contact his maid. I'm pretty sure his maid contacted whatever shaman or the Buddhist monk he had on call. God, I don't know. His rosary hung on my bedpost. I liked watching the cross hit it when we—well never mind. Apparently, my boyfriend had a fickle affection for religion.

"Do you want me to call your family? Friends?"

"No."

Reed's version of what happened in New York—the band had agreed to take a private plane with only staff for a meeting to discuss the album release and the touring schedule. The other guys arrived at the airport with girlfriends, hookers, and drug dealers. It was the typical out-of-control seven-hour party flight. Reed didn't speak to anyone when the plane landed and left in a separate car.

Phil scheduled the last minute radio interview at eight a.m. (which was five a.m. in California). Dene was meant to be there with Reed for the interview. Only, he had gone partying after their flight and never made it to the hotel.

Reed told Phil to cancel the interview when he found out what morning show it was. He described the show as "disgusting redneck, Christian, misogynistic propaganda."

Instead of booking the top rock stations in New York, Phil had scheduled an interview with a conservative radio show run by two jerk DJs from Alabama, who had a particular distaste for the band.

Reed's media contract was specific—his personal life was off limits. The minute they went on air the DJ took cheap shots, asking inappropriate questions and insulting him.

"But it had nothing to do with any of that, Jenny. I missed you. I saw an opportunity to run home, and I took it. You're different from any girl I've ever met." Those sweet words were supposed to make me forget everything else.

I had no earthly idea how to respond to this nonsense. Things were happening too fast. He made a late night phone call from the hospital, giving someone his room number. I dozed off, only to wake and see him sitting upright with his legs outstretched and head bowed.

A Buddhist monk at the foot of the hospital bed performed a blessing and placed a bowl of warm tea in Reed's hands. The monk left. It was beyond bizarre. Who was this rock star? What had he done with my boyfriend?

Phil returned the next morning with Reed's lawyer, a handsome man named Lou Reynolds. In a power move, Phil wore a blue suit instead of his tacky touring clothes—he looked like an irate blueberry. Reed's brother, Daniel, tall with short brown hair, came along to mediate. Void Records had hired Phil Watson to babysit the wildest rock band in the world—he had the experience. At his age, he knew this was his last big gig. Phil didn't care about the band.

Phil Watson cared about his payout.

If that meant sliding cocaine across a mirror to get the guys on stage, he did it without regret. Reed's relationship with Phil was hate-hate.

Mine would be too.

"She needs to leave," Phil said.

"I can go."

Reed motioned for me to wait. "Whatever you came to say, Lou, say it."

"I don't know if I'm comfortable—" the lawyer hesitated.

"He's too stupid to listen to reason," Phil said.

"You're in a lot of trouble this time," the lawyer said.

"CNN has established that," Reed said.

"Dude, listen," Daniel pleaded.

Lou sighed. "New York is talking serious jail time. They have warrants. If they decide to extradite, they can walk in here, arrest you and send you back East. I'm trying to work it out so you can take the jet. You'll be booked, bailed, and come home with the least amount of press possible. We may be able to get this pushed under the table before it turns into a bigger spectacle."

I pretended to be unaffected by the thought of the guy I was dating being extradited to New York.

"And I care, why?" Reed said.

"Because this will fuck your life up. Your career, the band, everything," Phil snapped.

"Phil, give it a break," Daniel said.

"We've taken care of the hotel bill, the damages. Convincing them to drop the charges was $20,000." Lou Reynolds slapped his papers against the bedside table.

"I owe you a bonus, huh?" Reed said.

"I'm the messenger," the lawyer said. "You and Dene need to make amends so you can get on the road. The radio station is a different story. They are looking at a $100,000 fine from the FCC, which they'll pin on you. They pressed charges for destruction of property. The DJ and two other employees pressed assault charges, which they will drop for the right amount of money."

"I'm not paying that fucker off. I didn't put my hands on anyone."

"This is out of control, brother," Daniel said. "You guys are going to end up dead and broke. Void wants Dene in rehab before they'll consider putting you guys on the road. You sitting in jail will not fix this. If you have a felony, you can't leave the country on this tour. Two hundred people don't know if they have a job this summer. It's not just about the band anymore."

"I don't care," Reed said.

Phil jumped up, spittle flying from his lips. "Listen, you selfish prick, everything is not about you."

"Sit. You work for me. I told you I didn't want to do the damn interview."

"You're pissed off they called you on your shit." Phil said. "You know what this prick is really like, sweetheart?" Phil turned to me. "Don't believe a word he says. You're not the first pretty girl who's fallen for his shit. You won't be the last."

Daniel pushed Phil towards the door. "You're upset, man. Come back when the two of you can work this out."

"Nothing to work out when Reed has his head this far up his own asshole." Phil aimed his finger at Reed. "How many pills did you take on the plane, fucker? Did you tell your little girlfriend over there that pneumonia is code for prissy, little, attention-whore rock stars that grind up Percocet and Oxycodone and snort them off bathroom sinks on last minute cross-country flights? You think you're not a junkie 'cause some L.A. doctor put your name on a prescription bottle? You're in for a rude awakening, pal."

"Phil, there's a big difference between you and me—you're replaceable," Reed said. "Get the fuck out."

Daniel made Phil leave, then turned to Reed. "Bro, you got to calm down with Phil. He's an asshole, but you know he's looking out for you. I swear he didn't know about the radio shit, that's not like him. There was some format change that got lost in translation."

"I don't care about Phil Watson. Sort this out in New York. If I need to do a few days in jail, I'll do it. What I'm not cool with is that radio prick getting any of my money. Pull our songs from the station, effective immediately. Lou, every time my name is used, sue the shit out of 'em. Make this guy wish he'd never met me. He's not making bank on this. Call New York, tell 'em I'll turn myself in as soon as the doc says it's ok. Fix it. But remember two things: that DJ gets nothing, and I don't do apologies."

"Alright," the lawyer said.

"We'll do what we can. Get some rest, bro," Daniel said.

Evan Reed was in a hospital bed, and still literally and figuratively had the biggest dick in the room. This wasn't about the radio station. Reed was planting a seed—he was in control. He had power over these men—lawyers, managers and record executives. And with that power came the ability to move the NYPD and judicial system around like chess pieces.

That's why he wanted me in the room.

I rambled off questions, not yet having been educated in the art of keeping my fucking mouth shut.

Reed un-muted the TV and gave me an icy stare. "We don't talk about this."

My back stiffened. "Look, if you're okay. I'm going home."

"I'll call my driver." Reed's eyes were fixed on a story about himself on CNN.

"I'll get a cab." I kissed his forehead. "I hope you feel better."

He grabbed my wrist. "You have no idea what you've gotten yourself into, sweetheart. I've tried to protect you. When you walk out that door, nothing in your life will ever be the same. Nothing."

He looked back at the TV.

No hug. No kiss. No goodbye.

Hospital security led me out the back of the building. Reed's driver was waiting, as were the blinding flashes of camera lights.

"Miss Stone, how's Evan?" someone shouted.

How do they know my name?

I shielded my eyes from the lights.

"Is he going to pull through? Jennifer, how do you know Evan Reed? Is he going to jail?"

I walked past Reed's black Mercedes to a cab. The reporters followed. The driver took me to Sasha's apartment. I panicked at the fare. I had Reed's money. I pulled a $100 bill out and gave it to the driver, and ran to Sasha's shop, using her spare key to get inside.

"Sasha?" I said, locking the door and snatching her curtains closed.

She ran downstairs. "Are you okay? Reporters have been calling me for hours. Is Evan Reed seriously your secret boyfriend?"

I tried not to cry.

"Oh Jenny. Sit. Kitchen. Now." Sasha made hot tea. The kind that makes you spill out six-months-worth of pent up emotion.

"Being with Reed was easy. Now it's so complicated."

"Go lie down in my room, honey. Rest."

The scent of eggs, toast and chamomile tea pulled me out of bed the next morning. Sasha was waiting patiently, sipping from her cup. She asked how I was doing.

"I can't believe you didn't tell me who he was—everything you said made him sound like a nice guy. But he threw one hell of a temper tantrum, Jenny."

"I keep hoping the media is blowing it out of proportion. They are so unfair."

"According to MTV, he fought a DJ, threw furniture out of a fifteenth story window, got on a plane and flew across the country like it was nothing. That's got to say something about him." She shrugged. "Or, I don't know. Maybe he had a bad day."

I half-smiled. "One hell of a bad day." It was different hearing it from a reasonable person, and not from people who acted like it happened every day. I remembered what Phil said—*Jail, this time.* Still, part of me wanted to defend him. "That's not the person I know, Sash, he's unbelievably kind and sensitive. My boyfriend is not the same person on TV doing all that damage."

Reporters called my job a dozen times.

Reed left messages.

"Hey, it's me. I haven't been able to reach you. I want to see you before I fly to New York."

I didn't call. I needed space. I counted his money to make sure I knew how much to give back to him: $9,800. I stuffed it under my mattress, hoping this would all go away.

My job let me go later that week. *Negative media attention.* I refused to ask my parents for money; this wasn't their fault.

Reed was the last person I wanted to be indebted to. I found his lawyer's address in the phone book and dropped the money off.

"We don't take packages from fans here," the secretary said. Then she opened the envelope. "Oh, you must be Jenny." She didn't explain.

"Can I get a receipt?" I asked.

Reed turned himself in to the NYPD. The city sent him straight to jail. Most of the charges were dropped, but the judge was determined to make an example of him and sentenced him to jail for thirty days. His lawyer appealed—time served with two months of community service, a mandatory anger management class and one-year probation.

Reed's lawyer leveraged the significant monetary loss for local venues. By locking Reed up and cancelling shows, the city risked riots from fans. It was in the best interest of New York Fucking City to cater to Evan Reed. He called me once from jail and twice more upon release. I didn't answer.

The record company capitalized on the publicity, booking as many late night shows as they could. Reed did a short interview with Larry King. Drunk, unshaven, wearing sunglasses.

This was not the person I cared so deeply for.

Every time Larry asked a question, Reed looked at his drummer off camera and laughed. The record company intended for him to come off remorseful, like he'd learned a lesson. He was toying with them. Instead of apologizing, he said, "It wasn't my intention, but whatever, people make up their own minds."

A late night host introduced the band as, "straight from jail..."

Where was that sweet guy I'd been falling in love with? Charisma and sarcasm seeped from the man on TV, but not an ounce of remorse.

MTV did a sit-down interview with Reed. He said, "Things got out of hand. My label forced me to do things I wasn't cool with. People weren't doing their jobs. I let an insignificant prick push me into losing my temper."

"Any remorse about what happened in New York?" the reporter asked.

"Pissed I let this asshole get under my skin. I've spent the last few years trying to change. But whatever. People believe what they want."

"Your female fans have been dying to know—is there anyone special in your life?" The reporter pried.

"Do you ask Paul McCartney that? Dylan? Is this the Golden Globes? You gonna ask me where I got my (bleeping) dress? Always with these (bleeping) questions."

"No offense. Asking for the fans."

Reed sipped a glass that wasn't filled with Pepsi. After getting direction off camera he answered, "No. No one in particular. There was one girl, but you know how that goes."

He was so vague he could have been referring to anyone.

Chapter Eight

A few days after the MTV interview, I answered the phone, hoping it was a job recruiter.

The line was silent. "Hello?"

"You're ignoring me? What's the deal?" Reed snapped.

"I'm busy." I lied.

"I'm thinking it can wait. What are you angry about?"

"Not angry. Confused."

"You can answer a fucking phone when you're confused."

"I can't do this, Reed."

"So, this is it? You're gonna bail? I deserve an explanation at least. Don't we have something here, Jenny? What bothered you so much you won't answer the phone when I call you?"

I hesitated. "Your fame game—you were in the hospital, then jail and on TV as if nothing happened. It's like you don't care."

"Honey, you promised you wouldn't fall for this shit. I play a character. The fans expect me to fit a stereotype. Occasionally, I fall into the trap. I didn't want to be in New York. I wanted to be with you. Don't you see that? Of course, I get angry if I don't have control of my life. Wouldn't you? The label wants a puppet they can pull the strings with. That ain't me. I'd had no sleep. This jerk pushed me. I don't care what anyone else in the world

thinks about me, except you. This wasn't about the DJ. It was about you. I need you."

"What do you want me to say?"

"Give me a chance? Don't give up on me so easy. You care about me, right? I didn't imagine it."

"It's too much."

"You knew who I was from day one. I've tried my best to protect you. Don't take us from me right now. You have no idea how alone I am without you. There are hundreds of girls who want to be with Evan Reed the rock star. You don't care about him. You care about me. Nothing would have happened in New York if you'd been there. You take care of me and call me out on my shit. I love that about you. Don't do this to me. I need you. Can you please come here and talk this out? If nothing else, you can break my heart in person. You owe me that."

"Reed..."

"I love you, Jenny."

After much pressure and an epic guilt trip, I agreed to fly to New York and spend the week with Reed. Sasha had bleached my hair punk rock white and cut it into a wavy bob, black underneath—it was supposed to boost my confidence.

"Daniel will pick you up at the airport," he'd said. Instead, Reed stood at the LaGuardia gate, balancing a four-foot tall, fuzzy teddy bear on his shoulders. He bit a red rose between his teeth, thorns and all. His white t-shirt read, *I fucked up. I'm sorry, Jenny* in black marker with a sad face.

"Do I know you?" I laughed.

"Nope. Isn't that the best part?"

Reed gave the giant bear to a little girl.

I hadn't kissed him, though I wanted to.

He stood across the aisle from me on the JFK Express Train to 57th Street in Manhattan. He held onto the high bar, stretching his back, smiling at me like a teenage boy. I was dying to tuck his now shoulder-length blonde hair behind his ears and drown in his sweet blue eyes.

"You gonna talk to me?" he said, biting his lip, super sexy, pulling out the charms with that boyish grin. "This is us."

I followed him off the train, the crowd pushing us towards the stairs.

Reed grabbed my hand pulling me to a group of street musicians, "Nah, come over here. I want you to meet some friends of mine."

Reed dropped a tip in the bucket, and grabbed what I recognized as his guitar, while the other guy pulled out a bass. The drummer tapped the high hat. The musician hammered out the unmistakable bass riff for Tommy Tutone's "867-5309/Jenny."

Reed tuned the guitar and launched into a solo, before singing my name.

A crowd gathered. A handful of people recognized him. Summer heat seeped into the gritty tunnels. Reed pulled his shirt off under the guitar strap and wiped his face. He'd drawn *Forgive Me?* inside a giant black heart on his sweaty chest. My heavy metal lover was so infatuated he was willing to play new wave/post-punk cover songs for me in the subway, in the sweltering June heat. Sweat dripped off his body. Reed smiled his million-dollar grin at me across the crowd.

"One more song? Okay. Go!" They launched into Simple Minds' "Don't You Forget About Me."

I didn't know he could sing these songs; his music was always significantly louder. The things he could do with that electric guitar rivaled Joe Satriani. I cheered for him with the fans who'd gathered on the platform. He gave a bow with the other musicians, handing his pricey guitar to the subway performer. "Keep it man," Reed said.

The man insisted on trading his own guitar for the one Reed was giving him. Reed put it in his case. He walked over, wiping sweat away from his brow with his t-shirt and pulled it over his head. "You ready?"

"That was wild." I laughed. "I can't believe you gave your guitar away."

"This one's got soul. If I write a hit on it, I'll bring his back."

"How long have you been planning that?" I said as we walked up the steps into the city.

"Doesn't matter. Did it work?"

I wanted to kiss him. My cold, hipster, artsy heart wasn't immune to the power of a rock star playing new wave covers in the subway. I hesitated.

Reed hailed a taxi and tossed my bag and his guitar case into the trunk. We rode across town to a high-rise hotel. The doorman took our things.

"I can carry my bag," I said. Reed picked me up over his shoulder. I laughed and tried to squeeze away from him. He carried me into the building and didn't set me down until we were in his hotel suite.

"I got you roses—red in this room, pink in the next—it's a double suite. You can have some privacy. I won't disturb you coming and going."

I stared in awe at the rooms.

He opened his guitar case on the bed and pulled out the second-hand guitar. He strummed the chords to U2's "Sunday Bloody Sunday." "I fucking hate Bono," he said and put the guitar down. Reed hated U2 the way '80s metal heads would one day hate Nirvana. Reed hummed, "How long will he sing this goddamn song?" He would never admit it was a damn good song.

I wore a long Sid and Nancy t-shirt over skinny black jeans and black boots.

I'd only been to New York once, staying with friends in a hostel. I loved the energy of the city. Tonight, I was in an executive double suite with a rock star. That wasn't why I went. I went to see if my Reed was real, and not Evan Reed the rock star with a temper tantrum. New York Reed was different from the guy who'd spent so many nights at my place—but he was winning me over.

"You still not gonna kiss me?" he asked.

I smiled.

"I guess I need to work a little harder then?" There was a knock on the door. "Speak of the devil. Amaya works for the hotel concierge. She's going to take you to the spa for a massage, facial, whatever you want, on my tab. Be back by five. We have dinner plans."

Amaya whisked me away for an unexpected spa treatment. I opted for a cucumber facial and hot stone massage followed by a quick dip in the indoor pool to cool off. When I returned to the hotel room, Reed had showered. He wore black slacks, shined boots, a tucked-in black button up shirt. He adjusted shiny metal skull cufflinks on his wrists. Smooth shaven, aside from his jaw line, his blonde hair pulled back. My rocker boyfriend had transformed into a Calvin Klein model. He patted aftershave oil on his skin and squeezed past me. "Can you get a quick shower, so we won't be late?"

"I didn't pack anything nice enough to go where you're going."

"Check your bed."

I walked into the adjoining room. On the bed lay a designer gift box with a short black lace Chanel dress—off the runway according to the pinned tag. A pair of shiny, black vinyl, ankle lace boots with a vinyl red bow at the open toes. It was like my boyfriend had walked up to a world-renowned fashion designer and said: classy, sexy, mod punk with '50s pin-up shoes.

He gets me. I eagerly showered and slid on the dress and boots. Perfect fit.

"How did you know my shoe size?"

"Observant. Hurry up."

Observant or obsessive? I was enamored when he walked around the corner wearing a black jacket, open collar shirt and loose tie. Have you met a person whose aura sets your chest on fire? You think, I'm going to die if I don't fuck that man. Like, right now. Except, you're in a fancy Manhattan hotel suite. He's the rock star boyfriend showering you with gifts and attention. And you're the jerk determined to end things. Reed was trouble from his newly-pierced tongue to his polished leather boots. *He should not look so good in a damn suit.*

A white limo waited outside the hotel to drive us a mere eight blocks to Maxim's of New York; a high society, black tie Parisian restaurant. It was elegant and romantic with art nouveau design, a floral glass ceiling and dark mahogany walls. A small orchestra played Gershwin and Cole Porter. We were led to a white-draped table in the dimly lit restaurant. This was a place for the local elite, not two renegades from California.

"Explain yourself." I nodded at the two extra place settings.

Reed smiled. "What? Are you not impressed with my impeccable taste?"

"I'm wondering what you have up your sleeve."

"Well, I'm trying to woo my way into your good graces. And I promised my label I'd be on good behavior. Which means schmoozing with bourgeois assholes tonight. If I charm this couple into investing, the label will fund my solo project."

"Corporate funding for metal music?"

"It is what it is. I'm going to tone back the guitars and sing for once." He gave me a mischievous grin.

"You're screwing them over, aren't you?"

"Steal from the rich, baby. Speaking of—" He stood and greeted a couple who introduced themselves as Marlene and Jordan Von Berstein. He shook Jordan's hand. "This is Jennifer Stone, my... girl—date." He raised a cocky eyebrow at me and winked.

"Are you enjoying New York this time, Reed?" Marlene Von Berstein asked, taking her seat. Her honey-blonde hair was styled into an elegant French twist. Tiny crystals were embedded into her high-shouldered evening dress. Heavy teardrop earrings matched the diamond and gold pieces adorning her neck and fingers. Money, power and golden charm.

"I've not destroyed anything, if that's what you mean."

"You do have a bit of a reputation," Jordan said.

"That I do." Reed picked up his drink.

"I love your look, Jennifer. Comic book heroine meets couture?" Marlene Von Berstein said.

I nodded, completely out of place in this fancy French restaurant with a New York financier and his upper class wife. It was obvious she was trying to decrease the tension of this meeting.

Reed was too relaxed. Tension was his element.

"Have you two been to the Met? My friend Jonathan Cross has several paintings there," Marlene said.

"I went the last time I was here," I said.

"Jenny is an artist," Reed interjected.

"Oh? What's your medium? Do you have a collection in any L.A. galleries?"

"Oil painting, abstracts. But I haven't..."

Reed interrupted. "Jenny is designing my next album cover."

"I am?"

"Well, we haven't talked about it yet—but yes." He laughed. "You should see her work, Marlene, it's amazing. I collected all of her pieces before I managed to hunt her down to meet in person."

All of them? That was new info to me.

"That's wonderful," Marlene said. "I fund an arts initiative in Manhattan as an outreach to inner city children, Jennifer. We're always looking for instructors. We have an open artist-in-residence position. I'll give you my number and you can let me know if it's something you're interested in."

"Wow. Thank you."

"No thanks necessary," Marlene said.

"Enough small talk," Jordan Von Berstein said, dismissing his wife. "Global Holding is considering investing in Void Records. Do you know why you're here?"

"Because I'm your biggest fucking obstacle," Reed said.

"To put it bluntly," Von Berstein said. "Your band is a mess. Your stunts last month were uncivilized. Tell me why I shouldn't buy out your contract and pull you off the label? At this point it's more cost effective than letting this train wreck ensue."

"Imagine by John Lennon," Reed said.

"Excuse me?" Von Berstein said.

"You pour your money into Void Records, and I'll write the next Imagine for you."

Von Berstein laughed. "You expect me to believe a heavy metal singer can write a song like that? You're not Bono."

"Bono can suck my dick," Reed said.

Oh god, please not a Bono rant. I placed my hand on his knee.

Reed handed Sony's latest Walkman and a pair of thin headphones to Von Berstein's wife. She adjusted the headphones, trying not to fuss her coiffed hair. Reed pressed play. Her head bobbed lightly, humoring him. She blushed; a youthful smile spread across her cheeks.

"Darlin' ask your husband if he wants that demo to hit the desk of some Geffen Records exec?" Reed said.

"Can he hear it?" Marlene handed the headphones to her husband.

Reed touched her hand. "Tell me what you think first."

"It's beautiful. Nothing like the loud noise of yours our son blasts in his bedroom."

"How does it make you feel?"

She hesitated and closed her eyes, "Like...I'm in love and the whole world is watching."

Reed let her pass the headphones to her husband.

Jordan Von Berstein listened to the song. He took off the headphones, "That's a hit song. Can you promise me you can give me an album like this if we invest in Void?"

"Whatever you want," Reed said. "Is that a deal?"

Von Berstein hesitated, and then shook Reed's hand, "It's a deal. I'll get the papers sent out to Void on Monday morning. Don't let me down, Mr. Reed."

"Wouldn't dream of it," Reed said.

Von Berstein insisted on paying. Marlene slid me a card with her contact information as we left for our hotel. "Call me soon, Jennifer."

"That was weird," I said back in the hotel lobby.

"It's about to get weirder." Reed pressed the elevator button for the top floor.

"What was on the tape?"

"Me singing a John Lennon song. Those assholes don't know anything about music." Reed loosened his tie and adjusted his collar.

The elevator opened to a cocktail bar. Void was holding a party for their executives and celebrity guests. Reed walked to the open bar and ordered drinks. I adjusted my dress, catching a glimpse of myself in the mirror. I looked killer.

"Was that Jerry Hall leaving?" I asked.

"Mick Jagger's old lady? Yeah, I think so. Prince is in the back corner if you want me to introduce you."

"I'm happy here with you." I smiled. This trip was overwhelming enough without adding the world's biggest pop stars into the mix.

"Good, I hate these people," Reed said. He ordered a second drink. "I can still kinda taste Von Berstein's dick. You didn't lose all respect for me back there, did you? I'm not normally one to kiss ass."

"Planning to redeem yourself?" I laughed.

"Girl, you have no idea what I have in store for Void. I've got to play the game for now. The payoff will be magnificent, trust me." He smiled. "I've been trying to wine and dine you all night, but I do have community service in the morning. My brother and his wife wanted to spend some time with you while I'm working this week."

"Chaperone me?"

"You know me too well." He smiled.

Several celebrities and recording staff introduced themselves. A waiter brought us another drink. After thirty minutes of people interrupting our conversation, I was tipsy.

Four scotches in, Reed pulled me off in a corner and gripped my hips.

"Please, Jenny, for the love of god, tell me I can take you back to my room and tear this dress off you?"

I kissed him on the lips. "I think Eddie Van Halen and Valerie Bertinelli are coming over here."

"Nope." Reed grabbed my hand and pulled me into the elevator.

I'm a total lush. I gave in. He was gorgeous, charming and I wanted to see what this tongue ring business was about. We barely made it into the room with our clothes on.

"Keep your boots on," Reed said, closing the door. He slipped my dress off my shoulders, down my hips. I kissed him and unbuttoned his shirt and pants. He picked me up and ripped open a condom. "You haven't been with anyone else, have you?" he asked.

"No."

"Good girl."

The next morning, he left a note on the bedside table. *Off to make amends to the city. Love—Reed.*

It was his brother Daniel's job to keep me entertained. The first of many times Daniel would be tasked with chaperoning me around a big city while Reed worked.

"Jennifer? I'm Daniel—Reed's brother. This is my wife, Sarah. I didn't realize you were the girl from the hospital." He shook his head. "Reed doesn't normally keep the same girl around this long."

"Daniel," Sarah interrupted, extending her hand. "It's nice to meet you, Jenny."

Daniel eyed me with suspicion. "I'm sorry, I have to ask, are you the reason we are here? This whole New York tantrum thing—Reed said he wanted to get back to L.A. to this girl he was in love with. I thought he was bullshitting me."

I laughed. "He was bullshitting you. I had nothing to do with it, I promise. Had no idea until I turned on the TV."

"I figured as much."

"It's not Daniel's first rodeo," Sarah said, like someone who missed her husband every time he had to fly out to calm his brother.

Back then, Times Square was one of the roughest areas in midtown—crime was high, the streets were littered, and lined with porn shops, drug dealers, prostitutes and homeless encampments. Instead, we walked to Stage Deli for their Broadway-themed dishes and overstuffed pastrami sandwiches. I liked that Daniel and Sarah were on my level; we didn't have to pretend to be comfortable in a fancy French restaurant.

"Where are you from, Jenny?" Sarah asked.

"I grew up in Phoenix. Moved to L.A. to go to art school. One more class next semester and I'll be done."

"Well, we're both from the great state of Kentucky. Known each other since high school, isn't that right, honey?" Sarah said.

"You went to school with Reed, then?" I asked, hoping Sarah would give me insight on Reed's early life.

Daniel moved his plastic fork around his plate. "Ah, no. Reed didn't live with my family. He went to a different school." He gathered his plate and took it to the trash, his way of telling his wife to change the subject.

Sarah glanced over her shoulder. "Okay, so, here's the deal. Reed and Daniel were not close growing up. They are now...unfortunately."

"You don't like Reed, do you?"

"Not his biggest fan," Sarah said.

"Care to elaborate?"

"He's complicated. Reed takes up a lot of our time. Daniel is protective. They had a pretty rough upbringing—Reed got the worst of it. But he puts unrealistic demands on people."

"He's never mentioned his parents."

"He won't. Their grandparents took custody of Reed when he was ten. Reed was troubled. Let's just say I wasn't surprised by what he did here last month. Typical Reed."

I looked at my plate. "It's strange, because he's never been like that around me."

"He will be. If you stick around long enough. I will give him credit—the past six months he's been on good behavior. He gets a little quiet off the road. He likes to go off the radar. Worries Daniel. Gives us a break."

"He can be needy at times," I said.

"An emotional vampire. I swear, he zaps the life out of Daniel. Look at him. Daniel is the younger brother."

"He is?"

"Looks ten years older than Reed, doesn't he? That's what Reed does to people. Reed is my brother in law—and yes, he does nice things for us. Daniel has a good job with him. But Reed is a twenty-four-hour, seven-day-a-week commitment. Something to think about."

"Ready to go, ladies?" Daniel asked.

The next morning, Reed and I visited a school in the Bronx. He read to a first grade class and played with the kids. They loved him. He was attentive and patient. He asked the principal what he needed for the kids to have new books, musical instruments, and for building repairs, then pulled his checkbook out and signed the bottom. "Pick a number, man."

That afternoon we met a journalist and photographer for an interview. Reed asked the photographer to take pictures of us together to send to him privately.

You've seen the pictures. People use them to this day on the internet to show the happy times between us.

I waited outside the hotel for him the next afternoon. He'd promised to take me to Brooklyn for pizza. I was flipping through a travel guide when a tourist with limited English asked me for directions to the Statue of Liberty. I gave him the map from the travel guide. He thanked me profusely. He was handsome, but it was a simple request for directions. I didn't even get his name.

Reed walked up a few moments later and kissed me on the cheek. "How's your morning been?"

"Great. Had yummy French toast at the restaurant around the corner."

"Who was that guy?"

"Lost tourist. Seemed nice."

"You need to be more careful who you're talking to."

I sighed. "Ready to head to Brooklyn for pizza? We can walk across the bridge if you're up for it."

"Not in the mood, we'll order something upstairs."

My feelings were hurt, but I didn't question him.

He stood silent on the opposite side of the elevator.

"Did I do something wrong?" I asked.

"Nope. You can do whatever you want."

"Are you jealous I was talking to that guy?" I said, amused.

"Doesn't look good. You standing outside a hotel, wearing what you're wearing, talking to strangers."

"What's wrong with what I'm wearing? You love this outfit when I wear it at home."

"We're not at home. It's a little short." He unlocked the door to our room.

I put my hand on his back, and he moved away.

"You're really upset about this?"

He pulled his boots off. "I'm looking out for you, that's all. How do you think it looks for my girlfriend to be standing outside a hotel, dressed like a slut?"

"Hold on—you don't get to talk to me like that. You've never had a problem with my clothes before."

"I do now."

Stinging insecurity twisted in my chest. I fought the urge to hide in the bathroom and burst into tears. He was pulling some chauvinistic macho bullshit and I wasn't falling for it. Something else had to be eating at him.

I changed my *offensive* clothes. When I bent over to go through my bag, Reed pulled me onto the bed and kissed me. I leaned back.

"Hey, look at me. I'm sorry, Jen. I don't want anyone getting the wrong idea."

"He was a tourist."

"I don't care. You're mine and I don't want men looking at you." Reed kissed me and slid his hand into my panties, pulling them off. He rose over me, gripping my wrists above my head, "I love you, Jenny." Jeans unzipped, no warm-up, his hips thrust into mine. Aggressive and one-sided; it didn't feel like love. He'd always made sure I got off, but this time he rolled over when he finished marking his territory.

I went to the bathroom, pissed off. Things happened so fast that he hadn't used a condom. I wiped myself down with scalding hot water before sliding on clean underwear. We always, always used protection, at his insistence more than mine. *What gives?* I knew I had to walk in the bedroom, unfazed. *Or what, Jenny? He'll think you're weak. He'll be the jerk he was at the hospital—and you're two thousand, five hundred miles from home with an empty wallet.*

Reed opened the door for the pizza delivery, slipping a piece out and taking a bite as he brought the box over to me.

"Yay, Domino's," I said, sarcastically.

"I'm sorry. I was being a dick. Let's eat and we'll go to the zoo."

I wore jeans. He bought cotton candy and kissed me on the carousel. I almost forgot he'd fucked me without a condom or emotion. I didn't want to ruin our last day in the city together. He spent the night telling me how much he loved me. He had early morning press and left a note: *I'll be back before your flight. — Love, E.R.*

At noon, he phoned me. "Jenny, I'm pissed. This interview started late. I can't make it in time to say goodbye. I'm sorry."

I needed to end things with Reed. How was I to know which side of him was real—the celebrity, the rock star, the criminal or the philanthropist? Was he the scared, vulnerable kid? The asshole who said I dressed like a slut? My sweet boyfriend? Or the new one I called the moody prince, who would arrive unshaven, likely drunk or high, wearing sunglasses, speaking in a deep voice.

The moody prince was the one who met me at the hotel at the last minute to kiss me goodbye. It seemed dishonest to leave without telling him the truth. I loved the guy, but this was never going to work.

He gave me a warm hug. "I couldn't pass up the chance to say goodbye."

"Reed, I know we only have a few minutes, but we need to talk."

"Gotta jet," he said. He kissed my fingers and pressed a folded piece of paper into my hands. "You don't have to go back to California, if you don't want to." He left me alone, holding the paper.

There was an address written on it and wrapped inside was a key. I checked the time. I was already running late for my flight. The hotel porter carried my bags to a waiting limo.

"Airport?" The driver asked.

Damn it, Reed!

Lexington Avenue. A high-rise, residential building. The doorman greeted me by name. I took the elevator to the fifteenth floor and unlocked the door to a newly remodeled penthouse overlooking Manhattan. Unfurnished aside from the bed—a cherry wood headboard with white feather comforter and pillows. I walked across new hardwoods. Floor to ceiling windows offered a postcard view of the city. I stepped back to catch my breath. Lying on the bed was a red rose and card. I lifted the envelope. An antique silver engagement ring fell into my hand. Underneath was a deed to the penthouse. Fingers trembling, I read the attached note:

"Yours if you want it—say yes."

My heart raced. *This is not why I came here.* I slipped the vintage ring on my finger, to see how it felt, promising myself that I'd put it back in the envelope. Tears welled; I recognized this ring. It was one-of-a-kind, from a Grace Kelly film exhibit we'd visited in Hollywood, weeks before his radio incident. A priceless artifact that had graced the hands of a movie star before she became a princess. While I'd been torn, questioning his feelings and mine—he'd made this happen.

The intercom buzzed, startling me. I pressed the red button to answer.

"Ms. Stone? Mr. Reed would like to know if you want him to have your bags sent up?"

I looked at the ring again, sliding it on my finger one last time. *Why did I doubt him?* That familiar voice rang in my ear—*run, now.*

"Are you there?" the building concierge asked.

I was overwhelmed. "Yes. Tell him I said yes."

"Magic Man," a track from Heart's *Dreamboat Annie* played on my mother's vintage record player—one of the few things Sasha shipped from my old apartment. My legs intertwined with Reed's. Dreamy bass and guitar swirled around our loft. I stared at his lashes. Sweet lips. I'd entered some sort of twilight zone; with a level of romanticism you only see in Hollywood movies. Cast under the spell of a beautiful young man.

Maybe I was naïve.

Maybe I should've listened to Ann and Nancy Wilson. I closed my eyes, my face against his chest, the turntable needle rolled into "Crazy on You."

I slipped into his dream.

The next few weeks were the hurricane Reed had warned me about. We painted, made love, and ate Thai takeout in bed. Every day he did something sweet to make me laugh. "God, baby you're beautiful," he'd say when we made love in our cozy sky nest in the greatest city in the world. He sat on our bed and played a love song he'd written for me. His eyes lit when he looked into mine at our favorite Italian place.

"This girl is amazing," he told our waiter.

I blushed. "I'm pretty cool!"

Reed laughed. "That's my girl. I can't wait to marry you and start a family, Jenny. I'm the happiest man on this planet. No one else has ever made me feel this way."

You don't stop to ask for directions when you're whisked into a fairy tale. One minute you're in your underwear, eating Cheetos at the foot of your bed, painting your toenails purple with Dollar Store polish, wondering how you'll make rent. The next, you're Rapunzel in a tower so high you will never get down. For all the good, bad, and unforgivable things that came next—in the beginning, it was a love story. If nothing else, I have to believe that.

Chapter Nine

One minute, I was a semi-anonymous artist in L.A. with a secret rock star boyfriend. The next, renowned fashion designers were calling me to schedule wedding gown fittings in New York. Can you imagine Gianni Versace calling your house? Charming, handsome Reed threw this my way to keep me busy while I was alone. He went from sleepover boyfriend to world-traveling showman; leaving for weeks at a time then flying back to New York for a few nights.

After his tantrum in New York, album sales skyrocketed. He joked in interviews, "Next time I'll skip the hard work and name the album *Central Park Riot*."

Band conflict took side stage as the album hit gold and platinum. The exact thing he'd wanted to get away from had catapulted the album. He would always wonder if the music would stand on its own without his outburst.

New York was the fantasy every little girl dreams of. I took up photography, and there were my good friends Gianni, Dolce & Gabbana. When you're alone in a big city, you don't turn down people who want to style your hair and let you sit front row at major fashion shows. I took a few modeling jobs in New York for magazine ads. I had opportunities to learn under marketing and design greats, using top of the line equipment.

The cover art for Reed's solo album with the purple/blue ghost face meld and the 3-D hooded figure images were created with vintage lenticular equipment from the MoMA archives. For a girl who'd been a struggling art student only months before, it was super cool!

I made use of our massive loft space, using an endless supply of art tools to paint a series of fifteen by twenty foot canvases to cover the blank walls. Those paintings later sold at auction for $10,000 each. So, there! A few still hang in a Brooklyn gallery if you want to check them out.

New York was a fantasy come to life.

Kaley was always in the back of my mind. I wished she was there to share in the excitement. I could hear her laughter in rooms she'd never graced—a constant reminder that I wouldn't be there without her. My art, my soon-to-be husband, life in New York—none of that would have been possible if she hadn't grabbed my hand and pulled me down the path to my destiny—and her demise.

I spent too much time alone, smoking cigarettes, thinking of her. Thinking I didn't deserve this life. When Reed wasn't around, I painted those images of her that haunted me. I had to get them out of my head. As soon as the canvases dried, I rolled them up and hid them in the closet. I needed to focus on Reed, on the present.

For a brief time, New York gave me him as a whole. Reed the boyfriend, Reed the singer—Reed in all his facets.

He religiously took antidepressants and mood stabilizers in NYC. He was sweet, funny, and bit his tongue about things that later would send him into a rage.

Our wedding date was set for November 14th, during a break in touring. The wedding plans got so out of control that we eventually got married on a whim. It started as an argument—which should have said something. I was smarter than this, but I can tell you exactly why it happens. You're on your own, things are going fine. Weeks pass while these men are out on the road. You feel lonely, you can't do this anymore. You're vulnerable. *Maybe he's not coming back, maybe he's with someone else?* He walks in the door and showers you with attention and gifts. He makes you believe you're the one and only thing that helps him keep his shit together. You're the reason he wakes up, the reason he breathes. It's you and only you, he swears.

Then he's gone.

Our life together was a never-ending tug-of-war with his career. What can you say to someone who is on the road for months, earning more money in one night than you'll make in your life, and entertaining thousands of fans across the world? "I want you to stay home?" No, you can't say that. You count your blessings. You find yourself exactly where you never wanted to be—completely indebted to another person, with no money and resources of your own. It's hard to start your own career when you are at the whim of another person's schedule.

I undervalued myself in New York. I did several internships, but I felt like an impostor. People were kind enough to share their craft. Those mentors told me many times that they would not have wasted their time if they hadn't seen talent.

Reed's fame might have opened doors for me, but I had to work ten times as hard to prove myself. Every time I had the opportunity to join a project, Reed's schedule interfered. When Marlene Von Bernstein contacted me to see if I was interested in a residency, I had to decline.

"I'll make a spot for you if you change your mind." She made a genuine effort to be friends and I pushed her away. I was marrying a rock star and she was the social elite, everything that wasn't cool in our world. It didn't matter that I wanted the residency, it didn't work for Reed.

In August, I planned to visit my parents, who I had not seen in six months. Reed returned home unexpectedly. He was angry that I was leaving—I should be home waiting for him. It was time to draw a line. I'd already booked the flights and they were expecting me. He shouted at me for using his money. I told him where he could put it... and so on. We hadn't seen each other in weeks.

"I'm sick of this shit!" I shouted at him.

The next moment, expensive lamps were flying against the wall. I grabbed a bag and tossed my clothes in it.

He snatched it away from me.

It was all quite dramatic. I'm surprised no Academy Awards were handed out that night. I dumped out my purse, threw his credit cards on the table and walked out the door.

He followed me to the elevator, grabbing my hair. "You forgot my ring."

When he let go, I turned around and punched him square in the face. I was not the type of girl to let anyone push me around.

Now I've done it. I wasn't sure how to follow up. I tried to run. He grabbed me, threw me over his shoulder while I kicked at him, and forced me into the penthouse. It was crazy, but other than the split second after I punched him, there was no fear. Two immature, pissed-off people taking it out on each other before having angry sex.

Equally responsible, equally battered in the end.

It's never okay to hit someone, but this fight was mutual. The next morning, we laughed. He had a black eye, and I had a busted lip where his teeth had brought blood when he kissed me. Should I have added it to the list of warning signs? Yes. But the angry sex was amazing, and in the end, the sex is all you remember, right?

"You still want to get married?" I asked after rescheduling my flight.

"Absolutely."

"Meet my parents or I'm out.'

"Alright."

He upgraded my coach seat to first class. We left for Phoenix in sunglasses and made it to my parents' house for breakfast. Reed charmed them. My mother pointed out my bruised lip and arm, though it was covered with makeup.

"It's okay, mom—I punched him. I kind of had it coming."

She walked over to Reed, lifting his sunglasses, "This is not good, the two of you." She gave both of us a stern talking to. My mother knew I was headstrong; if she opposed our relationship, it would push me towards him.

"Looks like you caught the wrong end of my little girl's left hook." My dad coughed. He wasn't one for conflict but had taught me to defend myself. He caught his breath. "Reggie Stevens down the street was throwing rocks at some little girls when Jenny was thirteen. She shouted at him to stop, and he didn't listen. She dropped the greasy bike part we were working on, marched across the yard and clocked him. Knocked a seventeen-year-old boy flat on his back. I didn't raise a soft girl." His assessment—if Reed wanted to hurt me, he wouldn't be walking around with a black eye.

My mom's mouth dropped when she saw my engagement ring. They congratulated us, but I saw the worried look in my mom's eyes—my parents didn't think we were serious.

I took Reed upstairs to keep mom from cornering me. That way I wouldn't have to ask about my dad's yellowing skin, his wheezing or the way his arms shook when he managed to push himself up from his recliner to shake Reed's hand. Reed took care of the medical bills so I wouldn't have to ask those questions. I loved him for it.

We smoked an old joint from my nightstand and listened to The Sound. Surrounded by posters of my favorite bands in my teenage bedroom, it was impossible not feel his rock star presence. I'd spent years inside these walls, dreaming about painting and travel, but this tall, handsome figure with long hair and an Iron Maiden shirt was something wild and foreign.

After almost a year together I'd managed to hide this part of myself—Jenny before California, before Kaley. Was he still going to love me after seeing I was just a girl from Phoenix who used to be an artist? Sometimes the rock star pissed me off, but I loved the lost boy from Kentucky fiercely. I smiled, wishing I could have known him then.

Reed kissed me. "Let's drive to Vegas and get married."

Caught off guard, I laughed. "This weed isn't that good, honey."

He took the hand that wore Grace Kelly's ring. "I'm serious. Leave your parents a note, we'll sneak out—which come on, you know you did all the time as a kid."

"And get married. Tonight?"

"It'll be morning when we get there. Come on. We can still do the big thing in November. This will be for us. Also, it's my birthday month."

"You're the worst." I smiled.

He picked up a photo of me and my dad riding dirt bikes together. "I dare you."

In hindsight, I can see he pushed for big things to happen (new penthouses, diamond rings, weddings in Vegas, etc.) when he sensed I might consider getting out. Things had to be in constant roller-coaster mode. I never had the chance to stop and analyze events as they happened. I wanted to leave my parent's house and the guilt over the peeling wallpaper in the bathroom, the leaky kitchen sink and squeaky floorboards my dad could no longer repair. All I had to do was ask and Reed would fix it all. How could I not love him?

"Let's do it," I smiled.

Fist Fight. Meet the parents. Wedding in Vegas.

Valet parked at sunrise, we dropped our bags in our room, showered and changed. Reed wore all black, with a silver chain and mirrored sunglasses. his long-sleeved shirt buttoned halfway. I bought a white sundress in the hotel lobby shop.

We looked at each other as we were leaving the hotel room. "Are we seriously doing this?" We went to bed again. Lust does not a happy marriage make. I can tell you that.

We took a limo to a rhinestone-adorned Elvis chapel. Graceland-something. It was a quick, "I do," kiss, and pink cupcake frosting on our faces. We were Mr. and Mrs. Evan Reed Williams—his full name.

"Never use Williams," Reed said. He hated his family name but hadn't made the effort to change it. "We'll take care of it in L.A."

It's insane that a simple matter of paperwork can legally entwine two souls for eternity. The thing we'd anticipated for months was done. We went for breakfast, then back to the hotel for a swim before retiring to the honeymoon suite for three days. Every time I thought the words 'my husband', was another excuse to fuck him. If it hadn't been for room service, we would have died in that room. I didn't want food or anything else, just Reed. *This is real. He's mine. I don't have to worry anymore. It's on paper.*

Reed promised we would go on a real honeymoon as soon as possible. The press had not homed in on our relationship since we had moved to New York. We wanted to keep it that way.

It was also bad timing. The band was recovering from negative publicity, having officially parted with the bass player, Matty. The label needed Reed to be the bad boy, poster heartthrob. A musician getting married affected records sales.

It was nice to have a secret between the two of us. I mailed photos to my mother, but otherwise it was our little secret.

Us against the world, remember?

He went on the road as soon as we returned to New York, flying to Amsterdam to meet the band. Back to the penthouse for me. This was in the days before Netflix and chill, so it was an expensive bottle of champagne, chocolates, and a stack of VHS rentals. I honeymooned alone, wondering if I'd done the right thing, getting swept into the fairy tale again.

The band was scheduled for two shows in Montreal, Toronto, then a break before the U.S. leg of the tour. Tickets waited for me to fly to Toronto to join them. Strangely enough—this was the first time I'd seen his band play an arena. (Big middle finger to the people who called me a groupie. I'd never seen this damn band play a full show!)

The Toronto hotel room was filled with roses, wine, champagne, chocolates, and a rack of designer dresses, all gifts he'd had ordered for me. I found a basic black mini dress with spaghetti straps and a lace top. Boxes of brand new shoes lined the bed. I had to remind myself it was real.

A driver took me to the arena, where the band's stage manager met me at the car and guided me through this crowd of fans to get inside the building. We did a tour of the arena and went backstage. I'd lived too many years with male friends to not recognize it as a complete farce. When wives and girlfriends were around, everyone was on their best behavior. There was a gourmet buffet, games for the crewmembers' kids. Grown, wasted men tried desperately to act clean and sober.

Reed came out of his dressing room to give me a kiss before he went on. "I'm glad you're here, Jenny."

When the band took stage, my heart was on fire. It was overwhelming to look out and see thirty-thousand people staring at you from side stage. Reed did this every night! On stage, he was intense, athletic and sweaty. He dedicated a song to, "This beautiful woman who has made my life complete."

Afterwards, we ran out of the stadium to a waiting limo. Screaming fans, followed by an echo chamber of silence. The rest of the band stayed for the meet and greets and parties. Reed had to get out as soon as possible, and I couldn't wait to get my hands on him in our hotel room.

After the shows, we went back to New York and left for a quick honeymoon in Hawaii. Because we never officially announced our marriage, we were able to do a few things under the radar.

It wouldn't last.

Reed asked me to go on tour with the band to keep him company. Musicians travel the world and never see anything—they walk off the stage to the bus and head to the next city and next show. The fans won't let them venture out. Even in smaller locales, hundreds of fans wait before and after the shows. We outwitted them a couple of times by staying at a different hotel from the rest of the band and crew. We had to go out in disguises; our luggage would be stolen; we had to kick girls out of the hotel rooms—they'd managed to get in before we arrived.

There's behind the scenes footage of us dancing on an airport baggage train one night, having a blast. Reed wore the infamous DIY *Hi Jenny* shirt on that tour during the last set to all the shows I couldn't make. He laughs and says, "Hi Jenny," at the end of the "Last September" live video. People everywhere shouted, "Hi Jenny!" It got the fans to warm up to me, which was nice.

Some stories should end when people are young, in love, and having fun.

If you're listening to "Last September," you still have time to turn back.

Chapter Ten

I loved touring with Reed. At first. Actually, I loved the sex on tour. We could ditch the fancy attire on the road. I had my boyfriend back. He'd come off stage, pumping with adrenaline from revving up the crowd and release it all into me against dressing room walls. We fucked before shows, after shows, in limos, taxicabs, and tour buses—whenever and wherever the mood hit.

"I fucking love you," Reed said.

I'd answer, "Shut up. Fuck me harder."

We lay down in a different city every night, my head rising from the pillow with a smile each morning. It was new and exciting. As the dates grew closer together, the nights in hotels were few and far between. I had to get used to sleeping on a smelly, bumpy tour bus full of drunken musicians, partying until they passed out.

After a month on tour, I didn't have the stamina to keep up with the constant partying. Anxiety plagued me. The young girls lined up after gigs reminded me of Kaley. Then there were the mean fans—the ones who spit and threw things at me. I started having anxiety attacks, but I didn't want to worry Reed.

The roadies were quick to make situations go away so he wouldn't lash out at the fans. One fan grabbed me in the crowd and ripped a handful of my hair out. I was a target, so I kept to myself with my books. This was not like me at all. I'd always been the girl with too much energy.

Fumes from the rumbling bus made me nauseous. I didn't feel like eating. Every bit of energy was zapped from me. I wanted to sleep, day and night. I kept a photo of me, Kaley and Kevin as a bookmark. I missed them.

One night, Reed left his jacket in the bus. He always wore it during a certain set, so I ran inside to take it backstage.

Riders specified Reed had a separate dressing room from his bandmates. Hot tea. Fresh towels. He didn't want anyone in the room while he warmed up.

I broke his pre-show ritual opening the door.

"Hi Jenny." He wiped the back of his hand across his nose, sliding a small mirror out of my view. He'd told me a hundred times he wasn't taking hard drugs—he couldn't, they made him crazy. Maybe it was stupid to trust him in the first place, but it was the first time it was blatantly obvious he'd been hiding something from me. I couldn't confront him before he stepped onstage to entertain thousands of screaming fans. Instead, I gave him his jacket and went back to the bus. He was my husband. I had a right to say something about this.

He came on the bus after the show, like he did every night, with a sweat-drenched towel around his neck. It had been a good show. He tried to kiss me. I pulled away.

"What's wrong?"

I had to give him an ultimatum. He'd lied to me. This wasn't weed, or the occasional pills, it was cocaine. I hated myself for trusting him so naively—it wasn't the drugs that bothered me—it was the secret.

If there was one, there were more. That vulnerability made me angrier.

He opened a beer, waiting for me to say something as he rubbed the beer cap between his fingers. I wanted him to tell me. After a few awkward minutes, he flicked the beer cap across the counter.

"Silent treatment?" Reed rolled his eyes. "You sure you want to do this?"

I tucked my feet in my chair and opened my book. It was childish, but I couldn't speak to him. He didn't deserve to speak to me.

He stared at me from the doorway. Shaking his head, he stepped off to light a cigarette.

"I just played a sold-out show to 30,000 people, honey." He laid the flip lighter on the dashboard. "I'm sure I can find a girl who wants to talk to me."

He slammed the door, stood outside, finishing his cigarette, and I assume waiting for me to follow him.

How do I talk to him about this? I'd seen his tantrums, even been on the receiving end of a few. I didn't want to be the person he exploded on. It hit me, I had no one to turn to on the road. No wonder I was miserable.

I woke to the bus moving. His side of the bed was empty. I jumped up, panicked that he'd missed the bus. I peeked through our curtain. Reed sat at a table, playing solitaire. He gathered the cards from the table, slid them in his front pocket and followed me into the bathroom at the back of the bus. He put his arms around me and kissed my neck.

"Still mad at me?" He shut the door behind us and pushed a strand of hair behind my ear. "Don't shut me out. Talk to me, please?"

My fear—if I said the words, he would deny it. I'd have another lie to deal with. Where would we go from that?

"You're the best thing in my life, Jen, you know that, right? Whatever I did, I'm sorry. Please believe me."

"You know what you did."

"I didn't mean what I said. I was blowing off steam." He dug into his pockets, placing a wrapped condom on the counter. "I didn't have sex with anyone. I could have. But I didn't. You believe me, don't you?"

"You're hiding things from me."

"You mean the dressing room? It wasn't what you think."

"What exactly was it?"

"A one-time thing. A pick me up. I'm exhausted, baby. Everything hurts, but I have to give those kids the best night of their lives. I need something to get me through these last few shows. I don't have the energy to go onstage."

"Then don't. I'd rather you not go on if you have to use cocaine before every show."

"Not an option."

"You were hiding it from me."

"I didn't want to upset you. I swear. I've used a few times this tour to go onstage, that's all. I never use anything afterward but weed or a few beers. You know that."

"I don't."

"Don't be like this. Tell me what you want me to do."

"Be honest. Don't hide things. Doing coke to get onstage is crazy."

"It's rock n' roll. Part of the job. I wasn't hiding. I didn't want you to be disappointed in me. It won't happen again."

"Okay." I sighed. No point in arguing with him.

"Are we alright?"

"Yeah."

"Thank God." He exhaled. "I thought you were leaving me. I'd die if you left me."

Chapter Eleven

Backstage was abuzz the following weekend. Nominated for three MTV Europe awards, Reed's band was playing two nights in a row in London to sold out crowds. Special guests were scheduled onstage both nights.

Jett Harlan was the singer for British legendary heavy metal band Silvertron, an act on par with the likes of Black Sabbath, Deep Purple and Iron Maiden. To insiders, Jett was a god. To an outsider like me, he was another old rocker wearing the same velvet, purple jacket he'd worn on his album cover in 1965. His wife, Suzy Harlan, a fashion designer, tried desperately to keep up with the younger girls. She wore tight leather biker gear, silver jewelry and winged black eyeliner. Her stark white hair was teased high as the moon. Backstage onlookers parted like the sea when they walked by.

My beautiful husband, who thought himself god's gift to the world, was barely fazed by anyone that wasn't a Rolling Stone. He told journalists he was honored to share the stage with Jett—but criticized the iconic rocker behind closed doors. Jett's band hadn't put out new music in a decade, reveling in the success of their youth—the kind of thing that annoyed the hell out of Reed. Still, Jett was rock royalty; even Evan Reed had to share his stage.

Rehearsal went smoothly the first night. The second night, not so much. I was in line at the food tent when I saw Jett and his wife Suzy near the front of the line.

The starving gossip girls were on attack. "Look at that old hag. If she only knew!"

Suzy was a bit weathered, but still beautiful. Few women over forty-five can pull off leather hot pants and fishnets. The younger women were killing themselves to stay thin and ahead of every trend. Suzy Harlan had an air of authenticity. She owned a boutique in London, selling clothes these girls craved—and were critical of her wearing.

Jett took credit for her work. I doubted that he'd contributed anything to the clothing line that shared his name. Can you imagine, creating a successful business in women's fashion and naming it after your husband?

The girls were envious. Suzy was not a girlfriend or a groupie—she was a wife. *How will things change when they find out Reed and I are married?*

I knew I'd never fit in with those girls. I tended to hang out backstage in a tank top, tight jeans, and Chuck's or Docs. I didn't mind a little leather, but I was glad Reed didn't expect me to dress like some trophy hooker.

Suzy's roots ran punk rock, not pretentious like the girls glaring at me for being in a damn food line! This was hard to get used to—feeling judged every single moment of the day.

Buried deep into Stephen King's latest novel, I almost missed the commotion at the front of the line. I looked up as Jett Harlan shoved his wife and slapped her across the face. He jerked Suzy's arm and grabbed her by the hair. She managed to pull away. She flipped him off and walked to the nearest restroom, her black halter-top covered in shepherd's pie.

Jett walked past me, wiping his prized velvet blazer with a napkin. The gossip queens gawked. Everyone else went back to business as usual. It was eerie. A man attacked his wife, and other than the jealous girls who now had a story to tell, no one seemed fazed.

This was not cool. I left my place in line and followed Suzy to the restroom. She stood at the mirror, wiping off her shirt, and pulling loose strands of teased hair from her head. Her silver bangle bracelets clinked against matching earrings. Her cat-eyes made their way to mine. "You think you're better than me, don't you? I see how you're looking at me. *'It's such a pity.'* You don't have a clue you're looking in a mirror."

"I'm sorry he did this to you, Suzy."

"Save your sorrow, sweetheart. You're gonna need it. That fucker you're with is a million times worse than Jett ever dreamed of being."

What nerve did she have? Reed was nothing like Jett Harlan. We would never be some old washed-up, has-been rocker couple. My chest turned red with anger.

I ran into Reed walking out of the restroom. He grabbed my arm and I jerked away.

"You, okay?"

"I need a walk." I headed down the concrete breezeway toward the venue exit. Reed followed.

The light drizzle was calming in the summer heat. I missed California and air conditioning—the one thing cities like New York and London didn't have enough of. We sat on the edge of the loading bay while the roadies carried the bands' gear inside.

"What's going on?" Reed said.

"Nothing."

He tugged the tongue of my leather Doc Martens. "Come on, it's not nothing. What's wrong?"

"You missed that entire scene in the meal tent?"

"Rehearsals, babe."

"Your band's hero attacked his wife in front of everyone. He spat at her, shoved food in her face and ripped her hair out."

"Jesus," Reed said.

"I went to make sure she was okay, and she had the nerve to go off on me."

"Honey, don't trust any of these girls on tour, they're glorified starfuckers. Suzy is the worst. She's not someone you want to be friends with."

"I wanted to make her feel better. But she was saying awful things."

"What did she say to you?" Reed asked, defensive.

"It's nothing. I shouldn't be upset with her. Jett is the jerk."

"I'll talk to him."

"No. Leave it. I don't want to make things worse."

"I can't have people upsetting you."

What if Suzy repeats what she said to me? Reed would lose his cool knowing she'd compared him to Jett. We were nothing like them and we never would be.

I fixed a plate, managing a few nibbles before getting nauseous. Something smashed down the hallway. Shouting. Crew members surrounded Jett's dressing room.

Reed. Fuck. He was going off on Jett. What a sight for the crew—these two legendary rock stars arguing with each other. The younger putting the older in his place.

Reed's voice boomed. "Jett, you better get your bitch in line."

Shit. Reed wasn't taking up for Suzy, he was defending me! Ashamed and embarrassed, I wanted to hide, but Reed was expecting me side stage.

I hated sitting with the band girlfriends. That night, it was mutual. Dene's girlfriend wouldn't even stand to let me get to my seat. The other girls didn't make eye contact. Suzy's seat was empty. I needed to find her and apologize. *I'm such a selfish jerk.*

I hoped she hadn't left for the hotel. A roadie said she was waiting for a cab. He wanted to say more, but kept his mouth shut.

Suzy stood on the loading dock smoking a cigarette. She had a freshly bruised eye and swollen lip.

"I guess we all know who the queen is now, don't we?" Suzy stared into the night. "You're naïve, but I never pegged you as a snitch." She took another draw from her cigarette and flicked it. "Don't say I didn't warn you."

I never saw Suzy Harlan again. She and Jett were in an accident later that week on their motorcycle. Jett's 4.0 blood alcohol level sent them head off the slick highway asphalt into a field. Suzy died on impact. Jett Harlan only did thirty days in jail for vehicular manslaughter. I lay awake wondering if I was the only person who saw the bruises on her face before she died. Those bruises were my fault—it was my husband who told Jett to get his old lady in check. Kaley, Suzy—how are women subject to such violence? I was grateful Reed wasn't like those men.

Rock n' Roll stops for no one. Not even legends. Reed told the staff we were married. The roadies who'd once been friendly started to avoid me, and when they did speak, it was, "Mrs. Reed." The other girlfriends ignored me. *Fuck them. I never liked them anyway.*

Always with the bandleader, I was privy to meetings and parties the other girls weren't invited too. I hated catty drama, and it was true, I didn't particularly care for most of them, but their exclusion made me insecure. Reed's air of superiority had seeped into my brain. It was the only way not to feel hurt. Besides, Reed and I didn't fit in—it was us against them, always.

Reed praised the band merch I designed. I was getting respect from other bands; hanging with the cool kids while the mean girls glared at us from a distance. People realized I wasn't going anywhere, that this wasn't some fling. This was real.

Cocky, ego-driven singers from the opening acts were always chatty. I made friends with the younger guys like Jamie London from No Spaces. A deep-voiced singer—panties flew off the moment he walked into a room with his shiny, honey-streaked hair drifting down his back. I was only a little fazed, having grown accustomed to the company of sexy, immature rock stars. The other women's jealousy was thick in the air. Hanging out with Jamie, harmless flirting and banter, smoking weed and laughing after a gig reminded me of Fish and the gang.

These friendships were always temporary. Another tour leg would start with a new opening act. I made great memories, but I was lonely on the road. And needy. The old me would have hated what I was turning into; this girl who needed Evan Reed to feel happy.

I'd always considered myself tough, but I wasn't cut out for the viciousness of rock n' roll. Reed said you had to be someone else on the road. That didn't work for me. Instead, I retreated to the bus with my books. Being ostracized by the other girls made me miss Kaley terribly. I tried my best not to think about what happened to her, but the more time I spent alone, the more those thoughts crept in.

It didn't help when I asked Reed when I would be paid for the artwork I'd done for the band. We were staying at an apartment in Toronto while they recorded a song for a soundtrack. I hated asking him for money, and I wanted to send something to my parents.

He didn't say anything at first.

I stammered, "I-I-I wouldn't ask, if it was for your solo project, but I did the work, this is for the band."

"You want to get paid?"

"Yes," I said.

His finger pointed an inch from my face. "You have the fucking nerve to ask me to pay you? Are you serious? You stupid bitch. I've spent half-a-million dollars on you this year. Your loans. Your parent's bills. Jewelry, designer clothes, anything you've asked for. I bought you a fucking loft in Manhattan. Seriously?"

I was in tears. "You're right. I'm sorry."

Reed picked up an expensive vase and hurled it across the room. "Fuck you, Jenny."

Chapter Twelve

The band was scheduled to play several nights in Los Angeles, then shoot a video for the film soundtrack. Paparazzi hounded us at L.A.X., shouting, snapping photos. Onlookers pushed and shoved past security to get close to Reed. We were separated from each other by the crowd. Paparazzi rushed him. A cameraman accidentally smacked me in the face. Reed's security guard pulled me aside, lifting me over a barrier. Reed attacked the camera guy and punched him in the face. It took two bodyguards to pull him away.

I left with a bruised cheek. Reed left L.A.X in handcuffs. The camera guy pocketed three thousand dollars to drop the charges.

After that incident, the paparazzi stalked me. Calling me by name, asking personal questions. I couldn't get lunch or go inside a store. I hadn't figured out how to handle them at that point. (You never do). I prayed they wouldn't find out we were married. Even when I tried to go to Sasha's salon for a haircut, they followed me there and waited.

She locked the door and closed her curtains. Rattled, I lost the keys to the rental car. I cried—which of course they photographed, captioning the picture: "Rock Star's Girlfriend Breaks Down Over Bad Hairstyle."

I found a payphone to call Reed. He told me to go inside the closest store and wait for him. He arrived with two bodyguards.

Marcus would become my constant companion. I felt like an idiot, but the paparazzi were intense. Aside from the brief moments we'd been able to sneak away, this had been Reed's life 24/7 in Hollywood. No wonder he'd avoided the Strip at all costs.

Drained emotionally and physically, I was anxious and crying for no reason. "My iron is low, or something."

"Go to the doctor and get it checked, babe," Reed said.

I kissed him and headed out for the day.

"Can I get meds for anxiety?" I asked the doctor when he came in with my lab results. "It's probably a vitamin deficiency or lack of sunlight." I laughed.

"Let's get you on a good prenatal vitamin first. That should help you with the nausea and morning sickness," the doctor said. "You're pregnant."

"You're not serious," I said. Then hurled into the trash can.

"I take it you weren't anticipating the news. Your chart says you're skipping meals—that's not good. I'll have the receptionist set you an appointment with our OBGYN. Do you remember the last time you had your period?"

I shook my head. "No. I travel constantly, they're sporadic. I must have missed a pill or something."

At least I wasn't going crazy. I'd lost my birth control for a few nights, but we'd used condoms. *This cannot be happening.*

Reed wanted kids. I wasn't ready. Terrified by paparazzi, the thought of having to protect a baby from them was daunting.

Commuting from L.A. to Malibu with paparazzi following us was impossible. We stayed in an L.A. hotel while the band filmed the video. I had yet to see Reed's mansion. Another crazy fame side effect—living somewhere, does not mean you actually "live" there. What kind of life would our child have if it wasn't safe for us to drive to Malibu?

Tell him the truth, you're not ready for a baby. I slid my key in the door to our room and took a deep breath.

"Reed, we need to talk." I sighed.

A blonde woman on TV, wearing Cover Girl's entire line of makeup, had Reed's full attention. He ordered me out of the room before I could speak.

"Downstairs, now." He slammed and locked the door behind me.

I was about to tell him the most important thing in the world and the door was slammed in my face.

Motherfucker.

I ran to the hotel lobby in time to catch the end of the interview.

Breanna Lee was a model-turned-porn star Reed had dated before me. Later, I learned their relationship did not end until things were serious between us.

Remember when he said he had a mean dog at home? *Yeah.*

They lived together in his Malibu mansion. She came home one day to find her belongings outside the gate. Reed stopped taking her calls when he found out she was having guys at his place while he toured.

When Breanna found out about us, she retaliated with a lawsuit and tell-all interview.

Many things were kept from me after we were married. Televisions stayed unplugged, newspapers would be missing sections. My bodyguards were instructed to turn tabloids in the opposite direction in stores. I believed Reed was protecting me, but I was slowly being isolated.

Closing me out was the wrong move on this particular day.

"Need a drink?" the bartender asked.

"No."

On TV, the blonde woman's long lashes batted dramatically against her striking blue eyes.

The journalist asked, "Breanna, how do you feel about Reed's new marriage?"

My head dropped.

The porn star's eyes widened. "Reed can't be married to someone new. He's still married to Melanie Martin. That's why we couldn't get married. Everyone knows that, but he gave me this." She held her hand up, displaying a giant diamond ring for the camera. A ring that could have eaten my cute little Grace Kelly ring.

The bartender poured me a drink.

When you're married (or not married, in my case) to someone as temperamental as Reed, life comes with an extra layer of fury. Nothing that happens to you belongs to you. When you're angry, confused, pregnant, and someone hands you a glass of Jack Daniels, your instinct is to down it. It's the only chance you'll get to process before this motherfucker walks into the room and steals the show. How do you deal with a problem brought to your attention on national television? The entire world knew more about our relationship than I did. It was like realizing you're with Henry VIII. Am I married? Am I not married? Is this child legitimate? What part of this will cause me to lose my head?

My normal reaction was to confront him. This metamorphosis had already occurred where I was becoming Reed's girlfriend, wife, or whatever. His and not my own. I stared at the exit. *Do I drink or run?*

It was a good thing I didn't go up to the hotel room because I may have been hit by the TV. That would have damaged the already doomed child in my womb, which, honestly, may have saved everyone trouble in the long run. I'd learned to walk on eggshells with Reed. The one place I should not go was to that hotel room with that man—that lying, manipulative, cocaine-snorting, possibly married man. I sipped the drink, then slid it across the bar and asked for a phone. I called another hotel and booked a room for myself and my illegitimate fetus.

Perhaps it was wrong of me to disappear. Things happen. Paperwork doesn't get filed. I was willing to accept that. But Reed had never mentioned being married in the first place.

The things you find out in tabloids: Melanie Martin was Reed's second wife. He'd married his high school girlfriend in eleventh grade. That marriage was annulled when her parents found out.

Melanie Martin was different. They were engaged, planned a wedding, ordered china, the full package. Reed caught her with a needle in her arm after a gig. They split up. She got clean. They reconciled. He cheated on her. She broke it off. He begged her to marry him, they had a quickie ceremony at the L.A. County Courthouse. His career exploded, she couldn't handle the fame.

His version: She was a controlling addict hooked on OxyContin. He tried to end things, she wouldn't let him. She attacked him. He hit her once, "to keep her from hurting herself." Her drug use coupled with his infidelities put her over the edge. According to rock and roll legend, she tried to overdose and failed, and he bought her a gun in a heart shaped box.

Reed signed his first major record deal while they were married. She was eligible for half of his earnings. He was determined to make sure she didn't see a dime. She refused to sign divorce papers.

Things tabloids don't know because they are covered up by record labels: he admitted they had an abusive relationship—but painted her the psychotic aggressor. He claimed she came at him with a knife. He shoved her away, causing her to "accidentally" fall down the stairs. He told police she'd tried to hit him with a car—but really, whose side do you believe? Was she trying to hit him or get away?

During their relationship, he'd gone from living comfortably in an $1100 condo from the initial record deal, to being a millionaire. He reconciled with her to get her to sign a postnuptial agreement. Taking advantage of her drugged state, he promised not to leave if she signed the papers. She signed away her rights to anything he'd earned. He stayed with her two more weeks, canceled her credit cards, and had her name removed from anything they shared jointly. He gave her an eviction notice. She refused to sign divorce papers again.

The saga continued.

Had their relationship details come out then it would have ruined his career. She finally agreed to sign the papers. Reed was under the impression it was taken care of. He changed lawyers and the paperwork was never filed.

Our Vegas quickie marriage was void. I was pregnant by a man who was married to another woman.

I watched the follow up at the second hotel. A guy at the bar looked at me and said, "I had a friend who went through the same thing. They couldn't find his ex, took a year for the thing to work itself out in court without her. His new lady was pissed!"

I sighed, lowering my head, my bangs covered my eyes. I wished I could disappear—drown in the bottle of vodka the bartender slid in my direction.

Leaked photos of Reed and I were plastered everywhere. *Is Evan Reed a bigamist? Exclusive tonight!* Suddenly, I was the King's "great matter." I got a taste of what Melanie had gone through when the hotel informed me my credit card was canceled. I had no job, no money, nowhere to live, no credit. I didn't know Reed and Melanie's full story, but I'd seen enough.

This was not the man I knew and loved. Was I allowing myself to live a lie because I'd managed to avoid his line of fire?

The hotel clerk said I had a call from Mr. Reed. I reluctantly picked up the phone.

"Jennifer?"

I cleared my throat. "Yes."

"I'm sending a car to get you. I didn't know if you were hurt or dead. I've been freaking out the past 72 hours."

"Why did you cancel the card?"

"What do you mean, why? I thought it was stolen."

"I don't want to see you."

"The car will be there in a few minutes—get in it and come talk to me. We've been through this before. You know none of that shit is true."

"So, you're saying you're not married to another woman?"

"It's a misunderstanding. You would know that if you'd stuck around."

"What about the horrible things you did to Melanie?"

"Lies. Get in the car. I'm tired. I've missed two days of work because of you. Don't make a big deal of this. Everything will be fine."

Strangers stared at me as I looked around the lobby. I had no money, no car, nowhere to go. "I want to know the truth before I see you."

He sighed, exasperated. "I'll repeat what I've said the past three days. Yes, I was married. I didn't mention it because it's not something I like to think about. I lived with that person one month while we were married and spent two years trying to get her to sign divorce papers. It's being handled. The minute it's over, we'll walk into the courthouse and get married again. Simple as that. My lawyer said the divorce was final. The clerk gave us a license in Vegas, how could I know?"

"My God, Reed. It's not the wedding license. They said you beat her up. You left her with nothing."

"You believe that? Jenny, after everything I've given you? Do you want me to tell you I was a shitty husband? I was the worst. Everyone begged me not to marry her. If I looked at another woman, she would threaten to kill herself. I never knew if I would come home to dinner or a corpse. It was psychological torture. That woman took three years of my life. I don't see why I have to answer to you or anyone else. How long do I have to pay for someone else's mistakes? You of all people know me better." I heard him tap the phone against the wall. "I thought you were different. You didn't trust me enough to come to me."

"You were caught in a lie and you know it."

"I have tried everything in my power to protect you, Jenny. I have never hidden who I am from you, I spared you. Media vultures will never stop digging things up about me, or you, for that matter. Don't think you're safe in this, honey. They want to pull us apart. When they do, they will destroy you—every guy you fucked, every joint you smoked in college, they're going to dig it all up. They will go after your family." The unmistakable thump of the phone hitting his palm, I'd seen him do this too many times when he was angry. "Jenny, they'll dig until they find out about Kaley. Tabloids live for those stories. You don't want her family dragged into this, do you?"

I held back tears. "They wouldn't do that."

"I won't let them, baby. No matter the cost. But don't be naïve. 'Rock Star's Wife Found Best-Friend's Corpse in a Freezer' is a headline no one is gonna turn down."

"Stop it." I cried.

"It's true. We need to lay low, play it cool. You're my wife. You're the only person I've ever been in love with. If you can't talk to me before believing tabloids, you need to tell me now. I can't keep doing this with you. Every time shit gets complicated, you run away."

"It's too much."

"If you're gonna second guess me, there's no reason for us to be together. These people have an agenda. They think I'll settle to shut them up. You saw with that DJ and the camera guy at the airport, people come into my life and intentionally fuck me over. Bree's talking all this shit—she was in my house fucking two guys while I was on tour. The maid saw them. Bree threw an ashtray and hit her in the head. You're listening to that bitch. Jenny, seriously? She fired the maid to keep her from telling me. I didn't find out 'til the maid sued me. Guess who had to pay since it was in my house? That's why that bitch's shit ended up on the sidewalk. I'm not a saint by any means, but I've never done anything to anyone they didn't deserve. And Breanna Lee of all the people in the world? She's a joke. I can't believe—after everything I've done for you, the things I've done to help your family. Who is gonna pay your dad's medical bills? You gonna let them get stuck with your student loans? Who do you think has been paying that? I wouldn't do those things if I didn't love you."

"Reed, I'm sorry, this is crazy."

"You're going to let the tabloid lies of a porn star and my crackhead, suicidal ex tear apart what we have?" That thump on the phone again. His rings clinked against each other. When he was angry, his fists balled so tight his fingers cramped. I pictured him shaking his hand, cracking his knuckles. Pacing as desperation set in, "Honey, can you get in the car when the guy gets there? He's going to take you to my house in Malibu. We can sort all this out. Leave me if you want, but you owe me the conversation."

I put the phone on the bar. I couldn't listen anymore.

The bellhop waved. "Your car is waiting, Mrs. Reed."

"Apparently not," I said. I bit the edge of my forefinger to hold back a scream. Reed was the last person I wanted to see. *But he's right, Jenny. You've got to hear him out. You owe him that.*

I was in the back of the Bentley, en route to Reed's house in Malibu—a place I'd yet to see in person. The old me would have walked out of that hotel to the abortion clinic off Sunset. That would have been the end of it. The old me didn't tolerate this shit. I didn't have a dime in my pocket to put in a payphone, definitely not the two-hundred dollars for the clinic.

Can you imagine if I did that and Reed found out? I shook my head, *Jenny, don't let him control you like this.*

Red light.

I opened the car door and bolted. No plan, just a sense of impending doom—a child in trouble who doesn't know what's going to happen when they step off the school bus.

I ran several blocks down the strip and ducked into a bar where an old friend, Mike, worked. The bartender let me use the phone to call him. An hour later, we were sitting in his dingy apartment near Sunset. Mike was cool. He didn't ask questions. He sat on his sofa strumming his guitar.

"You're welcome to crash here. There's a little food in the fridge if you're hungry. Some beer in the back."

"I just need a couple of hours to get my shit together."

"That's cool."

I watched Mike play Nintendo. I tried to sort my life out in my head, throwing out ideas to him.

"I can get you some hours at the bar, but I don't know how it's gonna be, you going from stupid rich to waiting tables," Mike said.

"I've never been rich. I had a rich boyfriend, who I thought was my husband, but isn't."

"That's pretty messed up," Mike said, killing turtles and oversized Mario ants. "You know that guy has done some real crazy shit. I didn't want to say anything, but he went out with this girl Kim that used to dance at the club. They did a lot of drugs in her apartment, she wigged out and he punched her in the face. We all do stupid shit when we're high, though. I know I did." Mario fell in a lake of fire. "Kim could have been lying, though. Strippers are mental."

"Can I borrow two-hundred dollars?" I asked.

Chapter Thirteen

I sat alone in the Los Angeles Women's Clinic for an hour. Reed told me to always wear sunglasses. Naked without them, I held a magazine in front of my face. Paperwork again—I didn't know what name to use. I couldn't put Jenny Reed—or Williams. That wasn't my name anyway, right? So why did it matter? I didn't have an emergency contact.

"Will someone be giving you a ride home?" The receptionist asked.

"Yes," I lied. I checked "no" in the married box.

I had an abortion procedure performed that day. Something went wrong. I ended up in the emergency room the next morning with unbearable cramps. Mike was at work; his landlord heard me crying. Blood pressure low, I was clammy, shaking with fever and chills, bleeding and confused.

Dropped off at the ER by a stranger. No identification, no money, no insurance. I was scared. I called Sasha after I was admitted, crying into her answering machine. I panicked, wondering if this is what Kaley felt in the hospital before she hurt herself; alone, afraid.

There was only one other person I could call. I gave the nurse Reed's number and let her explain what I'd done.

Marcus was waiting for me. "I'm real sorry you're sick, Miss." He opened the back of Reed's BMW, slid his 6'3" frame in the seat beside me.

You're not running this time, Jenny.

The driver followed a long winding path up the canyon. A funeral procession—botched abortion, dead Jenny. The girl I left on the floor of Mike's apartment was floating away from me. At the top of the canyon, fans huddled together on the sidewalk outside a massive white gate. A worker scrubbed "Jenny's A WHORE!" off the gate. The letters the rusty color of dried scabs. One fan was being held by a security guard. She broke free, ran towards the car, and spat at the BMW. She reached to the ground, then smacked a dead raccoon against the car window, her hands covered in blood.

I recoiled into the arms of the big security guard.

"It's okay," Marcus said.

"No, it's not."

First—it was terrifying. Second—I recognized the girl; a fan named Emilya. She'd grabbed my hair in the crowd at Reed's show. *Where did I see her? Argentina? Now she's here?* My eyes traveled up the tall fence. A security guard grappled with her, pulling her away from the BMW.

The gate opened. Our driver gassed it up the hill, the heavy gate clanked shut behind us. Twisted arms of bare trees framed the white house that towered into the sky.

"Don't worry, this place is locked down tighter that Corcoran. They're not getting in here," Marcus said.

"But out there?"

"That's what I'm here for. I'll put her on the bulletin board."

"A bulletin board of stalkers? Great."

"Standard precaution. They stick around so long you'd think they were on the payroll. Page me when you need to go somewhere, simple as that."

"We didn't have to do that in New York."

"We did," Marcus said, keying a security code in the back door. "You just didn't know."

My boot heels echoed on the marble kitchen floor. Following Marcus' lead, I slid them off. The kitchen was average size but opened into the entire house. To the left: appliances, an island countertop—also marble—and a laundry room. To the right there was another island with black cabinets, white top. Tall, black chairs with leather backs and silver metal rivets. Straight ahead was a massive living room with black walls. A black ceiling two stories above, white trim. A gothic chandelier dripped from the high loft. Long, black leather curtains covered the tall windows. Above them was a walkway that connected the upstairs level of the house. A black piano sat inside the living area. White fur pillows adorned an L-shaped sofa, large enough to seat twenty people. A matching fur rug lay beside the piano. Books and black roses were in a vase on the glass-top, coffee table. Everything was too perfect, too strategically placed. If one were to stand on the walkway above the living room windows, they could see everything.

Dark, cold. Drapes pulled in every room. The mansion was a museum, not a home.

To the left of the kitchen a small, carpeted staircase led to a balcony landing and three doors; the only real giveaway to the house's original design before its heavy metal makeover. The long hallway spanned the lower level, past the stairs farther than I could see. Behind the piano, an elegant staircase led up to a dark purple wall with a raised black velvet design. Massive speakers lined the walls. Beautiful, but dark.

Charles, the butler, introduced himself by the kitchen and led me down the right hallway. My mouth gaped at the white, satin-finished walls, glistening hardwoods and framed gold records. Collections I had no idea about—Alex Tremont's *Butterfly with Broken Wings* series suspended in glass cases. Three framed dark red and pitch black splatters of Ezra Orion's *Kill, Blood, Death.*

Charles opened the door to a windowless guest room on the first floor, lit by lamps. He pointed out the clean linens and laid fresh towels and pajamas in the private bath. Purple walls, white fixtures, walk-in shower and a large whirlpool tub.

Exhausted and not quite sure I wouldn't drown myself in the tub, I pulled on the pajamas.

Charles offered a sandwich, apologizing, "Usually, we have a menu prepared when Mr. Reed is home. We weren't expecting him so soon. Chef meal preps—three meals a day, two snacks. High protein, tight on calories and carbs depending on Mr. Reed's touring schedule. There's always fresh fruit in the kitchen. Don't hesitate to ask for anything, day or night. The maid, Mary, takes care of laundry, cleaning."

"Thank you," I said nervously.

"You're as lovely as he described, I hope it's not too forward of me to say. I admire your work."

"You've seen my paintings?"

"They're in every room. This is my favorite." He flicked on the overhead light and pointed above the bed. Exhausted, I hadn't noticed it. I ran my fingers across the canvas, feeling the layers and grooves. It was the one I sold the night I met Kaley and Kevin.

"I had no idea he owned this. Is he home?"

"Mr. Reed asked not to be disturbed."

"Let me guess, you do everything Mr. Reed says?"

"Don't we all?" He smiled. "I'll let you get your rest, Mrs. Reed."

"Please, just Jennifer."

"I'm not allowed to call you that, Mrs. Reed. Goodnight."

The morphine from the hospital had worn off. I woke several times in pain. My confusion and anger turned to despair. Paranoid in this big house with its long cold hallways. I was a stranger here. I reached for the bedside lamp switch.

Reed sat in a chair by the wall. His eyes, bloodshot. He stared at me without saying a word, a tiger readying for attack. The vein in his forearm pulsed when he rubbed his wrist and unfastened his watch, laying it on the bedside table.

"So, who did you fuck? Dene? Jamie London? I'll forgive you once. Because I know you wouldn't let a doctor rip my baby out of you." He'd been crying, and the one thing Evan Reed fought more than anything was tears.

Guilt poured over me. I didn't mean to hurt him. I was tempted to lie, to make this easier on us both—but I knew that offer of forgiveness was pure trickery to get me to give up a secret. "I didn't cheat on you."

His chest sunk. His fingers tightened into a fist. "I can't believe I was stupid enough to trust you."

"How do you think I felt?" I snapped.

Reed rolled his eyes. "You need to watch what you say to me right now, little girl. We don't talk about this. Ever. Otherwise, I'll do something we'll both regret." He held his thumb against his lips, lost deep in the darkness I'd created.

Where do we go from here?

The room was ice cold. I understood why he hadn't brought me to this house. The mansion was filled with treasures, but there was no love here. What could have warmed that darkness better than a family? A child's laughter filling its halls. I'd done more than take his child—I'd taken his hope. I wanted to hold him, tell him everything would be okay.

It was taking all his strength to hold back his anger. One small touch and he might explode.

I made the right decision—and it was my decision. But I wanted to fix this divide between us. He wasn't the scary guy from the media. He was the same person I'd spent the past year sleeping next to—my person.

He turned off the lamp, and climbed into bed beside me, his long hair falling against his face. He kissed my forehead for a moment. I sighed—I'd been justified in my anger about his lies—but I couldn't stand the thought of him hating me.

He buried his face in my hair, his breath hot. He moved his hand down the front of my pajamas.

I pulled away. "Not yet, I can't."

Reed didn't listen. He pulled my panties down hard, ripping the fabric. He was on top of me, his fingers inside, then his body. All of him. Too much. Biting into my shoulder, breaking the skin. Unwilling to express emotion through words, he punished the parts of me that betrayed him. Not loosening his teeth, his chest muscles tight against me, showing his strength. His grunting thrusts erupted into an animalistic anger-gasm. His palm hit the headboard with such force, I heard it crack. I watched myself from somewhere higher up, where cracked wood didn't sound like broken bones. I'd freed the monster. I shivered and quieted my lungs, afraid to breathe beneath him.

An hour ago, this hadn't happened. Now it had. Now what?

Leaving the mess of bloody sheets, I made my way to the shower. I sat beneath the water and tried not to let him hear me cry. *Hurt people, hurt people,* a voice said. *Not like this.*

You're crazy, I told the girl in the mirror. *Reed didn't do that. That didn't happen.* A basket in the on suite held everything an overnight guest might need—toiletries, bathrobe, and a bottle of wine. I drank it in the bathroom floor with the door locked, hiding the empty bottle under the sink. Stumbling and swaying into the bedroom, I face-planted into clean sheets, soft, fluffy like clouds. My bare feet dangling off the edges. Reed was gone.

His physician dropped by noon, said I should stay in bed and rest. He left Percocet for pain but didn't mention the bruises on my throat and thighs where Reed's fingers and teeth had dug into me. *Because it didn't happen.* I barely made it to the toilet to throw up the wine and lies I was telling myself.

Reed pocketed the pain pills and rifled through my belongings until he found my birth control. He made a production of popping each pill out of the packet and flushing them. We didn't talk.

My evening was spent beside him, trying not to hurl on his patio that overlooked his Olympic-sized pool, while his Hollywood friends jumped in and out of the water. If there was ever a day I didn't want to be caught in a bathing suit—this was it. Nauseous and dehydrated, I lunged for the tall glass Reed sat beside me. I choked—vodka, not water. My pain meant nothing to him.

"Please stop being mean," I begged, getting dressed for another party he dragged me to that week. Cocaine. Pills. He no longer cared what I saw. Easily accessible guns in every room—I'd had no idea how paranoid he was. Handguns, shotguns, an Uzi. A vault full of illegal weapons.

I'd made the right decision. No child could live there.

Hungover, nursing his hair of the dog with a bottle of whiskey at the foot of our bed, Reed gripped his temples. "Did you think about me? When you were getting rid of my baby, did I even cross your mind?"

"It was my decision—the right decision," I insisted.

"That's not what I asked you."

"I was scared, Reed."

"I didn't know if you were alive or dead. You called Sasha first, why not me?"

"I don't know."

"A little cowardly, sticking that nurse on the phone to tell me what you did."

"Reed, please."

"How fucked up am I, if the girl who swore she loved me would rather kill my baby than have a simple conversation?"

"You lied."

"So, you punished me. Does your revenge feel good? I left some irrelevant shit out. I've never lied to you. Whenever things get complicated, you bolt."

"Those things you hid from me—that's not my fault."

"I wanted to kill myself when I found out what you'd done," he said.

"But you didn't."

"I couldn't decide which gun to use."

I closed my eyes. *God, there are so many.* "I never meant to hurt you, Reed."

"You killed my baby. A baby that could've fixed everything. All I wanted was a family with you. You never loved me."

"Reed, I loved you."

"Yeah? You picked a fine fucking way to show it." He pointed at my hand. "Did you wear that Grace Kelly ring when you did it?" He half-laughed. "I sold a house to buy that ring, Jenny—a fucking house. That's how much I trusted you. But nah, I'm still white trash from Barren County. Not worth a conversation. I would have been a good dad. I would've taken care of you both. You know what, though? If I'd really known you, I would've driven you to that clinic." He laughed. "I would've gone Manson family on your ass and cut it out myself."

"You're sick," I snapped. "You expect me to believe I'm the only girl you've ever been with that had an abortion? From what I saw on tour, your band has a fucking doctor on call."

"Wasn't my first. Was it yours?"

"Seriously? Your double standards are infuriating."

"Those girls on tour weren't you. It doesn't matter anyway, does it? You never meant a damn word that came out of those pretty lips."

Forget the other Reeds I'd encountered; Hollywood Reed was a nightmare. An arrogant, petulant man-child who lashed out at everyone. The maid forgot to put the milk in the fridge, he screamed at her until she cried. He wanted me to comfort him. I wanted to go home to my mother.

Pills, drink, the guns—he was going to kill himself. I begged him to get help. He wouldn't listen. I didn't have time to think about what he'd done to me that night. Every waking hour was spent enduring his drunken, screaming rants or turning him over so he wouldn't smother in his own vomit. He shamed me for things we'd done in bed. "Perfect, innocent little Jenny. What would your mom think if she saw those pictures and videos? Her little girl tied up, begging to get whipped? Letting those groupies go down on you backstage so I could watch?" He was right, I'd set aside every inhibition to please him on that tour. He was regressing into this twenty-year-old rock star and hating himself for it. He drank to get drunk, then drank more to forget the things he'd said when he was drunk.

Sarah intercepted when I called Daniel. "I'm sorry, honey, you'll have to figure this one out without Daniel."

"Never mind," I said. I blamed myself.

"Happy?" Reed slammed his finalized divorce papers on the counter one afternoon. He didn't mention getting married again; I hoped he wouldn't.

Mike was at one of the Hollywood parties. He'd been worried since I'd never returned to his place.

Drunk, Reed grabbed my arm, pulling me away.

Mike followed. "Dude, we're just friends."

"She doesn't have friends. Get out!"

Mike stood in the doorway while Reed screamed, "Liar, whore, baby killer." He shoved me to the floor, threw his glass, shattering it before walking out.

Mike helped me up. "Shit. You okay, Jen?"

"Yes," I lied, tearing up. "Please leave before he comes back. Please?"

Marcus drove me home. I wished desperately that I had my own car so I could leave. I didn't even have a credit card.

Reed stumbled in later, ranting, reeking of sex and whiskey. Sleep was my only escape from him. He sat at the end of the bed drinking, nudging me with his steel-toed boot every time I dozed off.

"I hate you. You're just like my mother," he mumbled.

He slept on the sofa, his gun beneath his pillow. He played acoustic guitars in the hallway, then smashed them into the walls. He drank until he was spitting blood in our bathroom sink.

"You have to stop this. Get help," I pleaded.

"Fuck you!" he screamed, splattering his blood across my face.

His psychiatrist refused to give him more pills until he brought me in for a session. Reed ran his hands through his hair, slamming his fist into his therapist's desk. "Why did you do this to me?"

"Reed, you've got to calm down," the therapist said, after letting me endure three sessions of Reed screaming, throwing things and threatening me. "Jennifer, every time you come in here, you spend the entire session shaking, not saying a word. If you don't participate, he won't get better."

Of course not, asshole. I can't get a word in.

"Set a wedding date," Reed said. "That's what I want."

"You haven't mentioned getting married!" I shouted.

"Jennifer, can you agree to set the date to help establish trust with Reed?"

"Whose side are you on? No. I'm not doing that. Not after what he did to me!"

"Then move out of my house," Reed said.

Our driver wouldn't leave the psychiatrist's office without Reed. I kicked the back of his seat. "Take me home, damn it!" He locked the doors and rolled up the tinted privacy window. "You've got to be kidding me," I cried. "He's going to kill me."

We waited an hour outside the pharmacy for the prescriptions to be filled. Reed took a handful of anxiety meds and tossed me my bag. By the time we were back at the mansion, he was nodding out. "I can't do this anymore," he said with a dizzy stare. "You've gotta go." He put his head in his palms. "I don't care where." He slumped into the seat. "Just go."

I avoided my family and the few friends I had left. Not wanting to admit how bad things were. Reed was furious that I'd called Sasha before him at the hospital. If she called, I wouldn't have known, he kept the ringers turned off and disconnected the lines from outside when he was paranoid.

My mom finally managed to reach me. "Jenny, are you okay? I've been trying to call for a month. Honey, I wanted to tell you, we can't take this gift. It's wonderful, but we can't accept it."

"What gift?" She was right, it had been one hellishly, long month. I had no idea what she was talking about.

"The car. Honey, it's too much."

After Breanna's interview, when Reed couldn't find me in L.A., he called my mother and made idle chit chat, fishing for info. She'd mentioned a problem with her car and the next morning a brand new Lincoln was sitting in their driveway.

"Mom, keep the car, you need it."

See, Jenny—he's a good guy. You're fucked up. If I had ignored Breanna Lee's interview, we would be happy, in love, with a baby on the way. I asked my mom for my cousin Mary's number. No answer. After sorting through my bag of medication, I took the pills and went to bed.

Later, Reed was asleep with his arm draped over me, his bare skin touching mine. I tried to move. He held me tighter. He opened his eyes, red and tearing up. "Don't leave me, I'm sorry," he groaned. "I love you. I'm so sorry."

Reed was drinking orange juice in the kitchen when I woke again. Prescription bottles lined the counter. He took another handful.

"Therapy is at 3 p.m."

I took my pills.

Reed's medication dosage was so strong he couldn't hold his head up and fell asleep on his therapist's sofa.

I hated her. The way she gazed at him and agreed with his every word creeped me out. One in a long line of useless starfuckers. But I needed all the help I could get. If Reed didn't kill himself, he would overdose. He was trying to grasp some form of reality and failing miserably. *Don't discourage him.* Besides, what kind of sociopath suggests therapy?

I convinced him to see a new doctor. "A second opinion, that's all," I said.

He dozed off in the exam room.

"Why the hell would anyone prescribe dosages this high?" the doctor asked. "Has he been on any of these before?"

"Not regularly."

"Mr. Reed—can you hear me? These celebrity doctors will kill you. Do not let him go back to this doctor."

But it's his favorite one.

Chapter Fourteen

Reed's therapist knew the right way to stroke his ego and convince him positive changes were his idea. She praised him for his progress in our daily sessions. She also wanted private sessions with me.

"I'm not the one with the problem," I said.

"Then why are we here?" Reed slammed the door on his way out.

The therapist flipped her red hair over her shoulder. "Do you have any idea how much progress we'd made before you came along? Years of trauma work wasted. You most certainly have a problem, Jennifer."

"He raped me," I said out loud for the first time.

"He told me about an incident. We need to explore what that means. You believe he raped you and he believes you killed his child. Which is true? It's all a matter of perception, right?"

"You're fucking nuts."

I had to get him away from these people. How was she helping him by telling him everything he wanted to hear? The psychiatrist gave him any drug he asked for. His therapist would've sucked his dick in a heartbeat. Hell, she probably had.

"I'm done," I said.

His therapist sighed. "Jennifer, ask him about his mother. Have a real conversation with your husband."

"We're not married."

I took a risk walking into Reed's home studio. Sacred space. Fake wives and baby killers not allowed. He was writing in his black lyric journal.

"Reed, we need to talk."

"Therapy."

"We need to talk now, you and me. What are we doing here?"

"Avoiding each other. Unsuccessfully."

"Before all of this, we were happy."

"Until you believed a lying porn star and ruined us."

"You raped me."

"You killed our baby."

"Then why are we trying? What's the point?"

He put down his notebook. "Because I used to love the way you made me feel—the way you looked at me. But you're not that girl."

"I'm the same person."

"So, am I, but that doesn't matter to you, does it? You never loved me. The second I didn't fit your fantasy, you turned on me. So, what do you want? We've both done something we can't take back. We either walk away and live with that part ripped from our souls. Or we stay together and try to fix what we destroyed." He looked at his notebook. "It's your choice."

It made a sick sort of sense. Didn't it?

The refrain from that Guns N' Roses song kept repeating in my head. Where do our crazy asses go now? I wish I'd had Axl on speed dial to see if he ever figured that out.

Being unemployed allowed me time to perform a dangerous set of mental gymnastics. I was twenty-two. Reed was twenty-seven. Kids. We might live to be eighty. Was it fair to designate each other rapist and baby killer this early on? He knew I would make the decision he wanted me to—I'd spiral into some negative existential crisis of epic proportion and take it upon myself to save his damned soul.

We had to learn to coexist; not just in the same house, but the same universe. We'd broken something more sacred than trust. One of those things was legal in the state of California, the other was a crime. How much responsibility did I hold? What if I'd gone to talk to him right away? He would've lied. And it wouldn't have changed my mind. But the way he put it, it was my fault if we spent the rest of our lives hating each other.

I wanted to stop the pain. My body had suffered trauma without a chance to heal. The only place I'd ever rested well was with my head on his shoulder. And I was so tired.

His meds leveled out. The highs were not as high and the lows he managed to keep to himself. I couldn't understand how the guy I'd loved had just disappeared.

I wrote to him one night, *I just need some time, please?*

I hoped that once the screaming and fighting stopped there might be something left between us. *Will there be any of me left?* Sarah said he was an emotional vampire. It was true. Judging by the Anne Rice novels spilling over my bedside table, he was a Lestat, and I was desperate for a Louis. If I squinted just right from the corner of our bedroom, and he took a few more pills before collapsing into bed, I might get more than I bargained for. His manic energy and anger seeped out like blood leaving dying flesh.

Pleased to meet you, new Reed. This one was somber, quiet, and knew he'd done something wrong.

Really admitting it? Not a fucking chance.

"I'm going on the road. You gonna be here when I get back?" Reed asked one afternoon.

"I'm going to New York."

He didn't look up. "Leaving? That's your choice."

"A change of scenery, that's all. It's what I need."

"Fine, fuck it. If you want to go to New York, go." As he headed out the door, Reed slapped a sheet of song lyrics on the fridge.

"Regrets & Empty Promises"

– E. R.

If I ask you to stay, I'm the devil

If I leave, I'm the liar

Good looks and good intentions brought us here

We sacrificed something sacred, something holy

It doesn't matter who killed who

We're left with regrets and empty promises

If you leave, if I go–either way,

we're both alone.

Walking down the hallway we made love in

Pretending we don't see each other.

If you're gonna go, just go. (Don't go).

I fucked up. Forgive me. Please.

Chapter Fifteen

I woke in Manhattan to a paramedic screaming in my face while shoving a plastic tube down my throat.

Aside from a bottle of wine that hit way too fast, and what was left in the cabinets, our loft in New York was empty. I'd gone there to clear my mind.

Away from Reed, my true feelings surfaced. After two drinks on my flight, I couldn't stop crying. The old man beside me in first class had awkwardly patted my arm. I'd almost hyperventilated in the taxi. This was over. Sane people would not stay in this relationship.

I would leave his engagement ring on the bed where I found it.

"Welcome home, Mrs. Reed," our doorman had said. Up the elevator, down the long hallway, I forced my keys in the doorknob.

My mouth dropped.

Our furniture was gone. My painted canvases were rolled into a corner, a fresh coat of beige paint covered the walls. An envelope lay on the kitchen counter, the words *Your Copy* looped in cursive writing. I tore it open—the condo association guidelines and a rental agreement from Mr. Evan Reed Williams to a new tenant with a purchase option.

He never intended on going back to New York! I stared out the loft window overlooking the twinkling lights of Manhattan. I collapsed to the floor. None of this was real. None of this was ever mine.

The loft was where I'd let myself fall in love with Reed. *He's erasing the good parts, selling the world where we were happy.* Tears rushed back. The marriage was a lie. New York was some fantasy he created.

Taking the pills was not something I considered when I opened the medicine cabinet and saw them sitting there in a perfect row. I stared at my reflection—my skin puffy from crying, black eyeliner streaked down my face. *The monster and the baby killer—that's who we'll be, forever.* My scarlet A would be crossed across my chest in period blood, he'd get "rapist" tattooed on his shoulder, right above the skull and roses.

I hadn't known a broken fingernail could bleed so badly. It had split and ripped right off when I'd hit the loft floor, scratching across the hardwood. Leaving D.N.A. A forensic trace that I'd been there.

Once he erased us, I'd be exiled from his world. He'd sing songs about me to other girls. This place would be a rotting dream buried deep in my chest.

My bloody, frantic fingers twisted the caps off the medicine bottles—prescriptions he should've taken to L.A. *Maybe he forgot?* I didn't remember putting them in my mouth. *I wouldn't have, would I?*

I just remember the familiar voice behind me that urged, "Take them all."

Reed held onto the stretcher railing, a look of terror on his face. "Honey, I'm so sorry. They wouldn't let me ride in the ambulance with you. Is she going to be okay?"

"Sir, wait in the hall," a nurse said.

"I'm not leaving my wife." He pushed past them.

Sitting by the hospital bed, Reed rubbed his hand down his face. His tired skin stretched like putty.

"What happened?" My dry throat croaked.

"You called Marcus from the loft. You weren't making sense. My flight was connecting at JFK, my pager went off. I left right away to find you." A tremor shook Reed's shoulders. "I didn't mean for this to happen, baby. I never wanted you to hurt yourself."

"I wasn't trying to hurt myself," I mumbled. "I needed the pain to stop."

"I know." Reed wiped his eyes. "What can I do to fix this?"

A series of nurses and doctors interrupted, filtering in and out of the room.

I thought about what Reed said. *Fixing this.*

"You can't sell the loft," I begged once we were alone. "Promise me, you won't. Everything was different there."

Reed looked at me with genuine sympathy. "Jenny, keeping the loft will not fix us."

My blood pressure was high and my head full of fog. It was easier to fake sleep than try to face this.

He pulled the phone into the bathroom, closing the door. I overheard him making calls.

"Daniel, bring her parents. I'm freaking out. She's really sick. I can't get that image out of my head. She was ice cold. What if I hadn't been at JFK? Okay, you'll get them? Thank you, brother. I'll call her mom and let her know."

His next call was to his assistant. "Aimee, it's Reed. How did they find that out? No, listen, you tell them it was a miscarriage. I don't want them to print that about her. It was a bad pregnancy, she's having complications." He hesitated. "Honestly, it's not your business. You know that was a one-time thing. My wife is all that matters to me right now. I don't want the media to know about the overdose. I'll talk to Mark at the agency Monday, and we'll sort something out. For now, can you do your job?" He turned on the bathroom sink, then dialed the rotary line again.

"Mrs. Stone, Jenny is pretty out of it. I know, honey, the doctors are good here. No, they still don't know. They think she had an allergic reaction to medication. My brother is on his way to take you to the airport. My label is letting us use their jet. I know Jenny's dad doesn't like to fly but the doctor thinks you should both be here. You too," Reed said.

He was protecting my mother from what I'd done.

"Jenny, we need to talk before your parents get here." Reed pressed his fingers on his lips. "I'm so sorry, I never meant for things to get this bad. I can't—couldn't accept what you did."

"Reed, not now. Please. Am I going to be okay?"

Reed's eyes welled. "I don't know. The doctors said when you take a lot of pills, your body shuts down. Your kidneys aren't working. You're hooked to a dialysis machine. Look at your arms, they're neon orange. You wake up lucid, then you're confused, seeing things."

"I feel okay."

I didn't mention the yellow haze in the room or the crows sitting at the foot of the bed. Nobody wants to be the chick at the hospital who points out the harbingers of death. Reed would grow smaller, distant, then come into focus like I was twisting a kaleidoscope in my mind.

Crow-face; not crow-face.

"Honey, the doctor said you're improving in some ways, but the kidney failure is putting stress on your other organs." He wiped his eyes. "Jenny, we're not legally married. I can't make these decisions for you. I didn't want to tell your parents you overdosed. Your mom would be devastated if she knew you tried to kill yourself."

"I don't remember taking those pills," I cried. "I didn't want to die."

"I know, baby. You've got to tell the doctors what you want. You have to sign something called a DNR to tell them if you want them to keep treating you."

Jenny, for fucks sake. What have you done? I didn't want to hurt my family. I had no idea a handful of pills could damage my organs. It was a quick fix and now I might die.

But I couldn't remember putting them in my mouth.

You're crazy and in denial! If Reed hadn't been at JFK, you'd be dead.

"Jennifer, my name is Doctor Patel, I'll get to the point. You need a kidney transplant. Dialysis can only keep you stable for so long with this much damage. We need to know if you want surgery and if you want to be resuscitated on the operating table. That could involve anything from CPR to cracking your ribs open."

Shit, this is serious.

"Save her," Reed said. "Money is not an issue."

"I need an answer from Jennifer." Dr. Patel disappeared into the fog.

"Jennifer, you dozed off. Do you want a transplant, and do you want us to resuscitate you?"

I had no idea what the white coat was talking about. A tattooed rock star stood at the foot of the bed, his head hung low. Kaley Dean was crouched in the left corner of the ceiling like a crab. Frozen eyes open wide, dead as damn doornail, a long stream of sticky, black blood oozing from her mouth.

Rubbery men the size of ants marched out of the black blood, across the edge of the bed, into the mouth of birds.

"ICU hallucinations. It's normal," the doctor said to the rock star who was looking at me like I'd said something crazy. The upside down, dead girl motioned for me to follow her. *Get out of here while you still can...*

I'm too afraid, Kaley. The bathtub. The needles. Take the pills. Take the pills.

Fuck. Make this go away. Make it all go away.

"Jenny, I'm here, baby. You're going to be okay." My mom rubbed my arm. Daddy was in a chair asleep at the foot of the bed.

"Where's...?"

"Reed is in recovery, honey. The doctor confirmed he was a match, and he didn't hesitate. Isn't that love, baby girl? He saved your life. I don't know if your daddy would give me a kidney."

My dad coughed, waking up and adjusting his overall strap, out of place in this Manhattan hospital.

Our eyes met, he clapped his thankful hands and squeezed my feet. His eyes were sad and tired. His smile, wide. "You scared us, buttercup."

Reed came to my room later, pushing aside his hospital gown to point at the stitches on his abdomen. "Isn't that badass, baby? Daniel is going to drive your dad home tonight. You're going to be fine. I've been here two weeks, your blood counts, enzymes and all that shit are stable."

"I've been here two weeks?"

"Two long weeks." Reed laughed.

"Your tour?"

"Don't worry about that."

My mom hugged me. "Jenny, your loft is beautiful. I've never slept in a bed that luxurious in my entire life! So many fancy hotel pillows. Your daddy won't admit it, but he loved that marble shower and white leather sofa. Why didn't you invite us out before?"

Reed squeezed my hand. "Everything will be okay, baby."

Chapter Sixteen

My mother stayed with me in New York while I recovered. Headlines read: "Rock Star Gives Fiancée Gift of Life." Journalists speculated, "Perhaps the troubled rocker has a soft side." The porn star who'd thrown our lives into madness was harassed by fans until she recanted her statements.

"Evan Reed is a saint!" his fans proclaimed. A perfectly timed love song was leaked: *"Let the blood wash away our sins, what's mine is yours, bodies tired, the heart is strong."*

Reed protected my parents from the truth, protected me from the media. He'd saved my life.

Shouldn't I be grateful?

Maybe it was all in my head.

Maybe he's not the monster.

Maybe I am.

My mother made friends with our doorman and drew tiny maps of the neighborhood. Scouting the local shops, she brought in fresh-cut flowers and organic vegetables to make her healing homemade soup. I cried, thinking of the pain I could have brought to her and my father.

How had I been so selfish? And wasn't this chance to spend time with my mother another gift from Reed? Her only complaint about New York were the astronomical produce prices and dirty streets. We had daily outings to

Central Park for ice cream and swan watching. She couldn't help but feed the pigeons, delighting when one landed on her shoulder. People flocked to my mother, businessmen and the homeless sat beside her, striking up conversation. She had the same sort of charisma Reed had, except hers was goodness. And Reed's—well, I still wasn't sure, but I wouldn't be alive without him.

"Are you okay?" My mother asked, sitting on the edge of my bed, rubbing my hair. "You seem sad."

I had an abortion. He assaulted me. I think I tried to kill myself. No, I'm not okay. I don't know if I'll ever be okay. But a crazy part of me misses him—loves him for protecting you from the awful things we've done.

If I'd said that to my mother, she would've packed my bags and I never would have seen Evan Reed again. While my dad was sick, I couldn't burden her.

"I'm okay, mom, just tired."

"You know you can talk to me, right?" My mother gave me another chance to bare my soul. "Reed told your father and me about the marriage license mix up and how upset you were with the tabloids harassing you. Why didn't you tell me, honey? He loves you dearly."

I looked deep into my mother's eyes. She had the ability to see through bullshit and straight to the heart of someone. If my mother believed Evan Reed was a good man, then I was wrong. He deserved a chance to prove he was the person I loved, and not the mistakes he'd been trying to overcome.

Maybe I deserved that chance too.

Chapter Seventeen

R eed warmed my mother's breakfast casserole after taking her to the airport. We sat in bed eating it from the glass container with plastic forks, like we would have done in my old apartment. Later, we went for a swim in our building's pool. Sushi Bar One for lunch, then spent two hours perusing the stacks in Strand Bookstore before dropping into a Warhol exhibit at MoMA.

My world and his.

"You were right about New York, Jenny. Everything feels right." Reed rubbed my knee. "Besides, we're even now."

I gulped. *We're even now? What does that mean?* Quickly filed under *questions I'm not asking today.* He was in a good mood. After the past few months, Reed in a good mood was a blessing.

At his insistence, we went to CBGB's to see Sonic Youth. "One vodka," he promised, on his third. We danced close in the crowd. I loved seeing

Reed in his element—how every eye in a music venue made its way to him and how he only looked at me.

"I love you, you know that, don't you?" he asked.

I was wearing a Kaley-inspired punk outfit of knee-high Doc Martens, a Reed-approved short skirt, fishnets, and a midriff baring shirt. We ran into a few of the models I'd met living in New York, and they formed a protective posse around me. While we waited in the bathroom line, Carla, a Calvin Klein model, nudged Kimmy, a punk model from London. "What the fuck?"

I'd watched enough interviews with Breanna Lee to know her from across the room. "Shit. What is she doing here?"

"Don't let her see you intimidated. I got this, get your man," Kimmy said. A new member of the mean girls' club, I pulled Reed in for a kiss, blocking his view.

Kimmy bared her sharp claws and a sharper pointed ring at the porn star. She motioned for security to take Breanna out. Kimmy pointed her sharp ring at Breanna's fake breasts. "Pop, Bitch." She laughed.

I held Reed's chin so he couldn't see my girlfriends antagonizing her. I ran the hand with Grace Kelly's ring against bottom of my cut off shirt, lifting it enough that my scar was visible to Breanna. "Fuck you," I mouthed. My hand behind Reed, flipping her off as she was led out of the bar.

Normal Jenny would have never done that. Normal Jenny would have followed Breanna out of the building to ask if she was okay.

But I wasn't normal anymore.

Vodka. Check. We partied hard—two kidneys between us didn't slow anything down. Sex that night was like our early days on tour. It went down somewhere in Manhattan; hot, dark, and not the sort of thing you tell your mother. We lay in our bed, our arms wrapped around each other. We'd survived the shit in L.A. Breanna. My fall apart.

Just like he promised

"You and me, baby," Reed said. "That's all we need."

The next morning, I sat with my sketchbook, staring out the window overlooking Manhattan while Reed whipped up breakfast. Sipping a Bloody Mary, I wondered, *can we make this work? Start over?*

"My assistant sent some things from storage in L.A. I have to sign a release to get them off the plane." Reed pulled me back into the world of *Weird Things Rock Stars Say for $1,000.*

Our driver took us to J.F.K. We entered through an employee entrance and were led towards the hangar where Void Records' private jet waited. A stewardess walked across the wet tarmac and poured us each a glass of champagne. Black trunks with the band's logo were being loaded into a cargo truck.

"I don't think that red box belongs to us." Reed motioned.

"Came on the plane," the airport worker said.

"Might be instruments for my label's other bands. Can we open it?"

"Whatever you want, dude." The worker instructed two other men to bring the massive red trunk down to a lower platform. They opened the lid.

"Damn it." Reed glanced at his pager. "Honey, can you look in that box to see if it belongs to us? I need to make a call."

A worker helped me climb onto a platform to get a better view. I noticed a symbol stenciled onto the side of the red box. My drawing. I peeked inside and unzipped a garment bag. Rubbing my hand across a mass of white tulle, ivory, silk and crystals. "What's this?"

Reed jumped up behind me, rested his chin on my neck and slid his arm around my hips. "That's the $60,000 wedding dress Versace designed for you."

"I didn't think it was finished. You didn't buy this did you?"

"Keep looking." Reed stepped off the box onto the tarmac.

Still tipsy from my morning drink, I tried not to fall in the trunk. I pushed the dress this way and that for several minutes, marveling at the shimmering fabric. "I don't see anything else."

I turned around.

Reed was on one knee. A trail of candles ran to the record label's private jet. The airport workers had taken off their orange vests and work overalls. They'd been wearing black button-up shirts with red ties underneath. The flight attendants held dark red roses, silver skull Void logo pendants pinned to their short black dresses.

Fire, skulls, roses. I was about to be inducted into some heavy metal cult.

"Jennifer Stone, will you marry me?" Reed looked at me with the sweet blue eyes that had tripped me up at the Rainbow. "I didn't do things right last time. I'm going to make it up to you."

This can't be real. The jealousy when you saw Breanna was real. You still love him. And whatever went down with that hot wax and fire play in the city last night was definitely real.

Those lips. Blue eyes.

Jenny don't.

I fell right into the trap like there hadn't been four million blazing warning signs. *Don't be an idiot! Don't do it! Stop!*

But he saved my life. He protected my parents.

"I promise, everything will be different," Reed said.

Fatal last words, huh?

For a moment, I saw the person I loved. Any other day I might have said no, collected my things and got the hell out of there. But he caught me at the right moment. He always did.

He'd given me his fucking kidney and he wasn't screaming at me anymore. I owed him. He saved my life. I knew if I left him, he would never let me forget that. Maybe this would fix everything.

I said, "Yes."

He smiled, and the airline employees cheered. Jet engines rumbled. The co-pilot came down the steps and waved everyone over. "Come on. We can't waste jet fuel."

Reed led me up the plane steps.

"Where are we going?" I asked

He closed the door of the private bedroom, took off his jacket. When I sat on the bed, he kneeled on the floor and pushed my knees apart.

"Don't worry about it." Reed buried his lips between my thighs.

"Ladies and gentlemen, please take your seats and buckle in. It's going to be a bumpy ride to Hawaii."

Reed grabbed my wrists to keep me from moving. My hips lifted from the bed when the plane took off. We spent the next five hours fucking dangerously, making up for every night of the past three unbearable months.

Surfing, tanning, sex, and getting each other's names tattooed above our surgery scars filled the next week.

"How's my kidney doing?" He joked.

We snuggled skin to skin in the same chair under a beach umbrella reading *Helter Skelter* together. This time, I embraced his lifestyle. Private beaches, rock star sunglasses. Cocktails for breakfast and lunch, skipping dinner. Alcohol-induced laughter. Our every whim catered to by the resort staff. We took photos on the beach, my sarong and floppy hat blowing in the wind. His dark blonde hair, bare tattooed chest. Sweat shining in the sunlight. Running away from the older couple who tried to pick us up in the resort bar.

"Will we be like that someday? Rich, old, trying to pick up some young couple?"

"I hope so." Reed laughed. "I talked to that guy yesterday, he owns an island! We need to get an island."

"I wish."

Reed rubbed his tanned and sweating hand on mine. "Hey, we need to talk about something. When do you want to get married?"

He caught me off guard. "I don't know."

"I'm going on the road in two weeks."

"No," I whined.

"Management keeps adding shows. I don't know when my next break is. It could be six months, a year even. We can figure it out later, or we could do it next week."

I rose from the beach chair. "Next week! We don't have anything planned."

"Calm down. Everything we ordered before is in storage. My assistant found a wedding planner who can sort out catering and invitations."

My stomach tightened when he mentioned his assistant. "That's too fast."

"You love me, I love you. We already did it once. We're making it official like we planned, right?"

"Yeah, I guess."

"Good, then there's no problem." He smiled. "Next week it is. Don't get mad...I want to do it in L.A."

"No. You know what that place did to us."

"Hear me out. It's convenient for everyone, especially on short notice. Otherwise, we have to fly everyone to New York and put them in a hotel. And the house is perfect. You didn't even see everything. There's a beautiful cliff spot that overlooks the valley. You can see the ocean. I've always wanted to marry you there."

"I've seen the house and I don't want to go back there." I sulked.

Reed's brow furrowed. "It would be easier on your parents to go to L.A. Your dad is sick, honey."

"No, don't bring my dad into this. And this is too fast."

"Do you want to wait?"

I shrugged.

"Jenny, our vows should mean something. Isn't the house perfect for that? We can't be afraid of what we've been through together. We survived. Let's give the universe the ultimate fuck you. Come on, you know I'm right about this. Logistically, financially it makes sense. Private jet proposals are expensive. You didn't have insurance in New York."

"It's not what we talked about."

Reed pulled me close. "Baby, I want to make this wedding perfect for you. I can do that at my house. Flying people around the country is out of our budget. Throwing other schedules into the mix is going to make it a complicated nightmare."

"It makes sense but..."

"Jenny, sometimes it's like you're afraid to be happy." He touched my cheek.

"I'm not afraid," I shook my head. "I just..."

"Listen, we'll only tell your parents, my brother, and Dene. We'll invite the band, close friends and say it's a party. It'll be our secret. When my tour starts, you fly back to New York to do that residency with Marlene. I know how much that means to you."

"Really?"

"Scouts honor."

I smiled. "Okay."

He nudged me. "Let's have a punk rock Cinderella ball theme. Everyone will show up in their best wear, we'll spring the wedding on them. Rock n' roll, right?" He grinned.

"Can we keep the guest list small?"

"Whatever you want, babe."

Chapter Eighteen

Our second wedding was on the hilltop behind the mansion. Under the tree, in the sunset, overlooking the ocean—exactly what Reed promised. Our friends and family were there. He wore a black tuxedo, I wore the Versace dress. We laughed, danced, and had champagne. He introduced me as, "Mrs. Evan Reed—for real this time!"

He spent a fortune refurnishing the house for the wedding. Taking down the dark shades, using a lighter color of paint, having a skylight installed upstairs.

I, on the other hand, couldn't wait to get back to New York. Diamond encrusted champagne glasses arrived from Marlene Von Berstein. *Please let me know if you need anything* was written inside the card.

Reed's assistant abruptly quit an hour before our wedding. She saw me in my wedding dress and slammed her clipboard onto a table, knocking over a bottle of wine, shattering it on the floor.

"You deserve each other." She scowled, storming out.

Reed's phone conversation with her at the hospital slid through my memory: *"You know that was a one-time thing. My wife is all that matters to me right now."*

Sasha pinned my loose hair. "Whatever that was—let it go. This is your day, Jenny." She sprayed a halo of Vidal Sassoon. "Besides, she's not even cute."

"Honestly, what do you think of Reed, Sash?" He had gotten over his grudge against her, insisting I ask her to be my maid of honor. The gold bracelet dangling on her wrist was a peace offering.

"He's complicated. I had to keep him from coming in to see you this morning. He saved your life." She touched up my forehead. "Starting today, don't take any shit from him."

Walking down an aisle of rose petals to meet Reed at the altar felt like a dream. He stared at me in my dress the way he had the first time we made love. Like we were the only beings in existence. A million women would've killed to be in my red heels. *No one knows our darkest secrets—they don't need to.*

He fumbled his vows, laughing. "How many songs do I remember every night and I can't get this right?" He pulled a folded sheet of paper from his pocket. "Jenny, without you, I'm nothing. The sun rises with your smile. I gave you my kidney, but you brought me to life. I promise to cherish you and keep you safe 'til the end of our days. In the words of the great Shel Silverstein; endings are sad, so let's have a happy beginning and a happy middle."

My fingers shook, unfolding the paper I'd kept close to my chest. *If you say these words, Jenny, you must give your everything and put the past behind you.* I glanced towards the driveway. Escape. Then back at my parents' proud smiles and Reed's blue eyes. A tear trickled down my cheek. I smiled. "I thought love was something lost, not found. But you found me, you held my feet to the ground, taught me the joys of sand between my toes, ocean waves on my chest. You gave me life when I lost it. I want to spend the rest of my life with you." *I mean that, don't I?*

Reed smiled like sunshine.

Yes, I do.

We sealed our lives together with rings and a kiss. Reed scooped me into his arms and carried me down the aisle as everyone cheered. Cake covered, we sprayed champagne at each other. One drink after another found its way between my manicured fingertips. Reed took off his suit jacket and loosened his tie, while I changed into my party dress in the pool house.

"I want you. Now," Reed said.

"Not yet." I grinned and ran out to our guests.

Our trip to Hawaii had been a pre-Honeymoon escape. The California wedding was a two-day affair including a champagne waterfall, a Jägermeister delivery truck, and overnight stays for his friends at the mansion.

Once my family was driven home, hedonism became paramount. Laughter and dancing filled the backyard as more guests arrived at the wedding after-party. Spinning in dance, we were passed from one group of congratulatory hugs and cheers to the next. Another drink in his hand, another in mine. Imagine every party you've been to in your life, then dump a million dollars of drugs, lighting, and fireworks into the mix. Cocaine. Naked flesh. Everyone was high, dancing. Two girls kissed Reed on our stairway. Everywhere he turned, someone was trying to touch him.

I pulled him away, locking our bedroom door against the chaos. We fell over each other. I helped him undress.

Massive bass speakers blasted Tiffany's "I Think We're Alone Now" from the yard.

Reed swayed. "Jenny, God. I'm so in love with you. But I'm going to throw up."

I helped him to the bathroom toilet. I doused him in mouthwash and put a bath towel over his shoulders.

"Let's sit outside," he said. We opened the big window in the bedroom, and I let his drunk ass lead me out onto the ledge to a nook in the roof. We snuggled close, holding hands and watched our insane guests shoot fireworks into the night sky. Belinda Carlisle's "Heaven is a Place on Earth" played.

Reed pawed at my party dress. "Take that off."

"Negative," I said.

"I need another drink." He moved towards the window and almost stumbled off the roof.

"Double negative." I pulled him back from the edge. "Do these people expect me to make breakfast in the morning?"

"Fuck me." Reed laughed, burying his face in my cleavage. Someone from the ground yelled. "Turn that shit off!" They played Motörhead, then a fight broke out. Eighties pop princesses won out for a few more tracks. Then, real drums, real guitars and someone who sounded a lot like Joan Jett ripped into "Cherry Bomb."

Cops came with bullhorns and left with drinks. Reed snored between my breasts. I watched the blood red sun rise over Malibu. *A new beginning.*

I laughed, nudging Reed to go inside so I could kick two hundred people out of our house. Reed hurled again and brushed his teeth. Drunken king of his castle, he shouted from the landing, "Get the fuck out!" He called his security guard. "Seriously, dude, where's the caterer and van service? Aimee was supposed to take care of that."

"Aimee quit." I crossed my arms.

He grabbed my hips. "That's what we wanted, right? The two of us."

"Yeah."

"Grab a skillet. These assholes aren't going to feed themselves." He raided both fridges and pantries for eggs, cheese, peppers, potatoes and pancake mix and shouted across the living room. "If you can stand up without throwing up, I need you in the kitchen dicing and slicing. If you're gonna throw up, grab a trash bag and head outside, clean up."

Within an hour, we had a fully stocked mimosa station and a continental breakfast bar for half the white trash actors and rockers in L.A. We sat outside watching the zombie stragglers pick up trash. Reed draped his leather jacket over my shoulders.

"Not exactly the most romantic wedding weekend, huh?"

"It was fun." I smiled.

He rubbed his thumb against my chin. "We okay?"

"Always."

Reed was riding high on his *Rock Star Saves Sweetheart's Life and Marries Her in Secret Wedding Ceremony at Sprawling Malibu Estate* status. For once, he was getting positive media attention. Instead of drunken brawls, we made the cover of *People* magazine, his arms around me. Smiling. Tabloid darlings. He reveled in the attention, pushing me for more interviews and photo shoots.

It made me uncomfortable. What did I have to talk about, besides him? I'd been rebranded by the media as the sweet girl next door. Piece by piece, I was losing my identity.

"I know you want this residency with Marlene in New York. It's not a good time," Reed said, two weeks after the wedding.

"You promised, and I made a commitment to Marlene. She booked my flights, Reed. It starts next week. It's too late."

"What part of what I said did you not understand? It's not convenient."

"Why?" I clenched my fists, trying not to raise my voice.

"Seriously? Do I need to give you a reason? I said no."

I walked out of the room before I cried. If I argued, he'd accuse me of pouting. He would be in Chicago then out of the country when I left. I was going to New York, and we'd deal with it when he came home.

Reed intercepted the welcome package Marlene sent with my flight details. "I told you to cancel this."

"Marlene must have sent it before she got my message. I'll call her." I kissed him when he left for his Midwest press tour.

"He's going to be so pissed," I told Sasha when she drove me to LAX the next day.

"What's he going to do? If he gives you a hard time, call me. I'll hang in New York with you. Why does it matter? It's not like he's home anyway."

"Exactly. He wants people to believe we're this perfect couple now. If I'm not in L.A., he thinks the tabloids will say we're split up. There's only so much Los Angeles a girl can handle."

"Agreed, honey. So, this art thing, you're good, aren't you?"

"Used to be."

"Why haven't I seen any of your new stuff?"

"I've barely painted since he and I met."

She rolled her eyes. "Yeah, you haven't done a lot of things since you met him. Go make art. Don't worry about Reed."

I waved bye to Sasha. She was right but I didn't want to think about how I'd changed since I'd met Reed. I didn't paint or see my friends or my parents. I shrugged the thoughts away. *Now is not the time.*

I slid on my sunglasses, made it through security, and treated myself to a martini in the flight lounge. I could finally focus on my work, not Reed. Musicians are artists—he'd have to understand. Like Sasha said, what was he going to do?

While in line to board my flight, I heard an all too familiar Texan drawl behind me. "What's a pretty little girl like you doing in domestic when you could be on a private jet?"

"Phil-fucking-Watson."

Reed's road manager winked and tipped his cowboy hat. "The one and only. I reckon you know why I'm here, sweetheart."

"Catching a Delta flight to hell?"

"That's real funny, 'cause you got a first class ticket." He handed me an envelope. "I've been instructed to round your ass up and get you on a plane to Chicago."

"Fuck off, Phil."

"Gate 38. You walking or am I gonna have to tote you?"

"I'm going to New York."

Phil grabbed my wrist. "No, honey. You're not." He pointed across the terminal. "I've got an asshole rock star over there, high as hell, refusing to get on a plane to do his radio tour until you go with him. You remember what happened last time? 'Cause I do. I don't wanna call our next gig *The Cabrini Green Riot Tour*, do you? Chicago won't play nice."

I looked at where Phil was pointing. Reed was leaning against a wall at Gate 38, scribbling in his black lyric journal.

"I thought he left yesterday?"

"Did he? Or did he wait around to see what your bitch ass was gonna do?" Phil said.

"I'm going to New York."

Phil twisted my wrist until tears stung my eyes. "Don't make me throw your ass over my shoulder in the airport." He pulled his toothpick out of his mouth. "A little word of advice, sweetheart, act like you're happy as fuck to see that asshole, or your day is gonna get worse."

Reed kicked away from the wall when we got close. Not speaking until we were on the airplane, me trapped between them both. He thumped his pen against his lyric book.

"Damn, these seats are tight," Phil said, settling in. A flight attendant stood several aisles behind us, demonstrating seat belt safety and flotation devices. I nervously shook my foot, waiting for whatever mean thing Reed was going to say.

The thumping of his pen grew louder. He breathed heavily. "What the fuck did you think you were doing?" Reed growled and slammed the fist holding his pen into my thigh, burying the tip deep in my flesh.

"You fucker!" I slapped Reed in the chest.

He shoved me in the shoulder towards Phil. Searing pain shot through my leg. I aimed my elbow for his chin. He grabbed my arm; I went at him with my teeth. Phil gripped my hair from behind the seat. Blood ran down my bare leg.

"You stabbed me in the knee, you freak." I shook, trying to fight tears.

"Y'all stop this shit or you're gonna spend the night with a Federal Marshall, something neither of you little assholes are prepared for," Phil said. He saw Reed's trusty ink pen buried deep in my flesh and jerked it out.

"Oh my god," I moaned. A river of mascara poured down my face. Phil gave Reed's pen back and tossed a jacket in my lap.

"Is everything okay here?" the head stewardess asked.

"Yeah. Darlin', can you get me a Bloody Mary and put this young man in that empty seat in first class? These two lovebirds need a break."

Reed didn't wait for the stewardess. He snatched his bag and moved to the front of the plane.

"I warned you, didn't I?" Phil said. He pulled off the sweaty bandanna from under his cowboy hat and tied it tight around my bleeding knee.

I cringed.

"Stop being a drama queen. It's a flesh wound. Not like he shot you or something."

"What is he on?" I managed.

"Candy, honey. It's all candy with him."

"I'm ecstatic to be in Chicago!" jacked-up Reed said on air with the Chicago's WXRT rock station. "Band is doing good. New single coming out."

"I bet you get bored at these things don't you, sweetheart?" the DJ asked me.

"Oh, she doesn't want to be here," Reed said. "Do you, honey?" He took a sip of his drink. Eyes wide, slurring. "We were just in L.A.X. where she was trying to leave me."

"Seriously?" I grumbled.

"Wow, well that's certainly good song material," DJ Ted said. "On your tour—"

"Why don't you ask her about it? Apparently, what she wants is more important than what we need. Go on, tell him, honey. Tell him why you were running off to New York behind my back."

The DJ fumbled. "It's Jenny, right?"

"It's an art residency—you know that," I snapped at Reed.

Reed laughed. "So, the media is selling this sick lie about our fairy tale love story. Our vows were supposed to "mean something." He used finger quotes. "And the first thing you do when I turn my back is lie."

"This is not the place," I said.

"Who gave you a free pass? Do you seriously not remember what happened the last time you snuck to New York behind my back? You're so fucking selfish, you don't see when I'm trying to protect you from yourself."

"So, about that tour..." DJ Ted said.

Reed nudged my sore knee. "Honey, I got one good kidney left, you want that one too?" He leaned into the mic. "Man, when you tell a girl you'll do anything for her, be ready to back it up. Some girls want blood. I've got a mansion in California that would fill a Chicago block, and that ain't enough for her." He flicked a paper clip at me, finding even the tiniest ways to antagonize me.

My chest felt hot. To get to the exit sign I needed to get past Reed. *Was he worried I might hurt myself again? I read this all wrong.* The room was warm, I felt faint. *Did I start this? God, am I crazy?* I bit my nails. My bracelets clinked together like an off-key tambourine.

I looked at my shaky leg, the aching one with Phil's bandanna tied around it. *That's real.*

"You stabbed me," I spat, like an insane person.

Reed took out his earpiece, stood to leave. "You killed our baby, you dumb bitch."

I wish I'd sat in shock, and just watched him leave. But I had a half-Irish kidney that didn't belong to me. I charged him like a wailing banshee and shoved him out the exit into the hallway. He stood calmly, smiling, while I pushed and screamed in his face. "I knew you were lying. This was all a game to you!"

Phil leaned against the doorway at the end of the hall, chewing his toothpick, entertained.

Reed feigned concern. "I don't know what you're talking about, Jenny. What's your problem? Look, if you keep this up, I'll have to put you back in the hospital."

I punched him in the face. "I'm not crazy!" I screamed, completely unhinged.

Reed gripped me by my throat and lifted me off the floor. He smiled. "Prove that now."

"Alright kids, break it up." Phil grabbed my arm.

"Take this dumb bitch back to L.A." Reed said.

"No, no. Please. No," I begged. *Stop, Jenny. Take a breath. Take ten. Walk away. Why are you doing this?*

Fighting resumed in the limo. Reed kicked. I shoved. He pinned me to the floorboard, his hand gripping my face. I bit the web of skin between his thumb and forefinger hard enough to bring blood, then kneed him in the dick, collapsing him to the floor.

Phil laughed. "I guess you showed him, didn't you, sugar?"

"Fuck you, Phil."

I pulled away from Reed, back into the seat.

He caught his breath, lunged at the door handle, grabbing me by the hair, and pushed me towards the open door.

Phil's giant hands gripped both our necks like a mama cat, pulling us firmly into the car, and slamming the door. "Alright. Play fair. I don't have time to hide a body in Chicago. One more screw up and you'll wake up with a restraining order, got it?"

Reed and I didn't talk until we were in our hotel room. It was the St. Regis, in Rosemont, by O'Hare airport.

He tended the cuts and bruises I left on his face in the mirror.

"You never trusted me, did you?" Reed said.

"You didn't forgive me."

"Sit down."

I leaned against the whirlpool tub in the middle of the room. He pulled Phil's rank, blood-crusted, tour bandanna off my knee. I cringed.

"It's gonna hurt," Reed said. I nodded. He poured a cap of peroxide onto the wound. "I didn't mean to do that on the plane."

"Why didn't you just let me go to New York?" I cried.

"Jenny, you tried to kill yourself the last time you were in New York. You almost died. You can't see why I don't want you there alone?"

I shook my head. "We're a mess."

I woke up the next morning in Chicago, alone. A note from Reed and plane tickets waited for me at the front desk.

Jenny, we need a break. — E.R.

Chapter Nineteen

I went back to L.A., where I waited for him to call and tell me everything would be okay.

Evan Reed dumped me via fax machine.

My favorite butler, Charles, helped me pack a suitcase. We had been allies. Now he was making sure I didn't take silverware or priceless demos.

"This will blow over," he reassured me.

"I don't think so."

But it did—after two weeks of me crying on my cousin's sofa. I'd picked up shifts at the restaurant where she worked. Reed called everyone he knew until he found me.

One night his tour bus stopped in front of the restaurant.

"Well, are you coming or not?" he said.

Of course, I would. I was addicted to his chaos. I couldn't do normal anymore. I was accustomed to daytime sleeping. Pills to wake. Pills to sleep.

The constant movement of buses and planes. I grabbed my bag and left another shitty job for Reed. Even when I was angry, I was still addicted to him—to the sex, the drama. I was sick of how he treated me during his mood swings, and shocked at how bad I missed him when we were apart.

Promises were made. Rehab. Exercise. Healthy food. He stopped the drugs, took his meds. A millionaire hotelier named Philar Burton convinced Reed to join as co-owner in a new hotel he was building. We flew to Barbados to enjoy the beaches, clubs, and sailing. Private beach access, a villa we could use any time we needed to get away. A peaceful break from our L.A. chaos.

Some moron decided it would be a good idea for the band to extend the never-fucking-ending tour. My dreams of New York were pushed farther away. I couldn't be trusted there without him, and he was never coming home.

He was hospitalized in Russia for "exhaustion"—rock star for fits of rage, shattered TVs, and drug overdoses.

It was my job to fly out and reason with him. A record executive accompanied me on a twelve hour flight on the label's private jet, another hour by car to the hospital where Reed was locked in a psych ward. I was terrified. The U.S.S.R. had a fear of rock music and a fondness for electroshock therapy. Reed's band were already taking a risk traveling there.

I screamed at the hospital admin. "Let me see him now."

"I won't change hospital policy just because you have money, American woman."

"Can your security handle a riot when I let the fans know you are holding their king against his will? Let me see him."

Reed was wearing a straitjacket. Dark circles under his red lined eyes. He spat pills in the nurse's face. This man was ill—not pissed off because he wasn't getting his way, but sick like a certain Saint Bernard that didn't get its rabies shot.

I convinced him he had to calm down so I could get him to a U.K. treatment facility. We bribed an orderly who was a fan of the band and he let us slip Reed out the back door in a laundry cart.

We kidnapped a rock star from a U.S.S.R. mental ward.

The U.K. hospital put him on a new medication, and I spent the next few days in a hotel watching my zombie husband play Nintendo.

"What are we going to do about him?" His management pressed me at home.

Daniel pulled me aside. "Reed is using cocaine with his prescription meds. He needs treatment."

Reed agreed to sleep on his useless psychiatrist's sofa for a week. She bent to his demands like the rest of us. During his chaos, I'd failed to notice that I'd missed my period.

Chapter Twenty

I learned the hard way not to tell your crazy husband you're pregnant in an attempt to cheer him up. Karma will slap you in the face.

Reed told me a fan sued him, saying her child was his. DNA proved he wasn't the father, but that didn't make the experience any less stressful.

After a night of screaming at each other, I went to the emergency room and lost our baby—the one that was going to fix everything. The doctor asked whether I'd had an abortion in the past, saying, "there was some damage."

Reed grabbed his jacket and stormed out of the ER, leaving me in tears. He came back later to take me home. We stayed in bed several days, ignoring the outside world.

He wanted me on the road.

Buses, planes, limos. Shows. Drinks. Drugs. Sleep. Repeat. Reed was using cocaine and filling my hands with pills. Losing ourselves had become easier than facing the world.

Five gynecologists in Malibu assured me the miscarriage could have happened to anyone and that I shouldn't have any future problems. I stayed in a constant panic that things were going to get bad again. Eating pills like candy helped.

Money was becoming an issue. We couldn't get insurance and our bills were astronomical. How many times can one man be sued in a year?

A hundred and fifty two, for the record.

Reed was fined for missing shows, and constantly dealt with frivolous lawsuits. His accountant demanded a meeting. Reed's most recent album had sold 14 million copies. There were tour tickets, merchandise and song royalties.

"The good news—you made twenty million dollars this year. The bad news—you're broke," the accountant said.

Reed laughed. "What? How?"

"Lawsuits. New cars. Hospital bills. Drugs. You have to sell something before you lose everything."

"Can we liquidate the investment property in Barbados?"

"The hotelier you palled up with was into some shady deals. He's not returning my calls. I don't know if there's anything recoverable there."

"But I gave him ten million dollars," Reed said.

"You did do that. Had you asked, I would've told you not to. You have to make tough choices, or the bank will foreclose on your house, the cars, everything. These things get ugly fast."

Reed reluctantly sold the NYC condo. He hired a new accounting firm to look into his business and found out Phil had embezzled thousands of dollars from him. Phil wasn't the only one. Dealing with millions of dollars was not something any young musician is prepared for.

I'd spent the day in Los Angeles with an art gallery that wanted to buy my old pieces. I came home and Reed was sitting at the kitchen counter doing something I'd never seen—reading his bills.

"What's going on babe?"

"I'm going on tour."

"No. What happened to taking a year off to write? Start a family? That was our plan."

"Every asshole I know has been stealing money from me." He handed me a bill from the utility board. "Our electric bill hasn't been paid in three months. That Jag you spent the day in should have been repossessed last week. So yeah, until my lawyers—who I can't afford to pay, by the way—sort this out, I'm going back on the road."

The band released a live CD+VHS and went on tour. While half the groupies in the U.S. fucked my husband in sleazy hotel rooms, I stayed home to sort out his money problems. The amount of greed that resided in everyone Reed trusted was devastating. He couldn't afford to fire them until there was enough evidence to prosecute. Most of the time it was more cost effective to settle with them. We were able to get over two million dollars back, which paid the lawyers. That paled in comparison to the amount stolen.

I took as much stress off Reed as I could, but we barely saw each other. When we did, it was sex, and off to another show. The band played four nights a week. Understandably, he was furious about losing millions to people he trusted—who wouldn't be? I didn't worry when he started tracking every penny he gave me.

He laughed, scanning through my check register. "Jenny, I've never seen a checkbook this detailed. You keeping notes for when you leave me? If so, your math is off by fifty cents."

I shrugged. "I just know how you are. Don't want to forget where I was on some random Tuesday last summer."

He put his arms around me. "I'm not that bad. My accountant is going to move the money around a little, so just tell me when you need extra and I'll take it out of the bank for you."

I didn't tell Reed I was pregnant again. I wanted to make sure things were okay before giving him false hope. After the miscarriage, I wasn't very hopeful, myself.

Every time I planned to tell him, something came up and he couldn't make it home. At Christmas, he went straight to court to sort legal issues before the holiday. I was four months pregnant and showing. The doctor assured me twenty times everything was normal.

I pulled Reed into a restroom before an awards show. "Hello, wife," he smiled, thinking we were about to get it on. I opened my coat.

Reed did a double take, from my eyes to my round belly and lifted me up, kissing me. "Is this really happening?" His eyes went wide, and he smiled like a five-year-old on Christmas morning.

Everything in the pregnancy went wonderfully—until he gave me Trich. For those of you who didn't go to Sex Ed., Trichomoniasis is a sexually transmitted infection that can cause premature labor.

Reed was on tour when the doctor gave me the diagnosis.

Reed called late one night. I told him everything was okay with the baby and was as sweet as I could possibly be.

"I love you," he said.

"Then you should get an STD test before you come home again." I slammed the phone down. It was obvious he was cheating. I was naive to have thought otherwise. My goal was to have a healthy baby, get my tubes tied, then deal with whatever other shit life handed me.

As much as leaving made sense, I had no place to go. I had to keep my baby healthy and safe. The rest would have to wait.

Hayley was born exactly two weeks early at 3:32 am on March 2, 1989. Her daddy canceled a show and took a last minute flight from Philadelphia to make it in time to witness her birth. Her eyes were blue like his, her hair strawberry blonde. I've never seen a father prouder than he was of our Hayley. Despite his tough guy exterior, Reed had this classic '50s idea of the perfect family. Fatherhood was a chance to redeem himself. He expected me to grab an apron and forget the drama it had taken us to get us there.

Hayley was perfect. Healthy, happy, rarely fussy. Reed adored her. Everything was right in the world—except sleep, once you have kids, you will never sleep again.

He could be such an ass, but when I watched Reed with her, I could feel those old feelings of intense love I'd once held for him. I wanted so desperately for him to pull off this daddy thing. *Maybe he'll change for her.* I expected him to give up rock n' roll for Christmas albums any minute.

I loved her tiny cheeks and perfect pink little lips. Her first year passed quickly. She was sitting upright, eating, then crawling before early walking. Reed would lie in bed by her crib and watch her sleep. He didn't want to go anywhere he couldn't bring her. I had to make him leave the house to accept an MTV award.

"Everything will be different, okay?" He promised so many times I could've tattooed it on my forehead.

I tuned it out. I wanted him to be able to do it for her sake. He was there for everything—her birth, her first tooth, and her first birthday. If we argued, he insisted on going in the other room away from her. He didn't want Hayley to grow up the way he had.

I understood why. The few things I'd gathered about his childhood during late night drunken rants, and admissions from Sarah and Daniel painted a horrific picture. But things had gone so wrong for so long, I wasn't sure how much longer I could stay.

Part of me still wanted to save him, despite everything. I sacrificed myself for him, but now Hayley was my priority. This desire of his to have things perfect came from a place too deep to be rational. I needed a plan to leave before things got bad again—but I was afraid. He'd lost his mind when I had the abortion, what would happen when I took our living, breathing baby girl?

I told myself that regardless of how things turned out with us, he would be a good father. He was obsessed with protecting Hayley and keeping her safe.

But every parent has an off day.

Chapter Twenty-One

B eing Hayley's mother brought me a sense of joy and peace I'd never dreamed of. I was surprised when she was around eleven months old, I found myself pregnant again. Twins.

Reed was beside himself. This was the dream, right? Somewhat-sober Prince Charming, the house on the hill, a beautiful little girl and two more on the way.

Sons, this time. They were perfect, not a blip on any test. My cholesterol was awesome, which surprised the hell out of me, considering the only thing I'd been able to keep down were chocolate malts and Famous Big Boy Bob's cheeseburger combo meals. Those milkshakes were all I could think of. My over-excited husband brought them to me every day. Sometimes, twice.

We picked out paint for their nursery. I painted a cute little mural with baby elephants snuggling with mommy elephants and goofy giant gorilla daddies. Reed's label hosted a huge baby shower. We donated the gifts. We'd been too afraid to have one with Hayley—too worried about jinxing everything. This was our chance to redeem ourselves. We would be a happy little family.

Then we went to that birthday party.

On August 13, 1990, there was a birthday party for a little boy named Trevor. A cute six-year-old who loved fireworks, kites, and shiny spinning things. His dad was a producer who often financed the band's ventures. Every year he held a huge party and invited the band, stage crew, and families.

Perhaps we were obligated to haul my seven months pregnant ass and our little girl to this party near the valley. There was a flaw in that plan. In the end, no one is to blame. Fate slid all the wrong pieces into place.

Our Hayley was only seventeen months old, not even big enough to go in the bouncy castle. The party was held at a small park on a hill, along a bend of a busy highway. Massive trucks cut through that part of the valley, down the road along the hill. There was normally a fence at the bottom. As fate would have it, the fence was being replaced. It was going to be a much nicer fence than the one that should have been there that day.

We'd made the kids stay away from the street all afternoon. Two roadies drinking from Budweiser cans sent them up the hill to play in the bouncy castle. Families had picnic blankets spread out across the grassy hill. Everyone wanted a good spot to see the fireworks.

Hayley played with the other kids while Reed watched from our picnic blanket. Seven months pregnant, I had to pee a dozen times a day. I was determined to make it to the top of the hill without rolling down like a giant balloon. Reed was excited about the twins. He'd promised to take off touring to be with us. But he was tired that day. The band had come off a mini-tour in South America. As always, he promised things would get better soon.

I made it up the hill. Such a lovely, sunny day. Little Trevor, the sweet birthday boy, whizzed past me with a shiny spinning wheel; long, silver ribbons twisting and twirling behind him in the wind. His soft, brown curls brushed against my fingers. I instinctively touched my belly—my boys.

"You're glowing, Mama," Ian Hawthorne, a guitar tech from the last tour said. "Restroom is to your left."

His smile wasn't normal. It started pleasant. Then his mouth moved in slow motion—*concern? Fear? A stroke? What is happening?* Everything slowed. I heard screams. The world was spinning. Too fast.

Before I could turn around, I heard the sound of an eighteen-wheeler braking on the highway. Tires screeched as they melted and ripped pavement from the ground. The smell of burnt rubber filled the air. Sound ceased to exist. The universe was holding its breath.

It rushed back in blood curdling screams.

A little silver ribbon floated up into the clouds.

I grabbed my stomach. Ian pulled me to the ground. He put his arms around me, held me tight and tried to shield me from the terror in the road. "Don't look."

I could see it on the other families' faces.

Little Trevor, the birthday boy, ran up the hill without his spinning wheel, tears streaming as he screamed for his father. An adult grabbed him. Not me. My white summer dress and the ground around me grew wet. Ian, the trusty guitar tech, didn't budge.

"No,' I said, gripping my stomach. I knew. I knew.

"I barely looked away for a minute," Reed swore later.

Isn't that what they always say?

Chapter Twenty-Two

Everything happened in slow motion. Wives and girlfriends pulled their kids away. A crowd gathered at the bottom of the hill by the truck.

Why isn't Reed bringing Hayley up the hill? Grief filled my stomach and I gasped for air. My soaked thighs stuck together in the heat. I struggled against the man holding me back.

"No, no, no," I pleaded and managed to lean aside enough to see what Ian was protecting me from.

Reed was in the middle of the highway on his knees. His arms covered in blood, holding together what was left of our little girl. I couldn't get to them. Sirens. Screams. A paramedic put an oxygen mask over my face and tried to calm me.

I still run it through my head at night and in the shower. How he could have grabbed her just in time. How the truck could have easily missed.

How we should have left early as planned. I wished every way possible that we could take it back.

Our angel, the one who saved us, was gone.

The record company offered to reschedule Reed's fall tour, but he insisted on leaving. He couldn't look me in the eye. His hands shook constantly. He smoked a pack of cigarettes every few hours. We couldn't go near her room or her things.

He blamed himself and I tried not to. It could have happened to any family there. She'd been chasing a ball the big kids had dropped. Reed looked away when someone spoke to him and when he looked back, she ran. He called her name. She stopped and smiled, her little ringlet curls bouncing in the wind.

Everyone repeated the same story: Reed hesitated—she was walking back towards him, but she stopped. She giggled at him and chased the ball down the hill. He was on his feet, running, but wasn't fast enough. She was out of his reach when the truck's tires squealed. He was so close the truck clipped his shoulder, dislocating it, and knocking him into the ditch.

"It should have been me," he said.

He was so close. It could have been both of them.

Walking on earth was the biggest feat in the world. I know there was a funeral. There were decisions to be made. But I don't remember it and I hope I never do. My soul was hollow.

I stayed with my parents. Reed stayed on the road with the shows, the drugs, the groupies. He shaved his head. He had the date Hayley died tattooed on his knuckles. He stopped returning my phone calls. Tabloids rumored he'd overdosed in a Paris hotel. His manager assured the media it wasn't true. They never should have let him get on the tour bus. The record company didn't care about Reed or his family, only about money.

A wave had knocked my soul out of my chest. All the oxygen in my lungs was sucked into an infinite black hole that would spit out death howls and rivers of tears.

Grief is dehydrating. It's unforgiving. A battering ram to the senses. Tree limbs sinking, swaying into the abyss.

It felt like shit. It felt like quicksand. It felt like smothering in death, over and over. It felt like a bottle of pills on my tongue, my own finger shoved down my throat in a panic, gagging hot tears when I looked down at my still growing belly. Trying to figure out a way to go back in time and abort myself. It felt like fire in my throat. Like muscle and veins ripping beneath my flesh. A stripping of body from bone, from humanity and reality. A hellish limbo where everything you loved is gone and this person-thing you once cared for refuses to come home, refuses to comfort you, refuses to acknowledge that this was real and that you aren't losing your mind.

But most of all—it felt like nothing.

The universe had stepped in to remind us that we were nothing.

I touched the walls of my parent's house, hoping the wood panels would suck me in. When I had the strength for anger, I wished it had happened to someone else. If I could inflict it on anyone else, I would have. We were cursed. I had always known that—yet, I'd stayed. The teenage girl who'd grown up in that house, longing to paint and travel the world was dead. I didn't know her anymore.

The progress Reed had made, real or imagined, was gone. He didn't hide his indiscretions—the groupies, the hotel rooms. My parents couldn't console me. I needed Reed.

Numbing the pain allowed him to escape. I couldn't. I was pregnant with our twins and when the doctors realized I'd gone crazy, they put me on bed rest.

It was a miracle I hadn't lost them that day in the park. I thought of the guitar tech, Ian Hawthorne. How he'd held me so tightly. How quickly that wall of heavy metal machismo had dropped from his chest. A stranger comforted me more in a brief moment than my husband had the entire time I'd known him.

My parents were tasked with waking me and making me eat. My mother washed me, not like a child, but like I was her eighty-year-old mother. The weight of Hayley's loss was so heavy, I knew I would carry it to my last breath. Someone, somewhere was pulling the strings and laughing at me. I'd find myself dressed and not know how it happened. People stopped mid-conversation when I checked out.

Reed was halfway around the world. I burst into tears when he called, begging him to come home. The line went dead.

I had a dream that I was drowning. The house had flooded, and waves were covering my body. I woke hot, but quickly realized it wasn't sweat soaking my sheets. The boys in my belly weren't moving.

The nudge of their tiny feet and hands were my only comfort after Hayley's death—they had kept me alive. My hands and gown were covered in blood when I crept down the hall to my parent's bedroom.

"Mommy, I need you," I cried.

Reed canceled a show and came to the hospital. The doctors performed an emergency C-section. Victor was stillborn. The umbilical cord had wrapped around him, cutting off the oxygen to him and his brother. I heard Storm cry as the anesthesia kicked in.

It will be okay. I saved one. That's better than nothing, right?

But I didn't save anyone. The universe dangled a tiny bit of hope, then ripped it back. Reed's brother said nurses rushed Storm to the NICU. I never had a chance to hold him. My mother was tasked with telling me that my son was gone. To this day, she says it was the worst moment in her life.

When Daniel told Reed, my husband walked out of the hospital, left in a taxi, and boarded a plane. He played a sold-out show in Detroit, another in Red Bank, and three more without mentioning us.

When your kids die and your husband disappears, your church friends bring you dinner and help you get on your feet.

When you live in a bubble, after the camera lights stop flashing, there is no one. My parents didn't want me to go to Malibu. I had to, in case Reed came home.

Marcus was waiting with the car because they don't let crazy women on planes. We cried together. Doors locked, him in the driver's seat. Me in the back. He loved Hayley. She'd adored him. His job description prohibited hugs, as did my spousal contract, but he held my hand across the seat for something less judgmental than a moment of prayer—a moment of silence between us for my dead baby, the girl he called "little one."

My parents didn't keep hard liquor in the house. Their blueberry and plum wines weren't strong enough. I'd stolen a bottle of Crown Royal from their neighbor's cabinet. My head stayed between my knees, as I puked whiskey on the floorboard from Phoenix to Malibu. My post birth body leaked urine through my dress onto the BMW's leather seats. Forget the books I'd escaped into while on Reed's tours, I was a living, breathing horror show.

Marcus and I pulled into Hollywood Cemetery before going to the mansion. He said it was the first time he'd ever planned a funeral. I just couldn't do it again. To make matters worse, the director let me know the check for Hayley's service had bounced. The house account was empty. Reed had been withdrawing thousands for drugs.

According to Forbes, my husband was a multi-millionaire. In reality, we were broke. I had to ask my brother-in-law for money to bury my children.

The record company let me know that we had to keep this to ourselves. One death was good for business—but this was too much for the public.

I didn't have the strength to push back. My parents, Daniel, Charles, Marcus, Sasha, and I attended a small graveside service for the boys. My husband never came home.

Sasha tried to help. But it was too much. She couldn't handle the screaming and crying. I got it, I was past my limit too. I had pills, alcohol and Charles the butler to keep me company. I paced the Malibu Hell

House's long hallways for hours, hyper-focused on Reed's absence. My bedroom was empty. Hayley's crib was empty. The new nursery was empty. I slept in the hallway outside their doors, nothing but my pillow and the floor, weeping. My limbs like rubber, I lay awake on the cold tile, staring off into space.

A fly managed to get inside the house, I watched it walk across the floor and land on my face. I didn't move. I prayed for maggots and rot, flesh-eating bacteria that would speed my deterioration. I would have killed myself; I didn't have the strength.

Our Haitian maid quit, convinced we were cursed. Me, sitting at the foot of the stairway screaming for hours hadn't helped. It wasn't a mansion it was a mausoleum.

Desperate, Charles left my running shoes in obvious places. On the verge of giving up, he told me to get dressed because the house had to be fumigated. He lied, handing me my sneakers. "Go for a walk. You need fresh air."

I didn't want air, fresh or otherwise, but I went on an angry walk into the woods. *How can the sky be blue? How can the sun shine?* I wanted to punch a blue bird. Black out the sun. How could the world keep turning when mine had fallen apart? I sat on a log and cried.

Those tears were cleansing. Maybe it was the earth, the air or just the fact that I managed to breathe before the reserves overfilled. Although I didn't feel better, the fresh air and exercise helped.

Charles kept sitting my shoes out where I'd trip over them. I had to get out of that house before it killed me. I let go. I ran for hours through those long trails. I ran until my heels bled. I ran harder. I packed a bag. A bottle of water, a journal, and a sleeping bag. I hiked the Hollywood Hills. I saw deer, rabbits and a lone fox. I wore holes in the soles of my sneakers. Pair after pair. I kept running.

I wasn't eating. I hadn't had more than an energy bar here and there for two weeks. On November 11, three months after Hayley died, I was hospitalized for exhaustion—and they weren't kidding. I weighed 110 lbs. God, when they stopped me from running, I went bat shit crazy. I no longer recognized myself in the mirror; I saw Kaley, thin and frail, stuffed in a freezer like a piece of meat. I had visions of empty cribs and dead babies and dreams filled with frozen crab girls, twisting and winding a web with their spider legs.

You should have listened.

During those long runs through the Santa Monica Mountains, from Point Mugu to Griffith Park where I'd met Kaley, I had a premonition. Directly or indirectly, Evan Reed was going to kill me.

Whatever light had been inside him went out with Hayley. If nothing else, she and the boys would never know who their father became.

So, who knows? Maybe there is a God. One with a really fucked up sense of grace.

Chapter Twenty-Three

I was angry when I got out of the hospital. I had to know why he was doing this to me. How could he go on as if nothing happened? I needed his validation—to prove this was all real and that I hadn't gone mad.

His brother stopped answering my tearful phone calls.

"I don't know what to tell you, Jenny."

I went to the source. I flew to Chicago and rented a car to drive to Barren County, Kentucky. For the first time, I confronted Reed's mother. I had to understand him.

Yellowed scenes from our tabloid lives covered her walls. My eyes focused on the dancing sunflower in her window. I forced down a stale Little Debbie zebra cake with a fake smile, trying not to choke on the cloud of cigarette smoke.

Until the moment I sat on the sofa across from Betty Williams, I did not think a life worse than mine existed. Her smoke made me dizzy. The horrid creature's words whizzed by me in tobacco wheezes. I got exactly what I asked for. What was wrong with Reed started in her womb.

"Reed was a little bastard," his mother said. "I've seen your house in *Star* magazine. Can you believe he lets me live like this?" She lit another cigarette and pulled a folded tabloid photo of Hayley from her side table. "He didn't even let me know my granddaughter was dead."

She took a draw from her Virginia Slim. "Guess I can't blame him. He had it rough. The boy wasn't right, though." Her fingers trembled. "You see, I had a daughter that killed herself about six years ago. Then my husband, Clem, walked right out the front door and shot himself in the head. Evan didn't even come to his own stepfather's funeral. Probably just as well, Clem always hated him."

"Why?" I asked.

"Clem was a good, upstanding Christian man. Evan has all these crazy ideas about things that he says happened."

"What happened to Reed's biological father?"

"Me and Clem had our problems before he found the Lord. We got addicted to meth, Clem got arrested. I slept around with a few men in town for money."

"Wait, what?"

"I was in love and I did what I needed to do to get my man out of jail. But Clem didn't appreciate the little bastard when he came along. Wanted me to get rid of him. I tried. Gave him to his grandmother. She died, and his real dad got arrested, so police sent him back. By then, Clem had started preaching so he tried to do the right thing and raise him as his own, but Evan was ornery and disobedient. Even when he was real young, he would fight and bite. Didn't say a word until he was five years old. They had a speech therapist talk to him at school because they thought he was slow. Music calmed him down and she got him singing until he talked. Clem was good to that boy, but harder on him than the other kids. He might've hit him more than he should've, but I couldn't go against my husband."

"Mary, I need to go." I rushed outside, my weakened, postpartum body wretched, hurling sweet tea off the porch where her second husband shot himself. She told me more than my grieving heart could process. *I can't know these things. I'll forget I ever went there.*

"You need one thing to hold onto, Jennifer. You need one thing to get you back on your path to recovery. I know it's hard, but it's a small step on a long road. You have to keep moving," my therapist said at our next session.

Painting no longer existed for me. She insisted I take a drawing class. "Art is the purest form of therapy."

Exercise, vitamins, and a handful of pills every morning were supposed to pull me out of the black pit of depression of three precious souls ripped from my orbital being. I tried to stick with the class but doing an everyday thing with normal people was impossible. I hated them and their yoga classes and spa weekends. I hated their Beverly Hills fucking bullshit.

In classic Jenny Reed mode, I grabbed my bag and walked out.

My art instructor asked me to meet him for lunch to discuss why I'd left. He was handsome, but he was attempting to mentor me—it was nothing more. It was nice to have someone who wanted to hear about me. Jenny before the babies, before Reed—the girl who had friends and got lost in the beauty of color.

"I used to tell people I could taste color." I laughed; a sound I hadn't heard come from my body in months. I burst into tears.

"It's okay," my handsome instructor said.

I picked at the skin on my face that night, I hated the girl in the mirror. I called my therapist to tell her how wrong she'd been.

"It's okay to enjoy life, Jennifer. Do this for yourself. If not, you won't survive."

"I died in August. It's only a matter of time until my body catches up."

"Do you need to go back to the hospital?"

"No." That was the one place I'd been trapped with my thoughts before they pumped me full of pills

"You'll stick with the class?"

"Sure." If I played nice, the psychiatrist at her office would give me more Xanax. I'm not saying I had a problem, but I had prescriptions with four different doctors in town.

I was trapped in a nightmare limbo. I couldn't help but think about what happened in New York—did I really take those fucking pills over some pissy drama with Reed? I didn't remember taking them, and I was becoming quite adept at shoveling them in my mouth. If I wanted to off myself, this was the time. The visions I'd had of Kaley back then were a warning. I shrugged and took another Xanax.

I didn't tell my therapist about Kaley's keychain.

I didn't tell her about searching through Reed's nightstand for bullets because someone had unloaded my gun, or how I carried it with me just in case I got the nerve. Beneath condoms, pills, loose change, ten thousand dollar watches and twenty thousand dollar rings was a faded purple rabbit's foot.

Nope.

I took a handful of ammunition and slammed the drawer closed, locking it with the key I'd found behind the dresser. I loaded my pistol and slid it back underneath the mattress. Out of sight, out of mind. Lock the drawer, throw away the key.

One afternoon when I returned to the mansion, Charles had a frantic look, and held the cordless phone in his hand. "Mr. Reed," he mouthed. "The new maid told him you were out."

I didn't want to talk to him. After seeing that *thing* in his nightstand I'd entered a new realm of depression. I'd thought I'd traipsed right through all of them.

This place was blue, kind of sticky, medicated, and plump. But the pills were helping, lots and lots of them. Xanax, Codeine, Klonopin were a few of my favorite things to mix with lunchtime cocktails with strangers. Mumbling, "Fuck Reed," to anyone who would listen. Marcus was always there with the chariot to wheel me back to hell, where dear Charles the butler tried his best to make everything okay.

I giggled, snatching the phone from Charles.

"Good morning, sunshine," I slurred into the receiver.

"Where have you been?" Reed didn't care about me, but he was trigger itchy for control.

"Lunch, with a friend. Are you coming home?"

"Are you fucking him?"

"Are you?" I laughed.

Across the kitchen, Charles shook his head at me, whispering, "Don't."

"Who is he?"

"Reed, stop being dramatic. I had lunch with my art instructor. Nothing to worry your tired little manhood about. No one wants to fuck your busted up, brood mare."

Charles reached for the phone.

I jerked back.

"That's always what this has been about, hasn't it, Reed? You kept me around to make babies. Well, I'm right here, fucker." I cried into the phone. "I want my babies. You asshole. Do you even know their names? Victor. Storm. Or is it just Hayley? Every night I cry and pray that you will stop breathing. I hate you. I need you, but God, I hate you."

Charles tried covering for me after I threw the phone and left the room. He explained about the pills, the crying and the alcohol. A desperate attempt to gain some sympathy for me from my husband.

Instead, Reed canceled my credit cards.

"I have to keep seeing my therapist." I begged.

"Fuck. Jenny, of course, that's fine. God, I'm not the Antichrist. What kind of monster do you think I am?"

"Do you want me to answer that?" I said.

"Do you want me to cancel the therapy?"

"Don't."

"Did Charles schedule the movers for the nurseries? I want that shit out of the house."

"That's all we have left of our babies."

"I want it gone. I'm not kidding with you."

"Fuck you." I hung up.

Things at home weren't adding up. Sober and medicated, I figured out that Breanna, Reed's porn star ex, had still lived at the mansion when we first dated. The weekend before Thanksgiving, a temp worker at his lawyer's office sent a courier with a box of mail. I left it on the kitchen counter. Thanksgiving came and went without a phone call from Reed. I opened the box.

I came across a thick credit card statement. Hundreds of transactions with a $73,000 balance. I noticed a trend and found the other statements. There was a recurring monthly charge to Hôtel de Paris in France. I checked the itinerary taped to the fridge. The band hadn't played Paris in a year. I flipped through his Rolodex until I found a number. I gave them his real name—Evan Williams, and said I was his assistant. They confirmed he had three nights booked the following weekend. I compared the bank statements to his touring schedule. During breaks where he'd told me there wasn't enough time to come home, he'd been making side trips to Paris—for two fucking years! I called again.

"Hotel de Paris, c'est Francesca."

"I'm sorry to bother you again, I am Mr. Williams' assistant—I'm looking at his credit card statement and there seems to be a discrepancy on his last visit. The room service charges are a bit excessive."

"Ahhhhhh... Deux ordres de petit-déjeuner, deux ordres de temps de dîner de trois jours, six bouteilles de champagne, les deux douzaines de roses normales, massage pour Mr. Reed."

"English?"

The French woman sighed. "De petit-déjeuner—breakfast. Dinner, champagne, massage. The normal charges. I can print it for him when he checks in and have him review it in person."

"That's not necessary. I trust you're correct. He probably forgot—they were so expensive."

"With Mr. Williams, money is not an obstacle. If he asks for a 1920 Chateau d'Yquem, we bring him the Chateau d'Yquem. We'll bring him two if he asks. If he asks for a crate, we'll bring him the crate. If he asks for a barrel -"

"I get it. I am certain Mr. Williams knows whether he can afford a $4,000 bottle of wine. Thank you."

I counted the days to his reservation, then called his manager in Amsterdam.

"Reed's out doing press today, Jenny."

I redialed the Paris hotel. "Hello, this is Mr. Williams' assistant. I've been trying to contact him all morning from the United States, but the call isn't going through. Could you connect me? It's urgent."

There was a hesitation. "One moment." The line transferred.

"Bonjour?" A woman's voice answered.

I paused. "Hello... Can I speak to Mr. Williams?"

"He's occupied," she said in a heavy French accent, and giggled.

"I'm calling from the States, it's urgent."

"Hmmm... Hold please," she said. I could hear bits and pieces of her conversation with Reed in the background. She came back to the phone. "Who's calling?"

"Meredith from Glasgine and Fitch," I said.

She repeated it to Reed. He recognized the name of his lawyer's secretary. "Meredith?" Reed said.

"You lying, cheating sonofabitch!"

"Un instant de la vie privée? Merci," he said to the whore in his room. A door slammed.

"How did you get this number?"

"Doesn't matter. How is Amsterdam this time of year, husband?"

"Whoever gave you this number is fired."

"That's all you're worried about?"

"I'm not doing this over the phone, Jennifer."

"Oh! Jennifer is it now? I married you. I gave birth to your children, and I'm not Jenny, anymore? Don't bother coming home. I won't be here."

"Don't start shit with me."

"Jesus. You've got to be kidding me!" I shouted. "How long has she been your mistress?"

"You're making assumptions."

"Oh, so it's a different whore every time you make a side trip to Paris? Three nights a month in the same hotel?"

"You're out of your mind," Reed said.

"You piece of shit. It's on your goddamn credit card statements. This has been going on for two years!"

"I come here to write."

"I'm not an idiot!"

"I'm not doing this over the phone," he said, sternly.

"You've taken everything from me. Our babies are dead. I can't even take an art class, yet you were sneaking away to Paris to sleep with some whore this entire time?"

"I've been under a lot of stress."

"Stress! You want to tell me about stress? You said there was no money. I had to ask your brother to pay for our sons' funeral. I hope it was worth it, you piece of shit."

"I forgot a few bills."

"You were with her two days before Hayley was born. Instead of coming home to help me plan the funeral for your boys, you flew to Paris to fuck her. I knew about the groupies, but I had no idea you were hiding a mistress. You have an entire life I know nothing about."

He didn't respond.

I burst into tears. "You're unbelievable, do you know that? I want a divorce. If you die on a plane, that would be a goddamn blessing. I hate you with every ounce of my being. I never want to see your face again. And fuck you if you think I won't take everything you own."

There was a long pause. "I'm tired, Jenny. I'll talk to you when I get home. I love you."

Click.

Chapter Twenty-Four

After scanning various bank statements, I found wire transfers to France coming out of his money market account for $15,000 a month. *Is he laundering money in case he's sued again?* I located assets he'd never mentioned.

I had to get a good lawyer and be gone before he came home. I'd never cared about his money before, but I wanted to make him pay. I needed an upper hand before he arrived in the States.

My cousin, Molly, agreed to pick me up along with my things, and take me to my parent's house.

Deciding what to take was excruciating. I knew if I left, I couldn't come back. It meant going into Haley's room, into the nursery. I could imagine some stripper or random French whore touching their toys and unworn clothes. Those were my babies. It was all I had of them. I found a box of photos of Hayley, her favorite stuffed animal and the pajamas she'd worn the morning before the truck killed her.

My doctor had given me enough Xanax to numb a football team so I could exist with these things. There were a few trinkets from the hospital. Storm's baby gown. Their arm bracelets. Birth certificates.

For the first time I was confident. I could leave. I had to. Molly said she would pick me up around six.

At 5:45, I heard the gate alert and saw a limo pulling around the driveway from the kitchen security screens. It had to be Reed—anyone else would have needed my permission to get past security. I ran up the stairs and collected the important documents I'd packed in the suitcase and put them in my purse. I zipped the suitcase and hid it in the downstairs laundry closet. Worst-case scenario, I could grab my purse and run.

I shook as I waited for the back door to open; not sure if I could hold myself together. He had lost weight, and dark circles shadowed his eyes. His shaved head and new tattoos gave him the look of a cancer patient. A tuft of dyed black hair growing in down the center still said rock n' roll.

"You're not talking to me? I dropped everything to come home and make this right for you."

For days, my head had filled with images of strangers' legs wrapped around his hips while our twins died. Now he sat here with black painted nails, and product in his little bit of hair—even in mourning he had to look good for the cameras at L.A.X.

The fingers on his bad hand were shaking.

"Charles said you've been running."

"God, stop talking. I want to know who she is."

"You want to talk about France?"

"I want the truth."

He shook his head. "It's gonna make things worse."

"Tell me."

He leaned back in his chair and scratched his head. "Her name is Chloé. She's a few years older than me. A journalist. We met about ten years ago, on the band's first world tour."

"And you happened to reconnect while I was pregnant with our daughter?"

"There's more to it than that."

"I'm all ears."

"It's a pretty big deal." He hesitated.

"Are you married to her or something? Tell me."

"That's not true," I managed to mutter. You couldn't have knocked the wind out of my chest any harder if you'd hit me with a car. I slid into a chair by the kitchen counter. The world was spinning without me again. It wasn't fair. I couldn't make it stop.

"It's true, Jenny."

"No."

"Chloé and I have a son together," Reed said again.

"DNA?"

"I haven't met him yet, but he looks just like me as a kid. She doesn't want me coming in and out of his life. I pay their mortgage and his school. I didn't mean for it to turn into anything."

"How old is he?" My skin was hot. I rubbed my chest, rocking in my seat. I was going to explode.

"He's nine. It happened before you and I met. I found out right before Hayley was born."

"And you couldn't tell me?"

"I didn't want to hurt you. All the shit we've been through, I couldn't do that to you."

"Don't even." I almost slapped him. "You slept with her while I was pregnant with Hayley?"

He thumped his forehead. "Jenny, how many times have we tried to have a baby, and something went wrong? Every time."

"I trusted you."

"I don't know why."

"You go screw her whenever you're feeling it?"

His teeth ground. "Yes. I go to Paris and spend a few nights with her playing house in that hotel. In turn, she gives me pictures and updates on the boy. How he's doing in school, things like that."

"And that requires room service and $4,000 bottles of wine?"

"Wow, you did some digging, didn't you? What can I say, the woman likes a good bottle of wine."

"Do you love her?"

"I enjoy her company."

"Answer the question."

"She doesn't tell me that she hates me and wishes I would die on an airplane."

"And I suppose for that courtesy, you don't rape her after she's almost bled to death in the ER?"

"I don't love her. I love you. Despite everything you've done."

"You're not blaming this on me."

His knuckles tensed and the vein in his neck pulsed. "I love fucking her if that's what you want to know. She saved my life this past year. I wouldn't be alive if it weren't for her."

"You OD'd in that hotel, and you lied and told me it was a tabloid story."

"I didn't tell you anything. I told my manager to make it go away and he did. And yeah, after Hayley and the boys—I lost it. I went there for comfort. It didn't work. I shaved my head. I put on an old Jim Morrison record and shot up all the heroin I could get my hands on. She came in our room just in time. She pulled me out of the bath, called 1-1-2 and stayed by my side."

"Am I'm supposed to feel sorry for you? You should've come to me for comfort, not some whore."

"She's my son's mother. But she means nothing to me. Not the way you do." He wasn't getting his way. He shrugged. "I like the way she smells. She's intelligent, successful. She has long brown hair that curls and tapers down the curve of her spine, eyelashes to die for, and she gives a phenomenal blowjob. She does this thing with her tongue—let's say they should teach it in American high schools because girls don't pick up on it here. At least, it's not happening in this house."

"This is over, Reed. I'm done."

I put my bag over my shoulder and reached for the car keys on the counter.

Reed grabbed my wrist. "You're not going anywhere. What's in your bag?" He tugged at the strap on my shoulder. "Give me the bag, Jenny."

I let him slide it off my shoulder. He pulled out our marriage certificate. The babies' birth certificates. There was an envelope with bonds I'd found hidden in his studio. "Not yours," he said, tossing each item on the counter. A small cloth bag held the engagement ring and expensive jewelry he'd given me throughout the years. "Definitely not yours." He threw the priceless Grace Kelly engagement ring over his shoulder into the floor, and dumped my bag upside down, shaking everything onto the counter. He rummaged until he found what he was looking for. "Bingo." He dangled a key in my face. "Did you think the bank would let you in that box without me?" He put the key in his pocket, opened my wallet, and pulled the small amount of cash I'd managed to save. He flipped through the credit cards and bank cards, one by one. "Mine, mine, mine." He slid the empty purse across the counter, and then looked me over, taking inventory.

He pushed my hair back, rubbed his finger across my collarbone, and touched the silver locket I was wearing. He'd given it to me as a gift after Hayley was born. It held her photo. He let it go. Certain things are sacred, even to monsters.

"Let me leave."

"You are mine, Jenny. Do you want me to stop seeing Chloé? I'll do it for you. You sure you want me here every night?" A threat. "You might as well stop looking at the goddamn gate camera—nobody is getting in or out of here tonight."

"I'm leaving you one way or the other. It doesn't matter."

"Little Jennifer Stone, leaving me?" he laughed. "Over my dead body. Go upstairs. You don't want me in French hotels, then find a way to occupy me, sweetheart. I've got a lot of free time coming up."

"Go to hell."

"What was that?" He laughed.

I snapped. "Reed, I'm serious. I am done with your bullshit. I was done with you the minute I walked into that abortion clinic on Sunset. I never should have married you. Not the first time. Definitely not the second. And I never wanted to have your babies." I shocked myself, hearing the words come out of my mouth for the first time.

Reed slapped me in the face so hard the back of my head slammed into the wall. His breathing intensified, as he rubbed his wrist. "You have five seconds to leave this room."

Stunned, I was afraid to move.

His voice did not waver. "Do you want me to close my eyes and count? Move."

I ran upstairs to our bedroom, locked the door, and sat with my ear pressed against the door listening for his footsteps.

Professional DJ speakers in every room of the house were linked to the sound system downstairs. When bands recorded in his studio, he could play the music throughout the house. Or, if he was particularly temperamental, he could blast a deafening 120 decibels. This is exactly what he proceeded to do for the next six hours, playing the same high-pitched demo with repeating notes. When the windows were open, you could hear this sound system a mile away. The walls vibrated. Hour one was a migraine. By hour six, it was psychological torture. I was in the bed with pillows over my ears, weeping.

Then the gunshots started.

I bolted out of bed. I wasn't sure if he was shooting inside or at targets outside, but there was a revolver taped under my nightstand. I pushed our heavy dresser in front of the bedroom door and waited another hour for the damn music to stop before braving my way downstairs.

You cursed this house
You cursed this family
YOU.
The magic & divine,
You're twisted (in) time (inside)

He'd spray-painted those lyrics across the giant canvas I'd painted that hung in the living room. *YOU.* was sprayed in large letters on the opposite wall.

Leaning back on the fluffy white rug in the living room with his feet propped up on the piano bench, Reed played solitaire with a pack of Bettie Page cards. The glass tabletop was shattered. A bullet was embedded in the expensive oak hardwood and another in the wall. There was a shotgun on the piano and five other guns of various makes and models lying on the floor around him.

"You motherfucker," I said. "Psychotic, asshole. I thought you were dead."

He smoothed the deck and gently sat the cards down. "Go to that pancake house on Irvine and Canyon. Get something to go—something hearty, like that loaded chili hash thing they do, all the toppings, lots of meat, stack it, cover it up, cheese it, whatever. Bacon, sausage, and a couple of eggs on the side, and whatever you want. My wallet is on the counter with all that shit." He looked at my bare feet. "Don't walk in the living room baby, you'll cut your little toes." He rubbed his red eyes. "Get the food and I'll get this shit cleaned up."

"What do you want to drink?" I was too terrified to say anything else.

Chapter Twenty-Five

At the diner, I managed a few bites of my hamburger, three fries, and almost choked while crying in my strawberry milkshake—totally freaking the server out. I took the long way back to the mansion. Only god knows why I returned—maybe I subconsciously knew you could only get so far in a leased car with half a tank of gas? Maybe people just need to eat. Who knows?

The living room carpet was vacuumed. No sign of his firearms or the broken glass. The kitchen counter was clean. Things he'd strewn across the rooms had been put away. The bouquet of flowers he'd brought home was inside a paper bag on the floor. My ring was on the counter.

I sat his food beside it. I'd worn sunglasses to the diner to cover the bruise he'd left under my eye. I kept them on so we wouldn't have to talk about it.

At the top of the stairs, the twin's nursery door was open. *If he's destroyed their things, I will kill him.* I ran, hard.

He was sitting on the floor, folding and packing their things into boxes, sliding them carefully into the closet. He took the framed paintings from their wall.

I burst into tears. Reed followed me, catching me as I collapsed on the floor, weeping. He put his arms around me, kissed my forehead and held me tight.

"It's okay baby. I'm so sorry," he said.

"You weren't here," I screamed.

He rubbed his finger across the bruise on my face. "I couldn't, honey. I'm sorry." He helped me up. "Come on babe, it's time," he took my hand, gently leading me downstairs. He buzzed security. "Can you send Marcus with the car?"

Marcus let us out at the gates of Hollywood Cemetery. Reed gripped my hand, and we walked the long path, past the place where we'd thought it was so cool to watch Halloween movies together, near the graves and tombs of Hollywood's great stars, never imagining our lives would become a horror story.

Reed had managed to secure two plots before we'd gotten married. "Nothing says forever like joint plots," he'd joked. Neither of us could have predicted those two plots would hold the bodies of three babies.

I bit back my anger that he hadn't even shown up for the twins' funeral. If he hadn't already owned those plots of ground, the boys couldn't be buried next to Hayley.

I let Reed go to the graves by himself. He carried the flowers from the trunk. Marcus stood with me, holding a black umbrella. He didn't comment on the bruise spreading out from under my sunglasses, and I didn't mention it. Visiting this cemetery was as routine as brushing my teeth.

This was the first time Reed had been since Hayley's funeral.

Marcus gave me the umbrella. "Nobody will judge you for going to him, Mrs. Reed. Nobody's here but the three of us."

"I don't want to."

"He doesn't deserve your forgiveness, but he needs it. If I lost either of my girls, I'd walk into the woods with my gun and never come back. My job description forbids me from caring, but I do. Go on. It's the humane thing to do."

Reed collapsed on his knees in the wet grass by Hayley's tombstone, crying so hard his entire body shook. He hadn't allowed himself to grieve.

Marcus was right; it wasn't in me to ignore that level of pain. I walked over and put my arms around Reed. Cold rain fell around us, like that fateful night he'd been on my doorstep in the rain. Emotion hit me hard.

I pushed away the fact this was my bastard, lying, cheating, abusive husband, and focused on comforting this father lying soaked and inconsolable in the cemetery grass. If nothing else was real, the groans of grief emanating from his body were. I knew, because I had felt them too.

Marcus helped me get him into the car, then inside the house and into a warm shower. His ribs were sticking out; he had cuts on his skin, and needle marks on his arms.

"I never thought Hayley would be born. Things went wrong so many times, Jenny. I called Chloé—to talk. She told me about my son. I went to meet him. It wasn't what she had in mind."

I couldn't stand to hear him speak of her, but he needed to get it out.

Our bedroom windows were deep set; you could curl up in them, have your morning coffee, sex, or whatever in the sun. We called them thinking windows. Reed stared, catatonic, out those windows after we went to the cemetery. He smoked but wouldn't eat.

I checked on him but let him feel this thing he'd avoided coming home to. I committed to being the better person, to help him get through this. I would leave as soon as he went back on tour.

I wouldn't try to have another conversation with him about it. I didn't know which Reed I'd be dealing with. Helping him through this would give me a little more time to have a solid plan. I would get closure, even if he never did.

After a phone call, Reed came downstairs on the verge of a mood swing. Have you seen someone look angry drinking a glass of milk? Milk is nice and cold, refreshing and it compliments cookies. How could that make a person angry?

I rolled his medication bottle across the counter when he slammed the milk jug into the fridge. He picked up the bottle, turned over the label a few times, tossed two pills back, and left the room.

Marcus came up from the gate and handed me a letter—his resignation. "I'm real sorry, Mrs. Reed. I can't keep doing this."

"Why? You're the only one—" I decided to be honest, because, dude knew. "You're the only one who kept him from beating the shit out of me on the road. So many times—if you hadn't been there to intervene—who knows what would've happened. Don't leave me."

"He asked me to get heroin for him," Marcus said. "It's one thing if he wants me to look away when he gets his dealer to stop by. He's not going to use the fact you trust me to pull something over your eyes. I'm here to protect people, not to be a weapon in this war. Please, listen to me, I've seen these domestic violence situations play out so many times. This is not over."

That was the first time another person referred to our "situation" as domestic violence to me. As if I was the victim. As if this thing was not a secret. It was something other people spoke of.

I wanted to say, "It's not that bad, it's not like he hits me." Except he had. We couldn't take that back. I'd convinced myself our other fights were mutual. This was different. Marcus knew I was in danger with Evan Reed.

"I'm sorry Marcus. It wasn't fair of me to ask you to stay."

Reed was asleep. I could've run. I could've escaped hell.

Instead, I poured myself a glass of wine, grabbed a blanket from the hall cabinet, and fell asleep on the sofa.

I could have left the next morning. My suitcase was in the laundry room. The car keys were on the table. His wallet was lying on the kitchen counter.

I could have left.

I should have.

I wouldn't get another chance for almost two years.

Chapter Twenty-Six

R eed came downstairs wearing a pair of black jeans, tugging on a white t-shirt.

"My label called. If I don't go out and do the remaining gigs on this leg, they'll pull the plug on the entire tour." He poured himself a glass of orange juice and rubbed his hand across his brow.

"You're not ready."

"Doesn't matter. The album was good, but it didn't meet sales goals. Without the shows to promote it, we'll owe back our advance. If they cancel the tour, I've put two-hundred hardworking people out of jobs for the next year. And—the band wants to audition a new singer. So…"

"What are you going to do?"

"I worked my ass off to get this album out. I've killed myself trying to promote it. We've got songs recorded that the label will own if I walk away. Songs I wrote for you and Hayley. They have the masters."

"You have to grieve your children." I said.

Reed rubbed his hand across his face. "I've got twenty-four hours to let them know."

"When are the next gigs?"

"Sunday night in Berlin. I'd have to leave by Saturday. Did you get the food I wanted from the diner this morning?"

"Reed, that was days ago. What day of the week is it?"

"Tuesday."

"Do you know today's date?"

"Not off the top of my head."

"What month is it?"

He looked like he'd been asked to solve a complicated algorithm.

"What year is it?" I asked.

"Well, of course I know the year," Reed said.

"Tell me."

"It's right there on my tongue."

"What is your birthday?"

He paused and shook his head. "Why are you asking me these questions? Of course, I know. I can't get to it."

"Honey, you can't handle an international flight on your own."

"What else can I do?"

"Go lie down. Rest. I know you don't want to hear it, but you need to see a psychiatrist before you go anywhere. And the specialist about your hands."

"They've been doing that thing again. They lock. I can't play guitar."

"I know. I'll make the appointments. Go to bed."

He passed out on the sofa for twelve hours. When he woke, he looked through the box of mail. I watched his fingers shake and lock up. He waited for the shaking to stop and handed me an envelope.

"Deposit this royalty check. Should catch us up this month."

For a brief moment, we were in real life—me caring for him, him providing for us both—living paycheck to paycheck in a three million dollar mansion. If we couldn't do this, with everything we had at our disposal, how could the rest of the world handle it? I glanced at my graffiti-stained painting on the wall. We didn't want it to work, it was as simple and complicated as that.

I watched him from the kitchen as he tapped his foot, counting notes, quietly singing, "Show me a sign..." He grabbed a pencil and notebook and wrote lyrics. In the middle of chaos and uncertainty, he pulled a number one song straight out of the ether. But he stayed awake all night and the next day working on it. Sounds magical, right?

"Will you go with me to Berlin?" he asked Friday as if it was a reasonable expectation.

"No."

"Seriously?" He was dumbfounded.

"We're living in different worlds. That didn't change because you came home. Certainly not for the reasons you came home."

"You're going to leave me? Knowing the stress I'm under? If I do those shows, that's all I'll think about." He scratched his cheek, tapped the paper he was holding on the edge of the fridge. "Okay. What happens between us if I stay home? Where does that put us?"

"God, Reed, I don't know." We'd hurt each other in so many ways. I'd managed to convince myself those incidents were mutual, usually my fault. He'd left bruises before—my legs, my arms. This time he'd slapped me in the face. And this mistress in France—I couldn't excuse it anymore. If I stayed, it would escalate.

"If I go to the first five shows 'til the break, can you promise you'll be here when I get home to talk this out?" His hands shook. "We were best friends. If this is over, that's the least you can do."

I looked at Reed like the bat-shit crazy person he was. "We are not friends. We're not lovers. You cheated on me with the same woman for two years.

You hid a child from me. You abandoned me when our sons died. I want to help you because you need to grieve, and because at some point in my miserable existence, I loved you. But when I said done, I meant it."

"No separation. You're asking for a divorce." Reed's neck tendons tightened.

My eyes flicked to the panic button out of instinct. I remembered Sasha's advice. *Don't take any shit from him.* "I'm not asking."

"We've been talking, sharing, exactly what you wanted. For nothing?"

"Reed, you need to face what we've been through."

"We? You didn't see her. I was inches away. Where were you? You could've been watching her. It didn't have to be me."

"I won't let you use our child's death as a weapon."

"I can't eat. Drugs don't work. Sex doesn't work. Being on stage is the only break I get from seeing that truck. It's the only place loud enough to drown out the sounds of those tires on the pavement."

I cringed. "Stop. Whether you stay here or go on tour, I'm leaving."

"I need you," Reed said.

"I don't care."

I lived by the kitchen island when he was home—it was the closest place to the panic button and the back exit to the driveway. I saw his 9mm Beretta in his back pocket when his shirt rose. It made me uneasy, but it wasn't unusual. Guns were always strewn about the house.

He'd taken me to the range to teach me, insisting I carry the small gun he'd given me as a birthday gift, which I'd immediately given to Marcus to unload. My parents didn't own guns, I'd never touched one until I married Reed.

Now I'd gone numb to the sight of them. I slept with my loaded .42 under the mattress when he was home. It didn't faze me to see him walk in the laundry room with an envelope full of drugs, and a handgun in his pocket.

He came out of the laundry room, sniffling, wiping cocaine from under his nose. He tossed the package on the counter. An unopened syringe slid out. *Yay for party pack variety-kits for violent sociopaths!* In his other hand, he held the small red suitcase I'd packed the week before.

Shit. Instinctively, I took my seat behind the island.

Reed's nostrils flared. "You're seriously going through with this?"

"I told you I was serious."

He opened the suitcase on the counter, rifling through the things I'd packed.

"Is that all you are taking with you?"

"It's all I need."

"You got somewhere to stay? Your art instructor?"

"You know that never happened. I'm going to stay with my parents."

"Without a job or car?"

"For now."

"Nah, you tell me which car you want and it's yours. I have a rental house you can stay in, or I'll get you an apartment in Hollywood. You're my wife, I'm not leaving you homeless."

"I'm not staying in California."

The cocaine kicked in. His eyes shifted, he steadied his hand on the counter. "There's nothing I can do?"

"No."

He walked behind me, kissed my neck, grabbed my hair and twisted it tight in his fingers. "Sure about that? Let's go upstairs and see if I can change your mind. Or see if you can change mine." He kicked my stool, knocking me to the floor.

I scrambled onto my feet, eyes darting towards the panic button by the kitchen door.

He pulled the security box off the wall and ripped out the cords. "Now!"

I ran upstairs.

Reed pulled me down, punching me, ripping my clothes. *Now you've done it. There's no panic button.* I managed to get out of his grip. When I got into the bedroom, I was trapped. He shoved me into the floor and locked the bedroom door.

"What's your instructor's name?" Reed shouted, pulling the Beretta out of his pocket, shoving in the clip.

"Why?" I mumbled.

"I'm going to kill him. But I'm going to kill you first." He crouched over me on the floor and smacked me across the face with the butt of the gun.

Darkness.

Pain shot across my face. Nose broken. My eyes were swollen so tight I could barely see him on his side of the bed, shooting up heroin. I prayed he'd overdose. He leaned back on the pillow and refilled the needle, then climbed on top of me. A tourniquet was tied tight on my arm.

I screamed, kicking and fighting against him. He pinned my arm, thumping it below the bend to get a vein to pop. I used all of my force to rise and shove him backwards. I managed to slide my left arm behind me, pulling out the .42 from under the mattress.

Trembling, I could barely hold onto the gun. "Let me go!" I screamed.

He came at me.

I pulled the trigger.

Nothing.

Reed jerked the gun from my hands. He pulled the slide and showed me the empty magazine. He'd taken the bullets. My last resort, my only means of protection, gone. He threw me off the bed, his rage more powerful than any high. He pulled me down the stairs by my hair, out the door, across the gravel driveway to the car barn.

My bare skin scraped against the doorway and gravel.

He tied my hands to a rail in the barn. I prayed he'd leave me there.

Reed came back with a can of gasoline.

"Stop, please, Reed. Please." He doused me with gasoline. I screamed. No soul for miles. *How did we get to this? From vodka and roses to lies and dead babies, French mistresses and heroin—now gasoline? He's going to kill me. There is nothing I can do.*

He pressed a cigarette between his lips, looking me in the eye while he opened a pack of matches. He struck each match, holding them in the air.

I watched them burn against his fingertips.

One after another.

Each time I expected to go up in flames.

Go somewhere else. You don't have to feel this. Think about your mother.

My heart was about to beat out of my chest. I couldn't think about anything but flames burning my flesh—trapped, twisting and turning like I'd seen in horror movies. *Face him. It's all you've got.* His pupils were wide, black. He saw what I feared—dancing flames, swallowing me. An end to our nightmare. *See me. See Hayley. See something.*

One match left. The orange flame flickered, moving towards his fingertips. I choked back my fear, hating myself for being weak. My voice would not stop screaming, straining my vocal cords.

Please let it end fast.

Reed lit his cigarette, took a draw, then pressed it into my neck, burning my flesh. "Next time you pull something like that, you'll be dead, do you understand me?"

I nodded, weeping hysterically, piss running down my thighs in relief. Gasoline fumes and Marlboro smoke burned my throat and nose.

He tucked the matchbook in his jeans pocket and walked to the house.

The rope was so tight I didn't even try to get free. I threw up from the gas fumes, crying until I passed out, crouched in an impossible position. All alone in the dark. *He'll be back again. I can't do this anymore.*

The gardener found me the next morning. After using garden shears to cut the rope, he put his coat around me, and pulled me into his truck. He didn't stop at the house or at security.

When I told him I couldn't go to the hospital, he took me to the police department.

And I lied.

On December 12, 1990, I lied to a grand jury and said I wasn't sure who attacked me at the mansion. I gave the police a description of a crazed fan who had previously made it past the gate. "Reed wasn't home."

The prosecutor was determined to get me to admit Reed assaulted me. She tried to force me into identifying him as my attacker. She tried every possible way to reason with me.

I repeated the same lie until she made me do it in front of a jury. Pissed off, she slammed her binder down and walked out of the courtroom. She was part of a team who would later attempt and fail to convict O.J. Simpson for murdering his estranged wife, Nicole Brown Simpson.

The police forced me to go to the hospital that night. They made me get a rape kit. I could have nailed Reed. Whatever shield I'd managed to put up against his manipulation ceased to exist that night. Once someone tries to set you on fire, you are not the same.

A driver waited with my suitcase and passport when I was discharged from the hospital. I had clear instructions. I was to take British Airways Flight 315 to meet the band in London.

I obeyed.

I looked through the suitcase and changed in the car. The doctor had removed the stitches from the bridge of my nose. There was a brand new collection of Estee Lauder makeup in a gold bag. I used the high coverage concealer to cover the remaining signs of the attack. Enough cash tucked in the passport next to my tickets to buy food, nothing more. My driver walked me to the gate. Escape was no longer an option. A newspaper was folded in the suitcase: *"Art Instructor's Office Ransacked by Intruder After Death Threats."* Reed had tried to kill me, and he'd threatened to kill someone else.

I'd show up to the London gig with a smile on my face and pretend I was happy about it. He'd done me a favor, right—letting me live?

The media fell for the story that an insane fan managed to cross the fence and attack me. When Reed had left the house that night, he didn't know if I was dead or alive. Once in Berlin, he'd called his accountant to have a million dollars transferred to an offshore account—planning an escape on the run, just in case. We were broke, all right!

In a strange way, I believed I had the upper hand. *He won't hurt me again if he knows all I have to do is tell the truth. I'm loyal, don't you see? You win.*

Our staff said they hadn't seen Reed in the house that night. The butler and the gardener—my only allies—quit.

As soon as he found out where I was, Reed's lawyers had swooped in to find out what I'd said. When it was clear Reed wasn't facing charges, he addressed the media. To the public, he was a concerned husband, discussing the attack as if it had happened the way he said it did.

His lawyers coached me on what to say to keep him from looking like a suspect.

"It's in your best interest. You don't have a prenup. You'll be on the streets." God, I didn't care. He would find me no matter where I went.

And he was fucking crazy.

Chapter Twenty-Seven

R eed kept constant watch over me on tour: searching my bags, monitoring my phone calls, what I ate and what I read. He had taken things too far—beyond anything anyone realized he was capable of.

We had this secret now. One that no one could ever know. I was incompetent. Crazy. No one else would ever love me. He locked me out of hotel rooms, screaming at me in front of his staff and fans. They did nothing.

The night I arrived in London, after the attack, security delivered me to a posh restaurant in Kensington. Reed sat across the restaurant with two women on each side and didn't acknowledge me. Things were different now. Jekyll was dead, only Mr. Reed remained. The monster was out. He no longer had reason to hide behind the guise of kindness. At times, he was twisted with something that resembled guilt—but it wasn't, it was something else entirely. The truth was out in the open. If my Reed had ever been real, he was gone.

Something strange was happening to my body—constant migraines, aches, and pains even when he wasn't hurting me. I hated him, but I desperately needed his kindness. *Please,* I begged night and day for some sort of mercy from him. He couldn't let me go—he couldn't have the world see our marriage was a failure. Like my paintings, I belonged to him.

He blamed me for everything. He would hit me at the drop of a hat, then spend hours begging me to forgive me. "Why did you make me do that?" *I was drunk. I was tired. It won't happen again.* One minute he'd hurt me, the

next he'd say he loved me. I was his wife, the mother of his dead children. I would show him respect or regret it.

"When the tour ends, we'll sell everything. Start over." He was trying to convince himself more than me. "We'll go to New York. It will be different. I can fix this." He would be unbelievably kind and romantic. Dinner, flowers, the whole show. But there was always an agenda. *Smile for the cameras. Put on the lingerie I bought you. Act happy.* Other nights he'd threaten to kill me if I left our hotel room.

Sex. Drugs. Sex. Drugs. I'd given up pushing him away. There were nights he pretended he wanted more

"God, what's happened to us, Jen? We used to be happy. In love."

"You raped me."

"I'm your husband!"

"You beat me, covered me in gasoline and left me for dead. You abandoned me when our kids died." I couldn't soften this for him.

He rolled his eyes. "You can't let that shit go, can you? You're so fucking weak. That's the one thing I've never liked about you." He poured himself a drink from the bottle on the bedside table. "I'm trying to have a serious conversation with you about our future. Hayley, the twins, it's all my fault, right? You slept with your art teacher. You made this happen. And you forget about your abortion—you cursed us. Killing that baby is what brought this hell on us, and you goddamn know it!"

"I have never cheated on you."

"Lying bitch. You know you fucked him."

"You need that to be true, don't you? To live with what you did to me?"

He pulled my hair. "Shut up!" He slapped me. "You did this. I wanted to tell you I was sorry tonight, that we can find a way to make this work, but you don't care." He pulled on his boots and walked out the door.

He came back an hour later, high, and sat at the foot of the bed. "I need you to forgive me. We'll start over. No lies. No drugs." He rubbed his thumb across my sore lip. "This is not how I meant tonight to go, not another fight. We're soulmates. I can't live without you." He pulled out his Beretta Px4 Storm and laid it on the bed next to his lap.

I took a deep breath, knotting my fingers in the bed sheet.

"Reed..."

"You know I don't remember the first six years of my life. It's a blank. I don't know who my dad was. I know he was a bad man."

I've waited for him to tell me his truth and I don't care anymore. That beautiful broken boy who'd confessed his darkest fears that night in my apartment had never existed. This was another ploy for my attention. *Fuck you. Hold me. I hate you. I need you.*

Reed waited for me to react.

Empathy was not in my wheelhouse anymore.

He lit a cigarette. "My stepdad used to beat the shit out of me. I'm talking beat downs in the kitchen. He dislocated my shoulder, broke my arm. My mother sat there—that fucking bitch. I walked in on him in my sister's room. She was ten years old, and he had his hands on her. I tried to stop him. He pointed a gun at my head, told me if I said a word, he'd kill my entire family. He called DHR to get me out of the house. See what I'm up against? I don't know how to fight fair." Reed touched my hair. "I'm not him. I need you to forgive me. You think I'm useless, I can't have that."

"We can't go back, Reed."

He put the gun in his pocket. "Then I'm going for a walk. Can you give the fans some peace about this? Tell Chloé's boy something nice so he'll know he doesn't have to turn into this."

"Get help."

"I told you the only thing that will help."

"Reed, I'm serious."

Maybe I should have latched onto that moment, but I couldn't handle the lies anymore. I didn't know if he was trying to get attention, or if I'd hear that gun go off in the alley.

He came back, like he always did, smelling of whiskey and sex. He needed me to tell him he was a good person.

And I couldn't do that.

The moody prince was now the monster king and the only things that satisfied him were sex and violence. He fought with fans, bandmates—walls. From then on, I was a portable punching bag. "I gave you a chance," he'd say and spit in my face.

One night a fan accused him of rape. Her clothes were torn. She left the hotel in tears. I wasn't surprised when the police showed up at our room.

"What happened to that girl?" I asked him.

"Go to bed," he snapped. He showered and changed before curling in beside me. When the police came back, he denied everything. He put on his jacket and jeans and offered to go to the police station willingly. "You can ask my wife, I was here all night." They didn't ask me. All they needed was his word. He walked over to the safe, took out a roll of bills, and gave them to the officer waiting by the door. He even took the time to sign an autograph.

"Get your bag packed, we're going to L.A."

"What the hell did you do?"

I'm not sure what took place in the hotel that night. No charges were filed. I was terrified of him, but I would have told them the truth. If they'd bothered to ask. It never made the press.

Then fucking Arielle Waters happened.

Arielle was a journalist known for her behind the scenes, tell-all celebrity interviews.

A few nights after Reed's narrow escape, his drummer was arrested on drug charges. During a tour bus raid, half the crew ended up in jail overnight. The tour was halted for another rehab stint for several band mates.

Reed had a bad-boy image—a violent past, his present filled with tragedy. He jumped when America's sweetheart offered to interview him. This was his opportunity to play good again. "It'll be good for the band. Can I trust you? She won't ask about the kids. I promise. Are we good? Take this," he said, putting a Xanax in my hand.

A film crew took video of the chapel where we'd first been married and followed us outside our mansion. We smiled and pretended we were in love for the cameras. Nothing could have been further from the truth.

Arielle made idle chit chat to get us comfortable, slowly leading into the questions she wanted to ask. It was strange to hear how outsiders analyzed us.

"How did you know Reed was the one, Jennifer?"

The look on my face in the video is priceless. I tried my best to remember the good details. "I just... did," I stammered.

"Was it love at first sight?"

"No. He was cocky. But charming. Persistent. He showed up on my doorstep one night in the pouring rain, and the rest is history." Literal history. *Done. Over. Fucked. Forgotten.*

"Were you affected by his fame then?"

"It wasn't part of our world. We avoided Hollywood."

"When did you know Jennifer was the one, Reed?"

"Is she?" He laughed. "I'm kidding. It was her art. I knew before we met that she wasn't like other women."

When Arielle got around to asking us about the kids, Reed stopped her. "That's not something we want to talk about."

"I can imagine it has put a toll on your relationship. Do you feel it's brought you closer together?"

"I haven't been able to be there for Jenny the way she needs me to be. I could go on tour, block things out and shut down my emotions. Being on tour is not the place for relationships. You take things out on the people who least deserve it."

"What about drugs and infidelities? Is there anything you want to set the record straight on?"

"I don't know any touring musician that hasn't had to deal with those issues at one point or another. Jenny has supported me and tolerated my bullshit. I'd never get through it without her."

"Jennifer, you were attacked in your home earlier in the year by a fan. That had to be terrifying."

For a moment, I considered screaming that it had been Reed.

He interrupted. "I blame myself. To this day, I regret not being able to protect her that night." The camera settled on his tattooed, cigarette-burned hands holding my soft manicured fingers. His giant silver skull rings made for a great uppercut. I wondered if Arielle or the fans watching knew that.

"Reed, you never talk about your childhood. Is there anything you think would help us understand you more as an artist? For such a dynamic personality, a large part of your life is shrouded in secrecy."

"My childhood was not good. It's made marriage—relationships—difficult for me. But despite everything, I think Jenny and I are the rock n' roll success story. Most people couldn't live through what we have and stayed together. That transcends pain and tragedy. We'll be together until we take our last breath. I'm certain of that."

"Can we expand on your childhood? Did you know your father?"

"I said no. We're done," Reed pulled off his mic and left the room.

After our interview, the vulture went to his hometown and sat with his mother. She contacted Reed's high school girlfriend and first wife for quotes. The sweet one hour interview was expanded into a two-hour expose on "Evan Reed: Rock's Violent Troubled Superstar."

Reed was blind-sided.

He had invited the crew to watch it air in a hotel conference room. Arielle's staff had recorded live footage of the band. Crew members were excited to see if they'd made it on TV. Afterwards, Reed planned to preview the new live VHS. He had no warning about what Arielle Waters had done.

On national television, the world found out Reed's mother was a former prostitute. He was the castoff sperm of a sadistic John and convicted child molester.

"Is this thing on?" His mother asked, adjusting her mic on a silk paisley blouse. A rotating fan blew the National Enquirer clippings of Reed on her brown paneled walls. She held a glass of iced tea in one hand, a Virginia slim in the other. "I'll tell you what I told his wife. Evan was a terrible, disobedient child. Possessed by demons."

I felt Reed's hand on the back of my neck, gripping tight. I closed my eyes. *You're dead now, Jenny.* He had no idea I'd talked to her. His fingers twisted in my hair; his nails dug deep into my skin. *Please, not here.*

Arielle continued. "Betty, is it true that DCFS took custody of Evan when he was ten because your husband Clem was abusing your children?"

Daniel ran into the conference room and down the steps to turn off the screen.

Reed raised his hand. "Don't."

Betty Williams flicked her cigarette. "Clem Williams was an honorable, Christian man. Reed gets his issues from his biological father."

"Police records show that you were arrested for prostitution and Clem went to prison for manufacturing methamphetamine. They claim you sold your son to his paternal grandmother. After she died, your son was found alone in his father's trailer during a police raid."

"What the fuck?" Reed muttered.

His entire life, Betty had told Reed that his biological father died in prison before he was born. She'd never told Reed the man's name. He'd had no reason to look into his past.

Arielle-fucking-Waters walked up that old man's driveway with a goddamn camera. On screen, a sixty-seven-year-old man, with Reed's blue eyes, asked her to go away. She persisted until he let her inside. He didn't want to be filmed. The cameraman focused on his trembling, drawn hands. A favor no reporter had ever extended to Reed.

Reed's face was dead focused on the screen. His skin had gone cold like marble.

"I never messed with any kids. I'm saying that right away." His father's thick accent was low and shaky. Subtitles ran across the screen.

"But you went to prison, you were tried and convicted with overwhelming evidence," Arielle said.

His hands shook harder. He stuttered, "T'was the devil. Wasn't me."

"Do you know who your son is?"

"Betty came around, bragging about five years ago. Showed me some pictures. But Betty was always a liar."

"Have you heard his music?" Arielle asked.

"Nah, rock n' roll is devil's stuff."

"Why was he removed from your home?" Arielle asked.

"Nuthin' happened. Some kids and adults at the school I worked at said things that weren't true. Betty gave that boy to my mother for four hundred dollars and kept swindling her. She died. The police arrested me and took that boy. I went to prison for twenty-two years. What's this about? He dead or something?"

Arielle thanked him for sharing his side of the story. *Thanked him!*

Arielle re-traumatized Reed on national television in front of his staff and bandmates.

The buffet table barely missed my head when it flew across the room. Then the chairs. One crashed into the projection screen, ripping it.

I ran after him. His plan at playing the "good guy" on TV had failed, but no one deserves what Arielle did that night. I banged on our door until he unlocked it and pulled me inside. This was more rage than Reed could handle. After throwing half the shit in the hotel room, he collapsed on the floor, had a panic attack, and cried.

Certain songs calmed him. I found my Walkman, gave him my headphones, and pressed play on Dire Straits "Sultans of Swing." I knelt, unbuttoned the top buttons of his shirt, and rubbed his arms, chest, and hands to calm him down.

He flexed his stiff fists. His affliction was hereditary. Not just his hands, but all of it. He'd been lied to his entire life; the monster that lived in his dreams was alive. Little in the world scared Evan Reed, but the rock star—the indestructible force—was terrified of a sixty-seven-year-old monster who lived in an old clapboard house in Kentucky.

"Get my kit. It's under the bathroom sink."

"I'm not giving you heroin," I said.

"Get my kit," he said again, then crawled across the room and tightened a tourniquet around his arm with his teeth. His fingers were shaking, and he couldn't get to his vein. His hand cramped like the old man in the video. He looked at me, child-like and terrified with panic.

"No." I shook my head. "I can't do that."

His eyes flashed with anger. Instantly, the child I'd seen was gone. Reed gritted his teeth and slammed the syringe into his leg. It wouldn't satisfy him. His mother had failed him again, and here I was picking up the pieces. Somewhere, there was some woman who'd loved Reed's father, and his father had still been a monster. While there had been a momentary crack in Reed's humanity, he was most definitely a monster.

I thought of our twin boys. Had their deaths spared some young girl in the future? Was there anything in the world I could've done to stop such hereditary madness from passing onto my sons?

Reed mumbled, "That fucking woman. Of course, I'm going to feel abandoned and lose my shit when you try to leave."

"I'm not going anywhere."

He kissed my forehead and rested his head on my chest. "Good, because if you left me, I'd kill us both."

Reed terrorized me and I still protected him. I spent the nights after shows checking the pulse of the man who'd covered me in gasoline and threatened to set me on fire. I put him in the bath at every hotel, washed his hair, and soaped his scarred and tattooed shoulders. I got him in his towel and into the bed. I watched him sleep after he shot up, to make sure he didn't smother in his own vomit.

People ask, "Why didn't you do something?" Have you tried to take a needle from a man who tried to kill you? Would you?

Reed eventually came around, and so did those fists I'd spent weeks massaging and injecting with steroids when he was so high, he couldn't see three feet in front of him.

I played my part, his ever-dutiful punching bag.

I let him inject me with heroin, sealing a trauma bond like no other. The release was amazing. For one moment I knew what it was like to be free from his violence, and the death of our children. I understood why addicts endlessly chased that first high. Violently ill the next morning, I swore I'd never touch the stuff again.

Chapter Twenty-Eight

If Reed stubbed his toe, he'd hit me. His tea wasn't warm enough before the show, he'd throw it at me. He pushed and shoved me in front of half the crew, then flat-out slapped me backstage before a show.

How had I ever judged Suzy Harlan? At least she hadn't been in denial.

I didn't go out looking for something to happen with James Alan, the lead singer of Death Tree. Their band picked up the co-headlining spot on the second half of the never-fucking-ending tour. Reed's instability was causing problems. A big name was needed to hold the ship together.

If I breathed in another man's presence, Reed accused me of cheating. After so many nights caring for him during his heroin binges, I got sick of waiting in hotel rooms alone. I found isolated spots in venues to hang out during shows so I could try to read the damn Terry Brooks book I'd picked up in London Heathrow. I read the same paragraphs, over and over. I would never know what happened with the elves and faeries of Shannara.

I'd managed to get halfway through the book one night sitting under a tent, backstage in Detroit.

James Alan was tall, thin, and wore a fitted black button-up shirt with short sleeves, black pants, and black military boots. He'd spent time in the gym; his arms and chest were defined enough that I could see them under his shirt. His skin had color—a healthy look you didn't see on the pale addicts on tour. He had cut off his long brown hair after a recent rehab stint.

I didn't recognize him when he poked his head in the tent.

"Nice and quiet in here. Mind if I join you?"

"No, it's fine." I hoped he wouldn't.

"Reading Brooks? Do you have *Magic Kingdom For Sale. Sold!?* It's my favorite."

"No."

"I'll grab it for you when I go to my dressing room. If you're into Terry Brooks, you'll love it."

He leaned over to show me a quote. The musky, woodsy scent of his cologne lit up my senses, his skin dangerously close to mine. Something I hadn't felt in ages—sexual attraction. And danger. It was hard to discern the two anymore. He flipped my pages, running his finger down a line of text. "That line is a lyric in one of our songs."

I could almost taste the hot sweat on his skin.

"I have to go..." I exited the tent with haste.

James Alan went out of his way to say "Hello," ask me how my day was, and what page I was on. "Enjoying the book?" He said he identified with the main character Ben Holiday's loss. He didn't explain, but Holiday had lost his wife and unborn child in a car accident. I had a feeling James and I had a few things in common. He asked what other writers I enjoyed and recommended a book of poetry. He always found a reason to sit and chat with me.

"I can't keep talking to you, James."

"You're afraid your husband will see you interacting with another human and go ape shit? I'm not worried about him, honey."

I sighed. *Another man who won't listen to me.*

"But you're worried. He doesn't own you, you know?"

"I know."

"If you decide you don't want me to talk to you, tell me. If you're doing it so it won't piss him off, that's not a good excuse for me."

In Seattle, James said, "That kid from Gn'R told me about this coffee place called Starbucks. He bought stock in it, must be pretty good. Walk with me?"

"I can't."

"You can go for coffee."

It sounded simple enough, right? I glanced down the venue hallway to make sure there was no one around who would rat me out. "I'm going to run to the restroom, and I'll meet you out front, if that's okay?"

"I'll wait here," James said.

"It's better if I meet you outside."

Getting coffee should not be a covert operation. It shouldn't. Knowing our way around a heavy metal crowd, we both wore baseball caps. He put on his nerdy, black-rimmed reading glasses. Instant civilians. It was a mile walk from the venue, so we had time to talk before reaching the café.

We grabbed coffee and a newspaper to go. Rain poured the second we walked out the door, and James Alan held the newspaper over us. "Let's wait here." He ducked under an overhang on the side of the building. Then leaned in and kissed me in the rain.

"Don't," I said.

"Because of your husband, or because you don't want me to? Tell me you don't want me to, and I'll stop."

My shoulders dropped. I wanted him to kiss me—what kind of person did that make me? Someone who craved attention, kindness? Or the useless whore my husband said I was?

We snuck away for coffee every day. He made me laugh. He made me feel attractive. Always managing to steal a kiss; behind an amp stack, inside elevators, any venue office with an unlocked door.

He had a little stubble on his chin but kept his cheeks and upper lip shaved smooth. I loved the scent of his aftershave; how soft his skin was against my lips and nose and the way his hands felt on my hips. Being near James Alan made me happy—or at least, happy adjacent. I didn't know that was possible anymore.

James convinced me to go to his hotel room during Reed's set. There was a lot of downtime on the tour and Reed was always off getting high with groupies or doing some promo thing. I didn't care about the groupies. If they were taking care of him that was one more time I didn't have to.

James Alan was married. I also didn't care. Normally I would have but it had been so long since anyone had been remotely kind to me. He and his wife were separated and living in different houses. She wouldn't let him come home until he'd been sober at least nine months. If they were "together" I couldn't have been with him, but there was enough wiggle room in the situation that I didn't care. I didn't have the strength to care. We were open. I didn't want him to keep any secrets from me.

"Are you going back to her?" I asked.

"I'm not sure. What are your plans for the next twenty years?"

"Don't say things like that. You have kids."

"She's a good woman. She deserves better. I've been a shitty husband for ten years. Not much better than the one you have. That's why I know you need to get away from him."

"Never going to happen. He's been nicer lately. I guess a certain someone has been putting me in a good mood, so my existence is not as annoying."

"I can put you in a really good mood."

"I bet." I smiled.

During sex with Reed, James was all I could think about. A love potion of Oxytocin and fear. James was strong but gentle in bed. While sex with

Reed had been good in the past, it had always been about him. Even when he made me feel like a million dollars, he wasn't doing it for me—he was doing it to get himself off. I couldn't think of a single time he'd gone to sleep unsatisfied. James was good at making me happy when we were short on time.

Heroin killed Reed's sex drive. Unfortunately, he could interchange the two addictions. Unless he was too high to get it up, he wanted sex at least once or twice a day, sometimes more. It was exhausting.

If I knew I was going to see James, I tried to think of some excuse, but that was rarely ever a deterrent. I dissociated. I thought about James.

One night, Reed said he was going to go find someone else to get off with. "You're like corpse."

He wrote a song about it. He wrote many songs about me that tour—the words bitch, cunt and whore came up a lot in his lyric book. I'd betrayed him. It was the damn abortion. The unforgivable offense. Who knows if things would have been different if that hadn't happened? Would it have been a happily-ever-after story if I'd had that baby? Or would he have randomly shot me in the head at some point for over-cooking his eggs?

If you find yourself in this situation, don't stick around to find out. You'll regret it. Trust me. Go. Get the fuck out.

I had avoided groupies in the past, looking down on them. But I began to see them as saviors. When Shay Leigh gifted me books, a hand-knit blanket, and a box of homemade cookies, I was grateful. Did she blow my husband? Yes. But she saved me from getting my face bashed in on more than one occasion. I was jealous of the groupies' sisterhood. They got to go home at the end of the tour. Many of them had been made promises—relationships, visits that would never be followed through on. One night when things were really bad, Shay Leigh just lay in bed next to me and let me cry.

"Oh honey," she said, brushing her hand across my cheek. If I hadn't already been sneaking away with James, I'd have slept with her in a heartbeat just to feel something. But it wasn't like that—for a brief moment I felt part of that sisterhood of women.

She wore these arm bands with long metal spikes and was never afraid to get in Reed's face. "You leave her the fuck alone, Reed!" She shouted at him in our room one night, pushing him against the wall.

"What the fuck are you going to do about it?" Reed pulled his fist back.

Shay looked like the chick from Mötley Crüe's "Looks That Kill" video. Wild black hair and thick Egyptian eyeliner. She tilted her chin and side-eyed him. "Do it. Hit me, motherfucker and I will end you." She made sure I was okay, and then she fucked him so I wouldn't have to.

She wasn't someone you wanted to cross. She'd spent a week with Jett Harlan before Suzy died. He made a million promises, then took Shay's boots and told everyone on his tour that she was a whore. So, she spray painted a note asking for her boots back on the wall outside his house and it stayed there for over a month while he was on the road. She signed her letters "Shay F*n Leigh" and ended all her sentences with little hearts. We would've had a lot of fun together if I wasn't scared of my shadow. She was smart, wild, and didn't take shit from anyone. She was also free. Something that was lost to me.

James and I walked by her in a bookstore wearing our baseball caps, and she looked the other way. If she ever suspected anything happening with me and James, she didn't say anything. In the end we were the same; both fucking two rock stars on the same night. I just had a piece of paper that showed Reed owned me and a key to his house.

Not all of them were as nice as Shay. Some were vindictive and possessive. The fans were worse. Vicious and rabid, they would do anything for a chance with the band. A girl punched her own sister to get past the line. They broke in our hotel rooms and stole our things. One fan made it out of our room with a necklace that belonged to my mother. Shay chased her down and brought it back.

James' fans were just as bad. I had nightmares of falling into crowds and having girls rip me apart. Some fans tried the gift angle—making me trinkets to remember Hayley by and shoving them in my face on tour. Expecting a thank you and a hug. Did they actually think I could fucking forget? Fans felt entitled to our attention and we didn't have anything left to give. Well-meaning or not, those teddy bears and photographs were triggering. Roadies bagged them up and dumped them in back lots. Reed doused them with lighter fluid, and we watched them burn.

If nothing else, we still had fire.

Reed's band were concerned about the things he did in front of me. Wives weren't supposed to be around all the time. They were worried I would tell their significant others what they were up to. They never asked if I was okay. They knew better.

Shay disappeared onto another tour, leaving me to deal with Reed.

I punched a girl one night because she said, "Who are you, lady?" Reed sent her away. While he might humiliate me and fuck thirty girls in front of me, he wasn't going to let them disrespect me. I immediately regretted it when he pulled me back into his orgy. I witnessed more sex those few months than most porn stars see in their lives. I couldn't take enough showers. At least if I was there, I could make sure he used condoms so he wouldn't bring back anymore disgusting STDs. No one in the rock world took condoms seriously until Freddie Mercury died of AIDS.

Fans said, "Jenny married him—she knew what she was getting herself into."

I can promise you, I did not know I'd be forced into threesomes with strangers. It's the same fishnets, short skirts, and eyeliner every night. The sweet, "innocent" ones, the ugly ones, the laughable tough girls that thought they were going to teach me a skill or two because it was little wifey's first time with a girl? Ha!

Bands had competitions to see how many girls they bed in one night, and what was the sickest thing they could get them to do. Those girls smiled, clawing their way to the front of the line.

I hadn't known I'd get an STD from my husband while I was pregnant. I hadn't signed up for that shit. Some "band wives" get off on sharing their husbands. More power to them.

If you and I happened to be naked in the same hotel room in 1991—you were a willing participant in rape, because I didn't want to be there. I had the scars and bruises to prove it.

James was not selfish. Every time we met, he asked if I was okay, he told me to let him know when to stop, and more than once he told me to lay back and enjoy myself. He kissed me. Told me jokes, put on his glasses in bed, and read to me. James became my "tour husband." Everything my real husband was not. I never told him how bad things were in those hotel rooms with Reed. Consensual sex seemed like a privilege.

James and I had conversations where he asked my opinion instead of telling me what it was. He was writing lyrics about something that happened in L.A.

"Who is Rodney King?" I asked, looking at his lyric book.

James looked at me as if I was from another planet.

"Reed hasn't let me watch the news since we've been on tour."

James' face dropped. "Are you kidding me?" He explained how cops had brutally attacked King in L.A. He quizzed me: "The UN sanctions against Libya? The Dead Sea Scrolls? Jeffrey Dahmer?"

"I have no idea what you're talking about."

From that point forward, we always watched a few minutes of CNN, and he'd make sure to slip me his daily newspaper before he went on stage.

That's fucked up, right?

It wasn't that I didn't want to know what was going on in the world; I wasn't allowed. The two hours Reed was on stage, doing press, and screwing groupies were the only chance I had to escape the vacuum he'd created. We ate what he wanted, we watched football games, we did drugs, women—everything, his way. How could I watch the news when I couldn't even think without his permission?

James and I only argued once—he'd seen bruises on my arms. We'd talked about it. He knew I was afraid of Reed. It made him furious, but I made him keep quiet. One night we were in bed, kissing, laughing. He moved my hair and saw bruised fingerprints on my neck where Reed had pinned me against the wall and choked me.

James jumped out of bed and pulled on his clothes.

I held the sheet against myself, self-conscious.

"What are you doing?" I asked frantically.

"I'm going to beat his ass."

"You can't. He'll know I was here. Please don't," I begged. I couldn't lose my time with James. It was the only thing keeping me sane.

"I'll tell him about us. I don't care. This is done. He's not going to hurt you like that."

"And then what?" I asked. "Are we going to ride off into the sunset together? You're forgetting something—you're a married man, James. I'm not worth throwing that away. And what, when he walks out of that dressing room with a gun—which he will—then what? Are we going to draw straws over who he shoots in the head, first? Because he's that crazy."

"I'm not afraid of him," James said.

"I am."

He calmed down. "I won't say anything, for your sake. But the first chance I get, I'm kicking his ass."

I was terrified and comforted. For once, someone was willing to defend me.

Reed had no concept of consequences. If he found out I was cheating he'd kill us both. I tried to slow things with James after that, but he wasn't having it. We didn't always have sex, sometimes we'd lie in his bed, kissing, and watching TV. He booked his room on a different floor from the other bands to keep things safe. He volunteered DeathTree to go on first as many nights as possible so that everyone was at the venue when were together at the hotel.

One night, Reed made a comment about James' performance as James was leaving the stage. James punched him. Reed hit him back and busted his lip and they got into a fight backstage. It took four security guards to separate them; three of them to pull James off Reed.

James spit blood at him and shouted, "You need to get the balls to fight men instead of beating women."

Reed went on and played an adrenaline-infused set. His shows were best when he was angry.

James came back to the hotel after the fight and pulled me out of my room into his. I rubbed his cracked lip, and he lifted me onto his waist as soon as we were inside his room. I never came so hard in my entire life. He'd physically defended me when no one else besides Marcus had said a word to Reed about how he treated me. It turned me on, in ways I can't describe. Hotel guests made multiple calls to the front desk to complain.

Later, a woman in the elevator asked me if I'd heard a woman and man screaming down the hall.

"Fighting?" I asked, hoping she wasn't talking about me.

"Hell no, they were screwing so loud I thought the damn wall was coming down."

I laughed.

I was out of breath when I went back to my room. I waited for Reed to come back after his set. He was pissed about the fight and spent the night drinking, getting strip club blowjobs and almost missed the bus. *Small blessings.*

My relationship with James Alan was dangerous. It had to end, but there was a part of me so desperate to be out of Reed's control that I couldn't stop myself.

Tensions on tour increased. During a joint press conference, Reed referred to DeathTree as, "the opening act that can't get their shit together enough to warm up the crowd."

A reporter asked, "Are there any conflicts backstage?"

James said, "The tour is going great, just some no-talent singers creating distractions by beating the shit out of their wives."

Reed laughed the comment off. It was printed as "James Alan referenced domestic abuse occurring backstage as a distraction on the tour." Not calling Reed out. The rock press was wrapped around his finger. They adored him.

There was one month left on the tour—fifteen shows. James kissed me and said he loved me.

"Don't say that."

"I mean it. If I tell my wife I'm not coming home, will you leave Reed?"

I didn't know what to say.

"Will you think about it?" James sighed. "Do you love me?"

I nodded, too afraid to say it out loud.

"You have to leave him, Jenny. Even if you don't want to be with me, get away from him. I'll help you, whatever you need."

I flashed back to the barn, the cigarette, the matchbook Reed carried in his wallet—a sick souvenir to remind me to stay in line. I couldn't let James get involved.

"He'll hurt you. You don't know what he's like. It's so much worse than you know."

"I've been that dick, Jenny. I've been in that dark place Reed is not coming back from. He's too far gone. I'm not going to sit back and wait for him to kill you. I want to be with you, but more importantly, I want you to be safe. I talked to my lawyers and the record company—if he keeps pulling antics, I can have him kicked off the tour by next week. The label is already talking about which bands we can bring on to save this disaster of a tour. I'm sure I can piss him off enough to get him to go on a tantrum.

Give me a week. I can get you out of this. For good. You don't have to be with me but let me help you."

"What can you do? He doesn't let me out of his sight when he's off stage."

"Exactly what we do now. DeathTree will play the first set. You come to my room and stay until we get it sorted out. He won't know where you are. I'll get him off the tour one way or the other, and you stay with me on the road 'til the next town and we'll get you somewhere safe from there. No strings attached. I've got the money, you say the word."

I looked at the clock. Reed's band had taken the first set that night. "I need to get back to my room. He wanted me to have sketches ready for his new album artwork tonight. I haven't listened to the demos yet."

"Will you think about what I said?" James asked.

Chapter Twenty-Nine

I stopped at the snack machine for a Coca-Cola and bag of Fritos before walking down the hall to my room: #608. I paused at the door, shaking. I'd never be able to do what James was asking. *Could I?* It was my time to lady up and get the fuck out. He offered me freedom. *Reed fooled me too.* Could I get my smarts about me and escape? *I'll consider it, but not tonight,* I thought as I slid my key into the hotel room door.

I dropped my soda and bent over to pick it up. When I rose, it was a slow-motion nightmare.

I was about to die.

Reed sat on the bed in his stage clothes, his boots crossed. He was holding a book—*Magic Kingdom For Sale—Sold!* by Terry Brooks. No doubt reading the notes James had left for me in the margins.

I dropped my soda again. And the Fritos. Which sucked, because I was about to die hungry.

Why didn't I run? My foot was already in the door. I knew he would follow me. I didn't want him to hurt anyone else. *He has no concept of the word consequence.*

Coffee shouldn't be that complicated, right? *He knows it's not about coffee.* It was not about coffee or the Terry Brooks book in the corner of our hotel room, ripped to shreds. It was not about the man who bought the damn coffee and wrote those beautiful notes in the margins of that goddamn book. It was not the dripping of the faucet. It was not the bottle of soda and bag of chips I dropped when I opened the door and saw Evan Reed sitting on the bed, staring at me, his leather rock star boots propped up on the comforter. He held that book, the one with the marred edges and the love notes underlined in a code far too easy to ascertain.

Page 42, line 9. "I"
Page 88, line 12. "Want"
Page 108, line 15. "You."

I didn't need Terry Brooks. My Magic Kingdom was already sold.

"Close the door, Jennifer," Reed said. "Lock it."

I obeyed.

"Where have you been?"

"I went to get a snack. Why are you here?"

"It takes you an hour to walk down the hall to the snack machine. You're really going to pull that?"

"I went for a walk."

He smirked. "Anything you might want to get off your chest, dear? Got any big secrets heavy on your heart?"

"Aren't you supposed to be onstage?"

"Well, it's a funny thing. I had a scratchy throat, thought I'd come back for some hot tea, let the other band go on first. And it's kinda fucked when no one can find the co-headliner's lead singer. Apparently, that's a thing lately—he tends to ditch his duties backstage after his set, and barely makes it on time to go on stage the nights they play last. I heard a roadie tell their manager he saw him talking to "that lady Jennifer" at the hotel about some book. And shit clicked. I mean, you think you could trust a bitch to read a goddamn book."

"You know they have better tea at the venue," I said.

"Come over here. Now."

"And if I don't?"

"Trust me, bitch, you don't want me to come over there."

I walked over to the side of the bed, staying out of his reach.

"Get undressed," he said.

"No."

"Alright. We'll do this the hard way."

He rose from the bed, grabbed my hair, and pushed me across the room into the bathroom. He shoved me to the floor and ripped at my clothes. My head hit the tile. He was on me with the speed of a vicious animal. His hands gripped my neck like the mouth of a rabid tiger, slamming my head into the floor, over and over. My blood splattered against the tile, and I knew—this is how Kaley felt when Michael pulled her out of that bathtub, dying. I grabbed Reed's arm, digging my nails into his skin, trying in vain to fight him off. The rhythmic pounding of his fists reminded me of the chorus to The Misfits' "Die, Die My Darling." *This is all he needed. One excuse to send him over the edge.*

Reed jerked my limp head to face him. "How many times?"

I tasted my own blood. It ran down my lips, burned the back of my throat. I wanted to hurt him. "Every time you fucked me, I thought about him." Those were the words that would set me free. Would end this once and for all.

Fists. Parts of me cracking inside like sticks. I closed my eyes and waited for sweet death.

My spirit floated high, outside my body and away from Reed's rage. I'd never see James Alan again. I'd never see my mother and father. I'd never drink that damn Coca-Cola that had rolled out into the hallway.

Never would I quench the thirst for the things I'd longed for and been denied—love, my art, safety, security, my babies. I'd never know what happened to Ben Holiday. Would he rescue his friends from The Underworld, Abaddon? Would the King of Landover restore it to its former glory?

I had the sensation of flying. Had I found the dragon Strabo on my own, without the mind-controlling lo-Powder?

I heard the crack when my head hit the marble sink. A white explosion of light behind my eyelids, then sweet darkness. Finally. For the love of life, I was dead. I had to be.

But that would be grace, right? Oh, no. I wouldn't be blessed with death. Only the brief reprieve from torture that unconsciousness allows.

But death? Nah. Not for this girl.

Have you seen one of those movies where someone is tortured for so long, they forget what planet they're on? Reed never went on stage that night. I count those missing hours a blessing.

I wanted my mother. Because I knew it was finally over. Instead, Kaley came, whispering for me to follow her into the woods. *It's just a little farther*, she called me away from the living. Heat, something hot, scalding my skin brought me back—*he's lit the match. He's done it.*

I woke, naked in the hotel shower, watching as my own blood and thick saliva dripped from my swollen lips and swirled down the drain. I pressed my palm against the tile to brace myself. Water washed across the sharp stone pressing into my flesh—my tooth. *I have to get out of here*, Kaley thought. *Get out of the water, make it to the door.* Except, I wasn't Kaley. She was in my head—*or am I in hers*? The Rainbow. Michael. The Freezer. The Armani kit—the one with the good needles. The one that matched—no. Not his. You're mixing it all up, Jenny. Except I wasn't, was I? He had her keychain, the lucky rabbit's foot. Maybe he followed her home. Maybe he filled the needle and gave her something too strong. *Addicts are creatures of habit, Jenny.* The tourniquet. The ritual. The sound of skulls cracking porcelain. He's reliving the things that happened in that trailer with his father. *My legs trembled, like a newborn fawn trying to grab her footing.* Not the trailer. The white house with the eviction notices blowing in the wind. I was too dizzy to stand. *He knew you. He found you through Kevin and Kaley. You. That rabbit paw; worn purple fur gripped in his hand. Her father won it for her from a change machine on an Indian reservation. This freezer is so cold, Jenny.* Nails scraping against bathroom tile, breaking.

"I need you to stop," I mumbled through gummy saliva and blood. My body recoiled in pain when I tried to move. Darkness. Out again.

The faucet was turned off. A towel was placed on the burnt skin on my shoulders. "You can't stay here. You need to leave." A husky man with Suit's eyes tugged at me. *Maybe I never made it home from the Rainbow. Maybe I never made it home from the gallery.*

Hayley was real. Big trucks that run down babies and spill infants from mother's wombs are real. Blood poured from the wound between my legs, why not? It was pouring out everywhere else.

"You can't stay here," the man said, pulling my corpse out of the bathtub and down the hall to the freezer. He nudged me with the silver toe of his cowboy boot. His Texas accent, strong and nasal. *What about the medallion? Subduing the demon? Where is Ben Holiday? Where is James Alan? Isn't someone going to save me?* He said he couldn't help me if I wasn't willing to help myself. *Where is he now?* Gone, like a goddamn Rolling Stone. *Baby, I'm a fucking hurricane.*

"Should we call an ambulance?" A blurred figure in the corner said. The voice moved nearer. I could make out a maid's uniform.

Oh no, oh god no. I'm in that house on the hill!

"We'd be shut down if we called the cops every time a band left a hooker like this. Get her out of here. It's not our problem."

Hotel guests had called the front desk hours earlier about a woman being murdered on the sixth floor. The staff laughed, writing it off as rock star antics.

The maid put her hands on my naked shoulders. "I'll get you clothes from my locker. Don't move, okay?"

Moving wasn't an option. My vision blurred and my ears rang. I cried. The maid helped me into her clothes. Hotel security dragged me to the lobby to set me outside and let me die in the street. The men in charge thought I was a sex worker; they treated me like garbage. They catered to the animal who'd done this to me.

And there he was, walking into the hotel entrance.

God, no. It was daylight out. The bands and crew had left for the next town.

"There's your husband, Jenny." Kaley Dean stood four feet to my left, applying purple gloss onto her frozen lips, her face cracked glass, black nothing spilling and oozing down her.

Reed was holding a McDonald's bag with his bandaged, tattooed hand.

"Everyone's gotta eat," Kaley said.

"Oh god, what happened?" Reed ran over.

"Do you know this woman, sir? We've been trying to get her out of the hotel for the past hour."

"She's my wife. You were gonna throw her out?"

The man stammered. "Well, um—we thought you had checked out and that she was an... um... you know never mind..."

"Someone broke into our room last night. Honey, did you forget we changed floors? Babe, what happened?"

"Should we call the police? An ambulance?" the hotel manager fretted.

"No, no. It's my crazed fans. We've got a doctor on staff. We'll call the police from our room. I want to talk to your boss tomorrow. You were going to put my wife out on the street in this condition? What kind of place are you running?"

"I'm truly sorry sir," the man apologized repeatedly as Reed led me into the elevator.

My husband looked at me when the elevator closed. "Nice pants, sweetheart. You starting your shift at Burger King when this is over?"

Kaley leaned towards the elevator wall, running her blue fingers around the numbered buttons. "He's right, you know. You look like shit."

As the elevator slowly went up, I had flashbacks from the shower, moments of violence. His teeth. Fists. I didn't need to remember to know I'd been raped. My body burned from inside out. He'd held me under the scalding water to "wash James off" of me.

"This is my stop," Kaley said at the seventh floor. Her face merged with Suzy Harlan's for a moment. "Don't say I didn't warn you."

"Don't leave me," I mumbled, afraid to be alone with Reed. Dead Kaley walked through the closed metal elevator door.

Reed led me to his new room. I sat on the hotel bed, head spinning, and watched a six foot tall, blonde stripper walk out of the bathroom shower into the bedroom. *Dead babies. Strippers. Hooker girl in the bathroom floor.*

"I would like to call my mother," my voice said.

The stripper barely glanced in my direction. "Did you get breakfast, babe?" she asked my husband.

"Yeah. And some company. You have something she can wear?"

"I would like to call my mother," I said again.

The stripper looked through her bag and brought me lace underwear and a tank top. "Sorry hon, I don't think my other stuff will fit you. I've got a little black hoodie over there on the back of the chair. You can have that."

My head pounded, my body tremored my arms shook so bad—I was freezing.

The stripper nodded towards the bathroom. "Why don't you go in there and I'll help you clean up."

Reed flipped on the TV and nudged me with his boot heel. "Go."

I had to hold onto the bed. The stripper helped me into the bathroom. She didn't close the door. She had me sit on the toilet seat and tended to my face.

"Will you call my mom?" I cried. *I need to tell her I'm dying. I need to tell her I'm sorry for everything.*

"Honey, I'm going to give you a cold washcloth." The stripper leaned closer. "There are painkillers in the bottom of my bag. You put two of those under your tongue and I'll get you something to drink." A puff faced monster stared back at me from the mirror. "Here, this will help." She opened a container of white powder inside her makeup case. "Rub the coke on your gums and it will help numb you, okay? I'm going to get him to take me to work. I'll keep him occupied, try to rest."

My cocaine-laced, cracked fingernail slid into my empty gum hole. *There, there.* My missing tooth was in the front pocket of the maid's khaki pants. It was my tooth. I wasn't leaving it behind. My monster face was unrecognizable. I was relying on the kindness of the stripper in my husband's hotel room.

"You need to take her to the hospital or she's going to die," the stripper said.

"Move. You're interrupting the game," Reed said.

"Can I bring her something for the pain? I can get morphine before my shift."

He must have agreed. An hour later, I was entering a dream space and my pain was floating away.

When they parted ways, he asked if he could call her when he was back in town.

"Not after this."

But she didn't call the police, an ambulance, or my mommy.

Snitches get stitches.

We slipped out of the hotel in the middle of the night, to where a rental car waited for Reed and me in the parking lot. A few miles outside Dallas he pulled over to a service road. He slowed at a stop sign and touched my side.

Wincing, I drew away. My rib was cracked.

"Jenny, I'm sorry," Reed said. We were so far beyond sorry. "When we get home, it'll be different okay? We'll never talk about this again, understand?" He squeezed my hand tight, hurting my fingers. "DO YOU UNDERSTAND ME?"

What happens in Texas, stays in Texas. I nodded.

"I'm taking you to the hospital."

He turned the car engine on and pulled onto the service road. He drove several yards before braking and reversing. I assumed he'd missed his turn. The rental car lurched forward as he pressed the gas pedal to the floorboard.

A wooden sign at the end of the street read: *Woody's Bar and Grille—Get Your Fill.* The car tires squealed, glass shattered. The Woody's sign burst through my side of the windshield.

After several minutes, Reed woke in a daze and leaned forward. "You okay, Jenny?"

I was so sore, I couldn't feel anything new. "I'm okay."

"That's a shame, darling." Reed curled his fingers into my hair and slammed my face into the dashboard. I heard my nose crack. The TV cord connected to my brain popped, knocking my lights out.

I woke in an E.R. outside of Dallas, hearing my injuries were the result of a car accident. Reed told the press that this "accident" was the reason the tour ended.

The hearing in my left ear was permanently damaged. The doctor told me if my broken rib had moved a quarter of an inch, I would be dead.

Reed had minor injuries.

And that already-bandaged hand from where he'd almost bludgeoned me to death with his fists.

I never saw or heard from James Alan again.

Death Tree kicked Reed's band from the tour. There was a rumor Reed had a hit out for James. Reed won a little sympathy with the fans since his wife was injured in a car accident, but not much. He talked about the accident as if it were real. He could say this happened—and there it was.

No one questioned him. God help you if you did.

Chapter Thirty

I don't remember the months following the "accident" and Reed's exit from the '91 summer tour with DeathTree. I blocked out whatever happened after we returned home to the Malibu mansion. It's probably a good thing. Continuous blackouts from the husband-inflicted head injuries plagued me. I don't think Reed cared if he killed me, but one more punch in the face might be the last. He wasn't letting me go out that easy. If you'd shown me a picture of James Alan, I wouldn't have recognized him. I couldn't remember his name or why Reed had hurt me. Some days I believed the accident story. I wanted to.

Reed's shoulder had never healed properly from Hayley's accident. His hands bothered him. He quit heroin cold turkey at home instead of rehab. I'm sure someone looked after him. I was in no shape to help. Between the pain medication and head injury, I was lucky to string a sentence together.

Reed sent me to a neurologist. The neurologist sent me to a psychiatrist. My entire body shook. I couldn't complete simple tasks. Scans showed an untreated skull fracture, most likely from the marble countertop of the hotel bathroom. The inflammation of my brain trying to heal itself caused a secondary brain injury that almost killed me.

Multiple seizures led me to the ER again. Cedars-Sinai used an intracranial monitor to release the pressure. When that didn't work, I had to have an emergency craniotomy.

My life became a series of MRIs and CT-Scans. After the pressure on my brain was released, and the doctors patched me up, the shaking still didn't stop.

The neurologist wrote it off as a symptom of the brain injury. "Give it time," he said.

The psychiatrist said it was a classic sign of severe post-traumatic stress disorder. They didn't want to release me from the hospital, but Reed insisted we had in-home nursing care.

We didn't.

The outside world was non-existent for me. By the end of 1991, Freddie Mercury of Queen had died tragically from AIDS. A wave of panic swept through the hard rock community. A little band from Seattle, Nirvana, released an album called *Nevermind* and everyone lost their shit.

Reed loved and hated that album. It meant the end of an era. Luckily, his music had more staying power than most of the hair-sprayed bands of the day. He was over the guitar solos and '80s arena sound his fans loved.

Nevermind changed the playing field. In the summer of 1992, Nirvana would play a snippet from a track called "Rape Me" on the MTV Music Awards. Kurt Cobain started a feud with Guns N' Roses' singer, Axl Rose. Turning down a tour with Gn'R, Cobain said, "Rebellion is standing up to people like Guns N' Roses." The new guys were challenging the giants.

It was too late for some of us.

Reed considered the megastars of rock beneath him. He said, "I can shit out a better song than most bands are writing." While that may have once been true, times were changing. Rivers of black-tar heroin and tainted cocaine flowed through the streets of Hollywood, taking out members of Reed's inner circle left and right. His rhythm guitarist overdosed and was declared clinically dead for two minutes. That incident got him in check.

Sobriety was different this time. It wasn't the same man looking out of the mirror. He had fractured another person's skull—that's some serious shit, right?

James had been right, Reed was so far gone he wasn't coming back. We spent days in the house in silence, not saying a word to each other. Each trying to heal our wounds. One of us more damaged than the other—and I don't mean the one with the head injury!

The psychiatrist tried to help me through the PTSD symptoms. It's hard when you wake up every day staring at your trigger. Memories came in waves, then disappeared again. There were days I forgot about the babies—they were missing from my brain. *Small miracles.* This completely freaked Reed out.

He retreated into his studio, only coming out to make sure I'd had my meals and medication. He wrote a beautiful album about loss, remorse, regret, and betrayal (with a sadistic 10-track B-side demo he'd planned to set aside in the vaults for a few years). If I'd heard the new album and didn't know him, I would have fallen in love with him; his voice and the melodies so strong.

But now his voice terrified me and sometimes I couldn't remember why. I had never-ending migraines. One day my vision went out. He held me during a seizure, and we waited for yet another ambulance. Another day I forgot who Reed was.

Then I remembered.

And freaked the fuck out.

More tests. Another surgery. More medication. Rest. Recovery. After six months, the seizures slowed to a handful a month. As soon as my doctor gave the okay for me to fly in January 1992, Reed booked flights to Barbados. The place we'd loved so.

My doctors had encouraged me to paint. It would help my hand-eye coordination.

It looked like something a small child scribbled onto canvas. It was frustrating to be unable to get my hands to do what they created for. The beach helped. The waves, the birds, the sun and slow pace were a contrast to life on the road, and our house of terror.

Reed asked if I remembered the car accident. I told him no. And I didn't. He asked me about DeathTree and if I remembered James Alan.

"What's a DeathTree?" I asked.

Then the Rodney King trial and L.A. Riots happened on April 29, 1992. As we watched L.A. burn below us, I remembered everything.

Chapter Thirty-One

In late May of 1992, the band DeathTree released a track called "Riot!" about the atrocious racist police beating of Rodney King, and the injustices that followed. Singer James Alan said he'd written the song during the '91 tour while watching news coverage alone in his hotel room. He'd waited to release the song until after the trial, adding the last line after the verdict was read.

> *56-baton salute–No one will forget the atrocities of white men from Dallas to Los Angeles. Does that thorn of crowns sit heavy on your head, white boy? Nobody believes it was an accident. Whether it happened in Dallas or Los Angeles, Nobody believes it was an accident [Riot! Riot! Riot!] Let it all go up in flames.*

I didn't tell Reed I remembered Dallas. I pretended to forget things and made notes. I told my mother I was going to send myself letters to her address but not to open them unless it was an emergency. I wrote every detail I remembered from my time with Reed in case I became so injured that I forgot again. I wrote witness names, dates, times and places he'd hit me. When Reed wasn't looking, I searched his Rolodex and planners for names, phone numbers, and addresses; wrote them down, put them in an envelope and dropped in the nearest blue box. I asked doctors for duplicate copies of receipts and records. When I ran out of stamps, I'd tell Reed I'd lost them somewhere in the house, and he'd give me a few dollars to buy more. I told him I was having trouble painting three-dimensional objects and asked for a Polaroid and film so I could capture the things I wanted to paint.

I spent every waking moment in my art room, drawing and painting, trying to re-learn basic lines and shapes. Aside from a shaky brush stroke, I eventually made headway.

When Reed wasn't looking, I wiped away my terribly applied makeup, stripped to my underwear, and took photos of the scars he'd left on my body. I separated my hair and photographed my brain surgery scar. When he was outside, I took photos of the damage he'd done to our home. Most of it was patched over but some spots remained. He'd moved the guns. It wasn't safe to let a woman with a brain injury—especially one you tried to kill—near a gun. I took photos of things that belonged to our kids and trinkets. I took two photos of everything. One set I hid in an envelope inside a vent in the house and the other I mailed to my mother, writing *"Save for Jenny, DO NOT OPEN"* on the envelope.

I created art to rebuild the mental strength I'd lost, putting everything else out of mind.

After a while, Reed noticed that the work had come together.

"I need to draw you," I appealed to his ego.

"Okay."

He enjoyed the attention and let me take Polaroids and sketch his body. I documented every scar, mark, and tattoo on his skin. He'd sit in my art room playing guitar. It took everything in me not to shout at him that I remembered the truth.

I painted so many portraits of that goddamn man. I took Polaroids of them. Kept a copy, sent copies to my mother. *"Do Not Open. Save For Jenny"* I wrote again.

My mother was aware of the accident, but she had no idea about the abuse or extent of my injuries. She bought a safe to store the letters.

"Jenny, tell me what's wrong," she pleaded.

"I can't."

Maybe Reed was going to kill me someday, maybe he wasn't. Either way, I created a paper trail so someone could find my body and put him away for good.

I had thousands of Polaroid photographs and hundreds of sketches and paintings of Reed by the end of the summer. A magazine editor stopped by the house to talk to Reed about an upcoming interview. "Hi, Jennifer—Reed let me peek in your studio—would you mind if I took photos?"

I shrugged.

By the end of August, there had been two press features about how Jennifer Reed, the wife of rock star Evan Reed, overcame injuries from a horrific car accident through the healing power of art. Galleries begged for my work.

The paintings didn't look the same to me in photographs. I was painting lines, shadows, but on canvas his blue eyes told stories. Reed agreed to let the galleries show my work. The Polaroids I'd taken of his fists, the scars on his chest and arms, were enlarged by 6x7 feet. There is a beautiful black and white photo of him looking to the sky, his long hair blowing in the wind, the sun shining through dark clouds onto his face. I let the galleries take whatever they wanted. I wasn't interested in creating an art collection. I was documenting a life in case it came up missing.

I was merely an extension of Reed's ego and vanity—a prop wife when he needed me. Any press was good press after that last tour.

A publishing house was interested in releasing a book of my artwork, but they wanted it out by spring. Reed helped them put it together. There's a gallery in New Orleans that has a 6-foot nude I did of him splashed with paint—red, orange, blue—my danger colors. I had him strip naked in the art room and threw paint at him with my brush before painting him onto the canvas. If I had a favorite, that would be the one.

Those fast and furious paintings saved my life. I was building strength, buying time before Reed realized I was no longer as damaged as I claimed to be.

I asked him to open jars and pills. I did everything I could to make him believe my basic survival depended on him. I needed Osmitrol to make sure the brain swelling didn't return. I needed my anti-seizure medication, mood stabilizers, and anxiety pills to not work myself into a panic attack any time I was near him.

Work. Create. Don't kill this man in the bed beside you. I avoided conversation and eye contact. Those things would lead to sex, and I did not want to have sex with that man. The doctors made it clear, all it would take was another bump on the head for my symptoms to become permanent.

I had depressing days where I wanted to lie down and give up. I painted Reed as a voodoo doll on a cross, which he would later use as an album cover. I no longer had illusions about him. I knew exactly what he was—a monster. And I knew exactly what he was willing to do to me—murder.

There's nothing romantic about that.

I stayed alive. I painted and did my time. I kept moving so I wouldn't go crazy.

It happened anyway.

I didn't want to curate an exhibit, but the publishing company insisted. Reed wasn't keen on the idea; it meant I'd be out of his sight. He'd preface, "If you're not up to it, tell them."

Over a few days, I formulated a collection. I focused on the photographs. I wasn't where I needed to be with a paintbrush, and I needed the buffer. I wasn't ready to lay the canvas out on the table, so to speak. But the Polaroids were something different.

And I had a plan.

The Artist and Her Rock Star

Interview Magazine, November 2, 1992

Jennifer Reed will tell you she had nothing in particular on her mind during her latest series of work, roughly titled *He*. There's notably an absence of "She" in this collection of work. The majority of the drawings, photography, and paintings are of her husband Evan Reed. In the Museum of Contemporary Art installment, there are 3,001 nude Polaroids of Evan Reed from every possible angle. The artist won't be attending the exhibit.

"I'm private. He is not."

There are endless ways to analyze the work—perhaps it's raw adoration of her husband. Or maybe not? After five years together, mired in tragedy, it would be hard to believe that anyone knows Evan Reed more than the artist does. At first glance, this is a gift for the fans. On closer look, it's exposure. And not the flattering kind. Jennifer is notably absent from her own work unless you look closely—very closely. It's time-consuming to examine 3,001 photos. I had a lot of time last week when MCA offered me the opportunity to preview the collection.

When you walk into the exhibit, The Doors "Riders on The Storm" begins to play. As you leave, the audio sticks on a single line "killer on the run."

What happens inside that room, however, borders on schizophrenia. Hundreds of rows of photos dangle in a circle from the ceiling in the center of the room. A white step ladder sits, waiting for the viewer to approach, to climb inside—it's not easily accessible and it's not comfortable—this is by design. If you want the truth, you're going to have to reach for it. But you don't need to reach far. Methodically viewing each image in order, I found a pattern. The artist documents every hair and scar on her husband's body—until the hundredth photo—those marks, that smooth hairless skin, do not belong to a man.

Every hundredth photo another secret is slipped in. Bruises. Rope marks. Cigarette burns. X-rays. Ultrasounds. Broken fingernails. As this realization hits, Iggy Pop's "The Passenger" plays. I count through the photos quickly to find the next clue.

Your mind races when you uncover something secret and hidden—except it wasn't a secret was it? It's been so blatantly obvious throughout the years. The accidents, the miscarriages, the attacks by fans, the car wreck—oh yes, that car wreck. The 2500th photo is a shattered Texas road sign, "Woody's Lounge." Photo 2600—blank, an empty black Polaroid. 2700—a brain scan with a cranial fracture. 2800—a totaled sports car. Photo 2900 is a view of the ocean from the cliff on Evan Reed's estate. Photo 3000—the Hollywood Cemetery sign.

Photo 3001; Evan Reed, tied, naked upside down, ready to be crucified.

The walls around the exhibit are covered with larger than life photos from the same series. You get the sense you're being watched from every angle, at every second. My mind drifts to The Doors song that was playing when I walked into the exhibit. Was Morrison saying "killer on the run" or "kill her?

Maybe The Doors give me the creeps. Once this not so secret is revealed, it's hard not to think about it. It kept me up at night. Only a narcissistic monster with the ego the size of a rock star would have missed this exhibit's intent. If you're not careful, you'll walk right past it too. ~ Vivianne Gatskill, editor, *Interview Magazine*

I didn't think it was that obvious, myself. I was used to no one paying attention.

Reed looked up from the magazine.

I underestimated the fucks that anyone was going to give about my work. I'd been told it was useless for so long. This exhibit was breadcrumbs. By the look on his face, I should have left more because that trail would lead straight to a body.

He dropped the magazine on the table.

"Get dressed for your opening, Jennifer."

When that reporter managed to get me on the phone, I'd meant it when I said I wasn't going to the opening night reception. Once Reed realized I was getting attention, the pissy little Prince returned. He was jealous, angry that I'd subversively outed him. All I knew is that it wouldn't matter that the art reviewer from *Interview Magazine* picked up on this. If *Rolling Stone* didn't say it, if MTV didn't report it—it never happened in his world. That didn't mean he didn't have a plan to make me pay.

As usual, Reed had something black lace and skimpy hanging in my closet ready to wear.

Not tonight.

Sasha had been by the house earlier in the day to do my hair—signature blunt cut, shoulder-length bob, shock white-blonde, glistening black underneath. I put on a pair of flat-front black jeans, a white and black striped shirt and a dinner style, fitted leather jacket with my black Dr. Martens. I topped it off with winged black eyeliner and bright red lips.

I would be myself, even for a night.

Reed was performing at the opening. His hair had grown long again, his beard full. He wore sunglasses. He arrived at the gallery with the celebrity guests and art critics. I waited with my vintage Polaroid, snapping photos as stars walked in the door. I'm the one they don't see standing in front of them. I blend into the walls. These are the gods, and I am nothing. I snapped a picture of Mick Jagger and Jerry Hall. Guests filled the lobby. Waiters came out from the open bar, serving drinks and hors d'oeuvres.

I headed to the back of the gallery before the show. Reed was going to perform "Riders on The Storm", "Roadhouse Blues" and "Love Me Two Times" by The Doors. He promised the audience a surprise at the end.

My stomach twisted, I listened from behind the staging area as he conjured Jim Morrison straight from the grave. It was haunting. I leaned against the wall, wishing he were someone else and wishing I were somewhere else. Barbados, Hollywood Cemetery. Maybe nowhere at all.

A tall, lanky man with long, dirty blond hair walked up to me in the dark hallway, lost. "Is this where I should wait to go on stage?" the man asked.

I stared at Rhys Gold, my teenage idol, lead singer of The Sound, my favorite punk band.

He took a second look at me. "You okay, little girl?"

"Um, yes, Mr. Gold, sir—here is fine," I said.

"Call me Rhys."

I listened alone in the dark as Evan Reed and Rhys Gold sang a cover of "The Passenger." It should have been the most important moment of my career—and Reed stole it. Rhys Gold didn't know who I was, through no fault of his own. Stars played with and for the stars. The help stayed in the back.

Reed was supposed to introduce me at the end of the set. The gallery had gone over that with him several times. After the standing crowd slowed their cheers, Reed said, "Without further ado—He." He bowed, the spotlight went out, and the path to the exhibit lit up. Reed erased me from my art opening. He walked past me into the exhibit without a word. No one wants to meet the artist when the rock star is around. I didn't want the attention, but this match burned.

I'd stashed the lobby photos throughout the other photographs, hoping to capture reactions of the guests seeing themselves in the exhibit. Instead, I watched Evan Reed stroke his massive ego and brush elbows with his rock n' roll peers. It didn't matter the intent; I'd created him an altar where he could be adored by those he idolized. It was never about the art. It was about exposing him for the monster he was.

But here we were in Los Angeles, the land of gods and monsters. Evan Reed was both. He flirted with young women, choosing two brunettes, and announced he was going to the hotel. He motioned for me to follow him. I hesitated. He mouthed, "Now."

I picked up my bag and walked to the door, remembering that night so many years ago when I'd left my job with him, escaping Suit and Yuppie Scum. If only a blowjob would get me out of this—Hey, where'd Rhys go?

"If you're taking those girls, I'm going home," I said, leaning into him for a photograph.

Reed put his arm around me and grinned wide for the camera. "I made your pathetic dream come true. You owe me, little girl. I'm on to you. Smile and pretend you're happy to be here."

I'd fallen into a trap.

At the hotel, I watched him drink, snort cocaine, and fuck two strangers three feet away from me. Groupies for old time's sake. I took out my camera and took two photos. I left a Polaroid of the unconscious threesome on the bedside table and went downstairs to the bar.

I couldn't let him distract me with his games. I ordered a drink, used my sharpie to date the photos, and slid them inside envelopes. On one, I wrote to my mother, *"Do not open."*

I wrote the date at the bottom of a second photo and mailed it to Vivianne Gatskill, the editor of *Interview Magazine*. On the back, I'd written, "Does this answer your questions?"

The art reviews were all the same—it was "overwhelming." They referenced Gatskill's observations. "Is he a god or is he a monster?" Smothered by the crowd as they stood on that shaky ladder trying to figure out what the hell was going on—the wall closing in on them. One celebrity said, "It was so intense, all I could think is how the hell am I going to get out of this nightmare?"

I wish I knew!

Every time I went for a checkup with my neurologist, I darted to the gynecologist office to get my birth control shot without Reed's knowledge. With the press and planning for my upcoming book release, my follow-up visits were pushed off and rescheduled. I tried not to think about it so my head wouldn't hurt. I took two anxiety pills and kept painting.

My scars were healing, the shaved part on my head grew in. I was human again, with muscle and curves, not some bloody lump of flesh he left to die in a hotel shower. If I put on enough Estee Lauder extreme coverage, you almost couldn't see the scars he'd left on my face. And he needed somewhere warm to put his dick anyway. I mean, at least that's what he said on TV one night.

I could focus my energy into painting to distract my thoughts from going anywhere dark, but there wasn't a nook or enclave I hadn't already placed my psyche into so I could endure sex with that man. Part of doing the nude photographs and paintings of him was to build a tolerance to touching and being near his skin. That was different than him touching me. I recoiled at the thought. In the past, he would've taken what he wanted, but he couldn't risk scrambling my marbled head. I was worried that letting him inside me, when I most certainly didn't want him there, would push me into that dark hole I'd been trying to draw my way out of.

I couldn't handle saying no and being ignored anymore. But I wasn't going to pretend to enjoy it either. If he wanted to fuck a crying corpse, hell, I was his girl. I got lucky the first night. I guess it had been awhile, he misfired and passed out beside me. I couldn't stand his come on my leg but told myself this was the easy part.

After years of abuse, I'd made a habit of dissociating during sex with him. Now, I had to stay present to stay alive. I'd let my rage control me and now it had to set me free. I told myself to do my time and get out of that house alive.

So, I slept in Evan Reed's bed. I let Evan Reed put his dick in whatever warm hole wouldn't give me a brain concussion. I told him the doctor said I would die if I got an infection. He agreed to use condoms until he had a chance to get tested again. *Fine, thanks, done.* I told myself that my vagina was not a ripe juicy peach. It wasn't some virginal pathway to my spiritual being. It was no more special than my twice-broken nose or my cracked skull. It was a leg. An arm. A rib. He'd broken them already. I did my time. I paid upfront for my chance to rain Karmic hell on Reed Williams, Evan Reed or whoever he was.

And Reed, or Evan or whoever–came and came like he had a thousand times before. As long as my skull didn't hit the headboard, I considered it a workout. Prison push-ups. I didn't dissociate. I counted the seconds to hold myself in my body. If this was as good as it was going to get, they may well be the last moments and I'd be damned if that man would take another minute from me. *Karma. Karma. Karma.*

Don't get me wrong—I had no intention of killing Reed. Never. That was not my plan. I wanted him to pay. I wanted him to spend the rest of his life in prison. I needed to survive long enough to make my case.

My art book release was drawing near. Reed held a huge party in our courtyard to celebrate. Another chance to grasp this bit of publicity from my work and use it in his favor. The book contract listed me as a contributor. Somewhere in the stack of papers that needed my signature,

I signed my rights away. Not that it mattered. I hadn't been paid for my work in five years.

The party was beautiful, I'll give him that. His planner paid exquisite attention to detail. From the candlelit path, the peach and cream roses and ribbons, peach champagne, and small bites of cake, to the button on my husband's black Calvin Klein jeans, to the tip of his angry cock. She made sure this celebration in honor of my work was fully serviced.

Like the groupies, she made the mistake of thinking because she'd been that warm spot for Evan Reed that she had a right to speak to me. He knew the invasiveness of these women got to me. I couldn't stop him from sleeping with them. But they didn't need to be in my space, thinking because they'd been in the vicinity of his dick that they knew something about me. Talking to me, pretending it wasn't happening in front of my eyes.

He'd been making comments about me not getting pregnant. The prized bitch he needed to breed. I willed to death every sperm in his body.

The clinic on Sunset was open. I'd committed their number to memory. If he managed to knock me up again, I'd walk there barefoot if I had to. I'd fuck a wire hanger for sport before I would have another baby for Evan Reed.

He didn't care that I knew he was screwing the party planner. He targeted my insecurities. Manipulation, cheating; parading it in my face, bringing up babies and pregnancy, taking credit for my accomplishments. He was creating the perfect trigger cocktail for me to lash out at him at this party. To be the crazy wife. It was his way of hitting me without moving his hand.

I stayed inside the patio foyer. My charming monster was bestowing me with kindness, and I was ungrateful.

Part of this charade was the unveiling of the art studio he'd had built for me behind the house. He made grand gestures to sway media perception—maybe it made him feel better. I'd mentioned the paint fumes in our house were bothering me and hinted about the studio I'd seen downtown. I needed air that he hadn't breathed.

"You can paint at home," he said.

It was a long shot to ask him to rent me the studio. Of course, he'd gone this direction instead—giving me a gift to keep me trapped.

The studio was made of dark cherry wood, a mini-cabin shed with two double doors that opened the outside walls like shutters. I could paint at the top of the hill, by the tree where we'd been married. In a spot so high, it felt like you were sitting in clouds looking down at the valley and the ocean. But it wasn't a real gift. It was part of the game. If I sound paranoid—it's because I am. Once a man points a gun at your head, you trust nothing.

He walked by, kissing me, touching my hips to remind me he could do what he wanted and keep control. The party planner carried on as if she wasn't sneaking into the other room to have sex with my husband. It's a big house but not that big. I was used to him doing this by now—but not here in our own special hell.

Jenny, don't let him get to you through this woman. I'd worked so hard to hold in my rage, but I didn't know if I could handle myself with another tramp.

These women were pawns in his game. He used them for sex and to screw with my head.

I stood in the foyer, looking out the patio window at a hundred people on the lawn, talking, eating, dancing, and having a great time. Their expensive shoes touching spaces where rain had washed my blood away. The studio was tied with a huge white bow. Candles from the party tables flickered in the bay windows.

I found myself with a wine glass and a bottle of champagne, watching fireworks. I pretended for a brief moment that this fantasy was real. Maybe that little bit of pretending would help me keep it together the rest of the night and not cause a scene.

The party planner, whose peach dress and pumps matched the bows on the chairs, placed her hand on my shoulder. "Jenny, I hope I'm not out of line, but Reed told me about the problems you were having getting pregnant."

My heart dropped to the pit of my stomach and what welled up in its place was no less than the fires of hell. I wanted to punch her in the face and rip her intestines out of her peach dress. All of the horror books I'd read on tour with Reed were going to pay off.

She gave me an empathetic smile. "I know that can happen sometimes after an abortion—and I wanted you to know that you're not alone. If you ever need to talk-"

Trigger successful.

"We had three children, and three of them died, you cunt." I shoved her out of my way.

That's the last thing I remember.

Chapter Thirty-Two

Two hours later, I stood in the master bedroom looking out at the ocean. Fire truck lights flickered while the studio went up in flames below. I held a lit cigarette in my hand, a pack of Marlboro Reds, and carried a lighter in my pocket. It seemed like a good night to pick up a habit.

There was an official story about a candle and oil paint—a lie Reed concocted on the spot. After the fire was out and the guests left, Reed stormed into the house. I heard every stomp of his steel-toed boots coming up the carpeted stairs.

I sat on our bed, sipping from a champagne glass, smoking a cigarette, surrounded by photos of our dead children. Our happy little family. Scattered among them were the Polaroids I'd taken of my injuries.

We didn't take pictures of Hayley at her funeral. We wouldn't have—but someone did. And they sold the negatives to a tabloid. At least in those, she was dressed. She was reassembled with putty, glue, and two-inch thick makeup, not in pieces. The ones that were taken at the morgue were an entirely different story. Some creep had taken his own Polaroids and tried shopping them around. A gore company bought them and threatened to post them in web message boards. Reed paid half a million dollars to get the morgue pictures and stop the magazine from printing the funeral photos. Another hundred thousand to get them to only print a side shot of her coffin with a caption detailing her death.

I'd gone with the lawyer to get the photos. I hadn't opened them until now.

Sometime between punching a whore party planner in the face and setting a building on fire, I'd pulled the pictures out of my hiding place.

Reed was holding a cigarette, and a glass of whiskey, pointing at me and screaming. He was coming to hit me. A one-handed slap so he wouldn't spill his drink. He wouldn't be able to control himself, the whiskey would end up in my face—his glass against the wall. A cigarette stubbed out on my arm before he dragged me off the bed and beat the shit out of me.

Except he didn't. He stopped. His face froze like stone when he saw the photos.

For once, I was doing the screaming and he was listening.

"You blame me for everything! For a decision you gave me no choice but to make. I had an abortion, you asshole! Deal with it! YOU KILLED HAYLEY! She died because you weren't paying attention. When I had my abortion, I was protecting that unborn life from you and the psychotic world that surrounds you. Why weren't you protecting Hayley?"

He held the picture I'd shoved in his face, our daughter on an autopsy table.

"This is my life, thanks to you." I waved my arm at the rest of the pictures strewn across our bed. The words I'd been holding back came flooding out. "Look at me!" I screamed. "Tell me the truth!"

His eyes made contact with mine then rolled to the hell that awaited him.

"Did Hayley slip out of your reach, Reed? Or did you let her go?"

I couldn't have dealt him a heavier blow if I'd shot him in the chest.

He stumbled, reaching for something that wasn't there, and fell to the floor. There was no escaping the images scattered around him.

"I know you were there with Kaley, too. You bastard. I saw her key chain in your drawer and recognized your stupid Armani kit. It matches the one Kevin and I found in that house. She tried to kill herself with your drugs, didn't she? Did you bash her head into the sink like you did mine?"

"She wasn't my problem," he mumbled, his eyes adjusting to the horror around him.

I shoved a handful of the photos into his arms. I had no sympathy for him.

I walked over to the wall safe, where I'd seen him key in 3-02-1989. Hayley's birthday. She was one way I could get to him. I'd gone off the deep end and used her without mercy.

I took a zippered money bag filled with bundles of hundred dollar bills and the cloth bag that held his most expensive jewelry.

I had to leave the house before I doused it with gasoline and burned it down with him inside. I ran to the barn he'd tried to kill me in and shoved the keys in the ignition of his prized, black 1967 convertible Ford Mustang. Gripping the silver skull gearshift, I reversed out of the barn, pushed it into drive, and hit the gas.

On Canyon Road, at 60 MPH, I turned the radio on full volume. The Beatles screamed through "I Want You (She's So Heavy)."

I drove south towards the Mexican border.

Chapter Thirty-Three

I reached Hermosillo in Sonora, Mexico and rented a cheap hotel room for the week. I paid cash. Rolled out of bed after two days, bought a map, a Pepsi, and Fritos from the snack machine. I tore the Fritos bag open with my teeth and spat out the corner of the wrapper. I was starving. That Pepsi Cola tasted like heaven. I bought a pair of sunglasses and mapped out directions to Puerto Vallarta and the nearby Riviera Nayarit, places I'd heard about on tour.

It was a 12-hour drive, but I was up for it, having spent only a few minutes alone in months. I blasted the radio, playing anything I wanted to hear. I'd stolen a copy of DeathTree's latest album while in a record store with Reed one afternoon. Can you imagine Evan Reed's wife being arrested at Tower Records for stuffing a CD in the front of her pants?

I had flipped through the liner notes before tossing them in the restroom trash and sliding the compact disc between pages in my sketchpad. Until that drive, I'd never even had a chance to listen to the album. I listened twice, then played "Riot!'—the song about Rodney King—once more, before tossing it out the window.

By the time I made it to Puerto Vallarta, I needed a serious shower. I wanted to explore Riviera Nayarit, but it was dark, I was tired, and my Spanish was lacking, so I pulled into a resort and gave the Mustang keys to a valet.

The desk clerk gave me a hard time. "I can't rent you a private bungalow without a credit card. It's $1,500 a night."

"I need it for thirty days and I'm paying cash." I opened my bag and handed him a bank-bound bundle with a $50,000 strap. "You can keep the extra $5,000 for incidentals."

"Is it Mrs. Reed?" he asked, looking at my passport.

"No, it's Ms. and please don't call me that again. It's Jennifer. Not Jen, not Jenny and certainly not Mrs. Reed. Just Jennifer. And I'll need a safe in my room."

The bungalow was on the water. It had a glass floor and wide shutters that opened to a breathtaking view of the aquamarine ocean water. So quiet—me, the breeze, and sweet sleep.

Come morning, I had a late breakfast of almond-crusted French toast, then added Huevos Rancheros—fried egg over corn quesadilla, cheese, guacamole, red beans, and sauce. No one was there to tell me what to order or when to put my fork down.

I bought two bikinis at the resort gift shop—one brown with beads the color of the ocean and the other in pink because I'd never owned a pink bikini. I picked tank tops, board shorts, and a couple of flowy beach dresses, sandals, flip flops, and toiletries.

The cashier looked at me in surprise.

"These are nice, but there's an entire strip of clothing stores a short walk from here."

"I'm good. Can you tell me a good place to hear rock n' roll tonight?"

"Like, American?" she said.

"Isn't that the only kind?" I smiled. "Just anywhere I can find a long-haired dude with a guitar who speaks okay English."

"El Jardin, it's a little gritty but it's right off the beach."

"Thanks." I lugged my new clothes to my bungalow.

I showered, combing my hair for the first time after three days in the wind. I put on a flowy black tank top with Reed's silver bracelets and long necklaces, my jeans, and sneakers. Expensive concealer covered my scars. *London. Dallas. Los Angeles.* I exchanged cash in the lobby for pesos, tucked them in my pocket, and took a path along the beach to the rock bar.

A musician played Aerosmith's "Hangman's Jury" on a beautiful, handmade, 5-string Vihuela guitar, singing lines in broken English, between drinking flaming tequila shots. I wasn't there for the music. I glanced around the room until I saw the man I wanted. A thin guy in his twenties, slick black hair, long sideburns, black button-up shirt, black jeans, and snakeskin cowboy boots. I smiled. He grinned, motioning me over.

"¿Habla usted inglés?" I asked him.

"Si," he said as the guitarist switched from his Vihuela to an electric guitar.

I leaned in close and spoke in the man's ear. He smiled widely and bit his lip.

"You're a brave little girl," he said. "Are you sure?"

I slid $1,000 into his hand and smiled. "The rest when you get to my room. I only want it if it's good. Do you understand? Enough to last."

"I can give you everything you need, novia. See you in an hour?"

"Si," I said. I ordered a drink, then went to my bungalow, changed into my new bikini and went for a swim. I met Luces and Javier, two beautiful Cabana boys at the hotel. Friendly, flirty and getting off work. I invited them to my room. When the drug dealer arrived, I invited him in too.

Fuuuuck, that rush... I got it. I finally got it.

Only god knows what happened in the bungalow that night because I sure don't remember. It must have been fun because we did it again the next three nights. Luces' brother was a drag queen. She would come to the hotel, and we would dress up and snort cocaine. Drugs covered every surface. It was magical and liberating. I could do cocaine and not give a shit.

Luces and Javier hung on my every word. I bathed in the excess of it all—the money, the drugs, the spa—the ass on that Javier guy.

Come on–you didn't think I was going steal all that money and a '67 Mustang from that sociopath and ride off into the sunset like everything was okay, did you?

I lost control. That's what you do when you haven't had it in five years. I enjoyed every minute of my time there. I had to. Because that sort of freedom isn't free. The money in my bag was not free. As long as there was a chance that Evan Reed was alive, I would never be free.

I pretended to be someone else so I could survive. Somebody who could do something horrible like what I'd done in our bedroom, laugh, and forget everything that mattered. Someone like Reed. People say I did these crazy things and went to Mexico and partied for a month. The truth is I'd lost myself. I'd never been so vicious and cruel in my entire life.

As nice as it was, being stoned out of my mind didn't last. I blew a quarter of a million dollars in a month like it was nothing. It was time to go back to the States. To what, I wasn't sure. But I knew it was time.

I went to the spa, architecture tours and museums, instead of clubs. Trying to quit a habit on my own was hard. I'd done drugs with Reed, but I'd never partied on his level.

While walking to the hotel from a chapel, I saw the most beautiful man. Six-feet-five with long, honey-streaked, blond hair, and blue eyes. I didn't have time to panic, he lifted me and gave me the warmest hug.

"Jenny? In Puerto Vallarta? What a coincidence? You look great," my old touring pal, Jamie London, laughed and squeezed me. "Want a drink? I'm headed to the bar."

"Not drinking," I said, in my second day of sobriety. "Are you here with the band?"

Jamie's band, No Spaces, had opened for Reed. Now they were selling out stadiums on their own.

"No, we had a short leg in South America. Been on the road for six months. I needed a break before heading to the States. What about you? Here with Reed?"

"By myself."

"In that case, I'm starving, and you look like you could use something to eat."

The ground rules were set, and he was right, I was starving.

We had an early dinner at the hotel bar, laughed and talked for a couple of hours. I went to my room to take a nap (I was nursing a month long hangover). We made plans to go out that night. I woke at 9 pm and got dressed. We met at the restaurant at ten, a live band played in the background.

It was fun to share old stories—before things got bad. Most importantly, he didn't mention Reed. I'm not sure what he knew about our situation—word travels fast through those crowds—but he'd been out of the country a while. It didn't matter. It was an unspoken rule; when you're trying to pick up another rock star's wife in a resort hotel in Mexico, you don't ask questions. We were young and it was Puerto Vallarta...

"Are you coming off cocaine? Your hands were shaking at dinner. You know you can't quit cold turkey, right? You'll have a seizure," Jamie said.

"Bad month." I frowned.

"I figured." He walked me to my bungalow. "I've got something in my room that will help you ride this out." He brought me a prescription bottle of methadone pills. "I've had a couple of bad months myself."

He waited with me that night while I was sick. The next day he came at five p.m. to pick me up so we could go out again. I had to break up with both Javier and Luces the week before, though it was against my new religion to do so. Jamie kissed me in his room, and we slept together. He was beautiful; gentle and so caring. He told me he'd wanted me since the first time he'd seen me. I'd kind of expected that, but he was barely twenty-one when we met.

His wedding band was on the sink. I didn't know he'd gotten married. I remembered when Reed and I were first married, how it had to be some big secret. Jamie was only twenty-five. He looked and acted much older, but he was only twenty-five.

I wrote him a note to say goodbye. Underneath, I wrote: *Go home to you wife*, and placed the wedding band on top of the note.

I checked out of the hotel early so I wouldn't run into Jamie. Luces was waiting outside my door, and he helped me pack my bags. I kissed him goodbye and tipped him a couple of the hundreds I had left.

I didn't have a plan, but I couldn't live the rest of my life looking over my shoulder. I had to face Reed. I stopped overnight at a small hotel on the way to L.A. The next morning, I pulled up to the gate at the house and had no trouble getting in. The house was eerily quiet.

On the kitchen island was a stack of papers from the lawyer's office. Divorce papers. Reed had signed them. Yellow sticky notes indicated the spots I should initial and sign. There was a number for a notary and an overnight pre-paid postage envelope under the papers with a note to call his lawyer if I had questions.

Too easy.

I grabbed a snack from the cupboard and flipped through the papers. The settlement wasn't bad. It wasn't the half I was legally entitled to, but it was reasonable. Especially considering I'd just blown close to a quarter of a million dollars in cash. I sat the papers aside and looked around. I called out for the housekeeper, but no one answered. The tour roster on the fridge was blank.

It was odd for the house to be so quiet. I looked in the courtyard. The art studio I'd burned down had been removed. A few patchy places remained in the grass. I walked outside. *Why are you doing this, Jenny? Why are you here?*

I knew the answer. If Reed was going to kill me, I wanted him to get it over with. I couldn't live like this forever.

A blue, extended cab pickup pulled into the driveway, and Reed's brother stepped out. We walked into the house together.

"I guess you know why I'm here," Daniel said.

"Not really." I could think of a million things.

"He wants you out in twenty-four hours. Said to take what's yours. I'll help you move into the Brentwood rental house. The utilities are on in your name. He wants this done."

"The papers look fine, but I want a lawyer to look over them before I sign."

"Twenty-four hours. That's what he told me."

"God, you must think I'm horrible."

"It's not my problem, Jenny."

"Is he on tour?"

Daniel looked at me like I was crazy. "There's no tour. It was canceled."

"Canceled?"

"Yes. The tour and album were canceled. The band is over." Daniel narrowed his eyebrows. "You know Reed's in state, right?"

"The prison?" I asked confused, but hopeful.

"No, dear—the mental institution."

"God. Why?" Reed never sought treatment willingly. State was a place they put you, not a place you volunteered to go.

"I don't know what crack den you've been living in, but that's what happens when a housekeeper finds you OD'd, covered in blood, with pictures of dead babies and crazy shit written on the walls."

"Oh god," I said.

"Yep. So, did you have fun in Mexico?"

Word travels fast...

Chapter Thirty-Four

This had to end. I signed the divorce papers and moved into the rental house. I kept the '67 Mustang. We'd been to Mexico together—she was mine. I packed a small suitcase at the mansion—mostly reminders of the babies—and left everything else behind.

I gave up my life for Reed. I lost myself. What did it matter if I was "free" if I didn't know who I was anymore? He had controlled my entire existence. Maybe I did ride off into the sunset, but I came back alone.

I had someone check the rental house for bugs; recording equipment, video cameras, the whole deal. I was that paranoid. As awful as he was, Reed had always been there. Now, I was utterly alone in an empty house with my thoughts. Same prison, smaller cell.

A few days after I moved in, this red-haired, pregnant woman ran towards me, waving her arms. "Jenny! Jenny!"

Oh god, not one of his fans.

I unlocked my car, pretending not to hear her.

She finally made it down to my end of the street, panting.

"Oh, my goodness, I'm so glad I caught you." She took two deep breaths. "Whew, that was a workout."

"I'm leaving."

"Take this." She pushed an envelope into my hands.

Oh shit, I've been served.

But the pregnant lady was taking her bright red heels off, leaning against my Mustang, and rubbing her foot.

"Has anyone ever told you that you're hard to get in touch with?" she asked.

"Kind of my trademark."

She took another deep breath, put her shoe back on, and smiled. "My name is Elizabeth Elliot. I live down the street. Your brother-in-law was here a few days ago—well, ex brother-in-law? I'm sorry, he's sweet either way. He used to work on my husband's touring crew. We're past that business, thank goodness. Anyway, Daniel said you don't know anyone in the neighborhood. We always have a little get together to welcome new neighbors. It's Saturday. I hope you can come."

This woman seemed harmless; comical, even—*could it be a set up*? "Are you friends with Reed?" I asked.

"Um…" she hesitated, "that would be a negative, no. Is that okay to say? If you two are close, I don't want to say the wrong thing."

"We're not."

Elizabeth exhaled. "Good. My husband, Mark, was in a band in the '80s. Elias Rising. His hair was bigger then. Wait, there he is." She waved at a man down the street who had stepped out of a car. He walked towards us. Handsome, with dark brown hair that rested on the collar of his jacket, brown eyes, and a sturdy handshake.

"Hi, I'm Mark." He smiled.

"This is Jennifer, she's Daniel Williams' sister-in-law, or ex sister-in-law. She's the one we're having the welcome party for on Saturday."

I stuttered. "I-look this is such a sweet and unexpected gesture, but I'm not good with strangers."

The pregnant lady burst into tears. "Oh no, I'm so sorry! I'm intruding. It's okay. You don't have to come."

Mark stepped out of his wife's earshot. "Look, I know who you were married to and that it wasn't a good situation. Probably the last thing in the world you need is to hang out with my pregnant wife, but this is all she's talked about. If you can please, please humor her. She could go into labor any day now."

"Why would she plan a party for a total stranger?"

"Because she's nice. She's terrified about being a mom for the first time, her family lives out of state, and she needs a friend. It wouldn't hurt to have someone around with a car in case I'm not home."

My shoulders dropped. "Can we keep this gathering small? I don't do strangers."

"No problem. I'll tell her."

I became friends with Elizabeth and Mark Elliot and went to their welcome party. They brought food by my house afterwards. I didn't let them in.

Mark stopped by on his own, unexpectedly.

"Elizabeth wants to have you over for dinner, but she didn't have your number." He leaned forward and looked over my head into my little house.

This is it. He's not a nice guy. He's going to push his way into my door and then... I put my hand on the doorknob, ready to shove it closed.

"Jen, you okay?" Mark said. "You looked like you went somewhere else for a second."

I stuttered. "What-what else do you need?

"I lied, Dinner is not why I'm here," Mark said.

Here it comes.

"Elizabeth is nesting, which I didn't realize was an actual thing. And now she's nesting for other people—which is extra weird. She peeked in your window and swears you don't have furniture in your living room."

"I'm not staying here. As soon as I'm on my feet I'm selling this house."

"Please don't tell Elizabeth that. Look, we downsized from our last place. I have furniture in our garage. You can have it. If you say no, she'll try to drag the sofa down here herself."

"Geez, okay." I said, relieved that he wasn't going to burst into my house and rape me. *Maybe you can relax a little, Jenny.* I glanced over his shoulder and saw a black Cadillac parked at the end of the street. No, maybe not.

The next day, Mark and his friends loaded his truck with furniture and brought it to my place.

The black Cadillac was back.

Chapter Thirty-Five

I was stuck in traffic on the 101 when Reed's new song "Broken" came on K-Rock. I banged the dashboard, trying to move the dial to the next station, but the digital radio Reed had installed was stuck. I pulled off the front plate of the radio and put it on again trying to get it to register so I could turn it off. The slow and soft guitar riff at the beginning of "Broken" was familiar. Horns and engines protested against the rush hour traffic jam. Trapped on the 101, I burst into tears.

I hadn't heard a word from Reed since I'd signed the divorce papers. Other than the black Cadillac that kept parking at the end of my street, it had been radio silence.

Until now.

"But I miss you in my sleep/What was broken can't be fixed," he sang to me from the airwaves.

I gave the radio one last pounding. The thing was possessed, cosmically controlled by its owner. I put the Mustang in park, jumped out, walked, and then ran down the freeway emergency lane, screaming, "FUCK!"

A trucker got out of his big rig and led me back to my car.

"Lady, the traffic will be moving along soon, it's okay. I get a little panicked when I'm trapped too. Besides, it's a beautiful car. You don't want to leave that behind."

Another concerned driver walked back to see if I was okay. "I can call 9-1-1 from my car phone," he offered.

"I'm okay," I lied.

The trucker patted my shoulder. "Happens to the best of us." He went back to his truck.

I cranked the Mustang and put it in drive.

The song was over, but the DJ was talking.

"That is Evan Reed's new single off his latest solo album *Forget YOU*. That's capital YOU—period," the DJ said.

"That sounds final," another man laughed.

"The new album dropped Tuesday. Get your special edition copy at Tower Records this week, with a bonus track only available at the Sunset location. Dude's been through a lot and this album is a damn journey. The song "Broken" has debuted at number one. There's a short tour starting over at Hollywood Bowl next month. It's projected to sell out. If so, the gig will move to The Forum."

"Dude sells records. He might be a dick to work with, but he's a genius songwriter. Even this one: "Broken." The lyrics are simple enough on the surface but something deep is going on there," the second DJ said.

The Mustang's radio turned off. Traffic resumed and I made my way across the freeway to the Hollywood exit. I parked in front of the Tower Records on Sunset Blvd. and Horne Ave. The billboard above the store was the painting I'd made of Reed as a voodoo doll figure on a cross. Eyes, mouth and brutal fists stitched closed and tied above his head. I'd never signed a release. Not that it mattered.

Posters of him and his band covered the store.

"Hey, aren't you...?" said the cashier with jet-black spikey hair, covered in tattoos and leather and metal bracelets, more piercings on his face than I could count. His name tag read, *Zekk*.

"I'm not anyone." I took my purchase out to the Mustang. Sensing its Master's work, the CD player purred. I leaned back the restored leather seat, locked the doors, and listened to Evan Reed's latest album, *Forget YOU*.

I made it through "Broken" and a few other beautiful love songs. Before the live track titled "I Don't Belong Here," Reed said, *"I wrote this song for my mother and that bitch I married."* He played acoustic guitar into a misogynistic ditty about not trusting women. Loud, rumbling bass and electric guitars kicked in with a scream that I can only describe as a motorcycle descending into hell. *"I'm your abortion. Your miscarriage. One-thousand times, I don't belong here!"* This song was where the corpses from The Sex Pistols "Bodies" were set on fire and left to rot.

Reed screamed, "Mommy!" louder than Johnny Rotten dreamed of, with a level of anger and self-loathing that Kurt Cobain couldn't touch. The song erupted into something so loud and angry, I worried the car engine might explode. Between verses, he'd inserted audio from a phone conversation we'd had—I had no idea I was being recorded until I heard my voice loop. *"I don't want to talk it about it. I don't want to talk about it."* The clip showed up a few times later in the song as *"I don't want to talk. I don't want to. I don't want to,"* before the song spiraled into a crash of guitars and drums, loud vibrating bass. Reed released a guttural death like screamgasm, shouting, *"Fuck you, Jenny!"*

I skipped through the other tracks. He'd finished the angry demos he'd written after the DeathTree tour. Liner notes referenced, *"bitches who fuck other bands and steal your money."* There was a sweet song he'd written for Hayley, and another love song called "Unrequited."

The Times review said, *"The album can best be described as bipolar, as it cycles through love and misogynistic rage, sometimes clearly not knowing the difference between the two."* A review from *Metal Magazine* said, *"I get the idea if you sleep with Evan Reed, it's probably the last thing you'll ever do."*

The last song before the bonus track was called "Obsession." Reed repeated the lines, *"I love you. I hate you. I love you. I hate you. Come on home and let me break you."* "Love Letter from Hell" was incoherent babble mixed with spoken word poems playing in reverse while he screamed different lyrics on top of it.

The album went gold, then triple-platinum by the end of the week. Reed had done it. He'd gone out without his band and created one of the greatest albums of all time. At least that's what *Spin* and *Rolling Stone* said.

I considered it a love letter from a stalker who didn't yet have the nerve to call.

Chapter Thirty-Six

R eed went on tour. Elizabeth had her baby, a beautiful little redheaded girl named Sammi. Yes, Sammi Elliot—a nod to the delicious actor and *Road House* silver-haired hottie. I was anxious that they were in the hospital and not nearby.

Mark called to invite me to the hospital to meet Sammi.

"I can't."

"Elizabeth would love to see you."

"I can't do hospitals, nurseries—babies in hospitals. Tell her I'm so sorry. I can't."

"Oh God, Jen. I'm so sorry. It's okay, Elizabeth will understand."

"Congrats, Mark. Give Elizabeth my best."

I should have been excited for them, I'd tolerated the last few weeks of baby talk. But an actual baby—it wasn't fair. I walked to the liquor store, bought three bottles of vodka, and got wasted. I trashed my living room while listening to Reed's album.

He was wearing a t-shirt on tour that said, *"Fuck You Jenny."* His thousands of adoring fans chanted it back to him. He was king again. And me? I was drunk and alone. A nothing. Nobody. Exactly who he told me I'd be without him.

I was furiously jealous of my new best friends and ashamed of it. *Elizabeth is so sweet, she deserves a better friend than this.* I stumbled into my boots and leather jacket, too drunk to walk out my front door.

Hadn't I been sweet once? Maybe not. But how goddamn sweet do you have to be for the Universe to

allow you to walk out of a hospital with your baby? Maybe that would've made the hell Reed put me through worth it. *It would've made things worse.* I took my boots off and opened the second bottle of vodka.

Reed was talking shit about me at his shows. *"Getting married is the most expensive thing you'll do in your life—don't do it,"* he said. When he played his old songs he said, *"I wrote this for a sweet girl that's not so sweet anymore."* He didn't have to say my name, because the song did, the "Fuck Jenny" shirt did.

And his new music video was the nail in the coffin. I'd been drunk enough to turn on MTV and watch the world premiere of his video for that damn abortion song. It differed from the album version; the tongue in cheek acoustic country intro wasn't there. Instead, the intro was sweet, thoughtful music and lyrics he'd written for Hayley, before the song erupted into chaos.

The video showed him in his mansion, sitting on our bed—like I'd been the night of the party. He was holding a cigarette and a glass of champagne, surrounded by photos of our Hayley. Not the bad ones, just the sweet ones. He threw his glass and trashed the room, never losing hold of that cigarette.

I looked around my trashed living room. *Who have I become?*

In the video, Reed pushed past some supermodel, went down the stairs and out the door. The camera followed him as he stormed across the lawn into the barn where he kept the cars—where he'd tied me up and left me for dead. He came out with a can of gasoline.

My hands shook and my stomach tightened. He was doing this to punish me. Flashes of his tattooed hands on the naked bodies of different girls, their skin tones and hair changed, but their faces never showed.

The music spiraled. The camera panned to a set of the mansion. Instead of pouring gasoline on my flesh, he spread it across the house, across my paintings, which had been ripped from the walls. Upstairs he poured it on the bed and lit a match from a certain matchbook.

The scene changed to a home video he'd taken of me after he'd given me the insanely expensive Grace Kelly ring. Clean faced, my short, bleached hair tucked behind my ears. I looked like a person—like an artist, like me. The camera zoomed in on my face and my lips as I smiled. *"I love you,"* I said in the video. The music went silent. It shot back to the match hitting our bed, with Reed screaming the lyrics. *"100,000 times I don't belong here. You don't belong here-anywhere,"* he sang in this alternate version of the song. The bed went up in flames, then the rest of the house as the camera followed him. When it showed him outside singing the lyrics, you could see a small building on fire where my art studio had been. The camera panned to the towering mansion, in flames. His point was loud and clear—he could start a bigger fire. The line stuck with me: *"You don't belong here. Anywhere."*

The music stopped with another scene from the home video. I remembered thinking at the time that it was an odd question. Reed asked, *"How long will you love me?"*

"Forever," I answered in the video.

I turned off the TV. Forever is a really long time.

My phone rang. "Did you see the video?" Reed asked.

My body trembled, I screamed to the top of my lungs into the receiver. "I HATE YOU!" I slammed the phone down.

I pulled my leather boots on again, opened the bathroom cabinet, and dug through my makeup bag until I found the four-carat, round-cut vintage 1950s diamond ring—the Grace Kelly ring that had gotten me into this mess. I slid the ring on my finger like I'd done that night for him on camera. I grabbed the vodka and left the house. I was tempted to get in my Mustang, but I didn't want to hurt anyone else.

I stalked through the backyards of my neighbors, through a small patch of trees to the stretch of two-lane highway that ran behind the subdivision. Crossing the highway, I ran half-a-mile north along the edge of the road as cars passed by. I walked up the overpass that crossed the freeway.

Cars rushed past as I climbed onto the concrete barrier overpass. Big rigs rumbled beneath my feet. I put out my arms and balanced until I reached the middle. I almost slipped but steadied myself. I could hear his song in my head. *You don't belong here.* I knew the rhythm because he'd been humming it around the house. It was making me crazy. Cool air whipped against my skin.

"Hey lady!"

I almost lost my balance, rearing my arm to throw that goddamn $250,000 ring into the dark abyss. The good Samaritan who'd pulled over and stopped traffic on the overpass, grabbed me from behind before the ring left my hand. I gripped it in my fist.

The man lifted me off the ledge. He had dark brown hair and brown eyes; he was beautiful in the moonlight. So, I kissed him. When I let go, I put the ring in his hand. "Give this to your girlfriend."

That, ladies and gentlemen, is how you create a rock-n-roll legend! It's also how you end up on a forty-eight-hour psych hold at Cedars Sinai.

When the story hit the media, MTV pulled Reed's video. Kurt Loder from MTV News told the world that an onlooker had saved Evan Reed's ex-wife during a suicide attempt.

"The singer's former wife was apparently attempting to jump off an overpass into the busy freeway while intoxicated. Evan Reed has yet to release a statement, however, the incident occurred less than an hour after the world premiere of his latest video. MTV has decided to temporarily pull the video out of rotation as it may be a trigger for sensitive viewers. The pre-scheduled, three-day retrospective of Evan Reed's career will still air. MTV encourages any viewers who have thoughts of suicide to contact the National Suicide Prevention line at 1-800-273-8255. We extend apologies to viewers who were offended by the airing of this video."

MTV would later add the video back into rotation with an explicit trigger warning from the network, though they played it only after nine PM. Several radio stations dropped the song and a few of the bigger box stores pulled the album.

It only increased the album's popularity.

I never intended to jump off that overpass. Sure, I could have fallen. I could have put others in danger. But I wasn't trying to kill myself. It took two days to convince the psychiatrists at Cedars.

"You have an alcohol problem, then."

That's the first drink I'd had since Mexico.

The doctors at Cedars Sinai ran urine and blood tests when I was in the emergency room. A nurse called with the test results.

"Why is this such a big deal? I had too much to drink. It was a stupid mistake. Why are you bothering me?" I asked, defensive. It reminded me of the nurse who had called to tell me Kaley was sick.

"Your urine and blood samples came back, and both confirm you're pregnant. You need to make an appointment with an OB-GYN. I can give you a list of recommendations."

Phantom pains from my old head injuries pulsed inside my head. "You're not serious?"

"You're definitely pregnant," the nurse said.

I slammed down the phone. "Fuck!" Screaming, crying, shaking, I hurled every piece of glass in the vicinity against my living room wall.

I made an appointment at the clinic on Sunset. This time I wore sunglasses. Yeah, they'd botched it up the first time, but I figured what the hell? The place and I had a LONG history. And you know what? Fuck Reed. Fuck him. Fuck him. Fuck him. This was poetic justice. After all the shit he put me through, here I was sitting in the same damn clinic.

The nurse called me back to see the doctor after I'd given them another blood and urine sample. The doctor explained my options.

"I want an abortion. I cannot have this baby."

"Well, Ms. Stone, it's not that simple. You have options. Can you tell me when was the last time you had your period?"

"I rarely have them. My last doctor said it was because I was stressed and underweight. Can you give me an abortion? I can pay cash."

"You're definitely underweight," the doctor stalled. "Especially this far along."

"What?"

"You're 22 weeks pregnant. You can have the procedure, but with your medical history it's a little more complicated."

"That's five months. Holy fuck. How?"

"It happens. I've seen young girls who didn't know they were pregnant until they had labor pains."

"I've had three babies. I would know if I was pregnant." *Nausea.*
Tenderness. Bruising. Jenny! Out of tune with my body, I had ignored the
signs. *Drugs. Flu. Stress.* I was in a constant state of pain, illness, and misery
with Reed, so what was something new?

"At this stage and with your medical history, there are risks. It requires a
little more discussion. I prefer to be upfront with my patients, this is not a
quick and easy procedure."

"You don't understand. I cannot have this baby. Grab a hose, give me
a pill, whatever, just make this stop." My chest was hot with panic, I
remembered a *Washington Post* article I'd read while Reed and I were
together, *The Grandmother and The Abortion Kit* by Cynthia Gorney,
about a contraption made from a jar, tubing and syringe that created a
"menstruation extraction device." It sounded unsafe, unhygienic—and
absolutely necessary if this doctor didn't listen to me.

Five months.

This was not Jamie London's baby. It did not belong to the Cabana boys,
Javier or Luces. I'd gladly have it had been the Mexican drug dealer with the
sideburns and snakeskin boots. I'd rather it have been anyone in the world
than Evan Reed.

"Give it twenty-four hours. Call tomorrow and we can schedule your
procedure. In the meantime, I'll give you prenatal vitamins, which
regardless of your decision, I recommend you take. You're extremely
malnourished."

"I was so drunk last week I had to be hospitalized. I spent a month in
Mexico doing cocaine. My ex is a rock star-going-on-serial killer. I cannot
have this baby!" I sobbed.

"Twenty-four hours. I know about your recent suicide attempt. I don't
want you to do something you may regret. We don't have to do an
ultrasound, but I can if that would help make your decision. You don't
have to look."

"Just do it."

I thought of Hayley and the twins as she rubbed blue gel on my stomach. I didn't feel pregnant—maybe because I was utterly dead inside.

The doctor rubbed the wand over my stomach, and I heard a sound on the Doppler screen. A heartbeat. I'd heard it with Hayley and the twins—until theirs had stopped.

"You have a fully formed fetus, Ms. Stone. He looks perfectly healthy."

"He?"

"Yes, I'm sorry, that slipped out."

"He is healthy?"

"Yes, a little smaller than he should be. If you gain a few pounds, stay away from alcohol and drugs, you can have a normal pregnancy—we have the resources here to help you. Babies are a gift from God, Ms. Stone."

I looked her dead in the eyes. "You've obviously never fucked the devil."

The doctor sent me out of clinic with prenatal vitamins and a stack of pamphlets. Her minions swarmed me in the lobby, cheerful offering me cookies, rides to the clinic, and coupons for free prenatal care. I was in the middle of some reverse *Rosemary's Baby* bullshit. *Fuck.* I looked at one of the pamphlets: *Jesus Loves Your Baby*. I'd been in such a flustered state, I'd missed the re-branding outside the clinic. A fucking crisis center. I'd gone there knowing exactly what I had to do until she showed me the fucking ultrasound and got into my head. *Now I'm in a fucking crisis, lady.*

The doctor said she was concerned with my mental health—using it against me, to manipulate me the way Reed had.

Still crying, I pulled the vintage Mustang over on the side of the road. *Healthy.* I'd heard his heartbeat. I banged my fists on the steering wheel. I did not want Evan Reed's baby.

Do I want my baby, though? After all the shit he put me through, don't I deserve something? If I were sixteen, I wouldn't have this baby. If I were twenty-two, I wouldn't have this baby. But I was twenty-seven, with a miserably failed marriage, three dead babies, two miscarriages, an abortion, and a doctor who set the wheels of guilt in motion. I laughed psychotically.

gripping the steering wheel. "Jenny, you have a nineteenth century pioneer uterus! You're as fertile as a fucking Appalachian farm. You dumb fucking bitch!" Why couldn't Reed just let me take my damn birth control pills? Even he had to understand how insane and toxic we were together.

What the doctor had done to me was not okay. I thought about turning the car around and ramming it through the window of that fucking crisis center. She never once asked about the father or if I was in danger. She didn't care.

I lay in bed that night, eyes wide awake, turning. Tossing my pillows on the floor that was never as cold and hard as the marble that cradled me in the Hell House.

Healthy. Not like my twins, not like Hayley on that street below the hill. The thing was—if there was a three headed monster lodged in my fallopian tubes, that lying doctor would have convinced me to keep it.

And what if I did? There was no way I could ever tell Reed. I would lie. I would say the baby was Jamie London's. I'd go into hiding. Sell the house, move home to mom and dad. He had to understand why after what he'd pulled with that video. I didn't need his permission. I would talk to my lawyer and see what I needed to do.

I made an appointment the next day.

"What do you mean, I can't sell the house?" I asked my divorce attorney.

"You don't own it."

"What do you mean?" I said again. "Reed gave me the house in the divorce settlement."

"He agreed to give you the house once it was paid for. There's still a mortgage."

"Who owns it?" I asked. I'd never dealt with anything financial, or mortgage related since I'd met Reed.

"The bank owns the house. Once it's paid off, he's required to sign it over to you. The mortgage company said Mr. Reed lapsed on the payments. If they're not caught up soon, you're risking foreclosure."

"How much are the payments?"

"Two thousand a month. It's cheap for that neighborhood."

"You're saying I might lose the house?"

"Yes. I've put in a call to his lawyers. I can draft out a letter inquiring on the status. Do you have anything you could sell in the meantime to get it caught up?"

"No. Especially considering I gave a $250,000 ring to a total stranger."

"Please say that wasn't the Grace Kelly ring we told Reed's lawyers that you lost. Jenny?"

"It was my ring."

"No, Jenny. It wasn't. In your settlement you were supposed to return the ring. You said it was lost and there's an open insurance claim on it. You have to tell me these things. He could press charges against you. Not to mention insurance fraud if you signed those papers." My lawyer's hair ruffled when he shoved his hand through it.

"So, I'm fucked."

"It looks bad."

After everything Reed had done to me, I didn't think keeping that stupid ring mattered. Otherwise, I wouldn't have given it away. *Jenny, you idiot!* I could sell the car if I had to, but how would I get to my doctor's appointments? How would I get a job? When I pulled onto my street, I saw the black Cadillac with dark windows sitting at the corner again. Unless a rapper had moved into the neighborhood, I was being watched. I couldn't have this baby. No way, no how. I parked my car and walked to Elizabeth and Mark's house.

"You, okay?" Mark said before letting me in the house. He wasn't asking how my day was; he was asking if I was drunk or high before he let me near his perfect little family.

"I had a bad night, we talked about this. I promise—I'm good."

Mark reluctantly let me inside.

I waited at the table for Elizabeth to bring the adorable Sammi Elliott downstairs. I'd thought Elizabeth dyed her hair the bright red color it was until I saw little Sammi's head with a tuft of fire red hair, and cute, rosy, freckled cheeks.

"I'm pregnant," I blurted out after a few minutes of watching her with Sammi.

Elizabeth's eyes got big. "OH MY GOD! OH MY GOD!" Her tired mommy brain went from zero to overdrive in three seconds. I could see her planning playdates at the park and giving me hand-me-down clothes and toys. "Oh shit. Who is the father?" she asked as Mark walked into the room.

"He goes by different names. Lucifer. Satan. Reed."

"What are you going to do?" Mark piped in.

"You have to have it, Jenny. We can do mom stuff together. Please?" Elizabeth said, as if having this baby was as simple as rolling out a double stroller and scheduling carpools.

"It's complicated."

Elizabeth gave Mark the baby and a spit-up cloth. She threw her hands in the air. "There had to be a point in your relationship where you loved him, Jenny. That's what you need to think about."

"It wasn't real."

"But you believed it, right?"

"I don't get your point."

"All that matters is that feeling. Forget him. Hate him. But remember that feeling. When you look at your child for the first time, that's all you'll remember. But it will be new and different and a million times more wonderful."

"I've had that feeling, Liz. It was it ripped away."

"You're not the only one," Elizabeth snapped. "I'm sorry those horrible things happened, but this is your baby, not his. We will help you. Pardon my language, but f- that man. He doesn't own you."

Elizabeth was too sweet for the details. Too sweet to know what happened the last time someone offered to help.

"Let me walk you home, Jenny," Mark said. "That black car has been at the end of the street all week. I called the cops. You should too. It's only there when you're home."

"I know."

I wanted to get drunk. Elizabeth and her red-haired baby had gotten to me. I wasn't a kid anymore. I had every right to walk into a real clinic and rid myself of any connection to that sociopath. This baby was mine—my only connection to Hayley and the twins. I needed him. It had to mean something after the hell I'd been through. I wasn't sure how, but Evan Reed would never find out.

I called my lawyer the next day and pressured him about the house. I called Elizabeth's OB-GYN and made an appointment. I went to Trader Joe's; stocking up on healthy foods and vitamins. At IHOP, I ate pancakes, a waffle, eggs, three strips of bacon and a piece of toast. I had a baby to feed.

He must have been starving because I kept every bit of it down.

Chapter Thirty-Seven

R eed finally released a statement about the music video:

The video for "I Don't Belong Here" was an artistic interpretation of a toxic relationship, somewhat inspired by real events that occurred in MY LIFE. The truth is that person and I are no longer together because we were destroying each other. That said—it's ART. My team and I saw an opportunity to make a mini-film combining elements from the entire album. I hope it will be viewed as such and not tainted by the attention-seeking antics of a person who appears to be very ill. I have not spoken to my ex-wife since our separation, nor do I intend to. We've gone our separate ways for infinite reasons. I can only hope she seeks the help and treatment she clearly NEEDS. My concern is that MTV and other networks are using the desperate actions of one mentally ill person as a basis for CENSORSHIP. INTOLERABLE under any circumstance! If you're sick of bullshit corporate America controlling what YOU are ALLOWED to see and hear, get a ticket and come to my shows. Hear what all the music is about. See you on the road! —Evan Reed

So, what if the entire world thought I was insane?

Regardless of what happened with the house, as soon as I got the okay from the OB-GYN, I would move to Arizona with my parents. I'd already packed. The man from the overpass reached out to return the ring. Originally, I'd held onto it after Mexico and considered it my back-up plan. Now that Reed knew I had it, my lawyer said I had to return it to prevent theft charges.

Reed stopped mentioning me in the media and at his shows after his public statement. Good behavior for the press. At his gigs, he kept wearing that t-shirt and singing that song, inciting his fans. Hate mail and dead flowers waited on my doorstep. I received harassing phone calls day and night.

Reed's record label officially announced Neon God had broken up. The fans blamed me. I was their Yoko Ono. It turned out they were passing my address and telephone number around on a fan message board.

Reed's road crew followed the board. No one flagged those posts.

Since I had no financial interest in the house, and the mortgage was in Reed's name, my lawyer said for my sake, it was better to walk away. I would move to Arizona at the end of the month, find work and figure out my next step.

Elizabeth wasn't happy I was abandoning her. When she watched Reed's video and the press release, she broke out in tears. "God, I'm so sorry, Jenny."

I'd run across my welcome packet to the failed residency with Marlene Von Berstein. Newly divorced—it was her money, not Jordan's—she'd tried reaching out in the months before I left Reed. I was too ashamed to ask for her help now. I tossed the papers in the trash. Another dream Reed had taken from me.

My doorbell rang. I glanced out the peephole and saw a UPS driver. I wasn't expecting anything, but I was on my way out and opened the door.

The woman was not holding a package. There was no UPS truck outside the house. Nervous tick. A lazy eye that couldn't quite focus.

Dead Raccoon Girl.

Emilya Reyes had stalked Reed for years, targeting me after Breanna Lee's interview. She'd camped out in front of his gate for a month before the raccoon incident. The police said as long as she stayed a certain number of feet from the gate, she wasn't breaking any laws. She'd attacked me at two shows. I'd been walking to a seat with a bodyguard, and she came from behind, ripped a handful of my hair out, and disappeared into the crowd. She wrote *Jenny is a whore* on the white gate at the mansion my first night there.

Now she was standing in my doorway. She had the build of a linebacker. She was wearing the band's t-shirt and a special edition logo necklace under the UPS uniform. I'd designed it for the crew.

I glanced at the end of the street. The black Cadillac was not there.

Emilya forced her way inside my house. She had a knife; the tip of the blade pressed against my throat. Screaming, she punched me in the face so hard she knocked me onto the floor, and a rush of blood poured out my nose. She grabbed my hair and pulled me down the hallway.

I fought at her, but the blade was so close.

She shoved me into the hall closet and blocked the door.

Emilya barked orders into a walkie-talkie she carried on her waist. "Click. Click. Traitor is secured."

Reed had always warned me to be prepared for this. I'd spent so long thinking he was my biggest threat; I'd forgotten there were others.

Emilya was talking to herself. The walkie-talkie wasn't turned on. "Static. Bleep. Click."

She opened the door again, pulled me out of the closet and into the bedroom, where she demanded I undress to my underwear. She cut the straps on my bra, leaving me bare-chested, and shoved me to the floor again, spitting at me.

She screamed and kicked me in the thigh. I instinctively shielded my stomach, her blows came crashing onto my back and hips.

She growled and echoed one of Reed's old threats. "Bitch, I'm gonna cut you like Manson!" The single, most terrifying thing a pregnant woman could ever hear.

"Emilya," I pleaded. "You don't want to do this."

Her voice changed, picking up speed. "You destroyed the band. You ruined the lives of all fans of rock music in the entire world. You broke Evan's heart, you're a whore like the lyrics say."

"But they didn't break up, Emilya. Didn't you hear?"

"Liar," she paced, sweating profusely, scratching her messy curls.

"Reed and I are friends. It's an act, it's part of the show. You don't have to do this." She didn't believe me. I had to think of something. "We can call Reed. Speak to him yourself."

"This is a trick."

"It's not a trick. I can call and the two of you can talk this out, okay? You don't want him to be angry."

She agreed. I punched in our old private number and prayed he would answer.

He didn't.

Her breathing quickened.

"Let me try one more line. Sometimes he doesn't keep his phone with him."

She dialed the number and put on the speakerphone. This time he answered. I did exactly as he and I had rehearsed, using code names for each other.

"Hi, Bluebell," I said before he had the chance to say anything that could get me stabbed in the neck. "I have someone here—Emilya, on speakerphone—she's a big fan and I've told her you would love to meet her. She didn't know the band decided to stay together, but I've told her you'd be glad to come chat and smooth things over. Would that be okay, Emilya?"

Silence.

I hoped Reed had hit the hold button and not hung up. Surely, he would not let this girl kill me. "Can you tell Emilya that the band is okay? She's really upset." *Come on, asshole. You owe me this.*

Reed cleared his throat. "Yeah babe. That was a miscommunication. The band is fine. Can I talk to Emilya?"

Emilya shook her head.

"You're on speaker phone. Is that okay, Emilya?"

Her nose twitched. She wanted to kill me, but I'd planted the seed of uncertainty. Reed had answered his studio phone—he was thirty minutes away. I heard audible pauses on the line. I hoped someone was alerting the police.

Emilya pulled sheets of wrinkled paper from her jacket. She had the floor plan to my house, and the security code for the gate and front door. *How did she get this?*

Reed bought me time, asking about gifts she'd sent him and things she'd written in her letters. She had scared me before, but I'd never expected this.

Flashing lights reflected off the house windows. Emilya slammed the phone down.

"You don't want to go to jail, Emilya," I pleaded.

"Shut up!"

"I'll help you. There's a way out the back."

"I don't have to listen to you." She banged her head. The phone rang. As she said, "Hello," the front door burst open.

Police shouted, "Get on the floor! Get on the floor!"

I lay on my chest and waited for them to take her away.

Emilya fought while the officers handcuffed and pulled her out of the house. They checked each room from top to bottom. A female officer helped me to my bedroom so I could get dressed. Shaking, I pulled on a long sweater that fell past my knees, and a pair of jeans, while she patiently took my statement.

A male officer commented, "Why did you open the door if you weren't expecting a package?"

"Because my life sucks so bad, I wanted to be murdered, asshole," I said. Be careful what you wish for.

Reed walked in my front door as I came out of the bedroom. A second wave of terror hit, making my knees weak. Sunglasses. Shoulder-length brown hair. He was a stranger now, walking through the house, checking windows and doors behind the officers. He used his cell phone to call and ask for a new security system put in. He called a locksmith to come out and redo the locks that night. Then the police and locksmith were gone.

It was the two of us.

"I'll stay here tonight," Reed said.

"No. I don't want you here."

"I want to make sure you're safe. I'm worried about you."

"Not worried enough to release a press statement and tell the world I'm crazy?"

He tried to get me to look at him. "I don't care about press releases. Or albums. Or any argument we've had. Some deranged fan of mine held you hostage and threatened to kill you. None of that other shit matters."

"I'm sorry you drove over here. Please go."

"I'm here, let me help."

I moved to the far end of the sofa and pulled my knees protectively under the long sweater.

He handed me a folded blanket and sat beside me.

"You're not moving, are you?" he asked about the scattered boxes in the house.

"It's my neighbor. She's having a community yard sale. I told her she could store the boxes here. Emilya made a mess of everything."

"I'll clean it up."

"No, sit," I said.

"I'm sorry. It's these damn internet message boards. They can post anything. That must be where she found your address."

"Can't imagine how they got it..."

"I didn't give anyone your address. I wouldn't do that. I know things have gotten out of hand between us. I'll try to calm the flames."

"That would help."

"Jenny, I was angry with you when I wrote those songs. I was angry when we were together. But I got straightened out when I was put away, meds sorted. I know you don't believe this, but I barely remember the past three years. It wasn't me."

"Reed, don't..."

"Listen. I worked a lot of shit out—you, my mom, the kids, fucked up shit from my childhood. I felt free. I'd planned this beautiful, epic album. Day one in the studio, someone said Jamie London had bragged about screwing my wife in Mexico—all that anger came back. I lost it. My therapist reined me in—said to channel my frustrations through music. He underestimated me. I convinced myself it was art, I could do whatever I wanted, as long as I wasn't doing it in the "real world." I played the part of Evan Reed the rock star and I shouldn't have."

I nodded.

"When I called you that night, I felt guilty about the video. It was one thing to take part in it—working this angry shit out of my head—it was therapeutic. It was different when I realized millions of people had seen it. I never intended for you to hurt yourself."

"I would never jump."

"It shouldn't have gotten to this point."

"No, it shouldn't have," I said.

"Can I ask you a question, though? If I hadn't released the album or video, if I'd come to you like this, is there a chance things could be different?"

"Please don't make me go through this again."

He brushed a strand of my hair away from my face. "I love you, Jenny. I know I hurt you. But I was sick. It's a struggle to wake up every morning and deal with the unforgivable things that happened. What you did in the house that night was brutal. You saved my life though. I needed to face those demons. All of them. That shitty awful thing you did was the most loving thing anyone could have done for me. It opened my eyes." He laughed. "And you've got a lot of balls, little girl. How much cocaine did you do in Mexico? Cause I've heard stories. You took my car, a quarter million dollars and tried to throw a $250K engagement ring onto the 405. I mean, that's the stuff of legend. You should open a rock star training school. I'd learn a thing or two."

"Can you stop talking?" I asked. "I'm so tired."

"I'll stay and watch TV for a little while, just so I can make sure you're safe."

My eyes were so heavy. I'd never be safe with him.

I jerked away from Reed. I'd fallen asleep. He was rubbing my hair.

"Sorry, I didn't have the heart to wake you. I should get on the road."

"You drove yourself?"

He laughed. "I can drive."

"You never drive in L.A."

"I was worried about you." Reed leaned in to kiss me.

I put my hand up and pushed his shoulder away. "You need to leave."

"If you saw how beautiful you looked when you were asleep you wouldn't blame me for trying. I have a killer headache. Do you care if I grab a glass of water?" He walked towards the kitchen.

"Clean glasses are on the counter."

I heard him open a cabinet. *Fuck.* I jumped up from the sofa.

"Do you have Tylenol?"

"I'll get it." I rushed into the small kitchen, squeezing between him and the fridge. *No, no, no.*

He was holding the bottle of prenatal vitamins.

The radio station in my head picked up UFO's "Doctor." *Please for the love of god, no...* "It's just vitamins." I reached for the bottle as he pulled it back. "My doctor said I'm malnourished. I lost too much weight last year."

Reed flicked around the ultrasound photo I had taped to the side of the fridge. He put his arm above me on the cabinet, towering over me.

My shoulders dropped. The adrenaline from dealing with Emilya ran in reverse, rolling off my chest, down my thighs, planting my feet like cement blocks. I instinctively tugged at my baggy sweater. I was barely showing in my normal clothes. He would've never known if he hadn't gone in the kitchen.

"Tell me this doesn't say what I think it does. This is dated a month ago—twenty-two weeks. How long have you known?" His fist pounded the cabinet. "Goddamnit, Jenny, answer me!"

I shook my head. "Please go."

"You're six and a half months pregnant and you didn't tell me? How many times did I ask you? How many times did I tell you to take a pregnancy test? You lied the entire time?"

"It's not yours."

"Unless you were fucking the goddamn mailman, it better be. You weren't out of my sight." He gritted his teeth. "You were pregnant with my child, doing drugs in Mexico, and fucking god knows who?"

"I didn't know." My lips trembled.

He slammed his palm into the cabinet door again. "Don't lie to me."

"Check the date on the ultrasound. That's two days after I got out of the hospital. I swear to god, I didn't know."

Reed looked around the living room. "Community yard sale? That's bullshit. You've been asking the lawyers about selling the house. You wanted to disappear."

"I was going to stay with my parents. I can't stay here with people harassing me all the time. You see what happened with Emilya. Reed, please..."

"L.A. County Women's Clinic. Isn't that the place that butchered our first baby? You were going to get an abortion, weren't you?" Reed's shoulders twitched. He popped his neck on each side and breathed heavily above me. "You lying, fucking cunt."

My entire body trembled. Terror I thought I'd escaped ran across my flesh. *Please kill me. Please get this over with!*

The man was weighing his options. He closed his eyes, breathing deeply. He tapped the ultrasound picture on the fridge before sliding it in his pocket. He sipped the glass of water he'd poured himself. Sitting the glass gently on the counter, he exhaled and moved the arm that was blocking me from leaving the kitchen.

Reed grabbed his burgundy leather jacket from the back of the sofa and tossed his credit card and cash on my counter. "Send me your bills. And Jenny, if you're planning on leaving California, do yourself a favor and run a lot farther away than Phoenix." He slammed the front door on his way out.

In a matter of minutes, I'd gone from grateful, to more afraid than I'd been in my entire life. At least when he was hitting me, I knew what was coming.

Nothing prepared me. Nothing.

Chapter Thirty-Eight

I locked the door, before realizing the locksmith had given Reed a copy of the new keys. I collapsed on the floor. *At any minute, he can come back and kill me. I'll never be safe.*

The next morning, the black Cadillac was at the end of the street. Trapped again, I had to wait for his next move, and hope for mercy.

Mark and Elizabeth came by with Sammi. I didn't answer the door. I ignored their phone calls. The fewer people involved with me, the less Reed could hurt. No one was safe, especially the child I was carrying.

Two excruciating weeks of paranoid silence passed, until he called in the middle of the night.

"Jenny, I've been having the same nightmare for a week that something happened to the baby. I'm trying to do the right thing. I know you don't believe me, but I've done a lot of work with my therapist about us. I was the problem and I have no business trying to be a father to this child. I'll pay your bills, we'll have the same agreement I have with Chloé. But I need to know the baby is okay. My doctor recommended an OB-GYN in Malibu. I'm asking from one human to another, can you go to ease my mind? I swear to god, I will leave you alone. I can't fall off the wagon again."

It felt like a trap. I didn't trust his intentions. *This is better than waiting around for him to strike in the dark.* If keeping him sober would keep him away from me, it was worth a shot. "What's the address?"

The next day, I drove to the OB-GYN office. It was in a busy area. *Safe,* I reminded myself. *And it means better care for the baby.* The nurse was meeting with us before they opened; the doctor was on her way.

Reed leaned against the brick wall outside the clinic, his ankles crossed. Sunshine bearing down on his black clothes. He looked like he was in a rock n' roll photo shoot. *Live! From Malibu's Poshest Medical Clinic!* His beard was full. He took off his sunglasses. His blue eyes were bloodshot. *Maybe he is losing sleep. Good.*

"Thank you for doing this, Jenny."

The nurse unlocked the door and let us inside, taking me directly to an exam room. She handed me a consent form before she left me alone. "It's the normal stuff; sign here; and let's get you undressed to see the doctor."

After a moment, she popped back in to apologize. "Dr. Holbrook is stuck in traffic. She'll be here shortly."

My foot bounced. Something wasn't right. *Maybe I should get out of here. Nope, I'm being a decent human being. Giving Reed peace of mind, buying myself time. There are doctors here, Jenny, calm down!*

I didn't realize the nurse was requesting my medical records. While I waited nervously, checking my watch every thirty seconds, Reed's doctor—who wasn't in traffic—sat in her office pouring over my medical records with a lawyer. I'd never told my doctor who the father was, but I'd told her about Mexico, the drugs, the bad pregnancies, the physical abuse. It was all there.

Reed poked his head in the door and asked if he could come in for the ultrasound. He was being unusually calm and considerate. Vulnerable, sitting on the exam table wearing a paper gown, I nodded, tightening the blanket across my lap.

"You don't look pregnant."

I was hormonal, pregnant, and alone. ANY comment about my body sounded like an insult. *Stay civil, Jenny.* "I am."

Did he think I was making this up? Did he think I'd orchestrated the entire Emilya Reyes attack so I could pretend to be pregnant? Because I wasn't quite sure he hadn't had a hand in that. He could have easily been the person posting my info online. I remembered Marcus saying some fans were around so much they might as well be on the payroll. I doubt anyone was paying Emilya, but if someone gave her motivation—say, a special edition crew necklace, and put the right bug in her ear... *Paranoid. Hormones. Stop.* I was getting on my own nerves. *You're in a safe place with doctors.*

Reed noticed I'd tensed up. "I didn't mean anything bad. I know you're nervous, honey."

When the tech came in the room to perform the ultrasound, Reed gently grabbed my hand. How many of these moments had he missed? Here he was when it was so far beyond too late.

The tech pointed out the baby's heartbeat and showed his arms and legs to Reed on the screen.

"So, he's healthy?" Reed asked.

"Perfect," the woman said. "Congratulations. The doctor will be in a moment to go over some information with you."

The door closed. Reed dropped my hand. "When the doctor comes in, she will put you on bed rest."

"I'm fine."

"I don't give a fuck about you, Jennifer," Reed snapped. "I'm suing you for custody." He pulled a folder from his jacket and dropped it in my lap.

"You've been served," he said with a self-satisfied laugh, as if he'd been waiting half his life to tell someone that. He twirled his fingers. "Fuck you, Jenny." Then walked out.

Beneath the paper sheet, my knees knocked against each other. My heart sank to the pit of my stomach. I was on the verge of screaming. The doctor came in and immediately went into my medical history.

"Ms. Stone, I'm concerned about the safety of your baby. You were taking cocaine during your first trimester? Are you still taking drugs?"

"How did you get my medical records?" I asked.

"You signed a consent form. Your doctor faxed them over when I advised them you were transferring to our practice. Your husband—excuse me, ex-husband—has generously offered to pay for your care since you no longer have medical insurance. His credit card information is on file. All you need to do is show up for your appointments."

"I'm not changing practices. What is happening?"

"As a mandated reporter, I am required to report your drug use to DCFS. When that happens, law requires us to follow up with you. We will help you make informed decisions to keep your baby healthy. About the cocaine use—are you using now?"

I jerked away from her. "You can't be serious. How does he have you going along with this? You're a doctor!" I burst into tears. "I don't consent to any of this."

"You're not my patient, Ms. Stone. Per DCFS orders, I'm caring for your unborn child. And I am requiring you to go on bed rest. That will be explained after your booking."

I jumped down from the exam table and jerked my jeans and shirt back on. "What are you talking about? This is ridiculous."

Two L.A. County police officers waited outside the lobby. They arrested me on site and took me to the L.A. County lockup. Endangering an unborn child. It didn't matter that there wasn't a law at the time would allow the charges to stick. It didn't matter that I screamed Reed tried to kill me. It was now on public record—I'd openly admitted to using cocaine and drinking while pregnant. The world would see me as Evan Reed's lunatic ex-wife, the suicidal drug abuser. I hadn't believed Melanie Martin's story, yet here I was in her shoes.

I sat in a jail cell, puking my brains out while police raided my house, using a key Reed gave them, finding drugs and an unregistered gun that wasn't mine. Reed's lawyers leaked every horrible thing they could about me to the press. I was the druggie, the violent abuser. They threw me under the proverbial bus. When I bailed out of jail, they dragged me into family court so often it seemed they were trying to force me into labor.

I sat in the courtroom weeping for two hours, exhausted, mentally and physically. Reed was controlling my every move again. Everything I'd said and done was held against me.

A judge put me on house arrest. I could only go to doctor visits and court. I couldn't drive my car. My lawyer had to pick me up, and I had to wear an ankle bracelet.

The black Cadillac was at the end of the street 24 hours a day now.

"Jenny, there is no precedent for this case to stick," my lawyer assured me, even though I had the impression certain judges would make an example of me for the right amount of money.

While Reed worked to get custody of our unborn child, I worked with a less experienced team of lawyers to get a restraining order against him.

Most of this was unfolding in family court. The records were sealed, and the media only knew what Reed's counsel leaked. My lawyer found an emergency room doctor from Dallas to testify that my injuries were inconsistent with the car accident. I learned Reed had pulled me out of the hospital when the police asked questions. The maid from the hotel where Reed had left me to die came forward to testify on my behalf.

Luckily, I had a female judge that day, and after seeing the X-rays from Dallas and hearing the maid's testimony she removed me from house arrest and dropped the case. "Mr. Reed, I suggest you tread lightly in the court system," she said.

His lawyers went after me for theft of property. They served me an eviction notice. The Mustang wasn't listed in the divorce papers. I watched from a window as a tow truck removed it.

Lou Reynolds, Reed's attorney, came by my house. "Jenny, we go way back."

"Yes, you've spent your career covering things up for him."

"I have kids. I hope that you want the best for your child. That's what Reed wants." He opened his briefcase. It was full of cash. "Two-hundred and fifty-thousand. Take the money. Reed will drop the lawsuits."

"And what?"

"He wants you to sign over custody now and leave town when the baby is born."

"Get out of my house, Lou."

My lawyer said I'd have little to no luck fighting the theft charges filed for the car and ring. "You knew that car was not in the divorce settlement, it doesn't matter that he didn't ask for it. And you lied about not having that ring."

"I gave it back."

"It looks bad."

Reed would find a way to take the baby. Judges and lawyers believed him. If this child lived, god... it would be eighteen more years of this hell. That's if Reed didn't kill me first.

I took the elevator up twenty-five floors to the rooftop deck of the Excelsior Hotel. This was the place we'd stayed at the night our lives changed forever. I ordered a virgin daiquiri. I stood at the railing, waiting for the bartender to disappear, and tried telling myself the drop wasn't that far down. I would be free. Finally.

I asked to use the telephone. "Reed, I'm at the Excelsior. We need to talk."

Reed arrived thirty minutes later.

Chill bumps covered my skin. "You have to stop. I didn't come to the twenty-fifth floor of this building to talk to you. Stop or I will tell the media the truth about the barn. James. Everything."

"It's too late," Reed said. "You lied. You were going to take him from me."

I shook my head. "Then do me a favor. Push me. So, I don't have to jump. You're killing me. You've been killing me for years."

I said nothing in court the next day. Not a single word. No matter how much it frustrated the judge. I didn't cry; I didn't speak. They would use the truth against me. Saying what happened at the barn that night would mean admitting to lying, which meant further scrutiny of everything I said.

"Unless there's someone else who will testify," my lawyer said.

"Who? The maids, the staff? They're terrified of him."

"The gardener?"

"He only knows what I told him," I said.

"It's worth a shot," the lawyer said.

My lawyer called the gardener as a witness. "Mr. Smith, Ms. Stone told you it was a stranger who attacked her in the barn that night. He raped her. He stripped her clothes. Tied her arms and doused her with gasoline. A stranger. Did you believe her?"

The gardener shook his head. "No."

"So, you don't believe it happened?" my lawyer said.

"I don't believe it was a stranger."

"Objection!" Reed's lawyer shouted.

"Sustained," the judge said. "Where are you going with this counsel?"

"Well, we're talking about the custody of an unborn child, your honor. If it wasn't a stranger who attacked Mrs. Reed, that brings into question the safety of that household."

"I'll allow it," the judge said.

"If it wasn't a stranger, who was it?" my lawyer asked.

"Speculation!" Reed's lawyer shouted.

"I'll rephrase. Mr. Smith, why do you believe Ms. Stone lied to you about who her attacker was?"

"Because she was afraid of him." He pointed at Reed.

"She was afraid of her husband," my lawyer said.

"Scared to death."

"What's the point of this, your honor?" Reed's lawyer asked.

"Doubt," my lawyer said. "It's not a far reach to think a woman who was too afraid to report her abuser to the police is too afraid to speak up against him now."

I wasn't sure what would happen at the custody hearing—for my fetus—but I had a bag packed. I had every intention of disappearing if that judge had the audacity to award Reed custody of my unborn son.

On the final day of the hearing, Mother Nature sided with me. On January 17, 1994, at 4:30 a.m., a 6.7M earthquake struck twenty miles north of Los Angeles. It killed over sixty people and was felt across the state of California into Utah. Not only were many roads impassable, there was heavy damage in Santa Monica. Reed could control lawyers and judges with his money, but he couldn't control an earthquake. The courthouse was heavily damaged, closing the building for several weeks.

During the chaos, I slipped out of my house and into a friend's Jeep while Reed's lackeys were off guard. Over the next several days, I transferred from friend to friend and made my way out of the state.

Reed could stop me taking the baby out of the state once he was born. There was nothing he could do while I was carrying him. My lawyer made the court aware that I couldn't stay at my residence—the water was off, the power was out. I would stay with family until they rescheduled the court dates.

In the meantime, Riley Jacob Stone was born peacefully at the University of Utah Hospital on January 23rd, 1994, a week after the L.A. earthquake.

Reed expected me to go to my parents. So, I'd gone in the opposite direction.

I was afraid to hold my son. I was afraid to look into his eyes. I was afraid I might hate him. I was afraid to love him. I was afraid not to. When a nurse finally put him in my arms, I kept my eyes closed. Everything I'd ever loved had been cursed. Little fingers, little toes. What had I done? Could I ever really protect him?

Riley was a beautiful baby. Perfect, healthy and happy. My lawyer assured me regardless of what Reed pulled in court, it would be unlikely that any judge would remove an infant from his mother's care. Reed would make my life a living hell for as long as he could afford it. I wanted my son to have as many peaceful nights as possible before he met his father.

I had no intention of taking my son back to California. Judges in Utah weren't as swayed as the star-struck Hollywood judges—they granted a restraining order for both Riley and myself. My lawyer sent notices to Reed's lawyers. I waited for him to show up. I'd listed a furnished apartment as my address on the forms for the restraining order. I left a few personal items there, and instead stayed with a friend.

Reed should not have had access to the address—but he did. He set the alarm off at three a.m. Arrested for breaking and entering, he spent two nights in jail. The judge in Salt Lake City added harassment and stalking charges for Reed violating the restraining orders.

His lawyer argued that he desperately wanted to see his son. Devoted fathers don't cross state lines, violate a restraining order, and break into a house at three in the morning. In fact, the most skilled manipulators and criminals would have sent someone else. It was a setup, but any reasonable person would ask—what did he expect to accomplish at such an hour?

Instead of releasing the information to the media, my lawyers held back. A smear campaign would accomplish nothing in California; only allow his lawyers to build a bigger defense of lies against me. We let them sweat.

In a perfect world I would have asked Reed to be at the hospital to meet Riley. In our world, in the most fucked circumstances, I had to introduce Riley to his father at the Santa Monica Courthouse two months after he was born. I wore him in a baby carrier and held a stack of medical records showing he was in perfect health.

Reed held our son for the first time in the judge's chambers with both our lawyers and I there to supervise. Every time Reed's lawyer tried to make a new point in their case, my lawyer reminded the judge that Reed had broken into my apartment.

The Santa Monica judge ruled, giving us joint custody of Riley. The judge in Salt Lake City was not having it. He extended the restraining order against Reed, with supervised visits inside the state of Utah. For once, I had a sense of control in my life. Someone was listening.

For two months, Reed made the drive to Salt Lake City for bi-weekly supervised visits with Riley. Then he had to make a choice—his label wanted him on tour. The legal battles had put him in debt. I was grateful for the $2,000 per month child support the judge ordered him to pay. I was breastfeeding Riley and too paranoid to have him out of my sight to find work. My parents were taking money from their savings to help us out, and so they could make the trip from Arizona to Utah every week.

In Utah, everything had to go through the court. If Reed missed a visit, I reported it. If he wanted to see Riley longer, the court had to grant permission. The judge granted him a special eight-hour supervised visit with Riley the weekend before his tour at an office near the courthouse with a playroom. I could come and go as I pleased. The court-appointed chaperone would not leave Riley's side. I sat in the adjoining room where I could see and hear them.

Once Reed was out of the country, I could breathe a sigh of relief. I had no idea how I'd explain this to my little boy. "Mommy and Daddy aren't friends," was the best thing I could come up with as he got bigger. Riley looked at me with his innocent, unknowing eyes, bright blue like his father's.

Rocking him, I picked up Hayley's *Winnie the Pooh* book; one of the few things I'd salvaged from her far too short life. I pictured her in the doorway and told Riley about his big sister and imagined her climbing into the chair beside us. Long, lanky legs and arms like mine as a child, golden curls resting on her tiny shoulders. I didn't picture the twins. I'd long since convinced myself they were never mine. They'd popped into the wrong vessel and promptly ejected themselves from the universe when they realized the horror that awaited them. My two blond babies who made it out of the hospital, I imagined them together. The way it would have been without Reed.

As soon as his probation ended, we were back in court battling for custody. He could break into my apartment and judges in L.A. would still consider giving him full custody of our child. His lawyers tried to get a judge to force me to move to California to make visitation easier on Reed's schedule. They pointed out that he'd provided a house for us. I wasn't working. I wasn't near family. They said the only reason I was staying in Utah was to keep Riley away from Reed, which was EXACTLY why I was staying in Utah. It was not a secret. His lawyers dug for anything in my past they could use against me. Reed wanted full custody. He wanted to control me, and as long as his albums sold, he had endless money to do so.

My final saving grace came in the form of a twelve-year-old boy. My lawyers contacted Reed's former mistress in France. Investing every penny he had in trying to destroy my life, Reed had stopped paying Chloé's bills. He hadn't returned her phone calls in over two years.

It made my stomach turn to see this woman as she walked into court, knowing she'd been with Reed the nights before Hayley's birth and after the twins died. But I was grateful. Reed wasn't aware he was about to be bombarded. Chloé agreed to let their son Landon go on the stand. Reed had never spoken to or met the boy in person. If meeting in a courtroom was good enough for my son, it was good enough for hers.

(B—Addendum)

IN THE SUPERIOR COURT OF LOS ANGELES COUNTY

STATE OF CALIFORNIA

IN THE MATER OF JUDGE: MARLA YATES

RE: LEGAL COUNSEL 1–CALHOUN

ASSOC.LEGAL COUNSEL 2–ELAINE RICHARDS

RILEY STONE, PETITIONER: EVAN REED

MALE CHILD RESPONDENT: JENNIFER STONE.

CV-04-111

CUSTODY HEARING DATE: 18 JULY 1994

JUDGE YATES: This is CV-04-111, in the matter of Riley Stone. What I generally do is exclude the children from the Courtroom formal proceedings. I understand there was a motion to interview the child in the Courtroom and that the 12-year-old boy and his mother have agreed to testify?

LEGAL COUNSEL: Yes, your honor, we feel, along with the respondent that this particular witness should be allowed to testify in the courtroom as to identify the petitioner for a brief moment and then we'll have him step out. He is a witness only & is not the child whose custody is currently in dispute.

JUDGE: Motion granted counsel. You may call your first witness.

"Good morning, Landon. Did you have a nice flight?" my lawyer asked.

The blond boy with Reed's blue eyes nodded. "Yes," he said without the help of an interpreter.

"You've never been to the U.S. before, I'm sure your mother has something lovely planned for the day, so I'll make this brief. Can you tell me who your father is?"

Landon shrugged and pointed at Reed.

"Have you ever met your father?" the lawyer asked.

The boy looked at his mother then glanced at Reed. "No. I've only seen him on TV."

My lawyer presented the judge with a DNA test. "No further questions, your honor."

Reed whispered into his lawyer's ear.

"No questions, your honor," his counsel said.

Chloé went on the stand next.

"Can you tell me how long you've known Mr. Reed? And the nature of your relationship?" My lawyer asked.

The French woman answered with confidence. Her long lashes and wavy dark hair were as gorgeous as Reed had described. My lawyer used Reed's bank statements to show the recurring hotel bookings and the wire transfers to Chloé to support her statement. Reed glared at her the entire time, biting back his anger.

"No questions, your honor," Reed's lawyer said.

My lawyer called Reed to the stand to testify.

"You and my client were married in 1987, correct?"

"Yes," Reed said.

The lawyer fired off a series of yes or no questions. "You met Chloe while touring in 1981. Did you start making trips to France to see Chloé in June of 1988."

"Yes, as friends," he said.

"Well, that wasn't the case, but I'll move on. Can I draw your attention to the date February 27, 1989? Were you in France on that date?"

"If the credit card says so."

"And was your daughter Hayley born three days later, on March 2, 1989?

"Yes," Reed said.

"So, you two have spent a lot of time together."

"Yes."

"What happened on August 13, 1990?"

Reed hesitated. "My daughter was killed in an accident."

"Were you watching your daughter at the time?"

"Yes," Reed said.

"Relevance, your honor?" his lawyer asked.

"I want to establish that Mr. Reed is not capable of caring for a child, your honor."

"I'll allow it," the judge said.

"Your daughter was killed in a tragic accident while in your care, is that correct?"

"Yes," Reed said.

"She was hit by a truck, is that correct?"

"Yes."

"How far away from her were you?"

"Maybe five feet. The truck clipped my shoulder."

"Were you under the influence of drugs or alcohol that day?"

"No."

"You'd come off an international tour, correct?"

"Yes."

"I imagine you were pretty tired."

"Yes," Reed said.

"Did you tell the police your daughter got out of your reach because you didn't react fast enough?"

"I don't remember," Reed said.

My lawyer referred to the police report.

"Would you say your lack of sleep contributed to the accident?"

"Possibly," Reed said.

"Are you still a touring musician?"

"Yes."

"I imagine you're pretty tired coming off the road?"

"Yes," he said.

"Do you feel like you could care for an infant while you're recovering from touring?"

"I have nannies lined up."

"So, your infant son would be better cared for by strangers than his own mother?"

"Without question," Reed said.

"Can I bring your attention to September 10, 1990? Does that date have any significance to you?"

"No."

"No, it doesn't, or no, you can't remember?" the lawyer said.

"I don't remember."

"Your twin sons were born on that date. One of them was stillborn and the other died later the same day, is that correct?"

"Possibly."

"What did you do the afternoon after the second child passed away? Did you fly out of state to perform a show?"

"Yes."

"Your sons' funeral was held on September 15, 1990. Did you return home for the funeral?"

"No."

"Where you in France with Chloé (last name redacted) on September 15, 1990?"

"It's possible," Reed said.

My lawyer showed Reed his credit card statement and flight records and asked the question again.

"Yes, if that's what the records say, I probably was."

"Did you return to California for your children's funeral?"

"No."

"So, you weren't exactly handling your fatherly duties. How long was it before you came home to comfort your grieving wife?"

"A few months. I was having a rough time."

"Mr. Reed, a one-year-old child was killed while in your care. You did not attend or pay for the funerals of your sons. You have repeatedly violated restraining orders against my client who was the victim of multiple violent, brutal attacks throughout your marriage. You have been arrested on multiple occasions on drug charges and for violent outbursts. Not only do you have a twelve-year-old son that you never bothered to meet, you stopped paying child support two years ago. Yet, you are convinced you're more suited to take care of an infant than his mother—and you don't plan to take care of the child yourself, instead you plan to leave him in the care of nannies."

"Objection, your honor, this is not a question, it's an attack."

"Sustained," the judge said.

"Your honor, can I have a moment with my client," Reed's lawyer said.

"Make it quick."

When they returned to the courtroom, the judge said, "I'm letting you know that I do not plan to hear anything further. The defendant has presented more than enough evidence for this case to be thrown out. Do you have any suggestions on how you plan to proceed, counsel?"

"My client would like to withdraw the case, your honor." his lawyer said.

"I object. The plaintiff can't drag my client through this ordeal and change his mind."

"I agree," the judge said.

"We are willing to accept supervised visits on the condition that Mr. Reed stop filing these frivolous cases against my client. In the past year, his lawyers have filed fifteen separate lawsuits against my client. We would like to petition the court for monthly child support for both my client, and Chloé (last name redacted)'s child, in the amount of $10,000 for each child."

"I can't make a determination for the other child, however, Mr. Reed, I suggest you take up that offer. You might be able to pull the wool over half the judges in this county—but I can't be bought. As of now, the mother retains full custody of the infant. Mr. Reed, after looking over your finances and projected income, I don't feel $10,000 a month is proper compensation for what you've put this woman and your child through. I'm ordering $15,000 each month including back pay for the past six months, until the child is age one, at which point we may reconsider based on your income. You will be allowed bi-weekly supervised visits for no more than two hours. Miss one visit without making prior arrangements, Mr. Reed, and I will personally revoke your visitation privileges."

"Your honor, that strict schedule will not work for my client. His income is based on the ability to travel internationally."

"Your client came here to try to obtain full custody of this child—if he wants to be a father to his son, he'll pull his weight, or he'll be in contempt. Is that clear, counsel?"

"Yes, your honor."

"Your client will submit to weekly drug testing for the next three months. If, and only if, your client completes twelve months of anger management classes and intense psychotherapy, we will reevaluate the custody situation to determine if he is capable of bi-weekly unsupervised visits with this minor child."

"Yes, your honor," the lawyer said.

"Mr. Reed, if you consider bringing your bull into this court again, I will personally sign the warrant for the LAPD to visit your mansion to search for illegal drugs and firearms. Are we clear? I don't want to see you in this court again. Do not contact that woman. Do not drive by her house. Do not send her flowers. Got that?"

Reed nodded.

"Your honor, we also request that Mr. Reed stop sending security guards from HLC Security Group to watch my client's house without her knowledge or permission."

"Really, Mr. Reed?" The Judge rolled her eyes.

"Your honor, my client has provided those services without charge to his ex-wife. She was attacked in her home by a fan and has received numerous threats. The security is for her safety."

"Does your client need protection?" the judge asked my lawyer.

"Only from Mr. Reed."

"Drop it with the covert stalking Mr. Reed. If she needs protection, she should be able to afford it with the monthly support. Got it?"

[END TRANSCRIPT]

Finally, someone grasped how absurd this situation was. I didn't expect Reed to follow any of her orders. But I didn't hear from him for a while, which was always a blessing.

Chapter Thirty-Nine

Reed was allowed a two hour supervised visit every other Saturday. His lawyers appealed because of his touring schedule, and another judge bent for him. Nothing else changed; he had to follow the original judge's orders—the anger management, supervised visits, everything.

He'd lost. Obsessive, annoying drunk phone calls followed. He was too high to keep up with the supervised visits. His label sent him to rehab. For three wonderful months, I did not have to take his phone calls. I could enjoy my beautiful little boy. He was saying little words, humming songs and laughing. We played for hours together, free to go to the pool, parks, and shop for groceries like normal people.

Reed wrote me a thirty-page letter from rehab apologizing for his "wrongs." He was attending AA, SAA, NA, and anger management classes. He wrote that he hadn't had sex in thirty days and was certain he was going to die from withdrawals. "*When I get out of here, I'll make this up to you and Riley. I'm going to be there for him. I'm so sorry, Jenny, I never wanted to hurt you. I promise things will be different."*

He had a good run when he got out of rehab. He requested reconsideration on the custody case and an L.A. judge agreed to let him have unsupervised visits twice a month. I was terrified but the judge would not listen to me. The bigger scene I caused, the greater the rift it would create with Reed. Sober, taking meds, dating some actress. He promised to have a nanny there at all times.

"He doesn't know you," I said.

"That's not my fault, is it? My girlfriend suggested we get together the three—or four—of us and have a little family meal, and warm him up to being around us. This is not about me and you anymore, it's about what's best for my son."

"Our son," I said.

Riley had to go on these overnight visits whether I liked it or not. If Reed was willing to work with me, I had to take advantage of that. We agreed to interview nannies together.

"If there are any issues, you're the first person I'll call," he said. Family court had proved again, that I couldn't get rid of him. I had to play his game.

The pressure to move back to L.A. was strong. Reed put a down payment on a condo near a recording studio he now owned. He could stop by after he left the studio and walk Riley to the park. I had to know what was going on if Riley was going to be around him.

My lawyers agreed that it was not a good idea to let Reed take Riley from Utah to California. I took the condo. I knew it was only a matter of time before he fucked up again, so I did everything I could to appear to accommodate him. My lawyer said it would give me favor in court.

I invited him and his girlfriend, Michelle Trafton, to dinner. She was in her early twenties. I'd seen her on an episode of *Melrose Place,* and another Aaron Spelling show. She'd been a teen actress and model before that. Cute, witty, perfect legs, gorgeous hair—everything I wasn't. Reed was funny and charming; she was enamored.

I had an urge to warn her away, but what if this was real? What if he had changed this time? She would be one more person who could keep an eye on Riley.

The little family—plus one girlfriend—dinners became our normal Tuesday night thing. I liked Michelle. He didn't seem to be beating the shit out of her, so there was that. After dinner, they would go upstairs, play with Riley for about an hour, and get him in the bath and bed. Sometimes she would come down and chat while Reed read Riley his bedtime stories. It was sweet, if you didn't know our history. It gave me time to do the dishes or read a book (nothing by Terry Brooks—sorry, never again, strictly a Pratchett-Gaiman girl now).

Reed called several times a week to check on Riley and there were no awkward drunk in the middle of the night phone calls. I watched him with Michelle; he was respectful, cute with the honeys and sweethearts. *Is he changing? Was it me? Did I bring out this awful thing in him?* I was one hell of a starter wife.

We made homemade pizzas for dinner one night. Afterwards, he and Michelle took Riley upstairs. I could hear Riley laughing and having a good time. I was putting the dishes away when Reed came down and asked if I had shampoo for Riley's bath.

"Oh, sorry. I bought more." I reached towards the plastic grocery bag like a blind person, avoiding turning my back to him. I was alone with the Reed for the first time in over a year. He was way too close in the small kitchen for comfort.

"What are you doing?" I said when he reached his arm in front of me.

He took the bottle. "I'm getting shampoo for my little boy's hair. You alright?"

"Sorry, I just-"

"It's okay Jenny, I understand. If you need help with dishes, or anything else, let me know."

Was this an alternate universe where Evan Reed was a decent guy? Nah. Not even.

Michelle talked about the remodeling she'd done at his mansion. They had little jokes. He opened the door for her and held her hand in a way that signified love, not property. He bragged about her career and accomplishments. My maniac ex-husband—the perfect boyfriend.

I held my breath, enduring them until they left. After a few weeks of this, I would close the door and burst into tears. *It was me. The problems in our relationship were about me.*

The next time they came over, Reed left Michelle upstairs, reading to Riley, telling her: "I'm going to run to the store and get the cereal Riley wants for breakfast."

I'm sure Michelle thought that was the absolute cutest thing ever. She wouldn't have if she'd known as soon as he walked downstairs, he had his ex-wife on the kitchen counter with his face buried under her dress. I figure that she would have been surprised by that—I was.

One minute you're minding your own business, putting away the clean dishes, the next thing you know, you're on the counter with your crazy, rock star, ex-husband's head between your knees. And he's already made you come before you have a chance to tell him no. Without consulting me, he made me that "other bitch" that rock stars cheat with while their girlfriends are upstairs.

And it was like heroin.

No, no, no.

And he was the needle.

Stop, stop, stop.

I rage-hated him. He'd paraded himself as a new man in front of me with Michelle—an adoring, respectful lover. A kind, generous father. He stole the perfect moment. I wasn't going to fight back, not with his girlfriend and our child a staircase away.

Disgusted, tears ran down my face—but my body reacted to him. *Jenny, what the fuck?* I pushed him away. He leaned in and kissed me with wet lips, then ran back up the stairs.

I threw up in the sink, grabbed a bottle of scotch, a Xanax, and hid in the bathroom when he brought Michelle downstairs to leave. I took a hot bath, downing sips of the alcohol. Pouring it between my thighs, trying to scrub away the places he'd touched. He wasn't the guy he was with Michelle—it was only a matter of time before he turned on her.

But I'd seen him with Riley. As much as I hated Reed, he was a good father. I watched him with Michelle—gentle, loving, kind—the way he'd been with me in the beginning. *It's not real, Jenny.* But it could have been. If he wasn't so fucking damaged and I wasn't so desperate we could have been something close to perfect. It wasn't fair.

Reed was standing in my living room when I walked out in my robe. I jerked it closed. "What are you doing here? How did you get back in?" I glanced around for a weapon. My mace was across the room.

He held up a box of Lucky Charms. "Riley's cereal. You didn't lock the door."

"Leave." I pointed at the door.

He approached me, leaning in, catching a whiff of my breath. "Shit, you're fucking wasted, Jenny. With Riley upstairs?"

Panic. Fuck! "I'm sorry," I said, knowing I didn't owe him a damned apology. "I never drink around Riley. I over-poured. Please don't tell family court."

Reed shook his head. "I'm not going to tell them. I'll take Riley for the night and give you a break."

I put my hands on his shoulder. "No, it's fine. I'm okay."

"Jenny, you're fucking drunk. I'm not leaving him here. I'll bring him back in the morning."

But he wouldn't. I knew that. *He's going to take my baby.* I panicked. "You could stay here, just tonight," I said out of desperation.

"With you?"

My entire body was shaking under my robe. *No.* "Yes," I said and touched his arm. "Please?"

Reed's shoulder twitched, he glanced at the door and looked back at me. *Please just go,* I thought. He pulled his IBM Simon PDA from his jacket and turned it off, placing it on my mantle. He took off his jacket and nodded towards my room. "Well?"

Like drugs, it only takes one hit. With Reed, it was a punch. Always more than one girl could handle. He made me sick. I hated him. I was as damaged as him to let him fuck me after everything he'd done. Trauma bond, my therapist warned me.

My brain was playing tricks on me. *Maybe I can replace those bad memories. Delete them and slip in this instead.* I hated him, but there were things I couldn't get from anyone else—the intensity of our early relationship, New York, Hayley, the twins, our son.

I can't let this happen again. I won't.

He kept finding reasons to drop by. He knew how to exploit my guilt and insecurities.

"I care about Michelle, but I just need to know for sure that this is over."

I was anxious, scared, alone, and he knew exactly what to say and do to ease my mind. It was wrong and I hated myself for it. Despite the horrific abuses he'd inflicted on me, my body betrayed me. It was a biochemical reaction. Oxytocin, dopamine. The stress hormone cortisol releasing—because when he was inside me, for a brief time I didn't have to worry about him taking my son from me.

I broke down at my therapist's office. "I don't understand. I hate him. Why am I letting this happen? And why am I having these crazy thoughts?"

"Like what?" my therapist asked.

"Like, if I just go along with it, give him what he wants, maybe things will be better for Riley."

"Jennifer, your ex-husband is a narcissist and violent abuser. He doesn't care about you. He wants control and he knows how to manipulate you. Don't confuse the act he's putting on in front of you as reality. It's not."

"I want the fighting to stop, so bad. I never wanted to speak to him again. I prayed he would overdose so this nightmare would be over."

"Dear, the fighting is why we are here. He can't stop. And you know that. I see hundreds of abuse victims and what you're describing is not uncommon, but this man is dangerous. You've said yourself that he tried to kill you. This perfect dad thing he's doing—it's a game. He's playing a part to rope you back in. And when he does, he will hurt you. He's not going to stop just because your son is there. Do you remember what you said about Hayley? How he seemed jealous of the attention you gave her. If he gets back into your life, he will see your son as competition for your affection and make Riley's life hell.

"This man is dangerous, Jenny. Part of his abuse cycle is putting you through so much hell that he's the only one that can relieve it. No matter what he's done, he knows when to release the pressure. And I am ninety-nine percent certain this entire situation is a long con. Think about it—you went no contact. You escaped. And he managed to get back into your home, your life. When you've suffered abuse for so long, the attention, intense sex and emotions are like drugs. You think you will never fall for it again, then you relapse. Abuse victims experience something called abuse amnesia—he's been so violent that the moment he shows you a sliver of kindness, it's like the storm clouds have parted. Your brain absorbs this fake sunshine and you forget how bad it was. You're not crazy. You're not stupid, selfish, or unworthy of love. But you have to cut him back out of your life. Before it's too late."

My therapist was right. I felt so much shame for letting any of this happen. The next time he came to my place, he was wearing my favorite cologne, the one he wore when we first met.

"This has to stop. It's wrong. We're crazy and toxic together," I told him.

"But it feels good, doesn't it?"

He was right. It did feel good—the way pressing a tender bruise or injecting heroin feels good. "You tried to kill me," I blurted out. "Twice."

He sighed. "Do you want to talk about that now?"

"It happened."

"I was in a bad place and taking it out on you. You know my history, babe. I worked that shit out. I'm on a fistful of medication every morning. I go to my anger management classes. I go to therapy twice a week. I'm eating right, exercising. Michelle has me running five miles a day, entering us in marathons and yoga, all this positive shit. It's helping. I feel like a different person."

"Then why are you in my bed?"

"Valid. I'm a recovering sex addict. Not recovered enough. And you're right. I'm being a dick. She doesn't deserve this, and you don't deserve to be my piece of ass on the side. Though you do have a nice ass."

"You tried to kill me," I repeated to this man who was not the Evan Reed I'd ever known. "You've done everything in your power to make my life a living hell."

"I screwed up, Jenny. What can I do?" He shook his head and rubbed his hand against his lips. "Look, I'm gonna put my dick in my pants and go over to that church on Sunset because they have a late night SAA meeting. Might hit up NA or AA meetings on the way, to be on the safe side. I carry a card in my wallet with a list of meetings to keep my ass out of trouble. Yet here I am finding ways to fuck my ex-wife while my fiancée takes care of our kid."

"She's your fiancée?"

"About that..."

"Go, now."

"Ten-four, mama," he said.

He stopped at the door. "I know this question is going to bite me in the ass, but is there a chance that we could be more than this again?"

"No. We don't exist. Together, we are nothing more than a desperate, sad, insecure madwoman and a violent, homicidal man. We're both addicted to this madness. There's nothing good here. I suggest, if you have something better with Michelle, go save it."

He shook his head. "You've never held back the punches, have you?"

I shuddered. "Go check on your fiancée. You don't need to be here. Go to your alphabet meetings—all of them. You're doing good with Riley, don't let this mistake fuck it up. You fell off the wagon. I fell with you. Let's say we owed each other one and let it go."

Chapter Forty

My therapist said a slip off the wagon may have been a trigger, but it didn't cause what happened. Abused people return to their abusive partners and the most horrific conditions because it's all they know; they want to rewrite history—make one good memory to replace the bad. They miss the good parts of that person and of themselves. Reed was a master manipulator. He used jealousy and insecurity against me. I fell into the trap.

"But you stopped it before it was too late, that's what is important," she tried to reassure me.

The family dinners ended. Reed wanted Riley to come stay one night every other weekend, which made me nervous, but Riley was comfortable around his dad. Despite his many flaws, Reed was a great father. Michelle and the nannies would be there. I hoped family time had been for Riley and not an excuse to be with me.

I could not sleep at all when Riley was there.

My therapist insisted I keep boundaries with Reed. He wanted to take Riley during the week, and I said no.

"Jenny, you're being fucking selfish. He's my kid. You don't get to make the rules."

Michelle was filming on location in Canada and was no longer home to occupy Reed's time. When they fought, we fought. He brought Riley home late. He came over drunk, we argued, he shoved me. I called the police, they made him leave. Shit spiraled.

From that one drink, we were back at restraining orders, heroin addiction, attempted murder, suicide threats, and family court supervision. He lost thirty pounds, called me one hundred and fifty times in one week. He quit anger management, stopped his medications and raged out when he was manic. Paparazzi, airport employees, old ladies, poodles—nothing with a pulse was safe.

When he was strung out, I wouldn't let him take Riley. He punched a hole through the glass in my front door. He slapped his fiancée while they were watching Riley and she had him arrested. I took Reed to court to get a restriction on his visitation until he went to rehab.

I was so glad I didn't have any friends who could say they told me so.

Michelle broke things off with him. He showed up in the middle of the night, drunk, crying. I begged him to get help. Michelle begged him. His bandmates pleaded with him. He was going off the deep end, again. The president of the record label personally walked him downstairs and out the front door after he raged out during a meeting, pissing all over a conference room table. Having lost his latest source of narcissistic supply, his attention returned to me.

One night he shoved his way in the door and locked it behind him.

"No," I shouted.

He paced. "We are soulmates. You're going to pack your things and move home. I will kill Jamie London, James Alan, anyone you've slept with."

"Please stop, please go home," I pleaded, hoping Riley would not wake up. After his arrests, Reed was no longer allowed to have firearms, but his Beretta was in his back pocket. I was used to it at the mansion, but not in my house—not with my baby upstairs. I led him away from the stairs into the kitchen.

He kissed me, saying he loved me, and tried to unbutton my jeans.

"Reed, stop."

He pulled out the gun and ripped my shirt. Pinning me against the sink with his arm above me, the gun pressed against the wall.

"Mama?" Riley stood in the kitchen entryway holding his comfort toy Binky bear and rubbing his sleepy little eyes. "Mama, wad-der."

"Baby, go upstairs. Mommy is talking to Daddy. I'll be right there."

"But Mama."

I rubbed my free hand against Reed's cheek. "Please don't let him see this. You're his father. He loves you. Don't do this in front of him. This isn't you. I won't call the police, I swear. Just go home."

Reed hesitated, then zipped his jeans, slid the gun in his back pocket and left. He didn't even look at Riley.

Riley ran to me. "Dada's mean."

"Dada's upset." I picked Riley up, locked the door, and dialed the police. Two young officers arrived. The female officer walked around the condo looking for Reed while the male officer took my statement. I told him my name and explained what happened.

He laughed. "Seriously? Evan Reed, the musician is your ex-husband? I've heard that one before, lady."

Shaking, holding my crying baby—and the person who was supposed to "protect and serve" me was laughing in my face. He called the other officer to the door to tell her that this was a hoax.

"She's Evan Reed's ex-wife," the female officer said. "We're here five times a week. Dude's a total creep. Take the woman's statement."

The male officer apologized, "I'm sorry Miss. We get a lot of calls in Hollywood that turn out not to be true. There's not much we can do if it's your word against his. We didn't see him do anything."

"He came in my house, held a gun to my head, and tried to rape me," I said, with the calmness of a person who'd been through this a hundred times. "I need you to write that down so I can go to the courthouse tomorrow and get a restraining order."

"Yes, ma'am."

When I followed up the next day, a judge issued a restraining order against Reed. For me only. He refused to issue one for Riley. "Take that up with family court. Follow protocol."

"Fuck your protocol. He is going to kill us!" I stormed out of the courthouse with Riley on my hip. I sat on the curb outside in the parking lot and burst into tears. I had to figure out some way to make this stop.

Reed was arrested for disturbing the peace. He bailed out within a few hours and called, threatening to kill himself if I didn't move in with him. I called the police and told them to do a wellness check at the mansion. They wouldn't take me seriously.

"Check your records and see how many times I've had to call about this man. I'm not making this up. Do something!" I hung up and called his brother.

"Daniel, I can't take this anymore. He's going to hurt someone or kill himself. The police will not listen to me. Every time I call, they ask me if it's a prank."

"I'll check on him," Daniel said.

"Take the police with you. He's got guns."

"He's not supposed to have guns," Daniel said.

"Nothing stops him."

I triple checked the locks on the doors and windows, tucked Riley into bed, and went back downstairs. Resisting the urge to have a drink or knock myself out with Xanax, I turned on the news.

It was on all the channels.

"Rock star Evan Reed taken by ambulance to Cedars Sinai after suicide attempt. The thirty-three-year-old was found unconscious in his Malibu estate. There is no current update on his condition. The rocker has had a tumultuous year of arrests and stints in and out of rehab."

A representative from the hospital came out to give a statement to the media. I waited with the rest of the world to see if my son's father was dead.

"At 9:33 p.m., 9:50 p.m. and 10:10 p.m. multiple calls were made to the 9-1-1 emergency line by parties inside and outside a Malibu estate on 1206 Canyon Valley Road. At 10:15 p.m., a thirty-three-year-old male was found unresponsive. At 10:25 the thirty-three-year-old male was pronounced dead at the scene." There was a gasp among the reporters.

Fuck. I glanced back at the stairway to make sure Riley hadn't sneaked down. I turned the volume up on the TV. There was no way Reed was dead. He'd probably killed someone else, but he wasn't dead.

The hospital representative continued, "After several attempts paramedics on the scene revived the male victim. He was taken to Cedars Sinai and is currently in the ICU. We are notifying the patient's family. I can take a few questions, but we don't have many details at this point."

I couldn't hear the reporter's questions.

"It's touch and go at the moment. We can't release information on the patient's condition until the family is notified." The hospital rep turned the press conference over to a police officer.

"The only information we have at this time is that it was a non-life threatening gunshot wound coupled a with a massive drug overdose. It appears the gunshot may have been an accidental ricochet. That's the only information we can release at this time."

I took the phone off the receiver. Someone banged on my door at two a.m. When I looked out the peephole, I saw Reed's ex, Michelle, crying. She was shaking, traumatized. I let her inside. The young actress' life had gone off script.

"I'd never seen him this way, Jenny." She cried, rocking back and forth on my sofa, her young, athletic calves shaking. Her valley accent cracked, "He sat on the end of his bed with his pistol under his chin and a tourniquet around his arm, needle and spoon on the floor, shreds of paper where he'd written note after note and torn them up. I begged him to stop."

I listened as she described so many nights of my life. He'd screamed she didn't love him, and babbled incoherent nonsense about Riley, dead babies, and me. When Reed pointed the gun at his temple in the living room, she'd wrestled it away from him. It went off, hitting a metal guitar plate, ricocheted, and caught him under his rib cage.

"He didn't know he was hit." Michelle held her hands stiff in the air, physically trying to grasp what she'd seen. "He nodded out against the wall and fell flat on his face into the floor." She placed the 911 call from inside the house. "He was foaming at the mouth and turned blue. He was dead! He was dead! There was nothing they could do. They stabbed him with one of those big needles and he breathed. It was like a horror movie, Jenny. They won't let me go in the ICU."

The entire time she had been talking about Reed, I was watching her shiny, chestnut curls bounce perfectly against her neckline. *I wish my hair looked like that. I wonder what conditioner she uses?* Then I remembered. Revlon. Because she was in the commercial. Reed's little flying monkey was trying to pull me in. *You're a pawn, little girl—but that hair!*

"Jenny, are you listening?"

No, no, I'm really not. "I was on my way to bed."

Michelle sat down on my sofa.

"I don't know anyone who has died before. Even old people. I've never seen someone die—and then un-die. It was so scary. I know CPR. I auditioned for *Baywatch*. But I froze, I forgot. I mean, I could just tell he wasn't going to make it. It's like I knew." She was whimpering again, like he was a dead dog, or someone's grandmother, and not completely psychotic. "I'm questioning everything. Like, should I stay with *Melrose Place,* or should I audition for *E.R.*? I think I could do something more with my life. After seeing that. I just don't know." She cried.

I threw my arms in the air. "Why the fuck are you here?"

The poor girl looked at me as if I'd stabbed her cat. "I-I-I thought we could wait together, you might know something. I thought..."

"You came here to tell me that my ex-husband put a gun in his mouth, while my child is asleep upstairs? You expect me to feel sorry for Reed? Honey, no. You picked up the phone. You went over there. He's your problem now."

"B-but..." Michelle stuttered.

"You fell for this, honey. You're on your own."

"Why are you being mean to me?"

"You literally missed a bullet tonight, Michelle. Run while you can. If he wakes up in the morning, you won't get a chance."

"He's in pain, Jenny. He misses you and Riley. He's so lost."

I had to get her out of my house and hopefully save her stupid life. "Michelle, he's an abuser, he's a rapist, he's a psychopath—you're seeing something in him that isn't real."

"He's Riley's dad. How can you say these things? He could die." She sniffled. "He was right about you, you're crazy. Heartless."

"Michelle, if you'd let him shoot himself in the head, you would have been doing me a favor."

Those words will get you sent to prison, by the way. Just remember, always, that everything you say and do, can and will be used against you. Especially when you kick sweet, terrified chicks that remind you of yourself out of your condo the night your ex tries to kill himself. You don't get any bonus points when you shout you fucked him while she was playing babysitter to your kid.

"You are both insane. You deserve each other."

"And you're the dumb bitch wearing my engagement ring. Take your shit back to *Melrose Place* because I don't have time for it!" I slammed the door in her face.

Maybe I was the bitch she described to the media, but she didn't go back to him, so I probably saved her life. She would not extend any favors when I needed them later.

The press was outside the door when Daniel stopped by. "Reed is awake. He wants to see you, Jenny."

"Not my problem."

"You need to take Riley to see him. Just in case."

"If I give in, he'll do this every time he doesn't get his way. I have a restraining order against him, and I'm filing for full custody of Riley."

"I'll get him in rehab," Daniel said.

"Call me if you want to get Jayden and Riley together to play, but I'm done."

A judge allotted me temporary full custody. He said if Reed's condition improved and he completed a mandatory thirty-day rehab, he could resume visitation.

"Are you reading his file?"

"We have to give Mr. Reed the benefit of doubt," the judge said.

Reed recovered, spent three nights in jail on drug and firearm charges, and then did his thirty days in rehab. They let him go. Again.

He wrote an E.P. while locked up and spent a week recording it as soon as he was released. The record company did a quick press—they knew an expiring product—and cashed in. Two months after he got out of rehab, he was on a month-long mini-tour to promote his *Life After Death* E.P. The cover was a photo of his bullet wound.

Michelle never spoke to him again.

I wouldn't take his calls until we had another custody hearing. I was determined this time they would listen to me. They had to, right?

Charming, funny, "new guy" Reed was gone. The violent, raging asshole was back. There was no escape from him. Since I'd let him get lenient with visitations it was hard to get the courts to crack down again.

As much as I hated him, until that point, I'd wanted to help him. He was my son's father. I wanted him to get better so Riley wouldn't see him like this. But he would have raped me in front of my son. Reasoning with him was never an option. It never should have been. It took so long for me to accept that, and by then, it was too late.

Sometimes, you have to jump ship and do what's best for you, right from the get-go. You don't owe anyone anything if they're hurting you. Leave. Be done with it from day one. With violence and abuse, there's no second chance. I had cared more about saving him than taking care of myself.

I lay in bed every night and imagined how Riley and I could escape California. I had a new security system installed, triple locks put on the doors. I mentally mapped out different ways to get out of the house if Reed managed to break in.

When the renter moved out of the Brentwood house near Mark and Elizabeth, I sold my condo and moved back there with Riley. I wanted to take him and run, but Reed would find us, and I would go to jail for taking Riley across state lines. Then what? I couldn't risk breaking the law.

I contacted Marlene Von Berstein in New York.

"Jenny, I have been waiting on this phone call since the night we met. My father and first husband were narcissists. I knew when we met that Reed already had his claws so deep in you. I wish you would have called sooner." She offered me a teaching position at her art initiative and reached out to a lawyer in L.A. to help with the custody issues.

Even with Marlene's resources, the judge refused to give me full custody and block Reed's visitation. He required Reed to do monthly drug testing and have nanny supervision at all times. No matter how much I pleaded, the courts continued to give a documented, violent, raging, narcissistic, sociopath access to my son.

If I sensed Reed was high, I called the cops and he'd leave. But the days he appeared okay, I had no choice but to let Riley go. I wept when Riley was out of my sight.

Countless visitation issues forced us into mediation. When the counselor stepped out to make a call, leaving us in a room alone, Reed punched me in the throat across the table. I fought back to keep him from killing me.

Instead of using that as a reason to limit his access to Riley, family court decreed that Reed and I should have no contact and have someone from the state there during pick up and drop off.

Reed was out of money, so he used time to control me, just like he had when we were together. Visitation worked around his schedule. He was late on purpose, making any chance of career or social life impossible for me. He would then point out how irresponsible I was for missing whatever I missed—because he was late.

At some point, a judge had to listen, and put an end to this madness.

June 18, 1995, was different. On that day, everything changed. There was no turning back.

Chapter Forty-One

Sunday, June 18, 1995

W hen Reed hadn't returned Riley by three p.m., Sunday, June 18, 1995, I knew something was wrong. It was part of our agreement that we'd call to leave a message Sunday morning to confirm drop-off time. I had not received the morning message. I paced, watching the clock. I dialed his cell at 3:01 p.m. and it went to voicemail. I tried again at 3:10 and 3:15. I called his home number. There was no answer. At 3:30 p.m., Elizabeth came over.

The family services woman sat at my kitchen table, knitting. She rolled her eyes. "Honey, take a breath, you're overreacting."

At 3:45 p.m., I called Reed's brother.

"Jenny, I haven't seen Reed since he got out of rehab," Daniel said.

"He told me he was taking Riley to San Bernardino for your son's birthday."

"Jayden's birthday was three months ago. What's going on?" Daniel asked.

Reed lied. Of course, he lied. At four p.m., the family court worker wanted to leave. She told Elizabeth to stay with me and call the police if we had not heard anything by five p.m. Reed knew they would tell me to call the police. At 5:05, he wasn't there, so I called.

"Sounds like he's running late, Miss. Give him more time."

Elizabeth tried to reassure me. "This is typical, unreliable Reed. You know he can't afford to do anything else to get in trouble."

But he was always doing things to get in trouble, and always getting rewarded for it. He was always late—so they gave him more time. Supervised visits didn't work with his touring schedule, so they'd given him joint custody. Weekends weren't enough and he was trying to get Riley for a week at a time, which was never going to happen under my watch.

No matter what, he takes care of Riley. He loves to scare me, but he takes care of him. The weekend before Reed called right after three to tell me they were at the circus—the circus that opened at three, he'd done it on purpose. Riley had a great time. He came home with stuffed animals and cotton candy, saying, "Dada-fun."

Reed had said, "Mommy's mean. She doesn't want you and daddy to do anything fun. None of the other kids rode the elephant, did they? See Mommy, sometimes it pays to be me." He'd smiled. No one else was smiling.

Family court workers were wrapped around his finger. And oh, that suicide thing? That was an "accident". He'd had a little too much to drink. "Rock n' roll, you know?" A judge laughed at that, the same judge who told me that I'd be arrested if I didn't comply with the visitation order.

So, my options were—defy court orders, and get my son taken away. Kidnap my son, take him across state lines, get arrested, and have him taken away.

Or, let a suicidal, addict, rapist, sociopath take my son for the weekend. I'd only had two judges in the system who'd been helpful. The majority of the time some other judge came back to rule in Reed's favor. The family court worker would have never left early if it were Reed she was waiting with. I would have gotten in trouble, whereas, with a wink and a smile, those things were never written down no matter how many times he did it.

Look at the records. On June 18, 1995, the family court worker wrote: *The mother is a little agitated and overly emotional that the father hasn't returned with the child. He's only five minutes late.*

She didn't write that he'd never shown up. She didn't want to admit leaving before the five p.m. call to the police. They might have taken her seriously.

Reed called at 5:10. *Thank god.*

"Did you call the cops on me? I need you to come get the baby. I gotta be somewhere in an hour and I'm not going to have time."

I was too relieved to argue. "Elizabeth and I will meet you."

"No, not her. I'm sick of being judged by your friends. We can meet somewhere public. If you don't say anything to child services, I won't. Riley fell asleep. I didn't want to wake him. Can you meet me halfway?"

I had to get to my son.

"Where?"

"Exit 82. In Dozier. There's a shopping mall. We can meet in the parking lot."

"Where are you that Dozier is halfway?" I gritted my teeth. Dozier was an hour drive.

"Look, I'm tired. I'll listen to whatever you need to say when you get here."

"Reed, are you high?"

"Call me when you get here." The line went silent.

"Mark's coming home early to follow you," Elizabeth said.

"Take Sammi home. I'm going to take a quick shower."

I waited for Elizabeth to turn onto her street, then ran to my car. I couldn't wait on Mark. Reed was high. I knew it. Seeing Mark would throw him over the edge. He wouldn't hurt Riley—but I'd also thought he wouldn't use around Riley.

It only took forty-five minutes to get to the exit. I called Reed's cell. No answer. I followed the signs to the mall and pulled into the parking lot. My cell rang. I could hear kids in the background.

"Where are you?" I asked.

"KidzWorld. We waited in the parking lot. Riley saw the lights, had to go in."

Public was good—KidzWorld better. I parked in the middle of the lot. Reed always insisted that I carry a gun. He'd tried to enforce the rule after we separated. After living with him, I didn't want to see another gun, but Mark demanded that I keep a handgun in the house for protection. I brought it with me on days that I had to meet Reed. I opened the glove box and slid the small revolver into my purse.

For protection.

Kidzworld was packed. Reed and Riley were playing Skee-Ball in between taking bites of pizza. Reed was wearing sunglasses, and a black baseball cap turned backwards, his hair pulled back in a ponytail. A faded pair of jeans with holes, a white tank top, and a loose open flannel shirt. He had an unlit cigarette in his mouth, which he placed in the front pocket of his shirt when he saw me. He looked unusually young that day, like someone had scrubbed the rock star off of him. Just a young punk who'd knocked some girl up at some point; looking closer to twenty-one than thirty-three. He picked Riley up and let him drop a ball in the highest score. Riley laid his head on Reed's shoulder.

"Want pizza?" Reed asked.

"He's tired. I need to get him home."

Riley kissed me on the cheek, but he was content with his head on his daddy's shoulder.

"I wanted to have a good day with him." The dry distance in Reed's voice made me nervous. He picked up the diaper bag from the seat and used his free arm to toss in the miscellaneous toys and bottles. He handed the bag to me and looked around the table. He sighed. "Damn it. I left Binky Bear in the car. We'll have to stop by my car if that's okay."

I followed him to the parking lot.

"Sit in the car seat, buddy, while I look for your bear," Reed said when Riley fussed.

I stood with my hand on my hip, waiting while Reed circled to the other side of the car.

A group of kids sped by on their skateboards. They stopped and asked for an autograph. He normally didn't mind, but today it agitated him.

"I'm with my family. Give us space." Reed leaned the driver's seat forward to see if the bear was under the seat. "Here it is." He walked to the passenger side of the car where I was standing, to help get Riley out of the car. Reed's hand brushed across my wrist. Something cold and hard pressed into my back. The tip of his Beretta.

Oh god, what have I done? The same kids walked by the car. Reed waited. Once they were out of earshot:

"Get in the car, Jenny."

Chapter Forty-Two

I had done everything I wasn't supposed to do. I met Reed alone in an undisclosed location. I let him keep Riley between us. I went along with him in the restaurant to keep him from causing a scene. Now I was pressed between him and a black BMW rental car with Nevada plates, a gun against my back. He tightened his grip and twisted my wrist.

"Make this easy for Riley," Reed said.

Why did I let this happen?

I tried to stay calm.

He twisted my arm tighter. A kid sped by on a skateboard.

"Get in now and nobody else gets hurt."

We'd been in situations like this before—but not with baby in tow. Riley was calm in his seat. He didn't know anything was wrong. A million scenarios ran through my mind in a matter of seconds. I could try to fight, but the gun could go off and hit Riley or the skateboarders. If I managed to escape, I would be leaving Riley behind. If I screamed, Reed would shoot me.

He guided me into the passenger seat with the gun. Reed leaned over me in the seat, pressing his knee into my back, my head against the dashboard. He pulled a rope from the floorboard and tied my hands tight behind my back.

He leaned around me to buckle Riley's car seat. His knee was in my seat between my legs, and the gun in his waistband was at my chest.

"I tried to make this work. I tried everything I could possibly think of, Jenny." He picked my purse off the

ground, tossed it into the floorboard behind the driver's seat, and closed my door.

From the rear-view mirror, I saw him sign a skateboard on the trunk of the BMW. My cell phone vibrated in my purse. I kept it on silent when I was around Reed. He hated being interrupted. The kids left, and Reed got into the car and locked the doors.

"Keep your fucking mouth shut."

I stayed silent. He immediately pulled into a hotel parking lot next door. *He's been staying here the entire time.* He took Riley and opened my door slightly. He had the baby positioned so that I could see his gun.

"I need to grab a few things. Stay here and be quiet. Don't make this bad for the baby."

Reed slammed the door, setting the alarm with his keychain. I had to keep an eye on him with Riley, and at the same time tried to position myself to see if there was a way I could reach my purse.

He was out in minutes, carrying a suitcase, which he put in the trunk before putting the baby back in the car.

I remembered an episode of Oprah; she said never let your kidnapper get you to the second location. It didn't sink in that my son and I were kidnapped until Reed sped out of the hotel parking lot onto the ramp of the nearest interstate. He lit a cigarette and opened the window. *He's driving a rental car. No one knows where we are.*

An hour into the drive his cell phone started ringing. He ignored the calls. It was seven-thirty p.m. when we left KidzWorld. We crossed the Nevada state line at ten p.m. The baby fussed.

"Reed. Please we need to stop. He's so tired. He needs to be changed."

Reed ignored me. Riley eventually fell asleep, and I must have dozed off. I woke at three a.m. We were off the freeway, on some desert highway. Reed was wide awake. His new demo was playing.

The lyrics were not promising.

His phone was in the ashtray on vibrate. Thirty-two missed calls. Someone knew something was wrong. Reed saw my eyes on the phone, rolled down his window, and threw it out.

Finally, he pulled into a motel parking lot. It looked like some 1950s Miami hotel with palm trees. Except we were in a deserted no-man's land. I couldn't remember the last gas station we had passed. A payphone outside the hotel had a dangling cord, no phone.

The same instructions. Stay in the car. Don't make noise. Don't try to get anyone's attention. He left Riley in the car with me and set the alarm again. Seven minutes later, he came back with a room key.

He untied my hands.

"I'm going to let you carry Riley. If you try anything, I will put a bullet in your head."

My mind went blank. *I have to find a way out of this.* As I picked up Riley, I slid my purse over my shoulder.

Reed told me to stand beside the car while he pulled the suitcase from the trunk. He lifted the baby's bag out of the back seat and locked the doors.

"Walk." He followed me up the stairs to room 238. Inside the room, I let my purse slide to the floor between the bed and the nightstand as I leaned over to check Riley's diaper.

Reed latched the three locks on the door and put a chair under the doorknob. He flipped the TV on to some old movie station. Jerking the phone cord out of the wall, he sliced it with his pocketknife.

I stayed calm; tried to play normal. I got the baby ready for bed. He was hungry and there was no formula in the bag. Reed filled a bottle with tap water and handed him saltine crackers. I panicked wondering how long Riley had gone without formula. He had eaten a few bites of pizza at the restaurant, but he didn't have enough teeth to chew much of it.

"He needs formula, Reed."

"Tomorrow."

There was a small pack n' play in the corner of the room. Reed set it up for the baby. When Riley had been asleep thirty minutes, he moved him to the pack n' play, covered him with his blanket, and placed Binky Bear next to him.

Reed poured two glasses of scotch on the desk. He emptied a capsule into one glass, stirred it, and handed it to me.

"Drink it. It will help you sleep."

I did as I was told. He turned off the lights. Other than the flicker of the black and white TV western, the room was dark. Reed finished his drink. Mine was over half full. He hummed Alice in Chains' song, "Would?" Then took my drink from my hands and put it against my lips, lifting it to make me drink. The drink was too strong. I choked; it spilled onto my shirt and face. I wiped my mouth and tried to hold the whiskey down.

Reed pulled off his shirt. Pinning my arms, he kissed my neck and chest. I lay still, tried to conjure my old coping skills. My body trembled. They weren't working. He moved his hands over my breasts. I tensed when he put his hand between my thighs. He gripped my throat with the other hand. "I don't want to hurt you, baby. I can't help it."

"Please—not with Riley here."

"Stop saying his name," Reed said.

I tried to relax my body and put my mind somewhere else. He shoved his hands between my legs. I gasped and he put his hand over my mouth. He moved on top of me. He was looking me in the eyes. A tear ran down my face. He gripped my throat. He wouldn't stop until I orgasmed. I tried to close my eyes and think of anything I could that would help. Eventually my body gave in out of exhaustion and fear. It was hopeless.

The pills he put in my drink kicked in, and I fell in and out of consciousness, only to bolt awake to find him still thrusting long after I thought he'd got off.

He shook me awake when he finished. Reed rose onto his knees and pulled me up with both hands around my neck, choking me. He spat in my face. He shoved me on the bed, waking me several times throughout the night to have sex again.

After six a.m., I woke to see him cut a piece of rope with his knife. He tied my right hand to a bar below the right edge of the headboard of the bed, and I blacked out again.

According to the clock on the nightstand, it was afternoon when I woke to a crushing headache. My vision was blurred. and it took a moment before I first noticed the blood on my face and chest.

Had I been shot? I shivered, and immediately vomited on the floor beside the bed. I was so dizzy that lying down was like trying to catch my balance on a waterbed.

In the distance, I saw Reed put the Riley down, and walk towards me. I faded out and came to again with him nudging me to wake up. Blood covered the sheets, my hands, and arms.

He untied my hand, wrapped the sheet around me, and walked me to the bathroom. I stepped into the shower. Cold water hit like shards of glass, stabbing my face. My skin suctioned to the shower tile as I leaned into the wall to keep my balance. Panic swept over me. Texas. *Please don't kill me here.*

Blood swirled down the shower drain. Sliding downwards, I couldn't comprehend what was happening until I hit the shower floor. In and out of consciousness again. Was I in the hotel in Dallas? Was any of this real? Or was I reliving a nightmare?

The shower door opened. Reed stood over me, covered me with a towel, and helped me out of the shower.

I didn't recognize my face in the mirror. At some point in the night I'd become his punching bag.

Both of my eyes were black, my face swollen, covered in scratches and cuts. His rings had left indent marks in my skin. His hands marks on my neck. I was compelled to look. This was the last time I would see myself.

There was a broken glass on the counter, and a mirror covered in cocaine dust.

My chest and arms were scratched and bruised. I looked like the wrong end of a hit and run with an eighteen-wheeler—a sight I was too familiar with. My swollen lips twitched and quivered.

It's entrancing to see your own blood, your own death, your own fate happening before your eyes. I was looking at a mask, and I didn't see anything familiar or alive to help me stay connected.

Until then I'd tried to hold it together for the baby. My mind was giving up. I was shutting down.

Reed loomed in the mirror, breaking my trance.

"There's nothing that can help now, is there?" I asked.

He shook his head. "It's too late."

This is death. Somewhere in my mind a voice taunted, *he warned you. He said this would happen.* This wasn't something he could send flowers or gifts or lawyers to smooth over. This was final.

I was too worn down to stop it. I did a mental breakdown in my mind of my life with Reed. The babies. The lies. The abuse. If I closed my eyes, it would all go away.

Riley screamed, then wailed. I ran into the bedroom and grabbed him from the floor. He had fallen against the desk and hit his head.

"No!" Reed shouted and lunged after me. He was holding the TV remote in his hand and hit me across the face with it.

I winced in pain, putting my hands over Riley's head to shield him from the blows. I was naked, cowered over my baby boy and trying to protect him from his father. I wondered if this was happening for Reed, or if he was reenacting his own childhood. There was a pop, the room went black, and a lamp crashed into the wall.

Chapter Forty-Three

M y hand was tied back to the bedpost.

Reed was on top of me.

Surely, he couldn't rape me again.

I flashed back to the night in the barn behind the mansion. I remembered lying on the concrete floor, covered in gasoline, thinking, *he's coming back. He's going to kill me.* Is this how Kaley felt before she died?

In the barn, I'd thought it would be a relief to have this over, to end it. I had to push that away now. I tried my best to stay conscious. No matter what torture Reed inflicted on me, there was a terrified, screaming little boy across the room. A little boy who I was sure hadn't eaten in hours, if not days. A little boy whose fate would be left in the hands of this sociopath who was breathing heavily in my ear, uttering insults and obscenities that I'd managed to tune out.

How long had we been hostage in this sleazy hotel room? Was anyone looking for us? I prayed Reed had used a credit card to book the room. The cold blade of his knife pressed into my neck. Reed was frustrated. He'd been thrusting into my body for at least an hour.

He spat in my face and forced his lips against mine, his teeth grinding against my teeth. It was the drugs. He couldn't get off—and it was my fault for lying here—a lifeless rag doll. He wanted me to participate. I didn't think I could do it again. My insides were on fire, the dry friction had gone on so long. Reed gripped my neck tighter.

"Okay, okay," I whispered. I tried to conjure something—anything—that might calm him. "I love you. Everything is okay." I lied in his ear until I felt his body release. Suddenly he was a dead weight on top of me. I hoped to god that he'd stop breathing. Within minutes he was snoring, his bag of heavy bones smothering me.

I *have to get out of this room.*

I have to get this man's weight off me without waking him.

I have to save my little boy.

First, I needed to free my right hand from the bedpost. Reed had let my left hand loose. He'd wanted me to fight, but I'd been too exhausted to try. My left arm was useless, trapped and numb beneath his heavy sleeping body. *How could I do this without waking him?* I would have loved the satisfaction of shoving him off the bed, but I didn't have the strength. Why wake a sleeping tiger?

It was getting harder to breathe with his weight on my chest. I found space to wiggle, but I wasn't getting anywhere. *Think. Think. Think!* I had to get my sleeping arm between us. I tried and tried to ease my fingers between us, but it was useless.

Then it hit me. How many times had I rolled his snoring drunk body over? "Baby," I said sick-sweet and raspy. "You're snoring too loud." Nothing. "Baby!" I grunted louder. "The snoring—" This time he moved. It was a measly two inches, but it was two inches closer to freedom.

I used what strength I had in my right fingers to grip the bedpost and pulled myself towards the headboard. If I could get my shoulders in the slightest angle, I could push myself back with my feet.

Sharp burning pains shot through my calf muscles. I dug my heels into the filthy sheets twice before my left leg collapsed into the most painful Charlie horse of my life. My toes drew back. My teeth dug into my lip to muffle my cry. My body was revolting against me. My toes turned inward, pulling tighter and tighter by my useless muscles.

Get Riley out of this room. It was insane of me to think we could leave this room alive. I was in the middle of a double-murder-suicide, and I knew it. Reed would come to his senses and realize there was no way out of this. But he hadn't gone into this blindly—it was planned. He was going to kill us both. Riley was my son, but he was a pawn to Reed. I had to save him and get us out of this hotel room alive.

But I couldn't move. What if he overdosed or killed himself before he ended my son's life? My baby could die here, slowly and painfully, and no one would know until it was too late.

I forced my toes to straighten, and dug against the Charlie horse into the mattress, slowly inching up the headboard. After at least twenty minutes of slow movement, I was at eye level with my wrist. My left arm was tight against my body, pinned under Reed. *Now what?* I had to get my shoulder free so I could lean closer to my right wrist.

No matter how long it took, I'd have to chew my way through the rope. It was a thin twine, looped multiple times, and tied so tight my fingers were numb. I had enough movement in my shoulder to get a good grip with my teeth. I ground them against the threading of the rope. It went on so long, a blister formed on my lip. Finally, I was able to pop the thread, hearing a tooth crack. I gritted my front teeth together and worked through the pain. My teeth and arm were slick from my bleeding gums. The threads were getting thinner, but I was losing my strength and my jaw and neck were locking. I leaned my head back.

The strand of threads I'd been gnawing at for the past half hour snapped. My wrist slipped down. *This is something!* I lifted my head forward. I could move my fingers. My wrist went limp, and I was able to unwind it and slip from the blood-slicked rope.

For a moment—hope. I might get out of this room with my boy alive! I had to move quickly. Chewing through the rope, busting my tooth—that had been the easy part.

My legs were numb. Reed's hand moved across my hips—*no, no, no.* I froze, afraid to move. He was sleeping. His body covered the entire left side of mine, and now he'd wrapped his arm around my waist.

Focus. You've come this far, you can't stop now. I was weak. I hadn't eaten in at least two days. The only thing I'd swallowed in the past forty-eight hours was vodka, whiskey, and semen. I was thirsty and the bathroom was three feet from me. I could hear the faucet dripping.

I had to get to my purse. I could feel it with my fingertips. I had no other choice. I shoved Reed's arm, pushed him hard off me, and fell ass backwards into the floor. My feet were numb, but I grabbed my bag and slid it across the tile into the bathroom. If I could move, I could grab Riley and run for the door, but Reed was closer. If he stood, I'd never get past him. I pulled myself out of the floor, stumbled to the end of the bed, and grabbed Riley, pulling him into the bathroom.

I flicked the faucet on—it was a reflex—I had to have water. I put my chin under the tap and lapped it like a dehydrated dog. I cupped my hand under the faucet, then held it against Riley's dry lips.

Reed stood on the opposite side of the bed in the shadows. *I am Wendy. Jack has the ax. The bathroom door is open. Redrum, we're all going to die.* Things moved in slow motion.

I turned off the faucet and pulled my mangled hand from my bag. I must have turned the safety off. I slid my left hand around the corner of the bathroom door and turned on the blinding overhead light. I pointed the gun at him.

Reed stood across the room, by the hotel door, disoriented. When his eyes focused on me, he smiled—so sly, so sick, so twisted. "You've got to be kidding me," he said.

The last time I'd pointed a gun at Evan Williams—because that's who he was all along—he'd threatened to set me on fire and left me for dead. I had only one shot at this.

"Riley, close your eyes, okay? Cover your ears. Mommy and Daddy need to talk."

Riley followed directions and stopped crying. For a moment, the room was silent.

"You don't have the nerve," said the man I'd once loved, the father of my child, the monster who lived in my dreams and every waking hour.

Something in his eyes changed.

I must have pulled the trigger.

I must have.

Reed's hand went towards his chest. I saw the tattoo on his wrist—the little heart he'd crossed out with a giant X.

"We can talk about this," someone said. Was it Reed?

I remembered the audio clip he'd used of my voice in the song "I Don't Belong Here" "I don't want to talk. I don't want to," my voice had said in the video. Today I wasn't talking.

The second bullet hit him in the stomach. His eyes never left mine. The third was a misfire. My hand was wet, sticky with blood and water. The bullet clipped him in the right shoulder. This was never going to end.

"How long are you going to love me?" He'd asked in the home video.

"Forever." The world slowed down. Forever is a really long time.

I raised the gun and aimed it at his head. I pulled the trigger.

At 2:17 p.m. on a Wednesday afternoon, in a dead-end motel off the Nevada desert highway, I murdered a monster.

I grabbed my son, and at 2:18 p.m., I ran out of that hotel room screaming my lungs out, holding my one and only living child tight against my chest—into the brightest sunlight I'd ever seen. It was blinding.

The sight of us almost gave the maid a heart attack. I didn't see her. I didn't see the stairs, but I must have taken them. The hot pavement burned my toes, but I kept running.

I killed a man that day, but the monster—I'm still running from him.

I heard a woman screaming that day in the hotel parking lot, losing her mind. I didn't realize it was me. She was screaming about her babies and her body—hers and not his. And crying out over and over, "I don't want this!" As if she could give it back. As if she ever had a fucking choice.

But he did.

And he chose to hurt.

Again.

And again.

The hotel maid took Riley. I begged her to run, hide him. I believed Reed would walk out of that hotel room. And if he did, the police wouldn't stop him. Judges would not stop him. No one would ever stop him.

Wearing only Reed's torn white tank top, I was covered in my own blood from head to toe. Riley and the maid were covered in my blood. So much blood.

The hotel manager put blankets around us. He'd heard sounds—the cops were already on their way. "Should I call back and ask for more?" Only moments passed before the parking lot was full of flashing lights that sat gold against the evening desert sky. While the paramedics were looking at

Riley, the hotel manager came over and handed me a yellow pack of Peanut M&Ms and a cold Diet Dr. Pepper. The taste of freedom in America.

They brought what was left of Reed down the hotel steps on a gurney. He was breathing with an oxygen mask. As they passed me, his heavy chest rose high and the one good eye in his bloody, mangled face locked on mine before it fluttered closed the final time.

His chest collapsed into sweet peace.

He was free.

My bare knees hit the hard pavement as I fell from my seat on the back of the ambulance. I saw him look at me with his blue eyes over sunglasses in the Rainbow. I saw him standing on my doorstep holding a single rose. I saw him smile as he lay in our bed holding Hayley in the air while she giggled. I saw him look at me desperately as he held her lifeless body on the edge of the highway. I put my hand into the air and felt him move through me.

Across the parking lot, stood a young woman with purple dreads, wearing a vinyl black dress and boots. Two crows sat on her shoulders, harnessed to her with small chains around their legs. She lifted her hands in the air, clapped once and the transformer box on the power line blew. "You can get up now, girl," Kaley said and stepped into the fiery sun.

Chapter Forty-Four

I have no recollection of what happened after I saw Kaley. I'm sure it involved being transported to a medical facility, poked and prodded. Fingerprinted. I was arrested on first-degree murder charges later that week.

Seeing her chance to shine, Michelle Trafton testified against me, recalling the night after Reed's overdose when I said she would have been doing me a favor if she'd left him to die. Prosecution argued it was premeditated—I'd taken the gun with me, I'd taken it inside Kidzworld, endangering children. I'd gone with Reed to the second location. I'd taken the gun inside the hotel room. Instead of holding my child or getting therapy I desperately needed—my son was taken away from me and placed in the system until my parents could get custody. I endured an excruciating televised celebrity trial.

Fans blame Courtney Love for Kurt Cobain's suicide—but with Reed, I pulled the trigger. The prosecution ignored the shovels and two body bags in Reed's trunk. He'd intended to kill Riley and me.

Marlene Von Berstein hired a team of lawyers to file an appeal. Women's rights groups held feminist protests outside the court opposite screaming heavy metal fans. Letters, petitions, and appeals flooded in until a judge overturned the verdict stating it was clearly self-defense. I was released in the middle of the night.

Marlene had a car waiting to take me out of state.

"New York—the offer stands," she said. She wanted me to know that I had options again.

Freedom doesn't fix broken. I needed time to recover. Time to help my son heal. I wish I could wrap up my childhood and give it to him. I don't want to think about the dark hues of his beginning. His eyes are bright blue, but there are many, many layers to them. They sparkle and shine like broken glass. The outer areas are the brightest; they fade darker to his fierce black pupils. He's beautiful, brilliant, and damaged like his parents. Black and white thinking is his defense against the harsh reds and blues of his childhood.

My mother taught me to hold onto my gifts, to focus and perfect them. "Your gifts are yours Jenny, no one else's. You want to nurture, water, and feed them so they grow. When they are ready, you can share them with the world."

She was a wonderful mother.

My son, Riley, thinks in black and white and hides his gifts out of fear. What kind of mother does that make me?

His father gave him music and rage.

I gave him art and fear.

I know Riley is still terrified of what can happen when you combine the two. My father has been gone for years, but I wish there was some way he could be here to fix this.

My sweet son, I hope you wait to read this until you're older. I don't expect it to ever make sense.

EPILOGUE
June 8, 2008

If Evan Reed were alive today, he would be forty-seven years old.

You don't have to believe my story. I have tried to create a fair and accurate recollection of events, but I didn't write this book for you. It was written for our son, Riley. He wanted to know the truth about his parents—not the lies he's seen in the media. I hope this gives him the freedom to move on. But the reality is; this wasn't just my story. Reed is not here to tell his side of things. A lot of research went into this book. Fact checkers checked the fact checkers. People will accuse me of lying (especially if it gets them on TV).

I'm tired of fighting with them. I've said my part. It's Reed's turn.

8 May 1995

Jenny,

You probably know I'm in jail tonight. We've been doing this dance of ours a long time now, to be honest—I'm getting bored. Things are escalating inside me. Drugs and alcohol are a failed attempt to quell the demon. I created this monster to get through my youth—for survival. Somewhere along the way, all that fear, anger, and rage became ME.

My ID is saying I could crush you. I can lift a paw or open my teeth at any moment and destroy you. Even when you hate me, of all the people in the world you are the one who knows me for who I am. Good and bad. It sucks to be you, right? I could get away with murder and no one would care.

As Riley grows, I see myself and you– two people I have grown to loathe and hate and it's hard to love him. Our selfishness and pain are his burden. I hope I learn to love him more than I need to hurt you. This is ends badly, honey.

Eternally yours,

Your almost dead ex-husband,

Reed

P.S. You were right about Kaley. My drugs. My needles. Rest easy, I didn't fuck her.

(Editor's note—this letter was located with similar unsent documents at Evan Reed's estate after his death).

THE LAST WORD
THE ROLLING STONE INTERVIEW: JENNI HAWTHORNE by Jackson Tobias

"I feel free on the back of Ian's Harley. I feel safe surrounded by his brothers in black. There's a difference in being controlled by a man and surrendering to one. The press doesn't bother us in this fortress he built—to protect me and my son. He loves Riley, that's more important than anything else."

– Jenni Hawthorne.

"**O**ne interview. And I pick you," Jenny Reed (now Jenni Hawthorne) said, pouring me a glass of soda. "I'm sorry there's nothing to go in it—we have a no alcohol during the day policy here. You have to have rules in a place like this with a kid. Otherwise, it's chaos."

Jenni would know. Her life has been one of infamy and tragedy—love, betrayal, abuse—and murder have filled her pages. Now she's written a book, at the insistence of her teenage son.

"He's of the age now where he's reading things online that aren't the full story. He wanted me to set the record straight. It's not something I would've done on my own," she trails off. "Ian will be home soon, he can join us."

She gives me a tour of the house while we wait on her current husband, musician and biker Ian Hawthorne. She points at a painting of him on the wall. "That's mine." She smiles. "There's something about him, I found peace in the chaos."

I hear a garage door open and the unmistakable roar of a 1969 Harley Roadster. Jenni and Ian are an unlikely pair, but they've been together for twelve years.

"He saved my life. He's a talker, though." she laughs gently. "If you want to get anything juicy before he gets in, now is the time."

It's permission to dive right in. This woman lived through hell. I've had a chance to preview her upcoming memoir; it's not the story we know. I've been a research reporter for ten years—an expert on the saga of Jennifer Stone and Evan Reed—but the truth is, I had no idea. I was surprised when she reached out to me for the interview. She hasn't spoken to anyone outside a courtroom about her story since the incident.

Can I ask about your son? How is he? Has he read the book?

"Tread carefully. He is good. A+ student, well-adjusted despite the fact he was raised on a motorcycle ranch with a biker gang [laughs]. He loves books. He asked me to tell this story, and we talked about it, we talked about every chapter. And that's good, because now we have an understanding. He has the knowledge that would've been denied to him otherwise. I didn't want to talk to anyone about this for a long time. It's freeing to get the words out there. My son is very intuitive. I think he sensed that. He says he'll read it someday. That's fine. I'm glad he's not reading it now. There's way more sex in it than I anticipated. Details he doesn't need to know, but this was good for us because we needed to talk about this. It's his history, too. I've spent his whole life trying to protect him, but he's almost an adult, I needed to guide him. Our relationship is better because of the book. I hope the media has the sensibility to leave him alone. There's a lot here for a young man to unpack and come to terms with."

Have you spoken to a therapist together to guide you through this?

"Of course. I've always made those resources available. I've never purposely hidden any of these old truths. I avoided the topic if possible. But it was getting less possible. He's such a kind-hearted soul. The fact that he wanted to hear my version first, that is something men twice his age wouldn't consider."

Why did you pick me to do the interview, Jennifer? We have history together. Can we talk about that?

"We do have that. It's up to you. If you want people to know, write it. I'll plead no comment." She laughs her soft, gentle laugh again. "I didn't ask you for the reason you think, though. I mean, yes, we have a connection from the past, but I've read your work over the years, and I have seen your fair, unbiased approach. Even in writing about me, you were always a stickler for facts. Even when you called me a whore."

Yes, but you know I didn't say that. Not in those words:

"You implied. But listen, you had limited information at the time. It was frustrating."

But it caused a problem for you, for that I'm deeply sorry.

"Look, you had no idea. I knew that you were reporting a story. Luckily it got buried."

Can I mention it here?

"You'll ruin the book."

I'll let the readers decide for themselves. They need to hear your version, not rumors. But there was a story, involving a resort in Mexico, where I—well I will say I "mis-witnessed" something, and now that I know the full details it's good thing that story got canned. My employer at the time was not willing to take the risk. It lends an element of truth to your story—because for the

time, this would've been explosive, and it was covered up. And the information made it to your husband, Evan Reed:

"Well, your assumptions weren't entirely wrong at the time; it was the details."

I was a jackass trying to make a name for myself with a big story. I'm glad it was killed. As a young reporter, you don't always see the influence you can have on a story. I've steered away from exploitative stories since then. If anything, that situation made me a better journalist. People reading this interview will not have a clue what we are talking about.

"They can read the book."

I agree. I think it's worth it. It's a labyrinth. Once you get in there, there was so much going on. And no one knew:

"A lot of people knew. Your old boss knew."

There was a hierarchy.

"We were all pawns. Especially Reed. It was money. They hid stories if it would hurt sales. They never published anything for the sake of getting the truth out there."

Do you have any regrets?

"All of them. Everything."

People often say that in the end, it was worth it. I mean, there's your son.

"Everything. I've spoken to my son about this. No one should've endured what he did at such a young age. I would go so far back as the womb to erase every trace of what became—if there were a string to undo my life, I'd pull it in a heartbeat."

But you're happy now, right?

"I believe so. As much as one can be. There was no other way but up. Death or love. I was lucky that my hardheaded husband butted in when he did. There's a difference in being controlled and surrendering control. I was lucky he was there and that he loved us from the first moment. I don't remember a lot from that period, it was traumatic. He was a friend and insisted on taking care of us. It took a while for me to trust him, but it became something wonderful. I was a mess after everything that happened. Jail was not kind to me nor were the fans, I mean, I don't blame them. He saved me from myself on more than one occasion. He took care of us. He has protected us. Everything he said he'd do, he's done that and more. You don't know love until you're standing outside your house, the keys don't work, you've got no money, and you can't see your child—and Ian was there. He was waiting."

I can hear him singing to himself upstairs. We're beating around the bush, avoiding the tough parts. I know he's going to join us later, so I guess, are you ready? Your book kept me up at night. It made me question and re-evaluate why I love this music. You were a victim of the culture that rock music has thrived on, and it made you the villain. Do you think this book will change any of that?

"I hope things have changed, that maybe the story will bring awareness about domestic violence and abuse. I'm glad that my son and I aren't footnotes in someone else's story."

And you very well could've been. There's no denying the facts. It's there in his own handwriting. Evan Reed threatens to kill you and tells you that he will get away with it. I love that you had a fact checker check your fact checker.

"Every person sees things from their own point of view, but I tried to make it clear when I was dealing with my emotions, compared to, okay, here are the step-by-step events as they happened. I don't expect anyone to believe my side, they never have.

Can we go back in time? You and Evan Reed met in a chance encounter. It was a love story in the beginning. You'd both had tragedies in your life, and you bonded—it has everything a blockbuster love story requires. You went your separate ways, and the universe sort of pushed you together.

"It was all by design. I was young, naïve, and didn't understand the power of money. I hoped what was there in the beginning was real, but nothing in that relationship was left to chance. It was all planned. I knew better and fell for it time and time again. It's hard to explain, when someone manipulates you to the point that you're not yourself anymore. Your thoughts aren't yours, the criticism, the voice in your head—it's not you anymore; it's the abuser."

Were you blinded by the celebrity?

"No, that pushed me away. But I was blinded by the money—and not in the way that people think. Fans think I saw dollar signs, but it's not like that. He used money to manipulate people. It was like the time he casually left $10,000 cash in a jacket, or when he bought the loft in Manhattan—those are things most normal people only read about. To suddenly have things like that happening around you constantly, it's different. I knew it wasn't the real world, but I didn't drop enough breadcrumbs to find my way out. You get sucked into it. You get trapped. You need money to stay in, you need money to get out, and he made it impossible for me either way. I would say, "I don't want your money, I don't want gifts," and he'd buy me a million dollar penthouse in Manhattan, but he wouldn't give me money to fly home. He wouldn't let me work. He found a way to destroy every project I started. He gave me a house but wouldn't give me fifty cents for the payphone to call my mother.

Abusers isolate you. That's what they do. As a feisty young feminist, it never occurred to me in the beginning that these gestures were traps. I didn't want the loft at first. I mean, it was gorgeous, unbelievable, but he and I were in the middle of splitting up. But how do you say no to someone who won't take no for an answer? Who on his good days is too generous?

In writing the book, it flooded back how obvious the warning signs were. Big danger signs. But that's part of it. On top of everything, you feel stupid and humiliated. You think, "Not me, I'd never fall for that." Yet, you're the one in the emergency room for the third time this week with a different broken bone."

Yes, the things that you say happened in this book—the abuse—it would be hard to believe if you hadn't provided the medical and court records.

"But why is it hard to believe? You have no idea how hard and long I fought for those papers. And it's important because the man made me feel crazy. Gaslighting is serious. The fact the professionals who testified in court at the time, bold face lied against what these documents said, is mind blowing."

It is. I wanted to save face and prove that what I tried to publish all those years ago was correct.

"You wrote that I was, "a cheater. Another low-rent, brain-dead whore waiting around a Cabo resort for a dick to suck."

I did write that. And it's disgusting that I'd think such a thing, much less submit it. You were fucking with my favorite bands. I was angry—and Reed's music, encouraged that.

You should've confronted me. I probably would've spilled everything. I was lost and desperate."

I didn't have the balls to do that. The two of you were the dream, and to have that shattered was hard for a jaded fan who should've known better.

"I understand."

The magazine canned the story—they claimed it was too sensational, told me to never mention it again. It's frustrating as a writer when your stories are shelved. You said in the book that Reed heard about that incident in the recording studio, and it ultimately resulted in him lashing out at you in the "I Don't Belong Here" video but it was actually that article that set him off.

"Yes."

I felt so justified in spewing that at the time.

"But you've changed. That's why I asked to do this with you."

I was in the crowd after your trial, with all my fellow metalhead dude-bros shouting when it hit me. This was wrong. I spent a lot of time soul searching on why I believed any of it because I was there in London after you were allegedly attacked by his fan. I'd met you a few years before and your body language around him—everything was so different. But I didn't care then.

"It wasn't a fan. It was Reed. He was angry that I was leaving him. He beat and raped me, tied me up and threatened to set me on fire."

And you've never told anyone that story before now?

"Not until the book."

That's when you went on the road with him—on the Metal Messiah tour. The one that ended the band. He said he left the tour because you'd been in a terrible car accident, but you say in the book that's not what happened.

"No, it's not true."

But you told the media it was true at the time.

"I had to. His lawyers and the record company forced me. And I was terrified of him."

Are you worried, since you admit to lying to cover up the abuse, that people won't believe what you've written? You don't paint a pretty picture for yourself, you could've left the damaging stories about you out and no one would have been the wiser.

"Honesty is important, and my son asked me to tell the true story. I tried to be unbiased."

Does it hurt you that people call you a murderer?

"I mean, yes, of course, but their opinions don't matter anymore. If it hadn't happened the way it did, if the result was any different, my son and I would be in a hole in the desert. Reed would be alive, touring, and making music—which is what the fans want. I had to save my son's life. It took me a long time to accept that I'd done the right thing, but I had to save him. There was no other way out."

Thank you for inviting me into your home and sharing your story with me, Jenni.

"Thank you for listening and letting me tell my story."

Is there anything else you want to add? You've said this will be your only interview.

"I ask please, no matter your feelings about me, please respect my son's need for privacy. He's a child."

I've never in my career as a journalist allowed a subject to look over my notes before I've published a story. I have made an exception. The rock n' roll media owed her that consideration. She sent a short note that simply said, "Thank you."

I did have a chance to speak to her current husband Ian Hawthorne, a phenomenal musician in his own right. Though he tends to spend most of his time with his family and his Harley these days.

"My friend told me, "Stay away from that woman. Me and him ain't friends anymore. She's my wife. And that's my boy. I knew that the minute I laid eyes on her. That's the one. None of this other shit matters. I've got no comment on it, because none of it matters."

What is your life with Ian like, Jenni?

"We do normal things together. He drinks too much some nights, but it's okay. He's a stupid drunk. He laughs himself to sleep, and sometimes it's annoying if I want to get rest. But he lets me be me, it's the damnedest thing."

You were a guitar tech for Evan Reed's band before this happened, right?

"Naw, I never worked for him. I was a tech for Ozzy, but they had the same producer, and he invited the crew out. I was working on my own music. I knew Jenni from around. Had she not been married at the time, I would have paid more interest. I was attracted to her, but she was off limits. Not because of her ex. I would've never disrespected her. I didn't know the situation then."

You were there when her daughter died, is that correct?

"Yeah, I saw it happen. I was talking to her and I pulled her to the ground and sat with her until the ambulance arrived so she wouldn't see what I'd seen. It was terrible. I'll never forget that."

Did you feel an instant connection?

"I wasn't thinking about that. This woman's life was turned upside down, and I'd witnessed something horrific. It was a moment, but you know, she went her way, and I went mine. I just want her and our son to have peace with this whole thing. That man never loved them or he wouldn't have hurt them. No one deserves to be treated that way. No one deserves to go through something that horrific, especially under the guise of love."

Is there anything you want to say to other domestic violence victims, Jenni?

"No second chances. Get out. Get help. Don't wait until it's too late. You're worth so much more than what you realize. And things that seem too good to be true—always are."

Acknowledgments

Thank you to Bryan, Oli, Stef, Di, Adriane, Eve, David F., Renee, Linda, Sharon & Janice for being my first readers & keeping me on track. (Special thanks #Wolfpack! Leah, Gülay, Hanna, Ennie & Rebecca). Kat D., Cat Hellisen for editing and while we're on the subject of cats, "It's cats, Cat!" (you know who you are). Just not my cats because they are not helpful in writing!

I've had the privilege of experiencing so many story worlds through my writing the past few years. I've known Jenny Stone, Evan Reed and their story since I was fifteen years old. I didn't know I was an author for most of my life. I wrote bad poetry, blogs, hundred-page letters to my pen-pals and daydreamed my way out of junior high and into college. It never occurred to me that the little universes I created in my head were stories. Since then, I've dreamed up over two dozen novels—countless works in progress. Most of them come to me with a simple trigger—a single note from a song, a random quote from an interview. *Atomic Love* was originally titled *Rock Star*, and no one was ever supposed to read it. Stefanie Leigh and I met and became writing besties about ten years ago. We broke up for a long time (life). She had a daughter and started pursuing her master's degree. I moved to Chicago and had an awesome daughter. I kept working on a list of novels and forced a few people to read them. My confidence grew each time. In a secret folder, was *Rock Star*, which I tinkered on when I had a chance. This story was for teenage Jessie, no one was ever supposed to read it. When Stefanie and I reconciled (after swearing it would never happen—like several '80s rock bands...), she asked to see what I'd been working on. I figured, *what the hell do I have to lose?* We've seen each other at our best and worst. Within days she reached out and said, "This is the one! You have to finish it!"

Not this one! No way. Not a chance.

Then I told my husband, who had happily read so many of my early manuscripts, that I'd been secretly writing (blush!) this novel about this girl married to a completely insane rock star. He read it and agreed that the story worked. So that was it, my little high school daydream and these characters that wouldn't leave me alone were going to be a real novel.

Rock Star was never based on a single person. It was a combination of music, books, culture, things I enjoyed in the early 1990s and my imagination. I live for music (and it has saved me on more than one occasion). I met some of my best friends from the Metalhead Directory in *Metal Edge Magazine*. (Thanks Geri!). Gn'R, Bon Jovi, Iron Maiden, Skid Row, Rainbow, Dio, Metallica, Megadeth, etc. were always playing in my room. (And still do). Along with a slew of hairbands. Their albums were organized by artist and date below my favorite horror, music and true crime books. Everything by Stephen King and Anne Rice. Far too many serial killer biographies. Anything about Elvis. Jim Morrison's poetry. *No One Here Gets Out Alive* by Danny Sugerman was my favorite book. Graduating to Sylvia Plath, *Bitch* & *Prozac Nation* by Elizabeth Wurtzel, Darcey Steinke, Neil Gaiman and *House of Leaves* by Mark Z. Danielewski, listening to Nirvana, Neurotic Outsiders, Tori Amos, Poe, Hole and Ani DiFranco. Naturally on to Rancid, The Distillers and A.F.I. Then there was an Adam Lambert/Lady Gaga period. I traded serial killers and vampires for *Girl With A Dragon Tattoo*, Gillian Flynn's *Sharp Objects*, and these really bizarre books by Lynn Crosbie. Now it's Patrick Wolf,

Tegan & Sara, The National, Janet Egan's *A Visit from the Goon Squad*, Viv Albertine's excellent *Clothes, Clothes, Clothes. Music, Music, Music. Boys, Boys, Boys.* Patti Smiths' *Banga* album and every book she's written. One of my favorite Jim Morrison poetry lines from *Lords & The New Creatures* has a William Blake reference about eyes being windows to the soul. That poem was the chant of my youth, but it's not exactly true anymore. Augusten Burroughs sees directly into my soul now (and I know this because he keeps writing books about every random thing that goes through my scattered brain). Try and pry a Christopher Isherwood book from my hands. Just try!

Through all my various growth and stages, three things remained consistent—my love for: metal music, androgyny, Stephen King and tell-all rock n' roll memoirs. Ranging from groupies, ex-wives, to Patti Smith's *Just Kids*, Nikki Sixx's *Heroin Diaries*, Joe Perry, Billy Idol, Bruce Dickinson, Slash, Rudy Sarzo, Ozzy—if its music related, I read it. Duff McKagan's *It's So Easy: And Other Lies* and *How to Be a Man (and other illusions)* easily fit into my top ten books. I laughed and cried reading Duff's books—they felt honest. A lot of rock memoirs don't. (Which may or may not have something to do with the ghost writers—that Heart book—don't get me started. Or do—because I'm reading Johnny Depp give Joe Perry from Aerosmith a superhero's introduction and Ann and Nancy Wilson are reduced to boring schoolgirls, not badass rock n' roll trailblazers—not cool). But rock n' roll ain't always cool. And we know that.

Double standards against women, violence, sexual assault and domestic violence are embedded deep into rock culture. Even in the era of #MeToo we've been so slow to condemn the actions of our favorite musicians. (Unless they are black—and even then, it takes forever). Most memoirs gloss over the damage and chaos those men inflict on women. Some of them still make it a joke (looking at you, Mötley Crüe. And come on, Netflix, really?). In researching this novel, I pored over so many memoirs of rockers' ex-girlfriends, wives, and groupies. A lot of them were interesting, fun reads (Bobbi Brown is hilarious and honest about drug use, etc.). Mary Forsberg Weiland's promising *I Fall to Pieces* fell flat. The two books that I really felt didn't gloss over that era were Carol Ann Harris' *Storms: My Life with Lindsey Buckingham & Fleetwood Mac* and Roxana Shirazi's *The Last Living Slut.* The double-standards with which the related bands turned on those two women is definitive of rock n' roll. When women tell these stories, we're conditioned to think: *Yuck! Gross! Slut! She knew what she was getting into!* Men control the narrative—and their stories are *funny, cool and wild! Atomic Love* was written long before I read any of these books, but Shirazi's memoir really helped push me along in finishing my novel.

Atomic Love was never a love story but a brutal, dark, unrelenting answer to books like *The Dirt.* I don't want to trigger folks, but stories of domestic violence should make you uncomfortable. I intended to tell the brutal side of Jenny's victimization and the long term effects of being trapped in an abusive, narcissist's web. The novel could have ended after the scene in the Texas hotel or her art debut (editors probably agree), but narcissists don't stop just because a relationship ends. Their behavior often escalates as they wreak havoc on the lives of their victims. Riley was always essential to the story. Like too many kids, he's the collateral damage of an abusive relationship. It's hard to leave a character out when you've known them over twenty years.

Atomic Love is both a tribute to the music I love and acknowledgement that sometimes the things we love are toxic. In the #MeToo era, I think it's time to stop glossing over these stories—even in fiction—and question why we've been so slow to hold our music heroes accountable. But more importantly, how do we get it to stop?

Follow me on Facebook and Twitter and let me know if you want to know what happens to Riley next. I've heard a few things from the creative plane. ~*Jessie Rose*

About the Author

J essie Rose writes about rock stars, serial killers, vampires, and feminism. Jessie is co-founder of *The Beautiful Wild Magazine* which focuses on music, art, culture, and social justice. Co-founder of Love Letters to Russia, a project created to send positive messages to Russian LGBTQ+ youth. The author lives in Wisconsin with their husband, daughter and two cats. To find out more, visit: jessieroseauthor.com

Sign up for Jessie's Newsletter to find out about new releases & special events.

Stay in Touch

Find out what's next by joining my newsletter here:

https://www.subscribepage.com/jessie-rose-newsletter

If you enjoyed this book, please consider leaving an honest review.

I would also love to have you in my Facebook Reader group:

https://www.facebook.com/groups/1055934294907410

Stay in Touch

Resources

According to the National Domestic Violence Hotline: Anyone of any race, age, sexual orientation, religion or gender can be a victim—or perpetrator—of domestic violence. It can happen to people who are married, living together, dating or between friends. It affects people of all socioeconomic backgrounds and education levels. Elderly and LGBTQ+ people are at particular risk.

Domestic violence includes the use of physical and sexual violence, threats and intimidation, emotional abuse and economic deprivation. Some of the signs of an abusive relationship include a partner who:

- Tells you that you can never do anything right

- Shows extreme jealousy of your friends and time spent away

- Discourages you from seeing friends or family members

- Insults, demeans or shames you

- Controls household money and refuses to give you money for necessary expenses

- Acts in ways that scare you

- Controls who you see, where you go, or what you do

- Prevents you from making your own decisions

- Threatens to harm or take away your children

- Prevents you from working or attending school

- Destroys your property or threatens to hurt or kill your pets

- Intimidates you with guns, knives or other weapons

- Pressures you to have sex when you don't want to or do things sexually you're not comfortable with

- Pressures you to use drugs or alcohol

- Threatens to "out" you or ridicules your gender identity

- Physically harms or sexually assaults you

(https://www.thehotline.org/is-this-abuse/abuse-defined/)
National Domestic Violence Hotline: 1-800-799-7233
1-800-787-3224 (TTY) En Espanol
https://www.thehotline.org/
RAINN (Rape, Abuse & Incest National Network): (800.656.HOPE, www.rainn.org y rainn.org/es). RAINN is the nation's largest anti-sexual violence organization.
The Trevor Project:
1-866-488-7386. www.thetrevorproject.org The Trevor Project is the leading national organization providing crisis intervention and suicide prevention services to lesbian, gay, bisexual, transgender, queer & questioning youth.

Are you hurting your partner? Call the NDVH hotline for help: 1-800-799-SAFE (7233)

Victim Support (UK):

https://www.victimsupport.org.uk/crime-info/types-crime/domestic-abuse

Made in United States
Troutdale, OR
08/13/2024

21956604R00257